DISTANT SONS

ALSO BY TIM JOHNSTON

The Current

Descent

Irish Girl

Never So Green

DISTANT SONS

a novel

TIM JOHNSTON

ALGONQUIN BOOKS
OF CHAPEL HILL
2023

Published by
Algonquin Books of Chapel Hill
Post Office Box 2225
Chapel Hill, North Carolina 27515-2225

an imprint of Workman Publishing Co., Inc.
a subsidiary of Hachette Book Group, Inc.
1290 Avenue of the Americas,
New York, NY 10104

Printed in the United States of America.
Design by Steve Godwin.

The publisher is not responsible for websites (or their content)
that are not owned by the publisher.

This is a work of fiction. While, as in all fiction, the literary perceptions and insights
are based on experience, all names, characters, places, and incidents either are products
of the author's imagination or are used ficticiously.

Library of Congress Cataloging-in-Publication Data
Names: Johnston, Tim, [date]– author.
Title: Distant sons : a novel / Tim Johnston.
Description: First edition. | Chapel Hill, North Carolina :
Algonquin Books of Chapel Hill, 2023. |
Summary: "The actions of two young working men with secrets ignite
the passions and violence of a small Wisconsin town still haunted by
the unsolved disappearance of three boys in the 1970s"—Provided by publisher.
Identifiers: LCCN 2023021317 | ISBN 9781643753591 (hardcover) |
ISBN 9781643755465 (ebook)
Subjects: LCGFT: Novels.
Classification: LCC PS3610.O395 D57 2023 | DDC 813/.6—dc23/eng/20230512
LC record available at https://lccn.loc.gov/2023021317

10 9 8 7 6 5 4 3 2 1
First Edition

For Tad Michael Johnston
&
Randy Larson

Bleste be ye man yt spares thes stones,
and curst be he yt moves my bones.

—Shakespeare's tomb

DISTANT SONS

May 1976

As the days *grew longer the boys would hurry through dinner and grab up their mitts again and fly out the door—*

Wait for your brother!

—back to the schoolyard, back to their places in center, at second, on the mound, the clouds they kicked up from the infield redder now, more brilliant in the dropping sun, their own shadows taller in the dirt. Stretched shadows like forecasts of their future selves, then taller still, the elongate figures crouching, adjusting ballcaps, pounding long, misshapen gloves.

The brick wall that is the back of the school, so familiar and oppressive as they slogged toward it in a weekday sunrise—Watch your brother!—is remade at sunset with bricks of gold, bathing the players in the joy of the hour—of this almost-done day near the end of May 1976. Spring of the American Bicentennial. The war in Vietnam over and gone from their living room TVs. Ms. Wheeler with her short skirt, playing "Bohemian Rhapsody," the whole thing, on her record player. And Teddy Felt still staring at them big-eyed from the announcements case.

Teddy Felt with his black-frame glasses and his parted, mother-combed black hair. Fourth grader from Roosevelt, across town, who got off the school bus one day and never came home. Just . . . gone. One year ago this spring.

Teddy Felt, whose name, spoken into a girl's ear at close range (close enough to smell her hair, close enough almost to kiss her neck) would make her suck in her breath and cross herself.

All this and junior high in the fall—from kings to twerps in three months flat—and none of it is anywhere near their minds as they stand in the dusk, summer's smell of glove leather in the air, smell of their own dusty, sweaty, grass-stained bodies. *Their voices ringing on the golden bricks, and all of it conferring on each boy a feeling of his own greatness, his readiness, his sureness that the ball will come his way and will not get by him. Punching his mitt. Tugging the bill of his cap.*

Hum batter, don't whiff batter!

Only one of them can be right, only one boy's sureness borne out, and the ball itself chooses—it leaps from the bat with a diving, curving life of its own and leaps again from the dirt in a fiendish sideways juke, hell-bent on the gap between second and third, a run-scoring single the moment it reaches the grass. But it never reaches the grass. It is stopped, robbed absolutely by a lunging left arm, a backhanding glove: his. *Glove and boy wheeling all the way around with the flight of the ball before he halts himself, a hopping side step toward first, securing his grip on the ball and stepping into the throw, smooth as Morgan, deadly as Rose, the ball a pink moon in the dusk, the spiraling red stitches . . . the first baseman's mitt open like a fishmouth and the ball itself snapping shut the mouth with a deep slap of leather.*

End of inning. End of game.

That throw, the whooping of his teammates, still replaying in his heart as he goes among the pines, antic and happy on the needled path, heading home. The day's last rays shooting slantwise through the trees like arrows, and the boy moving in that riddled light as in a pink netting, lobbing the ball into the air before him in mini pop flies and rushing to field them underhanded Willie Mays–style, to the amazement of the play-by-play man—Hoo boy, some catch by Milner! That voice, the soft skid of sneakers in pine needles, the quiet slap of the ball in the mitt's webbing the only sounds in all those woods.

At the Assassin's Bluff, a low wall of rock from which a panther or more likely the Assassin himself would pounce, the boy's shadow lurches across the wall's craggy face, leaping to snag a shadow ball among the shadow trees. Beyond the bluff the path dives into the Valley of Bones and here he descends in his headlong lope—here misjudges the ball, bobbles it, chases it down the path, the play-by-play man's voice rising in urgency as the boy descends, as the runners advance, until the boy arrives breathless in the floor of the valley, that darker, colder gloom, and stops where the ball has fetched up at the foot of a tree, pocketed among knuckled roots. Gnarled roots like ghoul's fingers tensed in the earth for just this prize, the ball so white and small and perfect. Like a lure. And the boy feeling such a chill then to the back of his neck that he turns to see what has blown on him with its cold breath.

Teddy Felt, the silence says. Like a whisper in his ear, that old game, and it's as if the picture itself, big-eyed Teddy Felt in his black glasses, has followed him here, to these haunted woods, where it might at last become the living—or not living—boy himself.

Joey Milner, Teddy whispers, and Joey's heart drops, the cold rushes through him and he grabs up the ball and turns and flies—just flies. Wind and breath and pounding sneakers and thudding heart all one great sound in his ears, and Teddy's sneakers pounding too, thudding with the blood, and there's the terror-thrill of what is just behind, of what cannot be seen: Hands. Grubby, dirty little hands, reaching—

Joey! . . . Teddy Felt calls. Joey, wait up . . . !

FROM THE WINDOW *over the sink she looks again—and there he is, springing from the dark woods like a deer, as lovely and light as that. A joy to see, but when nothing more follows him into the yard, joy turns to annoyance, then to anger. Then to something worse, climbing into her breast.*

She opens the screen door and calls to the running boy: Joseph Milner, where is your brother? and the boy pulls up short, childish blooms on his cheeks, narrow ribcage heaving.

He's here.

(Wait for your brother!)

He's not with you? Her heart sliding. A woodenness in her legs, an emptiness.

I said he's here.

He is certainly not here.

The boy tugs at the bill of his cap. He wanted to come home, he says.

So why didn't you bring him home?

Because . . .

What—?

Because the game wasn't over. I made the last—

So you sent him home by himself?

I didn't send him home, he just went.

She looks beyond the boy, into the woods, and the name she has been fighting off breaks suddenly into her chest—Teddy Felt. Ten years old. Same age as her Duane. Teddy Felt who did nothing but get off the school bus at the wrong stop. A mother at home waiting for him . . . watching. Waiting.

He knows the way, Ma, says her own son. Her Joey. We've done it like a thousand times, he says, and the screen door slaps behind her as she takes her first steps in a changed world. Passing the boy, she hears as if through a wall of stones—Ma, he's around here somewhere. He's probably hiding.

Moving more quickly now, this mother of two, striding, not running, toward the trees and the darkness within them. Toward a possibility she'd not even allowed herself to consider one minute ago.

PART I

1.

February 2018

First the heat had quit. Then the engine light had come on. In his bleariness Sean looked long at his gauges—too long, nearly driving off I-90 at high speed and saved only by the shuddering of the rumble strip.

He could've stopped on the Minnesota side, town of La Crescent, but he pushed on for the Mississippi, and when he reached the other side, Wisconsin, he passed up two more exits before he began to smell the engine in the cold-blowing vents. He took the next exit, drove under the overpass, pulled over on the shoulder and shut her down quick. Popped the hood and got out, snugging down his cap in the wind. Cold, raw wind off the Mississippi blowing overland for Lake Michigan, water to water. The new day coming up in the east, the first pink bands of daylight staining the hem of blue sky, and the stars fleeing to the west in degrees of greater brightness, as if they might outrun, just this once, the advance of day.

The latch was hot but not too hot and he lifted the hood—and stepped back swatting at the cloud of acrid steam, spitting the taste of it from his mouth, "Son of a bitch."

Under the bumper the pool was already forming: bright chemical green in the dawn, rippling with the steady drip.

He stood and looked north: the distant glowing signs of gas stations, fast food, motels.

"You could've made it," he said to no one.

"Yeah, and you could've burnt out this engine," he said. Voice of his father. Of using your head. Of quiet disbelief when you didn't. "If you haven't already."

To the south the big rigs plowed the overpass eastward with the wind. Another two hours and he'd have made Madison. Let himself into his father's house, hit the shower, hit that old couch. Wake up to his father coming home, looking down on him. *I see my truck's still running.*

Your *truck?*

His father studying him. Older by a year—all of them: father, son, truck. *Where you coming from?*

Billings, Montana.

What was there?

Three days cladding a pole barn was there. A man named Dell Cortez he'd met just sitting at a bar drinking a beer. It happened that way sometimes. Sometimes he found something on the local Craigslist—Carpenter Needed. Handyman Needed. When they'd finished cladding the barn, Dell pulled five new hundreds from his billfold and his wife came out with a brick of banana bread still hot in its tinfoil. He'd eaten the last of it around midnight, just outside Sioux Falls.

Have you seen your mother? his father will ask.

No.

You need to see your mother, Sean.

Yeah. You know there's no food in that kitchen, right?

There's food. You gotta know where to look.

I looked.

Well, get up offa there, moneybags. You can buy me dinner.

And he would.

But he had to get there first.

He thought that once the engine cooled he could crawl along to a gas station, and so he moved to the lee side of the truck and lit his cigarette, and there he stood smoking it, a lean man leaning against the Chevy. A man merely taking his ease, he imagined, a man taking a break from the road, watching the new day come up. And but for the raised hood of the truck, so he might've been assumed to be and left alone. As it was, a white Dodge Ram with a load of cordwood rolled by, the driver slowing for a look at the Chevy, at Sean standing there, and at last pulled over. The reverse lights came on and the Dodge began backing down the shoulder.

Sean dropped his cigarette and mashed it under his boot toe.

The Dodge stopped short of the Chevy and Sean got a closer look at its load: lengths of cordwood all uniform in size and shape and stacked with great care and level across the top. As if the driver had indeed put a level to them. Sean liked him already.

The man cut his engine and stepped down from the cab and walked to the back of the Dodge. "Mornin," he said.

"Mornin," said Sean.

They wore canvas work jackets, the two of them, and they held each other's eye briefly before both turned to look into the open engine bay of the Chevy.

"What happened here?" said the man. He was older than Sean by a good two decades. His father's age, maybe. Early fifties. He wore no cap and his short silver hair stood stiffly in the wind.

"Well," said Sean, tugging the bill of his cap, "first the heat cut out. Then the engine light came on. And now this."

The man stepped back to see what Sean was tapping his boot at—the pool of green fluid.

"That's not good," he said.

"No sir," said Sean.

The man stepped forward again and leaned in under the hood and stared at something. As if he might grab hold of it and yank it out. "You got somebody coming?"

"No sir. I don't know anybody here."

The man looked at him. "I meant a tow service."

Sean looked to the north and said he thought he'd try to crawl along to one of those gas stations once the engine cooled down. The man looked too, then turned back to the engine.

"You'da been better off turning the other way," he said. "There's a good garage about four miles south of here." He pushed back his jacket cuff to look at his watch. "Probably just opening up right about now."

"I don't think she'll go four miles," said Sean.

"No, probably not." The man reached in and jiggled a dusty hose. "I were you, I'd call for a tow. Bud's Top Line Auto. That's the name of the garage."

Sean got out his phone and as he was thumbing the screen he saw as in some cartoon one of the Dell Cortez hundred-dollar bills flying like a bird from his wallet, then another, and another. "Bud's Top Line . . . ?"

"Auto," said the man. "Owner's an old buddy of mine."

"Bud?"

"No. Bud was years ago. Larry Hines is the owner now. Larry will take care of you."

Sean walked off a ways, leaving the man alone with the engine. After a while he came back to the Chevy.

"The wrecker's out on another call," he said. "Said he'd be an hour, maybe more."

"Did you talk to Larry?"

"Yep."

The man studied the engine. "How 'bout I just drive you on over there?" he said. "He's got coffee and a place you can sit till the wrecker gets back."

"You weren't going that way," said Sean.

The man shrugged. "Four miles," he said.

Sean dropped the hood on the Chevy and climbed up into the cab of the Dodge and hauled the door shut behind him. The truck shook to life and the man swung it about in the road and got it up to speed going south.

The truck was not new but there was no dust, no trash, no smell in the cab other than the wood smell and the smell of shave cream, smell of coffee. No cigarette had ever been lit there.

"Hurt your leg?" the man said.

"Sorry?"

"You hurt your leg?"

Sean held his hands to the dash vent. "My knee," he said. "Long time ago. It stiffens up on a long drive."

The man sipped from a travel mug and returned it to the center console. "Didn't fall off a roof, did you?"

"No sir."

"Old carpenter buddy of mine fell off a roof one time and never did walk the same after that."

Sean said nothing.

"I took you for a carpenter," the man said. "With that Knaack box in the back."

"Yes sir."

"Finish, or frame, or—?"

"Pretty much whatever needs doing," said Sean.

The man nodded. "I bent a few nails in my day. My younger days. I sell firewood now."

"That's a good load you got."

"Taking her up to a man at Lake Neshonoc. I doubt you know where that is."

"No sir."

"Saw your Colorado plates," said the firewood man.

Sean looked out at the gray new day. The gray nameless buildings. His brain was buzzing with the long drive, the lack of sleep. Nicotine.

"Family there?"

"No sir. Not anymore."

The firewood man looked at him. "Meaning they don't live there anymore, or—?"

"Meaning they don't live there anymore."

The firewood man nodded. He took another sip from the mug.

"Where were you headed? If you don't mind me asking."

Sean was slow to answer. "I tend to go from here to there," he said. "Grabbing work where I can get it."

The man nodded. "I did some of that, my younger days. Went to work on the BNSF line when I was twenty and, man, I rode those rails all over this country. Down to Brownsville, Texas on the Mexico border, on up to Winnipeg Canada. I was in Surprise, Arizona when my dad died, and the railway sent me home. 1988. Two years later Mom passed and all of a sudden I had a house, property. Met my wife. Started a family."

Sean didn't know what to say. It sounded like a whole life.

"You married?" said the man.

"No sir."

"Kids?"

"Nope."

"How old are you?"

"Twenty-six."

"That right?"

"Yep."

"Thought you were older."

They were sitting at a light. There was no cross traffic and it was a long light.

"Damn thing of it," said the man, "was why he stopped on those tracks in the first place."

Sean was watching the light. He turned and looked at the man. He thought he'd missed something—just blacked out for a second. Totally possible.

"My dad," said the man. His hands loosely on the wheel. "Had him a load of apples in the back he'd been all day picking. On his way to the market and he stopped on the tracks and he wasn't gonna leave those apples, by God. Sat there cranking at that engine, cranking at it, and the train just a-comin along."

The light turned green and the man drove on.

Sean watched the buildings. His own father was getting up, making coffee in the little kitchen, the empty little house. His hair a mess. Looking out at the day.

"Of course, the railway said he did it on purpose," said the firewood man. "Of course they said that." He lifted his mug and sipped. "My mother didn't even fight it. Said it would just make people talk. The neighbors. She couldn't stand what the neighbors would say."

He looked over at Sean. "How do you like this town so far? Man gives you a ride and tells you his life story. My mother is turning in her grave."

"Was it the same railway?"

"How's that?"

"The same railway that hit him? The BN . . ."

"BNSF. There isn't no other railway, not around here there isn't." He flicked his signal. "This is Larry's right up here." He slowed to pull into the lot, but Bud's Top Line Auto was a small operation, the lot was already packed with cars and trucks, and he flicked off his signal and pulled over in front.

"You don't mind, I'm just gonna drop you. But you tell Larry hello from Lyle."

"Hello from Lyle," said Sean. He opened his door and began to get out.

"And your name—?"

Sean turned back. "Sean," he said, and shook the man's hand. "Thanks for the lift, Lyle."

"Don't mention it, Sean."

Sean was turning to shut the door when the man named Lyle leaned toward him. "Tell you what, Sean."

"What's that."

"I just now remembered. There's a man lives out in the bluffs asked me a while back if I knew a carpenter. Had some kind of a job at the house out there needed doin. I told him I'd call my old carpenter buddy—guy who fell off the roof—but when I called him he said he was retired. News to me. Anyway, I don't know if the man found somebody or not, but I could put you in touch with him, if you were interested."

"What's the job?"

"That I can't tell you. He didn't go into details. Just needed a carpenter. He sells me his deadfall, time to time, this man. Or sometimes just wants me to cord it up for him, for his own use."

The man named Lyle waited. Watching Sean's face. "How about I just give you his number and you can call or not call?"

"OK."

"I'll text it to you."

"OK."

They got out their phones and after a minute Sean had the text. He read it quickly and put his phone away. "Thank you."

"Call him, don't call him. But he's only got the house line and you gotta let her ring. Kind of an old man. Living alone out there, just him and his dog. You can tell him Lyle sent you. He asks me, I'll tell him the truth—I gave you a lift and you're a carpenter looking for work. After that you're on your own."

"OK."

Lyle nodded, and stayed as he was, leaning toward Sean, looking at him. Sean waited.

"I won't tell you he's the easiest man in the world to do business with," Lyle said. "Somewhat set in his ways, you could say. But his money is US American, and it's cash."

"Cash is good."

"Cash is good."

Sean raised a hand. "Thanks again, Lyle. I appreciate you stopping."

"Well," said the firewood man, "I hate to see a man broke down on the road."

Sean watched as the man got the Dodge turned around and up to speed again going north, then he fished up his cigarettes and lit one and stood smoking, alone in that anonymous outskirts. One-story enterprises of cinderblock and sheet metal. A brick four-story with a corporate logo and eight orange squares of sunrise in the top two floors. Smell of the river in the air, the wide Mississippi, plodding along on this morning as on all mornings since a time unimaginable, before the first men stepped foot on the land.

Wisconsin. Land of his birth and childhood.

Drifting thoughts in a tired brain. He did not stand in that unknown place contemplating how it was he ended up here—*here*. The chain of happenstance and accident that had led to these particular circumstances and none other; he would have time, and greater cause, to think about such things later. Just then he had the problem of the Chevy. The pool of green fluid. The hundred-dollar bills from Dell Cortez.

He got out his phone and read the text from the firewood man.

"Marion Devereaux," he said, and wondered was it a misspelling—*Marion*.

"US American dollars," he said. He took a last drag and dropped the cigarette and stepped on it. Then he turned and crossed the lot to the glass door that said OFFICE in gold sticker letters, and went on in.

2.

OF THE STONEMASON Marion Devereaux little was known. He'd shown up one morning, midweek, at one of Randall Pratt's jobs, wearing great slabs of clay for boots. Slogging on up the hill and asking the man was he hiring. Like that. Out of the blue sky. Denim bib coveralls and a denim long-sleeve shirt buttoned to the throat. Not young, not old. Average height, average build. Brownblack hair combed back so you saw the scalp below, white as bone. Bright blue eyes looking out from under a ledge of brow.

When Pratt saw him again on the TV years later they were both old men but Pratt remembered the name. He knew the eyes in the photograph. The ledge of brow.

It had to do with a body—remains, they called it—and Devereaux was in the hospital with broken bones.

Pratt raised the remote in his trembling hand and shut off the TV. He didn't want to know about such stuff anymore—the things people did. He just didn't want to know it.

He sat back in the recliner and shut his eyes.

'75, that must've been, his mind went on. He'd been building those houses up in the hills above the Old Indian Highway.

No, the war'd been over awhile by then, so more like '76, '77. It rained cats and dogs that spring, that he could tell you.

He'd asked Devereaux the first thing he wanted to know: What can you do?

The man standing there, scratching at his neck.

I've done some of everything, he said.

Jack-of-all-trades, said Pratt. What'd you do most?

Most?

What do you do best.

Devereaux glanced in the direction of the jobsite. Not much more than a slab of concrete so far. The beginnings of the basement walls, cinderblock, two and three courses high.

I'm a good brickman, he said, and Pratt turned to look at the site. The three men standing there got back to work.

He turned back to Devereaux. I got me a overhand crew already, standing just yonder.

Devereaux nodded. Well, he said, I thought I'd ask. And began to turn away.

Well now hold on a second, buddy. I just got rained out nine days running and I was behind schedule afore that. How's your hand with cinder?

It's good.

Pratt stood studying him. All right, come on up here.

Devereaux followed, halting at the cement slab to kick and scrape the clay from his boots.

Never mind that, said Pratt. Wilby, give this man that trowel a second.

The man named Wilby handed over his trowel and stepped away from a wheelbarrow half-full of wet mortar. Devereaux stepped into Wilby's place. He looked at the low wall and he looked at the stack of cinderblocks and he looked at Pratt.

Go on and set one, said Pratt.

Devereaux picked up a stretcher block one-handed and, holding it in the air, he cut the trowel into the mortar and with a neat chop delivered the load to one of the end ears, then likewise buttered the other ear. He swung the block into place, mating the block to the previous block and sizing the joint by eyeball. He troweled off the squeeze-out and flicked the mortar back into the wheelbarrow, then began to tamp the block with the butt end of the trowel handle, tapping all along its topside as if listening for a false note, and perhaps he was. He stopped when the edge of block lay just under the mason's string and no variance to the line whatsoever. He scraped up the squeeze once more and mixed it into the mortar and then stood looking around as if he were missing something, the men watching him.

Give him it, Wilby.

Wilby pulled a slender tool from his hip pocket and held it out to Devereaux, and Devereaux nodded his thanks. He looked at the slicker, flipped it in the air and fit the larger end into the drying mortar of the previous block and pressed that same concave joint the length of the new block, then pressed it vertically in the head joint. He skimmed away the thin ridges of mortar with the tool's edge and leaned over the wall to repeat the process on the outside joints. He rang the slicker lightly against the wall to free it of grit and lastly he stropped it on his pantleg and handed it back clean to the man named Wilby.

No one spoke. Devereaux scratched the back of his neck.

I get better once I get going, he said.

Pratt said, Come on over here, and walked off to where they'd stood before. He looked back at the men, and the men began working again. Wilby said something to the other two but you couldn't hear what.

They're betting which one of 'em I'm gonna fire.

Devereaux looked at him. Pratt looked at Devereaux.

Where'd you learn to pick and dip like that?

From my uncle.

Where was that?

Sir?

Where'd he learn it to you.

Hereabouts.

I figured out east somewheres. You don't see it much around here. 'Specially not with cinder.

He worked in Massachusetts a little while. My uncle did. After the war.

Nam?

Yes, sir.

Pratt studied him. How old are you?

Twenty-nine. Thirty come August.

Did you soldier?

No, sir. They didn't take me.

Why not?

On account of I got one leg shorter'n the other.

Pratt glanced down. I didn't notice.

My left boot is special made.

There's boots under there?

Devereaux looked down at the caked boots. Yes, sir.

Pratt studied him. I can go ten dollars an hour, he said. Now—there's three more houses up here after this one, so a man could make more after a while, if things work out.

All right.

You drive a hard bargain, buddy.

Devereaux raised his hand as if to scratch his neck, but instead he shooed at some bug that wasn't there and dropped his hand again.

Pratt said, I'm guessing you're free to start right away.

Start right now if you want.

No, I want to give these boys a little time to get used to the idea of you. How's tomorrow morning?

That works for me.

We start seven a.m. sharp.

All right.

Sharp.

All right.

Bring some lunch. We got a spigot up here for water.

All right.

Any questions?

Devereaux glanced toward the men. You aren't really going to fire one of them, are you?

Pratt's mouth went a little bit crooked. You had to know him to call it a smile. I'm gonna sleep on it, he said. Anything else?

No, sir.

Nothin else you want to tell me?

Can't think of it.

How about your name?

Devereaux reddened and said his name.

Devro? said Pratt.

Yes, sir. It's spelled the French way.

You French Canadian then?

My people were, some ways back.

Well, you're gonna have to spell it out for me sometime. First name?

Marion.

Marion?

Yes, sir. He held Pratt's eye. Pratt put out his hand.

Randall Pratt. You can call me Mr. Pratt or sir or boss and not much else I can think of.

All right, Mr. Pratt.

All right, Devro. Go on, now, I'm a busy man.

Two, three months later Devereaux was gone again, remembered Pratt, in his chair, drifting in and out of sleep. An old man's recollections.

Gone like he came.

Load of cinderblocks too. Never did figure that one out, but most likely Devereaux who took them. Who else?

And the wheelbarrow, thought Pratt, drifting. *Man uses your wheelbarrow to cart away your blocks, you can see the tracks coming and going to his truck, but then he leaves the wheelbarrow behind.*

Doesn't just leave it, thought Pratt. *Puts it back where it was and turns it over so it don't fill with rain. Does everything but wash the damn thing . . .*

Go figure that one out.

3.

THE CHAIR HE sat in was metal and, like the metal table, was secured to the floor by L-brackets screwed to the legs, and the brackets pinned to the linoleum by Tapcons driven into the concrete below.

After he'd sat there some minutes, Sean keeled to one side for a look at the footings of the chair opposite, then sat upright again, his hands to either side of a threaded U-bolt fixed to the tabletop like a goal in some miniaturized game. The bolt's actual function was clear but in this case it stood empty while his uncuffed hands moved freely about. Farther from reach a small plastic microphone leaned in its steel housing, cordlessly feeding sound to those who watched from behind the mirrored glass, into which he'd looked exactly once, when he'd first come in, and not again.

He'd been in the room at least an hour, or what felt like an hour, so it must be what, one thirty, two in the morning. He needed a cigarette. His smokes were in his jacket pocket and his jacket was God knew where with his other things—his phone, his wallet, his belt; they'd not taken his shoelaces, not yet. He wore a flannel shirt, once a dark shade of red but now, these several years later, a lighter shade that showed the drops of blood where they'd fallen from the split in his lower lip. He tested the swollen split with the tip of his tongue and tasted the penny tang of his blood.

The knuckles of his right hand were likewise enlarged and bloodied.

Buddy, why don't you just shut up awhile?

Why don't you make me, tough guy?

Two geniuses, matching wits.

He was staring straight ahead at the metal door when the latch handle snapped downward, the door swept open and a woman stepped into the opening.

Just behind her stood a large man in a white shirt and striped tie, his eyes hard on Sean, but the woman came into the room alone and shut the door behind her.

She stood looking at him, Sean at her. Dark-gray jacket and pants, pale-blue blouse. No gun or holster that he could see. A badge clipped to the belt at her waist. Her eyes were dark and her dark hair was pulled tight and ponytailed. Older than him, but not a lot older—midthirties if he had to guess.

"Mr. Courtland," she said.

"Yes ma'am."

"Sean Courtland."

"Yes ma'am."

She sat down and began arranging loose sheets of paper, a lined writing pad, a retractable ballpoint pen. He'd not noticed the smell of the overheated room before she came in but now he realized it had smelled of nothing but himself, which must've been the smell of cigarettes and sweat and unwashed hair. And blood, maybe.

"My name is Detective Viegas," she said. "I'm with the ISB. Do you know what that is?"

"No ma'am."

"It's the Investigative Services Bureau. We're in charge of investigating what are known as sensitive crimes—crimes of domestic violence, crimes involving juveniles, crimes against the elderly, and sex crimes."

He held her gaze.

"I don't suppose I could have my cigarettes," he said. The last time he'd been in one of these rooms the detective had given him his smokes.

"Sorry," said the detective. She sat watching him.

"Sean," she said. "Do you mind if I call you Sean?"

"No ma'am."

"Do you know why I'm talking to you, Sean—why an ISB detective is talking to you?"

"Yes ma'am. But I'm not as old as I look."

"Sorry?"

"Crimes against the elderly."

The detective allowed herself a half smile, then with no smile said, "Do you think what happened tonight was a crime against you?"

"No ma'am, I don't."

She rested her hands on the writing pad. "The reason you had to wait so long, Sean, was that we weren't sure how we were going to investigate this, and therefore how we were going to interview you."

"Interview," he said.

"Yes. I want to hear your version of what happened."

"My version is what I told the officer."

"I just want to go over it with you. Is that all right?"

"Is it all right?"

"Yes."

"Is there a second option?"

"Yes. You could refuse. But that would only set other wheels in motion." She watched him.

"What do you want to know?" he said, and she consulted her papers.

"In the statement you gave Officer Keegan, you said you tried to stop another man, another customer, named"—she checked a separate sheet— "Blaine Mattis, from bothering Denise Givens, who was waitressing tonight at the Wheelhouse Tavern. Is that correct?"

"I know Denise from other times I've been in there, but I don't know the other guy. As I told the officer, I tried to stop a drunk from bothering Denise, and he wouldn't stop."

"So you struck him."

"The other guy?"

"Yes. Mattis."

"Yes ma'am."

"Then what happened?"

"He struck me back."

"And a fight ensued."

"Yes ma'am, it did."

"And who struck Denise Givens?"

Sean looked at his bloodied knuckles.

"I did. She tried to break it up and I hit her by accident when I was swinging at the other guy. I feel pretty shitty about that. I tried to stop the whole thing

right then but the other guy didn't care to stop." Sean flexed the bloodied hand. "The officer wouldn't tell me anything about her. If she was all right or not. I'd like to talk to her if I could."

The detective sat watching him. His eyes. His hands.

"You said you knew Miss Givens from before," she said. "Were you involved with her?"

"Involved? No ma'am. She was just nice to me. When I was in there. She was nice to everyone."

"And that was enough to make you sucker punch Blaine Mattis?

"No ma'am. He saw it coming."

"What made you think Miss Givens wanted your help?"

"I didn't. I just didn't like seeing her treated that way."

"Did you know she'd recently been dating Blaine Mattis?"

Sean shook his head. "I don't know how I'd know that." He patted his chest like a man looking for his cigarettes. Which he was. "But that doesn't change anything, does it?"

"Did you see him hurt Miss Givens—grab her, or strike her—before you hit him?"

"No ma'am."

"Did he threaten her verbally?"

"Threaten her? No ma'am. He just wouldn't quit with that mouth of his. Talking about her to his buddy or whatever he was. Loud enough so she'd hear it every time she went by."

"His buddy Mr."—checking her notes—"Raney."

Sean shrugged.

"And how did you hear what Mr. Mattis was saying to Mr. Raney?"

"Because I was sitting about two seats away."

"At the bar."

"Yes."

"And what was he saying? Mattis."

Sean ran the tip of his tongue over the back side of the lump in his lower lip. He looked at the microphone with no cord. "The officer took it all down," he said.

The detective watched him. "All right," she said. "So, hearing all that, you felt you needed to stand up for her? Defend her honor?"

He watched the detective. Her eyes were lit with the workings of her mind, but her face gave no indication of thoughts or purpose. She asked her questions and watched to see what reactions they caused. Like adding one chemical to another.

"I wouldn't put it that way," he said.

"What way would you put it?"

"I'd put it I saw a guy treating a woman who was just trying to do her job, a woman who puts up with asshats like him on a nightly basis—I saw him treating this woman a way she didn't deserve and I couldn't just sit there. I'd put it that way, I guess."

"Plus hitting him in the face."

"Eventually, yes."

The detective returned to her papers. She placed a new one on top and without looking up from it said, "Can I ask what you're doing here, Sean—in this town? You're not from here. You're from Madison originally. Your truck is registered to Grand County, Colorado."

"Yes ma'am. I was just passing through."

"Something stopped you?"

"Yes ma'am, my truck stopped me. It broke down. A man gave me a lift and told me about another man who needed some work done, and that man hired me, and that's why I'm here. Just making some money."

"And how long ago was that? That your truck broke down."

Sean looked up at the ceiling, and back at her again. "February twenty-third. A Friday."

The detective did the math. "Just over two weeks."

"Yes ma'am."

"And who are you doing this work for?"

Sean hooked his forefinger through the metal loop. "I'd just as soon not say."

"Why not?"

"Why not?"

"Yes."

"Because the second you talk to the man to see if I'm telling the truth, he's gonna fire me and I'll never see the money he owes me." Sean knew how this sounded: like one lie to cover another. But it was true: the old man wouldn't think twice about firing his ass and keeping his money.

The detective sat watching him. "And this address," she said. "68 County Highway F?"

"A place I've been renting."

"For how long?"

"Since March first."

"And how long will you be renting it for?"

He held her gaze. "As long as it takes me to finish this job," he said.

"And how long will that be?"

"Another week, give or take."

She turned back to her papers.

"Another reason you had to wait so long tonight, Sean, was that I was running down your priors and trying to get a sense of your . . . history."

He leaned forward on his elbows and squeezed his bloodied knuckles in the opposite hand. A shiv of pain dug around in his knee.

"The first incident was the most serious one," she went on. Omaha, Nebraska. You were brought in with some other boys for the assault of a young woman in a parking lot behind a restaurant. A Detective Lutz interviewed you."

"And let me go. I didn't have anything to do with what those boys did except trying to stop it."

"Two years later in Kansas City you put a tire iron through a man's windshield after you say you saw him grab a woman by the hair. Turns out it was his girlfriend."

"Again—does it matter what she was to him?"

"No, it doesn't."

"Plus I paid that jerk for his windshield and then some." Sean opened up his hands, almost as if inviting her to take them. "I've gotten into some situations, Detective. I've even spent a night in jail. But—"

He put his hands flat on the table and stared at them. His head was pounding.

"Mattis said you sucker punched him for no reason whatsoever."

He looked up. "What does Miss Givens say?"

"She says pretty much what you say."

"Then"—he shook his head—"why am I still here?"

"Because people lie."

"You think she's lying?"

"No, I don't."

"If she's saying the same thing I'm saying and she's not lying, doesn't that mean I'm not lying too?"

"As far as I'm concerned, yes. But it doesn't mean you didn't throw the first punch."

"I already admitted to that."

"Doesn't absolve you of it, I should have said."

He looked at the mirrored glass, the reflection of the two of them sitting there. The other cop, or cops, behind the glass watching, listening. He turned back to her.

"Detective," he said, "are you charging me?"

"No."

"Is someone pressing charges?"

"Not so far."

"Then why am I still here?" he said again.

She made no reply. Observing him in silence. Then she placed the papers on top of the writing pad and looked toward the glass. But if she made some kind of signal, or if just looking was the signal, nothing happened.

"I know you won't be going back to the Wheelhouse Tavern," she said, "but if you think of anything else you want to tell me, or if there's any more trouble with . . . well, anyone, give me a call." She took a card from the side pocket of her jacket and slid it across the table. "Preferably prior to any bloodshed."

He picked up the card and slipped it into the breast pocket of his shirt without looking at it.

She collected her papers, pushed back the chair and stood, and the metal door unlatched. The same big man in the striped tie stood in the doorframe.

"Officer Keegan will return your personal items to you at the front desk," she said. "You can go now, Sean."

When he stepped out of the station it was just past three in the morning. Cold and dark and nothing moving but the flags on the station pole popping in the wind, the halyard strumming its dull note against the hollow pipe. There was the smell of the river on the wind, and the wind rushed like a river west to east down Main Street. Sooty banks of snow all along the curbs. Early days of March in Wisconsin.

He went down the salted steps and stood on the sidewalk with his back to the wind and got his cigarette lit and took a deep hit.

Across the street an old stone church stood in its own footlights, godly and fortified. Gothic arches, notched battlements. Old green iron cross on a spiked green spire. In the large front window a stained-glass image of a robed figure standing with his hands at his sides, palms-out, like a man showing he was unarmed.

He heard the other guy's voice again—Mattis. The low litany of smut, then the vows of murder from the punched and swelling face. The stench of him as sharp in Sean's nostrils now as if his own clothes, his own skin, had been contaminated.

Behind him a door swept open and he turned to see a woman coming out of the station in her black winter coat. The detective. She came down the steps and walked up to him where he stood on the sidewalk.

"Is someone coming to get you?"

"No ma'am."

"And your truck is back at the Wheelhouse."

"Yes ma'am."

"Do you call all women 'ma'am,' or just women who might throw you in jail?"

"I don't know. I guess it's a habit I picked up somewhere."

She checked her watch. "I can drop you. That's me right there, the blue Prius."

Sean nodded. "I appreciate the offer but I think I'll just walk it. I think it would be good for me."

"All right," she said. And stood there. "Do you have another one of those?"

He brought out the pack and shook one up and she drew it out and leaned to the flame of his lighter, his cupped hand. She took a kind of sip on the filter and blew at the sky, and the thin stream vanished at once in the wind.

"You can really see the stars this time of night," she said. "Or morning."

Sean looked up.

"There's the Big Dipper," she said.

He was silent. Then he said, "Ursa Major."

"Sorry?"

"The name of the constellation is Ursa Major. The Big Dipper is just one part of it."

"Ursa Major," she said.

"The Great Bear."

She kept looking.

"One of the stars in Ursa Major isn't even a star," he said.

"What is it?"

"A galaxy."

"No kidding?"

"No kidding."

They stood smoking. Strands of her hair had come loose and she tended them absently in the wind. She took a last hit on the cigarette and dropped nimbly into a squat and stubbed it out on the concrete and stood again, all with an ease he had not known since he was a boy, if then. She walked over to a city trashcan and tossed in the dead butt and walked back to him.

"That split is pretty deep," she said.

"It's all right."

"You might want to have it looked at. There's an emergency room a few blocks from here."

"Thanks. It'll be all right."

She stood there. Then she said, "You have a sister?"

He watched her.

"Yes," he said.

"An older sister."

"Yes."

"Same here. Five years older. When I was eighteen, she told me she'd been raped when she was in college."

He held the detective's eyes, then stared at his boots as she told him more: That her sister was eighteen at the time, a freshman. That she'd gone to a party

at a friend's house and a boy she met there got her to go down to the basement with him, and there he raped her. On an old sofa that smelled of cat piss. She, the younger sister, had had no idea about the rape until she herself was about to begin college. Her sister wanted her to know what was out there. The detective asked her sister why she'd never told her—why she'd never told anyone—and her sister said it was because she'd been drinking that night, and kissing the boy, and because her name was Viegas. She said it was because the boy was white and on the basketball team and because this was five years ago—saying this last as if speaking of another century.

Sean's knee was spasming with pain, the old fusings cracking open, but he didn't shift his weight. *Do your damnedest,* he told it.

The boy, the rapist, the detective was saying, was now a dentist in New Orleans and her sister was director of a domestic violence program in Houston, Texas.

He waited for her to say more, and when she didn't he looked up again. Her eyes were dark and clear and held distant lights of their own.

"And you became Detective Viegas," he said. "Sensitive crimes unit."

She smiled faintly. "It isn't a direct line. Our dad was a cop when we were kids. A deputy sheriff."

"Was," said Sean.

"He became a lawyer." She began to rummage in a large coat pocket as she might've in a shoulder bag or purse.

"And she never told him—about the boy?"

"Oh, no. He would've killed him. Bite-size Snickers?" She held two of the square candies in her bare palm. Like dice she wanted him to roll.

"No, thanks."

She returned one to her pocket and unwrapped the other and popped it into her mouth and began to chew.

"Also," she said, "he never would've looked at her the same way again."

Something in her voice, the look in her eye—*she was talking about herself, not her sister. It was her, the detective, who'd gone into the basement.*

The thought pumped once in Sean's heart—and was gone. The power of blood, that was all: because it had happened to her big sister, it was as if it had happened to her too.

He understood—to a point. A younger brother could never fully understand something like that. Ever.

The wind gusted and the detective hunched her shoulders. "You sure you don't want that ride?"

"I'm sure. But thank you."

"All right. You take it easy, Sean Courtland."

"Yes ma'am. I intend to."

She got into the Prius and he watched as the car pulled from the curb and went smartly on its way.

In the sky to the west, Castor and Pollux, the twins, walked down the heavens toward the planet's edge. The wind gusted at him and he thought of his cap and where it might be at that moment. Under some table at the bar, or in the bar's garbage bin, soaking up the grease of burgers and fries.

Somewhere to the east an engine on the BNSF line blew its horn, a long and pitiful sound, like some solitary thing sounding out the night for one of its kind. Sean tugged his jacket collar high and set off in that direction.

4.

HE DIDN'T THINK he'd sleep for the pain of his mouth, the pulsing of his knuckles, but then suddenly he was running in a pine woods on a bright day, a stony path in the shadows of the trees, and he was running from a man who, when he turned to look, had the bloodied face of Blaine Mattis one second and the bloodied face of some other man the next, a man he didn't know. And he was running, not fighting, because he was a kid again—young and afraid and he didn't know where his sister had gone but she was ahead of him on the path, calling to him *Let's go, Sean! Move it!* But the stones were getting bigger and he was so slow, so pathetically slow, and he knew he would not get away from the man, and he called out to her to come back, come back for him, but she would not, she was too far ahead, and when he awoke it was not from fear but from the pain of her leaving him behind, abandoning him to the man with the bloody face, a pain inseparable, to his waking heart, from the pain of his failing to protect her.

He lay staring at the dark bands of ceiling beams as his heart quieted. Listening to the silence—or not silence, but a steady droning his brain identified, after a few seconds, as the old heating unit across the room, the hot air blowing.

He saw again the man with the bloody face—Mattis—and he made a fist of his swollen hand and felt the sensation of hitting her, the waitress. Denise. The sound of it. Her blood so red and quick. The immediate cold sick feeling in his heart.

He remembered, too, the satisfaction, the actual pleasure of hitting that other face.

He thought of the detective in the interview room, and then standing with her in the wind as she told him about her sister and the sofa that reeked of cat piss.

Why would she tell you that?

He stood in the bathroom in his bare feet, blinking at the brightness of the mirror. The seam in his lip had crusted over but one wrong move would split it open again. He thought Mattis had hit him just once, but the colors and abrasions on the left side of his face said otherwise.

Because she knew, he answered himself.

Because she'd fed your data into the department's best machines, and your whole story, your so-called history, had spat out on the ticker tape for her to read. She told you about her sister to say she understood about *your* sister. *I get it, buddy,* she was saying: Why you punched Mattis. Why you were always getting into the trouble you got into. *I may be a cop but I feel you . . .*

He filled his hands with tapwater and dipped his face to the cold shock of it. He bent lower and let the stream run over his lip and finally he drank—copper taste and the water so cold his eyeballs ached.

He got into yesterday's clothes, bloodstained clothes, stepped barefoot into his boots and clomped out onto the little porch to light his cigarette. First pale blues and pinks seeping into the pines to the east. The trees and the smell of them in the morning revived his dream, or the feeling of it, and it was a short journey from there to the dream's source: the high pines of the Rockies, the summer she was eighteen, a track star floating up the mountain on pink Nikes while he, age fifteen, fell increasingly behind on the bike. While the man in the woods got closer.

Across the clearing a light came on in the kitchen of the big house. A shadow moved across the scrim of curtain.

The big house, like the cottage from which he viewed it, was built of stones quarried from the bluffs, but for almost a hundred years the cottage had been the only house on the wooded land and the old couple had lived here when they were younger, and only later built the larger, modernized house, when their son was old enough to need his own room. They'd told Sean these things the morning they showed him the cottage, the old man running his fingertips over the darkened oak mantel above the fireplace, she running hers along the white, chipped edge of the sink, remembering not the years of dirty dishes, Sean imagined, but a baby boy, gazing up at her from the suds.

After the showing, outdoors again, the old man had asked if he might see Sean's driver's license, and Sean handed it over. The old man gave it a quick look and handed it back and then they stood awhile looking at Sean's truck and discussing it as if it, and not the cottage, were the object of their business. The old man asked about the Knaack box in the truck bed and Sean looked more closely at him: his seamed and weathered face, like an old sea captain's, the black watchman's cap he wore snugged down, the gray-blue eyes in their creases. Not a large man but standing straight and plumb, his black rubber boots planted in the snow. Niles Parnell, his name.

Come on up and have a look, Sean said, and Parnell laughed.

It must be ten years since I got up in the bed of a truck. Peggy won't have it. Least of all in winter.

Peggy had gone into the house to brew fresh coffee. Sean saw the old man eyeing the back of the truck. He saw the hook of a smile on his lips. Out of the side of his own mouth he said, *I don't believe she can see us from here, Mr. Parnell, and that truck bed is dry as a bone.* Parnell looked at the house, and turning back said, *You get on up first and give me a hand and let's be quick about it,* and Sean climbed up over the tailgate and reached down for Parnell's hand. In his winter coat and layers the old man could not have weighed more than 140 pounds.

Sean unlocked the box and lifted the lid and they stood looking down on the cases of power tools, his levels, his kitbags full of hand tools, all arranged in a tight jigsaw puzzle of organization that had evolved over time and which must be done in the proper order for everything to fit and the lid to close.

Parnell blew a thin white rope of whistle. *Mighty shipshape, Sean. Mighty shipshape.*

It's the only way it all fits.

Well, now I understand what kind of carpenter you are.

You do?

How a man treats his tools says a lot about the kind of carpenter he is. Says everything, if you ask me. And this here says you have an eye for space and a love of order.

Sean looked at the tools. Some had been his father's. Most he'd bought along the way with his earnings from one job or another. For a while he'd bought the tools he'd needed to finish whatever job he'd taken on, but it had been a long time since he'd not had the tool he needed.

There was the sound of a window sash lifting and then the reedy cry, *Niles Parnell, I see you in that pickup truck!*

Oh boy, said Parnell without turning. *Busted.*

I'm sorry. I'll tell her it was my fault.

No you won't, and she wouldn't believe you anyway. Just give me a hand down and let's go face the music.

On their way to the house, in no rush to get there, Parnell said, *I've got a job or two around here needs doing, if that interests you. It's OK it if doesn't. But we could work it into the deal if you cared to.*

I guess it depends on the size of the job or two, said Sean. *I kinda gotta focus on this bigger job.*

What job is that?

I'm building a new laundry room for a man. Moving his machines up from the basement. He can't go down the steps anymore.

I know that feeling. Who's the man, if you don't mind me asking?

A man named Devereaux, up in the bluffs not far from here.

Parnell did not pause or even slow his steps, he did not look at Sean, but something in him changed.

I assume you mean Marion Devereaux, he said.

You know him?

I know of him. How did you get hooked up with that old varmint?

Sean explained: the leaking radiator, Lyle the firewood man who'd put him in touch.

Parnell stopped and stood studying his boots. As if struck by the blackness of them in the snow.

I guess you'd hear it from somebody else if not me, he said, *so I'm just gonna say it. So you won't be blindsided down the road.*

All right.

Well. Years ago three little kids went missing from around here. Grammar-school boys. One a year, beginning in 1975 and ending in 1977. Forty-one years ago this spring, that last one. And one way or another some folks got their minds around to the Devereauxs, who lived out here in the bluffs. In that house—I assume it's the same house.

It's an old house, said Sean.

Loners, they were. Not altogether normal, as families go. Three of them: the old woman, her son, who'd got his bell rung pretty good in the war as I recall—Vietnam War—and her grandson, who was Marion Devereaux. Must've been about thirty at the time. His parents had been killed in some kind of house fire, is how he came to live with his uncle and grandmother. Anyway. Folks talked. Some folks.

Parnell looked sidelong at the carpenter. Reading his face.

Sean shook his head, just to do something.

The old woman died around that same time, Parnell said. *I remember that. I do believe the uncle moved on somewhere, and the house fell to Devereaux. Must be the same house.*

Sean was silent.

Peggy would call me a gossiping old woman if she could hear me, Parnell said. *Marion Devereaux hasn't bothered a soul I know of in all these years. He's just an old man now like me and I've got no business telling stories on him and his kin. I just thought you might as well hear it, is all.*

And the little boys?

They never did find 'em.

Sean blew out his breath. Jesus. Forty-one years. Forty-one years when a day of it could kill you—the panic, the searching, the praying. Worst of all, the imagining.

Parnell cleared his throat. *We lost our own son during those times. Older than those other boys. That's how I remember the year.*

Sean shook his head again. *I'm sorry,* he said.

The old man's coat shoulders rose and dropped. He looked off into the woods and said, *He hanged himself.*

Sean said nothing.

He wasn't but fifteen years old, Parnell said. *What does a fifteen-year-old boy know about life that he'd go and do a thing like that?*

They walked on in silence, but before climbing the steps to the back stoop Parnell stopped again and said in a lowered voice, *Of course there's another*

theory as to what happened to those three boys and why they never were found.
Might put your mind at ease. Might not.

What's that? said Sean, and Parnell aimed a forefinger at the sky. Sean
looked up.

Spacemen, said Parnell.

Now come on inside, he said, opening the storm door, *and let's get some coffee*
in you.

Ten—now eleven days ago that was, and Sean had seen little of Niles or
Peggy Parnell since. If he saw them at all it was as he was getting in or out of
his truck, and the wave they sent from the big house did not encourage or discourage interaction, and he went about his business. He settled in as the tenant
he was, and when he was finished with the Devereaux project he would load up
and move on.

Move on where? Parnell—anyone—might've asked.

To wherever the next job was. To the next place, or the place after that,
until the job crossed his path or he crossed it. He would stop and see his father
in Madison, a night or two there. Drive across town and see his mother, who
would make a fuss, cook for him. Fresh sheets in the other bedroom, where his
sister's old ribbons layered the corkboard, where trophy figures posed in stride
like gilded miniatures of the girl herself. He'd lie in that bed until he knew his
mother was asleep and then he'd get up and slip out, leaving the note on the
table saying he'd woken up early and decided to get an early start, *Love, Sean.*

He bent to crush the butt of his cigarette on the sole of his boot and
when he looked up again he saw the figure come out of the trees and his heart
clenched—*the man in the woods.* Then he recognized the winter coat, the black
rubber boots, the watchman's cap.

The old man trudged on toward the house, head down, hands deep in his
coat pockets. He climbed the steps to the back stoop, paused there to stomp
each boot once, then opened the door and stepped inside.

In an hour or two the Parnells would drive into town and go to church.
Perhaps they'd see Marion Devereaux there, who did not want Sean working in

the house on Sundays. A believer, apparently, the old crank. Scowling old child abductor of the bluffs.

Sean had not been to church since he himself was a child, and even then he'd believed not in heaven but in the heavens: The planets, the stars. The great spiral galaxies so distant they were pinpricks of light in the corner of a constellation named by the creatures of a small blue planet on the outer rings of the Milky Way galaxy, itself a pinprick of light in some other creature's sky.

He'd believed in spacemen.

5.

April 1977

THEY DIDN'T EXPECT *to see him but then there he was, standing just inside the door and peering into the darkness like a boy come to fetch his father.*

Devro, they called, and waved him over.

The man named Sheldon scooted out the fourth chair with his boot and the new man sat down. Three pint glasses of beer already on the table. Packs of cigarettes, lighters, a green Bakelite ashtray. Friday after work. Payday.

Above a general fog of smoke a denser layer seethed, a ceiling cloud glowing red, blue and green, as if hidden within it were weird, hovering aircraft. An early evening babble of voices and laughter. At the jukebox a young woman stood bent at the waist pushing the buttons, her face lit with jukebox light. The selected disc played and she swayed in place, then swayed to the bar and stepped between the knees of a man seated there who tracked her all the while.

As did Devereaux. Like a man unused to seeing such things.

The man named Wilby sat watching him.

Ever been in here before? he said, and Devereaux's gaze quickly shifted, as if drawn to some other thing of interest in the bar.

A time or two, he said. Not for some time, though.

A waitress was passing by with empties in her hands and Wilby reached out to detain her. She took his order for one more pint and when she moved on again he watched her go.

Turning back to the table he took a hit on his cigarette and squinted at Devereaux. Smoke?

Devereaux looked at the offered pack. No thanks, he said. Reckon I'll just breathe the air in here.

Wilby smiled and the men laughed. Devro, making a joke. Devereaux himself smiled.

The fourth man, a man named Petey, lit a cigarette with a plastic disposable lighter. Wilby sat turning his silver Zippo on the table.

That's a good lighter there, Devereaux said, and Wilby stopped turning it. Then stood it upright like a little book.

You recognize that emblem?

Yes, sir. That's Marine Corps.

Were you over there, Devro?

No, they didn't take me. My uncle was, though. He was Marine Corps too.

Korea, said Sheldon.

No, Vietnam.

Shit. How old is he?

He's five years older than me. He was a good bit younger than my mother.

Why not? said Wilby.

Devereaux turned to him. Why not what?

Why didn't they take you.

On account of I got one leg shorter'n the other.

No shit. I got one nut hangs lower'n the other but they still took my ass. Sheldon's too.

Devereaux turned back to Sheldon. You were there too?

Sheldon looked steadily at Devereaux. Yes I was. Right up to Saigon, man.

You'd never know about the leg to see you walk, Wilby said.

My left boot is special made. I limp some barefoot.

The waitress returned with Devereaux's beer. She set down the glass and with her open hand made a croupier's pass over the table. Everybody all set for now?

They were, and she moved on. Wilby watching her again.

You got a old lady, Devro? Sheldon said.

You mean a wife?

Yeah, I mean a wife.

No, sir.

The other three men caught each other's eye. They smoked.

Not married, anyway, said Devereaux, and they looked at him.

Well, now, said Wilby. A lady friend. What's her name?

Devereaux scratched his neck. Christine, he said.

Christine. Got a picture?

Not on me.

What's she do?

She's a schoolteacher.

What grade?

Junior high.

Which one?

Devereaux stared emptily at his inquisitor. Harding, he said.

Harding Junior High.

Yep.

My boy Caleb goes there, said Petey.

Where'd you meet her? Wilby said.

At the school, said Devereaux. When I worked there.

You worked at the junior high?

I was on the maintenance crew.

Maintenance crew, said Wilby. You were a janitor.

I did lawn care too.

Wilby studied him. How come you don't work there no more? They fire you? Consortin with a teacher, something like that?

Devereaux looked at him. No, I just quit. I make better money laying bricks.

Bricks and schoolteachers.

Jesus, Wilby, said Sheldon.

What? When did you become so goddam tender-eared? Christ, I admire the man. I admire you, Devro.

Harding is just four blocks from Hoover Elementary, said Petey, and the other men looked at him.

Petey met only Devereaux's gaze. My boy Caleb was friends with Joey Milner, he said. Still is, I guess. They went to Hoover together.

Wilby and Sheldon turned to Devereaux to see what he would say but he said nothing.

Joey Milner—? Petey pressed. Duane Milner's older brother?

They all saw a small light go on in Devereaux's mind.

That little boy that went missing, Devereaux said.

Yeah, said Petey. Second little boy. One year ago this spring. The first one was the spring before that. Teddy Felt. He went to Roosevelt.

Devereaux nodded slowly. Teddy Felt, he said.

Wilby and Sheldon tipped their ashes studiously in the ashtray. Silent. Like men resigned to something inevitable.

Petey glanced over his shoulder and looked again at Devereaux.

Caleb was there on the school grounds that day, he said. He was on the ball-field the day Duane Milner went missing. Caleb and Joey Milner were friends, like I said. Good kid, Joey Milner. Heck of an arm. Saw him turn a double play this one time—

Petey, said Wilby.

Yeah, said Petey. Anyway, Caleb says Duane Milner—the little brother—had his rocket ship with him that day.

Toy rocket ship, Sheldon clarified. Not looking up.

Toy rocket ship, said Petey. My boy says that kid was crazy for rocket ships. The moon. Star Trek. Anything to do with outer space. Says he had that rocket ship with him that day.

Petey fell silent again, and Devereaux looked once more around the table.

That's it, said Wilby. That's the whole earth-shattering story.

Devereaux nodded.

Did they ever find the rocket ship? he said.

Negative, said Wilby. The aliens took it with them, you see. They wanted to take it apart and learn its technology. They figured the boy must be some kinda astronaut.

He looked at Sheldon, but Sheldon was staring at Devereaux.

You see that movie Chariots of the Gods, Devro? Sheldon said. About the aliens? The ancient civilizations?

Wilby shook his head. Here we go.

No, not yet I haven't, said Devereaux.

Go see it. Take your gal. I didn't have to see it. I'd already seen it with my own eyes.

Devereaux looked at him. He looked at the other two men, then at Sheldon once more.

What did you see?

Sheldon said nothing. He seemed to be searching Devereaux's eyes. His very thoughts. Finally he shook his head and looked away. Like a man who would waste no more of his time with the likes of these. But then he turned back and looked at them one by one.

How do you explain the fact they don't have no clues, man? Not one little thing to go on.

That you know of, said Wilby.

Sheldon looked at him with something like pity.

Petey sat staring gloomily at his own hands on the tabletop. Let 'em try to take my kids, he said. Let 'em try. I'll blow their motherfucking alien heads off.

Wilby put a hand on his shoulder. You ain't got to worry, Petey. The aliens ain't gonna take your kids.

Petey stared bleary-eyed at Wilby. They ain't?

Naw, Petey. They'd take one look at those kids and say thanks but no thanks. Next house.

Sheldon blew a smoky hiss of laughter. Petey turned to look at him. At Devereaux.

Shit, he said. They'd be happy to get my kids.

I better get going, Devereaux said.

Where you going? said Wilby.

I told my uncle I'd help him out.

Wilby sat watching him. You know what I think? I think we all need to let off a little steam. Let the kids get out and play. Give the wives a break. Just have us a little goddam fun. He looked around the table. What we need is a barbecue. What do you all think a that?

That'd work, Sheldon said.

Yeah, said Petey. I'm in.

Devro? said Wilby. You can bring Christine.

Devereaux nodded. I guess it would depend when, he said. She teaches the piano on the weekends.

Ask her when she can get free one Saturday and let me know, said Wilby. That work?

All right, said Devereaux. He got to his feet. Thanks for the beer.

See you Monday, Devro.

Devereaux turned and began to make his way to the door and they watched him go and believed they saw the limp. Or saw what they looked for.

The metal door opened and late sunlight blazing head-on from the west shaped a bright corridor in the smoke, elongate and square-edged as a mine shaft, as a pharaoh's passageway, and stepping into that distorting light Devereaux himself was transformed—a gangly puppet-man, a weird-bodied alien going home— before the door shut again, taking light and shaft and Devereaux with it.

6.

COME MONDAY MORNING Sean took the twisting blacktop roads out of the bluffs and into town, passing along the way the Wheelhouse Tavern, site of his stupidity, the lot now empty, the windows dark.

He drove on.

He'd been getting his breakfast at the diner since his first morning in town—Larry Hines, the mechanic, having sent him there. He walked in now and sat at the counter and did not sit long before the waitress came to him with her globe of coffee.

"Hey, partner," she said, pouring.

"Hey, partner."

She put her other fist on her hip and shook her head. "Did you get the name of the bus?" Her name was Maggie. Middle forties, maybe. He liked seeing her in the morning, fielding the banter she threw at him. Friendliness with no danger of actual friendship, the rules understood.

"Do buses have names?" he said. "Like streetcars?"

"Sure, why not?"

"Then yeah," he said. "This bus's name was Stupid."

"So you ran yourself over."

"Exactly."

"I could get you some ice for that lip."

"That's OK."

She watched him. "You want the same?"

"No, I believe I'll take the number three for a spin this morning."

"Bold. How do you like your eggs?"

"Over easy."

"Runny?"

"Is there another way?"

"You'd be surprised what folks ask for when it comes to eggs."

"Runny, please."

"White or wheat or something else?"

"Wheat, please."

"Sausage or bacon or something else?"

"What's the something else?"

She shrugged. "Neither, I guess."

"Bacon, then."

"You got it. Anything else?" She didn't write any of it down.

"That's it. Except one more thing," he said, feeling his lip with his fingertip. "After it's cooked up, could you put it all in a blender and bring me a straw?"

She smiled. "One number three in a sundae glass, comin up."

He sipped his coffee and glanced around the diner: Four old men in a booth under the windows, their meals long gone, their hands wrapped around the white mugs. Same booth every morning, same orders. Widowers, perhaps, or just claiming their daily time away from the house. In the booth next to them two big men sat forking eggs into thick beards, one man the image of the other in their Carhartt coveralls. At a table for six a woman in a skirt suit, her neck swaddled in bright turns of scarf, raised spoonfuls of yogurt as she stared into her laptop.

The glass door swung open and two young women still in pajama bottoms shuffled in half-asleep and heaved backpacks into a far booth and fell in after them. One fair-haired under her wool beanie, one dark. Their faces, their outfits, their air of burdened lassitude, identified them as young college women not just confident in their right to appear in public however they chose without fear of reprisal or harassment—certainly not of danger—but who did not even give such possibilities the least consideration. They'd come to study, and by this act they endowed the diner with the same protections, the same assurances of safety and privilege that followed them everywhere on the campus proper.

If you could call it a campus. From what Sean had seen of it, it wasn't much bigger than his high school, with an open football field surrounded by the same red cinder track he'd watched his sister go round and round, leaving the other girls in her dust.

"Here you go, bus driver."

Sean sat up and looked at the plate of steaming food.

"How's that look?" she said.

"Good enough to eat."

"Anything else right now?"

"No ma'am."

"Okey doke," she said, and with a slow flourish produced a straw in its paper sleeve—a tiny magic wand—and placed it next to his silverware.

"Perfect," he said.

He popped the yolks with his fork and watched the bright fluid run.

He'd finished the eggs and toast and he had the last slice of bacon in his front teeth when two officers walked into the diner. They were young and they wore the brown and tan of the sheriff's department, the stiff-brimmed hats. One of them nodded at him and he nodded back and faced forward again. He listened to them getting out of their jackets, clopping those hats on empty seats, and he remembered the detective, Viegas, telling him the story of her sister and the sofa and her daddy the deputy sheriff, who would've killed that boy had he known.

Another waitress went to take their order.

Sean sipped his coffee, and when Maggie came back with the pot he said, "Just a splash," then sat watching the wheeling liquid and the steam that chased it around the inside of the mug.

A minute or two later a man came into the diner and walked to the counter and put a hand on the chairback to Sean's left and asked if anyone was sitting there. "All yours," Sean said, and the man sat down. When he shucked out of his jacket his movements brought the smell of the cold outdoors. More faintly of a river not yet frozen over. The man blew into cupped hands, rasped his palms together, then placed his hands one over the other on the counter and sat staring at them, at the counter, or at nothing at all.

Sean slid the menu over and the man thanked him. A man about his age, Sean saw—twenty-six, twenty-seven, maybe. Brown, windblown hair, dark whiskers on his jaw. Tan canvas jacket—a man of the trades perhaps, like himself. Silent and apart despite his nearness and wanting nothing from anyone but his first cup of coffee.

Maggie, passing, tapped the counter with her nails. "Coffee?"

"Yes, please," said the man, and she continued on to get it.

"What's good here?" he said, and Sean looked at Maggie, too far away to hear. He looked toward the man and the man said, "Thought you might know your way around this menu."

"I'm partial to the number five," Sean said, "but this morning I went crazy and ordered the number three."

"The number three," said the man. "How was it?"

"Entirely edible."

Maggie came back with the pot and poured. "What can I get you, hon?"

The man ordered the number 4, a breakfast sandwich, choosing bacon over sausage, cheddar over American.

"What about you, champ, anything else?"

"No ma'am," said Sean. "Just the check, please."

She placed it facedown on the counter and lifted his plate. "You did pretty good, considering."

"It's all in the footwork."

She laughed and moved on.

He got his wallet from his jacket and placed it on the counter. He lifted the white mug and sipped. The man to his left sipped too, then looked at the mug and set it down.

"It grows on you," Sean said.

"It had better," said the man.

"Yeah. I only kept drinking it because everybody else was."

The man glanced around at the other diners. Behind them, the sheriff's deputies were talking with food in their mouths, clinking forks and knives on the china plates.

"You're not a native, then," said the man.

"No. Just visiting. You?"

"Same."

Sean nodded and they fell silent. They sipped the coffee.

"Well," Sean said after a while. "I best get on with it. I hope that number four works out for you."

"Thanks. I do too."

He counted out a few bills and set them on top of the check, and he was about to stand when a third man arrived and took the seat to his right—took it, without hesitation or niceties. Whumping down and claiming counter space with his forearms, with the laced ball of his hands. Sean saw the bruised and swollen jaw, the darkly purpled eye, the red stain of burst capillaries mapping the eyeball—and turned away. He looked into his empty mug and shook his head.

"I thought I recognized that shit-green Chevy in the lot," said the bruised man. His smell, his personal odor, recalled the violence of that night, two nights ago now, even more vividly than did his face.

Sean looked up and said to the other side of the counter, as if speaking to one of the cooks who appeared from time to time in the pass-through, "A man who shits green maybe ought to rethink his diet."

"Funny man," said Blaine Mattis. "Funny man who punches girls in the face."

Sean looked Mattis in his broken eye and looked away again. "Listen, buddy," he said. "Why don't you just let it go."

Mattis looked over his shoulder and turned back. Sean looked too: The deputies. The back of the nearer one in his ironed blouse, hunched over his breakfast, the eyes of his partner staring back at Sean over the rim of his coffee.

Sean faced forward again and Mattis, leaning nearer, said, "Why didn't you just mind your own business . . . buddy. Know what that little bitch did? Got me served with a restraining order. How funny is that, funny man? You punch her in the face and I get the restraining order. Pretty God damn funny, right?"

Maggie returned then with her pot of coffee and, seeing the new man, stopped abruptly and shook her head. "You must've been hit by the same bus."

Mattis turned to her slowly. As a pasture animal toward some sound. The man to Sean's left leaned forward in his seat.

Maggie held Mattis's gaze. She gestured with the pot. "Do you want coffee?"

"No, thanks."

"Did you want to order anything?"

"No, ma'am. I just stopped in to say hey to my buddy here."

She looked from one man to the other and knew their story. She planted her hand on the countertop in a kind of counter server's stiff-arm and, looming nearer, said, "I know I don't have to tell you there's two sheriff's deputies sitting not twenty feet away."

"No ma'am," said Sean, "you don't."

The deputies had stopped talking and sat watching. The old men in their booth too. The college girls lifting their faces from their books like baby birds.

"In fact," Sean said, "I believe I'll just get my butt to work." He pushed the check and the bills toward her and she said she'd get him his change and he said, No, keep it, and stood. He lifted his jacket from the chairback and nodded to the other man, the working man, who nodded back, then he walked toward the glass door and stepped out into the brightness of the morning.

He stood as if taking in the new day, as if deciding what it called for, and finally he went around the corner to the parking lot and got into the Chevy.

"Tell you one thing, Blaine old buddy," he said. "I cannot have you following me around all day."

He didn't know what Mattis drove so he sat in the cold truck and watched the corner of the building—Mattis would have to come this way to get to his car. Unless he was on foot.

After a while he checked his phone. He'd been sitting there five minutes. He sat one more minute and said "Screw this" and turned the key and put the truck in gear. He tried to see into the diner as he drove by but could make out little beyond the glass—the old men at their booth, bald heads, white heads, all turning as one to watch the Chevy go by.

When he looked back to the road he saw the man in the tan canvas jacket walking along the sidewalk. He drove on—then drifted left, crossing the centerline, and pulled over in the oncoming parking lane. He cranked down the window and put his elbow out and waited for the man to catch up, and when he did he said, "So what's the verdict?"

The man slowed and looked at him. "Sorry—?"

"The verdict. On that number four."

"Oh." He stopped. "I took it to go." He patted the side pocket of his jacket.

"Ah," said Sean. The man stood looking at him. Like a man awaiting his next directive. "Hey, not to bother you," Sean said, "but did that other dude ever leave?"

"Which dude?"

Sean smiled, thinking he was joking. But the man didn't smile, and it crossed Sean's mind that he might be drunk, or stoned, though he'd not seemed so at the counter. "The one with the colorful face," he said. "The one talking to me."

"Oh," said the walking man. "No. He decided to order something after all."

"That explains it," said Sean.

The man stood there. He seemed to look the Chevy over. Maybe to see if the color matched the description he'd heard. "OK," he said, and raised a hand. And began to walk again.

Later, Sean would wonder why he didn't just let the man go. Why he didn't drive on.

But a few days ago he'd been standing on the shoulder just off I-90 and a man had stopped and helped him.

"Hey," he said to the walking man, who paused a second time. "You need a lift?"

The man looked up and down the street and again at Sean. "Which way you headed?"

"I can go any which way. Which way are you?"

"I'm up by the interstate. The Motel 6."

"That's a long walk for breakfast."

"Yeah," said the man. He touched his fingers to his forehead, near the hairline, lightly. As you might feel for some bump, or wound.

Car accident, maybe, Sean thought. Still getting his bearings.

"I had to see a guy," said the man.

Sean nodded. "Listen," he said. "I can run you on up there. Save you some boot leather, as they used to say."

The man half smiled. He looked up at something, squinting, and Sean looked with him: the clean-blown sky, a blue with no depth to it other than the high, thin stitch of a contrail.

"Didn't you say something about getting to work?" said the man, and Sean looked at him again.

"I did. But how I get there is my business. Including pulling over on the wrong side of the street."

"I saw that."

"I just have one question," said Sean.

"What's that?"

"Are you packing heat?"

"Am I packing what?"

"Do you have a gun."

"No, sir. But maybe I should."

"Why's that?"

The man looked at the truck, the curb, the other parked cars. "Seems like a pretty rough town."

Sean smiled. "It's downright lawless. Hop in."

"Well," said the walking man. "All right."

7.

THEY DROVE NORTH along a route parallel to the great river, but as the cab warmed, Sean realized the marine smell was coming not from the river but from his passenger, as it had when the man had first sat down at the diner. Something like the smell of an old canoe life jacket drying in the sun.

That, and the pungency of bacon.

"Go ahead and eat that sandwich," he said.

"It can wait," said his passenger.

"It won't be hot."

The man shrugged. "It doesn't matter."

"In that case, do you mind if I smoke?"

"It's your truck."

"Do you mind?"

"I don't mind."

"You want one?"

"No, thanks."

Sean pushed in the lighter knob and when it popped he gapped the window and blew the smoke toward the gap. After a while he said, "Car trouble?"

The man said nothing. Then he said, "Truck trouble."

"That's how I ended up here," Sean said, and the man looked toward the dashboard, perhaps to see the gauges.

"What happened?"

"Hole in the radiator. I was lucky I didn't burn up the engine."

"Got her fixed, though," said the man.

"Yeah, and emptied my wallet doing it. The man who gave me a lift told me about a man who had a job he needed done, and now here I am."

"Carpentry job," said the man, half turning, thumbing at the Knaack box in the bed of the truck.

"Yep."

Sean thought the man might say his line of work but he didn't.

"What's yours?" Sean said.

"Mine—?"

"Your truck."

"Ah. F-150. Two thousand one."

"What happened?"

"I don't know."

"You don't know?"

"The man doesn't know. He's trying to figure it out."

"That wouldn't be Larry Hines, would it? Bud's Top Line Auto?"

"No. Different garage."

Sean tipped his ash in the gap.

"Where were you headed? If you don't mind me asking."

"Oh," said the other man, gesturing vaguely toward the world. "No place special. I was just getting out of Dodge for a while."

"I know how that is," said Sean. Didn't say he'd been doing basically that since he was seventeen.

They came to an undeveloped stretch of the road from which the river could be seen and they watched it: The wide dark surface sluggish and steaming in the morning sun. White shelf of ice on the shore of some middle island. Dark, barren trees of Minnesota in the far distance.

"I didn't punch her," Sean said. "Just for the record."

The man looked at him, and looked away again. "None of my business."

"I mean, I hit her, but it was an accident. I was trying to hit him."

"Looks like you succeeded."

"Yeah."

"More than once."

"Yeah."

"Did you know him?" said his passenger.

"No. I'd seen him before but I didn't know him."

"What about her?"

"I knew her by name. Know her. She's a waitress at the bar where it happened. But it wasn't about her. Not in that sense."

"Which sense was it? Not that it's any of my business."

Sean shrugged. "The fairness sense, I guess," he said, and turned to the man. "Ya know?"

"Yeah," said the man.

An eagle appeared over the river, moving north as they were, white-headed in the sun, dark wings wide over the dark water, and soon enough it descended toward its own image and the white leg feathers came forward and the surface spangled and the great wings beat and the bird rose, its beak down in its talons as if it did not believe, as if it would make sure it had indeed missed its prey, and empty-footed it banked away toward Minnesota and out of sight.

They drove on.

"You fight a lot?" said the man.

"Do I fight a lot? No. I'm not a fighter. Neither is he, obviously. Of course, he was already staggering before I hit him." Sean shook his head. "A smarter man would've just walked away. By which I mean me," he said.

"Got it."

Buildings reared up again to obstruct their view of the river, and after a few blocks the road divided into separate one-way avenues, and some blocks after that they crossed a concrete bridge over a railroad right-of-way.

"So where was Dodge?" Sean said.

"Dodge?"

"Where you got out of."

"Over yonder. Minnesota."

"You didn't get very far."

"No. I'd have liked to get a bit farther."

"Hot on your trail, are they?" Sean said, and the man said nothing. Then he huffed a laugh and said, "Yeah. Thought I lost 'em at the river, but . . ." And fell silent again.

Sean drummed the wheel slowly with his thumb.

"Screw it," he said. "I'm just gonna say it." He turned to the man. "Are you interested in work?"

The man didn't answer, and Sean looked back to the road. "I've got this job that's turned into kind of a bitch," he said. "I could use a pair of hands. Preferably skilled."

The man was silent. Then he said, "I don't have my tools with me."

"I've got tools."

"I don't have my truck."

"Yeah, that's why I asked. I thought since you were stuck here anyway." He took a drag on his cigarette. "No worries," he said. "Just thought I'd ask."

The man watched the road. "Are you talking about now—today?"

"No. I gotta run it by the client, make sure he's cool with me bringing in another man. You can call me in the morning and let me know one way or another."

"I don't have a phone."

Sean looked at him. "There's not one in your room?"

"Oh, right. I forgot about that kind."

Sean pulled into the Motel 6 and took a pen from the visor caddy and cast about for something to write on. His passenger sat waiting; he brushed at a dark crust on his knee. Maybe the remains of dried mud.

"There you go," Sean said, handing the man the little white card. "If you don't feel up to it in the morning, give me a call around seven thirty. Otherwise I'll be here at eight a.m. sharp."

The man looked at what Sean had written in blue ink on the back of the card and turned the card over. It was a police detective's card and an *X* had been drawn from corner to corner in the same blue ink.

"Never mind that side," Sean said.

The man turned the card over again. "Sean Courtland," he said.

"Yep."

"Dan Young," the man said, and they shook hands.

"How long you been here?" Sean said.

"At the motel?"

"Yeah."

"Just a few days. Where you staying?"

"I'm renting this little place out in the bluffs."

"The bluffs—?"

"Just east of town. This big area of woods and . . . bluffs."

"Got it." Dan Young opened the door and stepped out, then turned to look into the cab.

Sean waited.

"What made you think I could help you out?"

"How do you mean?"

"When you pulled over. You were looking for help with that job."

Sean stared at him. He'd pulled over because he'd wanted to know if Mattis had left the diner. He touched his tongue to the crusted split in his lip.

But yeah, Dan Young was right: He'd wanted help. Needed it.

"Yeah," he said. "But you also looked like a man who could use a ride, so."

"What made you think I could help you?"

"I don't know. You had that look about you."

Dan Young half smiled. He stepped back to shut the door and Sean called to him and he looked in again.

"I got one for you."

"All right."

"Is that your real name—Dan Young?"

"Yes, sir. Why?"

"You're not actually on the run, are you, Dan Young? From the law? The po-lice?"

Dan Young held his gaze. "Do I have that look too?"

"No. But I once gave a ride to a man who didn't look like it either and I ended up spending the night in jail."

"Maybe you ought to stop giving rides."

"Yeah." Sean waited.

"No, sir," said Dan Young. "I'm not on the run. I'm just . . . on the move."

Sean nodded. "All right. Sorry to ask."

"No worries."

"I'll talk to you in the morning."

"Yes, sir."

"One more thing."

"Yes, sir."

"How old are you?

"I'm twenty-nine."

"Shit. You're three years older'n me."

Dan Young looked at him again. As if he were resetting his understanding of what he saw.

"So do me a favor," Sean said.

"What's that?"

"Stop calling me sir."

"All right."

"I'll see you in the morning, Dan. Unless you call."

"All right, Sean. Thanks for the lift."

Dan Young shut the door. He stood in the parking lot as Sean pulled onto the service road and drove back to the intersection, and he was standing there still when the green truck passed by the motel going back the way it had come in the far lanes of the divided avenue.

8.

FROM THE MOTEL 6 Sean drove east across town and on into the wooded bluffs, following the bends of the blacktop as it wrapped around the walls of rock, and turning, finally, onto the unpaved drive. The Devereaux house sat back in the woods some fifty yards from the road, and when he pulled up in front of it at a quarter past nine the house was still in the shade of the tall pines.

He stood in the open door of the truck looking for the old German shepherd dog to come down off the porch or limping around the corner, barking at him in her blindness until she heard his voice or caught his scent and began to wag her tail. But she didn't, and he swung the truck door shut and still she didn't come or bark and he thought maybe she'd died. The idea was already lodged in his mind when he saw the old man, in the morning shadow of the house, raising a pickaxe and bringing it down on the hard earth.

He watched Devereaux at his labor and wondered at such loss—at the emptiness of the old man's days to come, when the dog would not bark at the carpenter's arrival, greeting him with fierceness and then happiness, trailing him as he carried tools or materials in and out the back door, underfoot despite the old man's scoldings—the dumb old girl grinning at the carpenter with her yellow teeth and gazing at him with her milky eyes, wagging her tail when he spoke to her. Sean was so committed to the fact of the dog's death that when the dog rose from the ground not far from the old man's feet the world tilted and his heart swung and he waited for the old man to cry out and drop the pickaxe and fall to his knees. Instead he paid the dog no mind and she came limping out of the shadow and into the light and Sean laughed and reached down to take her face in his hands and look into her clouded eyes.

"Are you going deaf too?" he asked her.

Devereaux went on chopping and Sean walked toward him, the shepherd following. When he saw them the old man paused and held the tool at waist level. His knobby walking cane leaned against the house next to the wheelbarrow. Years of lifting stones and cinderblock had left him back-bent, his knees permanently cocked. Holding the pickaxe he looked a stricken old rampager, a hunchback Viking, improbably standing in the wreckage of battle. He stood as though planning the next blow and Sean saw that he labored not to craft a grave or any other kind of hole in the earth but only to free the tire of the wheelbarrow from a small pond of ice, the result of Sean having left the barrow upended there against the side of the house instead of almost anywhere else he might have left it.

It was the oldest wheelbarrow Sean had ever seen. Boxy and dented, rusted like a sunken ship. The icebound tire couldn't have been the original but looked it: bald and sun-faded and cracked. Yet it held its air.

Devereaux looked up toward the roof and gestured with his bristly chin. "The gutter sags there."

Sean looked. The gutter indeed sagged, and was hung with dripping icicles.

The old man looked down at the ice. "And the water don't drain here."

"Shoot," Sean said, "I shouldn't have left it there. I'll bust it loose, Mr. Devereaux."

Devereaux made a kind of grunting sound.

"Did you need it?" Sean said, and the old man looked at him. Eyes bright blue in their deep wells. He wore no glasses that Sean had ever seen and didn't need them. He did not hover over Sean while he worked, but if he passed by he was likely to stop and ask about some imprecision or unfinished task, and Sean would feel those blue eyes going over every detail, and he'd begun to take more time even with the rough work. Devereaux had insisted on a bid for the finished job, not time and materials, and Sean knew he was not going to make the money he'd wanted. But at least now with a second man he'd finish sooner.

Unless that man, Dan Young, called to say no thanks. Unless he just kept moving on.

"Need what?" said Devereaux, his eyes on Sean.

"The barrow," said Sean. "Did you need the barrow?"

"Need it?"

"Yes sir."

"What for?"

"I don't know. I figured since you were trying to bust it free you must need it."

He stared at Sean. "I'm trying to bust it free 'cause it's froze up in ice."

"Yes sir."

"What if you need it?" said the old man.

"Yes sir. Why don't you let me bust it free?"

"Because I reckon your time might be better spent on other things. Especially so late in the day. What happened to your face?"

"I was in a fight."

"A fight."

"Yes sir."

"What over?"

Sean shook his head. "Nothing."

"A fight over nothing."

"Yes sir."

Devereaux grunted and turned back to the tire. "Have it your way. But I guess I'd kind of like to see this job finished someday."

"Yes sir. That's what I wanted to talk to you about."

Devereaux looked up again.

"I'd like to bring in another man to give me a hand."

"What man?"

"A man I know in town. A carpenter."

"Same man who fought you?"

"No sir. Completely different man. A good man."

"How do I know if he's good or not?"

"I guess you don't, except that I'm saying he is."

"I don't like just anybody coming into my house."

"No sir. I understand that."

"Didn't much care to let you in, tell you the truth. But I can't keep going up and down those stairs."

"I understand. That's the reason I want to bring this man in, so I can finish this job sooner and get out of your way."

"I suppose you expect me to pay for a second man."

"No sir. He'll be figured into the bid."

"You'll lose money that way."

"Yes sir. But I'll finish the job sooner so I can get on to the next one."

"How'd you say you know this man?"

Sean held the old man's eyes. "I've worked with him before. We ran into each other and he was looking for work."

Devereaux turned toward Sean's truck. "Where is he?"

"I'll bring him with me tomorrow."

Devereaux looked at the pickaxe. As if he'd forgotten he was holding it. He seemed to test its weight.

"Let me meet him before you get all carried away. I want to meet a man's gonna be coming into my house."

"All right." Sean gestured toward the axe. "You want me to bust that tire out?"

"No, I don't. I'm doing it."

"All right. I'll get to work." He turned to go around the corner of the house where the back door was and he put out his hand to stop the old dog from following, but she didn't see the hand or didn't heed it and trailed after him on into the house.

THE JOB WAS to relocate the washer and dryer from the basement to a small first-floor room just off the kitchen that did not yet exist but which must be created by moving one wall and grabbing floor space from a dining room that had not been used in many years, if ever, the old man taking his meals at the kitchen table or in the living room in front of the TV. Decades-old plaster fell away under Sean's hammer and crashed in sheets onto the Ram Board he'd laid down over the hardwood. Lath strips creaked and sprung from the studs in dusty explosions, and the studs were thicker and broader than modern two-by-fours by a full half inch, having been milled in a day when lumber dimensions were actual and not nominal. The studs were rough-hewn and dark, and when you cut into them there was the dusty smell of ages but also, inexplicably, the smell of cinnamon.

At the end of that workday he swept up the space and stowed his tools in the corner of the new little room and said good-bye to the old dog and left as he always did by the back door. He had learned in the first days of the job that he need not make any effort to say good-bye to the old man unless he was in view, and on this day he was not.

He'd worked later than usual to make up for the late start, and he'd intended to go back to the stone cottage and get cleaned up and eat something and get to bed early, but when he came to the end of the Devereaux drive he stopped and sat there. Holding the wheel in both hands. The swelling on his knuckles was down, the scrapes crusting over.

"Don't be stupid," he said.

"Stupider," he said.

Finally he turned right, not left, and drove into town.

The near-empty parking lot foretold a lonesome bar on an early Monday night and so it was. No music. No clack of billiards. No voices raised against the din. No din. Smell of fresh hay chaff and the soft crush of it underfoot.

Behind the bar Little Jeff watched his approach, no expression on his face and no movement to him other than his hands as he turned a pint glass in a bar rag, the jump of muscle along his forearms. The bartop itself was a slab of lacquered walnut worn to the raw wood by human hands going back perhaps a century, and Sean placed his own hands on it as he'd done two nights before, as he'd done on other nights, and Little Jeff shook his head.

"Why am I not surprised to see you again?"

Two men to Sean's left raised their faces to look at the bartender, then swung them to look at the man he'd addressed. The two men were in their sixties, easy, seventies maybe, and they'd been there awhile. The nearer of them tipped two fingers and said, "Afternoon."

Sean did likewise. Then to Little Jeff he said, "Is she here?"

The bartender set down the pint glass and picked up another. "She's working."

Sean nodded.

"I won't keep her," he said. "I just want to see that she's all right. Then I'll go."

Little Jeff looked him over: his eyes, his busted lip, the rest of him that he could see. He set down the glass and flung the bar rag over his shoulder and turned and pushed through the swinging aluminum door.

Where he had stood there was now a view of the backbar mirror, and standing in it was a man with stiffened hair and a fattened lower lip. In the hair and in the whiskers of his jaw were bits of white dust like baker's flour. Sean ran his hand over his face and stopped short of running it through his hair for fear of the dust raining from him like dander.

The two older men watched him in the mirror, and he watched the near one raise a hand and rap backhanded on his—on Sean's—upper arm. He turned and the man turned too. Bleary hazel eyes in a hedge of eyebrow hairs.

"Young man," said the man, "do you know the time? Not for myself, but for Mr. Bonner here, who asked that I ask. There's that cliché of a clock, of course," he said, tossing his chin at the Pabst Blue Ribbon clock above the backbar, "but that is bar time and cannot be trusted."

Sean looked to the other man, Mr. Bonner. Thinner of face, larger of nose, but otherwise not much distinguishable from his companion. Then he hunted up his phone from his jacket and read the screen. "Six thirty-two."

The man turned to the other. "Six thirty-two."

"Il est six heures trente-deux?"

"So he says."

The second man, Mr. Bonner, leaned forward, the better to see Sean's face. To look into his eyes with the drunk's great patience. His great wisdom.

"Plus tard que je pensais," he said.

"Sorry?"

"He says it's later than he thought."

"Mais pas trop tard," said the other.

"But not too late," said his translator.

"Not too late for what?" said Sean.

The man shrugged. He turned to Mr. Bonner. "Pas trop tard pour quoi, chéri?"

Mr. Bonner bunched his lips, and with his eyes still on Sean's he said, "Ne savez-vous pas?"

"He asks do you not know?"

"Tell him I don't."

The translator did and Mr. Bonner shrugged and turned away. "Dans ce cas," he said, "vous êtes déjà perdu."

The translator did not translate.

"What did he say?"

"It doesn't matter."

Sean looked from one to the other.

"I'm sorry," said the nearer man. "Questions of time confuse him."

"Then why does he ask?"

"I don't know. It began when he lost his wife."

"When did he lose his wife?"

"1969."

Sean was silent.

"It was the war, you see. The Indochina War—the second one."

"Vietnam."

"Yes. He fell in love with the eldest daughter of a French rubber baron."

"A what?"

"A French rubber baron. A Frenchman who owned a rubber plantation. They were wed, Mr. Bonner and the daughter, and two months later the entire family was assassinated, the plantation burned to the ground while the young soldier was off fighting General Giáp in the jungle. The young soldier returned and stood among the ruins, the smoke. The blackened bones of three generations. Little boys, little girls. He himself a boy of nineteen."

Sean looked at the man. Then he looked at Mr. Bonner, who stared impassively at the backbar mirror, or in its direction. They were part of Sean's sentence, these two characters, envoys of punishment, and he knew he must listen to them until she appeared. That she wouldn't otherwise do so.

Mr. Bonner said, "Qui est-il?"

"Who is who?"

"Le mec à votre droite."

"He is the man who tells time."

Mr. Bonner frowned. "Dans ce cas, demande-lui quelle heure il est."

"I just asked him and he told you. Il est six heures trente-deux."

"C'était il y a des heures."

"It wasn't hours ago, my dear. It was minutes."

Sean watched the round window in the aluminum door. He felt he'd been standing there a very long time. He turned to look at the section of floor where he thought most of the fight had taken place, as a man might gaze on the spot where someone he'd loved had last been seen alive. Of the fight he saw no sign—no trace of scuffing and skidding in the chaff or in the wood below the chaff. No dried drops of blood. Nor did he recollect the particulars of the fight except for the moment when he struck her. Seeing that again, her shocked and bloodied face, he shuddered and turned back to the bar, and as he did so the waitress pushed through the door and came to the bar opposite him. As though to take his order.

No blood on her face, no shock. No warmth or coldness in her eyes, or much of anything, though they seemed the brighter, the greener for the bruising underneath one of them—the left. The lurid half round of blue and green and yellow.

"Jesus," he said.

Little Jeff had come out behind her and stood as before, wiping down his pint glasses. Joyless as a bodyguard.

She waited for Sean to look up again, to meet her eyes, before she said, "The good news is it feels worse than it looks." Then: "That's a joke. It doesn't hurt." She touched the bridge of her nose. "OK, it hurts," she said, "but at least now I can breathe." And by way of demonstration, or for the pleasure of it, she raised her face and inhaled through flared nostrils.

"It wasn't—?" he said, and reached vaguely toward his own nose.

"Broken? No. Though you should've heard the crack I heard."

"I can't even tell you how sorry I am," Sean said, and Little Jeff said, "Sure you can," and the two sitting men tracked from the young woman to the young man to the bartender as each spoke, watching from under their brows.

"I'm really sorry," he said before them all. "I asked to see you, at the station, to see if you were OK, but they wouldn't let me . . ."

"I wonder why," said Little Jeff, and Denise turned to give him a look.

"And then yesterday was Sunday," Sean said, and lost his way, narratively. Dry taste of hay dust in his mouth.

"I asked too," she said, "but you were in some kind of top-secret room getting the good cop–bad cop treatment, I assume. Did they rough you up?"

"It was just one cop and she was all right."

"Detective Viegas."

"Yes."

"Yeah, she was all right."

"What did you ask?" he said.

"If you were OK."

His head jerked involuntarily. He opened his mouth, but had nothing to say.

She held his eyes. Then closed hers. She put a fist on her hip and turned to the other men and buffed a small space in the air, as if clearing steam on a mirror, and said, "How're you all enjoying this? Is this all right or do you need a better seat?" She had not lived in Tennessee since she was a little girl but that had been enough. The sitting men, so chatty moments before, were driven back into their hunches by the sudden and twangy scolding.

Little Jeff raised a pint glass to the light, then placed it with care on a rubber mesh behind the bar. "I'm just standing here working," he said without looking at her, and Sean alone saw her eyes roll.

She looked at him again. Then she turned and walked the length of the bar and raised the gate and stepped through it and kept going. She carried a spray bottle and bar rag, and as she strode before the booths along the far wall she looked at him standing there and with her look beckoned him in some way. He too walked away from the bar and joined her where she stood wiping down a tabletop. After a few strong strokes she turned and faced him. She was not as tall when she was not behind the bar.

"I took out a restraining order on that numbnuts," she said.

"Yeah, I know."

"How do you know?"

"He told me."

"He told you?"

"Yes."

"When?"

"This morning, at breakfast. At the diner."

"Are you kidding me?"

"No."

She stood there, her mouth making shapes but no sounds.

"Nothing happened," he said. "All very civilized."

"Yeah, I bet." She searched his eyes. Shook her head.

"I didn't do it because I was afraid of him," she said. "In fact after the other night I'm pretty sure I could take him in a fight—no offense."

"None taken."

"I did it because I don't want to see his idiot face in here anymore," she said. "And because I thought it might help your case."

"My case?"

"Yeah. The one where you get charged with aggravated assault and put in jail."

"Oh, that case." He jutted his chin and scratched at his throat. "I think just telling the truth was probably enough."

Denise spun the bar rag once around her hand, once back the other way.

"Anyway, it felt like the right thing to do," she said. "The restraining order. That idiot didn't even show up for the hearing this morning. Which was fine with me. The whole point is not to see his face again."

Sean saw Mattis's face, bruised and swollen, grinning at him at the diner counter, and said nothing. He knew he would see that face again.

"Did you have that lip looked at?" she said.

"What lip?"

"What lip."

"Yes I did," he said. "I looked at it."

Her eyes were on the wound. Then on his eyes.

"Do you know those two guys?" he said, and she turned. The two men were facing forward again. Little Jeff was clinking bottles in a cooler.

"I mean, they're regulars," she said. "Mr. Bonner and Mr. Bergman. Why?"

"I just wondered if you'd ever heard about Mr. Bonner's wife. And her family."

"What about them?"

"How they were all killed in the war. In Vietnam. I guess they were French."

"A French wife killed in Vietnam," she said.

"Yeah. He only spoke French. The other one translated."

She nodded. Then she said, "Mr. Bonner taught economics for like a thousand years at the university and he's about as French as a glass of Bud Light."

Sean looked at the men, then at her again. The mirth in those eyes.

"I think maybe they were having fun with you," she said.

"Or maybe you are."

"Do you speak French?"

"No."

"Then how do you know he was speaking French?"

"Good question."

She raised an eyebrow at him.

"I gotta get back to work," she said.

"Go," he said. "I just wanted to make sure you were all right. And say how sorry I am."

"Stop. It was an accident. Although you have to admit, this look is pretty badass." She raised her face and turned it left and right. She looked like a woman who'd been punched in the face. "Oh, get over it." She stopped posing and cocked her thumb at the door. "And get out. And don't come back."

"OK."

"No, seriously. You shouldn't come back here for a while."

"OK."

"Also you have white stuff in your hair."

"Yeah, I—"

"Oh," she said, "wait here." He watched her jog back to the bar, back through the swinging door, and when she returned she was holding his cap, a little out of breath when she said, "Here's your hat, what's your hurry?"

He took it from her and stood looking at it. "Thanks," he said.

"De rien."

"What?"

"Nothing. Bye."

OUTSIDE IT WAS darker, colder, and he stood looking up at the early stars. He had a physical sense of his heart rising, of the thing itself lifting from dark spaces to a kind of light. It was because she'd forgiven him—only that.

Then he saw the detective. Stepping out of the Prius and crossing the gravel to him.

She stopped and stood before him with her hands in her coat pockets. "Mr. Courtland."

"Detective Viegas." He looked back at the tavern, then at her again.

"Relax," she said. "I'm here to see Miss Givens. Though I distinctly remember advising you not to come back here."

"I know," said Sean. "But I needed to see her in person, and I didn't know how else to do it."

Viegas stood watching him. She tossed the loose hair from her face. "How did she take it?"

"Take what?"

"Your apology."

He held her gaze. "She was cool. We're cool."

"Everyone's cool."

"I wouldn't say everyone," he said.

"Do you mean me?"

"I meant the bartender."

She shook her head. "Imagine."

"Yeah," Sean said. "Anyway, she told me the same thing."

"What's that?"

"Don't come back here."

Viegas watched him. She seemed to take stock of his abraded face, his crusted lip.

"And Mr. Mattis?" she said.

"What about him?"

"Any sightings?"

He weighed not telling her, but he'd just told Denise, and Denise would mention it—and so he told Viegas about Mattis at the diner that morning.

"That was it?" she said. "Just a chat?"

"Yes ma'am. There were a couple of sheriff's deputies sitting right there."

She watched him. "Do you want me to talk to him?"

"And say what?"

"To keep his distance from you."

Sean pushed at the inside of his fat lip with his tongue. "No ma'am," he said. "He doesn't worry me."

She stood there, watching him. "OK, Mr. Courtland," she said at last. "Good-bye again." And without taking her hands from her pockets she continued on toward the back door, her bootheels loud in the gravel, the black wings of her coattails flapping.

9.

DAN YOUNG WOKE up with his heart thudding, and nothing he saw assured him. Morning light shaped out the curtains, enough to see by, but what he saw was meaningless: the window itself, the framed images on the walls, the cheap and characterless furnishings.

No idea where he was.

Worse: who he was.

To whom did this pounding heart, this eyesight, belong?

He floated, his mind floated, in a kind of anonymous terror, until it seized on the black shape of the TV and he remembered watching the morning news, and through that slim crack of memory poured the rest—the return of history, which was the return of the body itself, a physical weight that pulled him down from midair to the bed where he lay with his heart slowly calming.

Dan Young.

The Motel 6 near I-90.

Wisconsin side of the river.

He raised fingers to his hairline, expecting to feel the stitches, but the stitches were out.

Then he remembered pulling them out himself in the bathroom—when was that?

Yesterday morning, before the long walk into town. Before breakfast. Or breakfast to go. Before the man with the busted lip had given him a ride.

"Shit," he said, and turned to the bedside table, and was pitched once more into confusion:

5:10 p.m. said the clockface.

What he'd thought was the light of morning became the light of afternoon, and the new day was in fact day's end and he'd overslept by almost twelve hours.

He had set the alarm but had not set it correctly. Or he'd slept through it.

But he hadn't booked the room for another night—he knew that much—and someone would've knocked on the door: housekeeping, management. Or the phone would have rung, the busted-lip man himself calling, whose name was. Whose name was.

Sean Courtland.

Dan raised up on one elbow and took the handset from its cradle and listened for the dial tone, replaced it again and lay there watching it. As if having been disturbed it would now ring.

"You didn't oversleep, dummy," he said. "It's still Monday."

Sean Courtland had dropped him off at the motel that morning and would not be back until tomorrow, Tuesday.

In the bathroom he washed his face and leaned nearer to the glass and drew his hair back to expose the thin red seam at the hairline, the small puckerings where the sutures had crossed the welted skin. Maybe it was more than a flesh wound. Maybe something had been altered fundamentally in his brain. That would explain the bad dreams. The waking up in unknown rooms. Unknown identity. The panic and the pounding heart.

He stared into his eyes, looking for signs of damage. Of a mind knocked somewhat off its moorings. And by pathways inherent to that same mind and beyond his conceiving he smelled rust, and felt the iron clothesline post, sunwarm and scaly in his hands. Two young boys were hanging on each arm as if on some rude balance scale, and the structure indeed inclined suddenly to one boy's favor, and there was the sensation below of concrete, like a great tooth ripping in its socket, and both boys dropped to the grass barefoot and running. Terrified, laughing, running.

SHE PUT HIM in a window booth and placed a menu before him and he sat looking out the window. The day fading but not gone, a last blaze of light in the branches of the trees this side of the Mississippi.

She came back with his water and he turned from the window.

"All set to order or do you need more time?" She flipped a page on her pad.

"That depends," he said.

"Oh boy. On what?"

"On can I get breakfast or not."

"Well, let's see. Is this still America?"

He ordered eggs over easy. Bacon. Wheat toast. A buttermilk pancake on the side. Coffee. Orange juice.

"That it?"

"That's it."

"Okey dokey, I'm on it."

"One more thing, if you don't mind," he said.

"Lay it on me."

"Can you tell me what day it is?"

"What day?"

"Yes, ma'am." He opened his empty hands. "I lost my phone."

She looked at him. "It's Monday, sweetie. All day."

"I thought so. Just double-checking."

"Sit tight," she said. "I'll be right back with that coffee and OJ."

An older couple came in and were greeted by another waitress and shown to a window booth of their own. Before they sat down they pulled knit caps from their heads and stood tamping down each other's charged fine hair as if putting out little fires. The man helped the woman out of her coat and hung the coat on the booth hook, then hung his own over hers. Their scarves they left on. After a moment they began discussing what they would order in the voices of two people who no longer noticed that they repeated everything they said, and at volume.

He ate his late breakfast, and when he looked out the window again headlights were plowing the new darkness.

He dug up his fold of cash and with it the key card for the motel and another card he didn't know he'd picked up from the dressertop. It was the business card on which Sean Courtland had written his name and number. On the other side was the detective's name and number, and he sat awhile looking at that.

Detective Corrine Viegas of the Investigative Services Bureau.

"Can I clear some of these plates for you?"

He turned the card over. "You can clear them all," he told the waitress. "Thank you."

"I'm not rushing you. You can sit here long as you like."

"Thanks, but I best get moving."

The waitress put the check on the table and began gathering his plates.

"Can I ask you one more question?" he said.

"Absolutely."

"What's that statue of, across the street? I saw it when I came in."

She peered into the window, though there was little to see there other than her own reflection. "That's a statue of three Indians playing lacrosse," she said. "Native Americans, I should say."

He looked into the window, nodding. As if he saw it now.

"They invented it," she said. "I don't know if you knew that."

"I think I did but I forgot."

She looked at him again. "Where you from, sweetie?"

He thumbed in the direction of the window. "Across the river."

"Minnesota."

"Yes, ma'am."

She smiled. "It's always nice to meet folks from faraway lands. I hope you enjoy your stay."

She had turned to go when he raised his hand, and she turned back.

"That couple over there." He nodded toward the old couple in the booth.

She looked. "That's the Parnells. They come here every Monday night for dinner. Very sweet."

"Do they eat pie?"

She looked at him. "He likes apple but she's partial to banana cream."

"Do you have those?"

"Is it Monday?"

He smiled. "Can you put one of each on my check and bring it to them when they're ready?"

She looked again at the old couple, and once again at him. "Can I tell them who it's from?"

"Just say it's on the house."

"I'll say they had an admirer. How's that?"

"That'll work."

"You take care, sweetie."

"You too."

10.

May 1977

IN THE TREES, *in the warm and fragrant dusk, birds moved restlessly—hopping, chittering, shaking their feathers. Shape of the owl on a jutting branch, the devil's prongs of her eyebrows, her dished face half turning eerily . . . Bat shapes dervishing on an indigo sky. And above the treetops to the east a crown of paler blue, like the glow from some resting, immense craft—in fact the light of a rising moon.*

Also in that dusk, fixed in place at the head of the drive, Marion Devereaux. So still for so long now that when he moved at last the birds hushed.

He walked up the drive, keeping to one of the wheel ruts where the gravel was hard-packed. Two cars stood side by side in the shadows: a faded blue '69 Pontiac and a '76 Chevrolet so white and glossy it seemed bathed already in moonlight.

Devereaux stepped up onto the stoop and raised his fist to rap on the screen door and just then, as if in response to this gesture, as if he were some house-calling conductor with a baton, there was music. A piano—the instrument itself, bright and immediate and so near at hand the metal screen shivered with its notes.

Devereaux lowered his fist. He wiped his open hand on his pantleg.

Just inside the screen door on a rug stood a pair of rubber boots, cherry red, toes to the baseboard. A clear plastic umbrella leaning on the wall. Jackets hanging on hooks. Beyond the short length of hall there was open space, yellow light, a framed painting on the far wall.

It was a whole tune she was playing. Devereaux put his face to the screen and closed his eyes. The music grew louder, more excited. Then abruptly it calmed, slowed, until a last deep note sounded and hung in the air, and when that too was gone there was no sound at all—the birds had settled, and if there were bugs in the woods it was too early in the evening, or too early in the year, for their droning.

In that stillness Devereaux raised his fist again and rapped on the wooden frame of the door. Unlatched and flimsy in its jamb it banged sharply and there was a little cry of surprise from inside the house. Chair legs scraped, hard heels tapped a hardwood floor, there was the wish-wish of cloth and then her face at the end of the short hallway—only her face: wariness, perplexity—then the rest of her stepping into view, coming to the door, to the figure framed in the haze of screen and no change to her expression.

Marion . . . ? she said.

Yes, ma'am, said Devereaux.

Good grief. You gave me a shock.

I'm sorry for that. This door rattles some.

She shook her head, her black hair swinging. Bright and swingy blue-black hair. Her lips bright with lipstick.

What are you doing out here? She did not open the screen door.

Devereaux looked down, then up again. Well, ma'am. I was passing by and I thought maybe I'd catch you for just a minute, if you were home.

She looked beyond him, toward the two cars. Passing by? she said. Did you walk here?

No, ma'am. I parked up the road a little ways. I didn't want to scare you with that old truck rumbling in here.

His gaze shifted, and she turned and looked behind her. A man stood at the end of the hallway, leaning on the wall, hands in his trouser pockets. Small careless grin on his face. He nodded at Devereaux.

It's just Marion, she told the man. From the school, she said.

Devereaux half raised a hand. Howdy.

Howdy, Marion. I'm Richard.

Forgive me, said the woman, whose name was Christine Wheeler. Marion Devereaux, this is Richard Getz. Richard is . . . His daughter is a student of mine. A piano student.

Did you hear her playing? said the man. Getz.

Your daughter?

Getz smiled. No, this one here.

Oh, said Devereaux. Yes, sir. She sure can play.

She sure can.

Richard, said Christine. Will you give me a few seconds here? I don't want to keep Marion any longer.

You bet, said Getz. Nodding to Devereaux. Nice to meet you, Marion.

Same here, said Devereaux.

Christine pushed at the door and Devereaux backstepped, teetered at the edge of the stoop, then clomped jerkily down the two wooden stairs to the ground. The door clapped shut behind her and she stood looking down on him from the height of the stoop, arms crossed over her stomach.

I just can't imagine why you're out here, Marion. She smiled. As if it were some joke he must be playing.

Like I said, said Devereaux, I just thought maybe I'd catch you for a second. I didn't know you had company.

How would you know?

He seemed to think about that. He looked in the direction of the cars and back again.

Is everything all right, Marion?

Oh, sure. Sure. I got some new work. Masonry work for Randall Pratt—he's building those houses out Old Indian Highway?

She shook her head again, her swingy hair. That's good, Marion. I . . . She shrugged her thin shoulders.

Yeah. I work with these guys. Pretty good guys. Well, one of them, Wilby, he's throwing a barbecue. For the crew and their families and such as that.

She nodded, lips holding a small smile. Hearing him out.

Well, said Devereaux. I just thought you might like to go. To the barbecue.

She stood looking at him. The crease between her eyebrows, there from the beginning, deepened. Marion—she said. Marion, that's kind of you. But I don't think I can do that.

I know you got the piano lessons on the weekends. Some days.

Yes. But it's not that. It's . . . Well, it's Richard, Marion. I'm seeing Richard. It just wouldn't be right.

Oh heck, said Devereaux quickly. It ain't like that. It's just a friendly barbecue is all it is. You can bring him too.

She smiled. She shook her head. I couldn't do that, Marion. I'm sorry. I—we just couldn't do that.

He shrugged. That's all right. I didn't think you could. I just thought I'd ask.

It was kind of you. Thank you.

Well. He half turned away. You all have a good night, then.

You too.

He was passing the rear end of the Chevrolet—he seemed about to reach out and touch it, drag his fingers along its smooth flank—when she called his name, and he stopped, turned back. She stood with the screen door in one hand, her other hand on the jamb, her mouth open. But then she closed her mouth and gave him a kind of wave. Good night, she said, and turned and receded in the square of screen and vanished around the corner.

In one of the windows a curtain lifted, not by any breeze, and from there they watched: Devereaux standing beside the Chevrolet, hands in his pockets and the hands restless. Like a man rooting for keys. Presently he moved on down the drive—was he whistling?—back to the blacktop road, where he paused again. As if he knew they watched. He turned to the mailbox and spoke to it. Or seemed to. Then he walked out to the middle of the road, turned left, and passed from their view, and still they watched—the young piano teacher and her guest, who stood just behind her, looking over her shoulder, the sound of the ice in his glass close to her ear, sound of his breath.

What was that all about?

She shook her head. He came to ask us to a barbeque.

Us?

Me.

What did you say?

I said I couldn't, of course.

Why didn't you invite him in?

She ignored that.

I'd have liked to talk to him. Getz rocked the ice about in his tumbler. I'd've asked him how you two kids know each other.

He worked at the school. He was the janitor. I suppose I was nice to him once or twice and he took it the wrong way.

Was the janitor, *said Getz.*

Yes. He's got some other job now. Building houses or some such.

He was fired from the school?

I don't know, she said. Maybe.

Getz raised his drink and the ice crowded noisily up against his teeth and rattled again in the lowered glass.

I think you should've let him in, he said. His breath hot on the side of her neck.

Oh, why won't you just be quiet? she said, and shrugged her shoulder where he was trying to kiss it.

He walked off toward the kitchen and she stood alone at the window. As she'd stood at her classroom window that day four, five weeks ago, staying late to grade tests. First warm Friday of April and the window open, so she'd heard their voices, and when she'd looked she saw the three bigger boys shoving the smaller boy around, calling him a pussy, calling him the flaming homo, that bright, brassy hair of his. She would have yelled at them or gone out there herself but just then the janitor, Marion Devereaux, had come from the back of the gymnasium and the three bigger boys stopped shoving the smaller one as he approached in his green-gray uniform, the boys grabbing at each other in mock fear but watching the janitor carefully, and she never heard what he said but soon enough they backed away, smirking, and when they were some ways off they called back such vile things at the boy and his protector, such trashy, ugly things, and she stood as the only witness.

The boys at last quit and sauntered away, the janitor standing with the smaller boy, and when all was silent again he'd set his hand on the boy's shoulder and said something to him she couldn't hear, and after a second the boy shrugged off his hand violently and walked toward the baseball diamond. When he reached the pitcher's mound he turned back and yelled, Creep! Goddam creep! Don't ever touch me again! and turned and ran toward the woods, that red hair so bright in the afternoon sun, as if it were indeed on fire. The janitor—she always said Hello, Marion when she saw him, she made a point of that—the janitor watching the boy go, and she'd felt he was about to turn, that he'd seen, or sensed, her standing there, and she'd moved quickly from the open window.

She'd meant to tell Principal Wegman about the bullying only—the names of the bigger boys, the janitor's coming to young Parnell's rescue—only that. But somehow when she was sitting in front of the prim and serious older woman, her boss, the rest had come out: the boy running off, yelling what he'd yelled. And when she was finished the principal sat watching her without expression. Toying with a blue Bic pen.

So Mr. Devereaux touched him—the Parnell boy?

He put his hand on his shoulder, said Christine. That's all. To comfort him. Trying to be kind. I think David was just upset, understandably. From the bullying.

And you didn't hear what Mr. Devereaux said to him—to David?

No, ma'am.

Or to the other boys?

No, ma'am.

Wegman tapped the pen on her desk blotter. I've heard from other teachers that they call him the Creep, she said. Some of them. Have you heard this?

No, ma'am. Not until Friday.

Wegman looked off toward her bank of windows. I have parents walking their kids to school now, Ms. Wheeler. Walking them home. They want assurances the children are in sight at all times. She shook her head. I don't blame them—two missing boys in the same district in two years. If my boys were still little . . .

She thanked Christine and said she'd let her know if she needed to talk to her again. But she hadn't needed to talk to Christine again. And if she'd talked to David Parnell, or his parents, or to those other boys and their parents, Christine never heard about it. And she never saw Devereaux again at the school. Or anywhere else, until tonight, standing on her stoop, his pale, childish face caught in the screen's shadow.

Strange that she should see his face through the screen and also the screen's pattern upon it, but that was what she would remember, and would vividly see again, whenever she thought of that night in the years to come.

11.

Tuesday morning they took I-90 out to the Home Depot and Sean backed into a loading space near the building and they sat finishing off breakfast sandwiches, taking last swigs of coffee, before tossing open the truck doors.

Inside, he told Dan Young to grab a second cart and they wheeled the two carts aside to let other shoppers pass by.

"We need framing materials and we need plumbing supplies," Sean said. "What's your druthers?"

"Plumbing."

"That's the more complicated one."

"I used to work in a plumbing supply store."

"You're kidding me."

"No, I'm not."

"Can you sweat copper?"

"Yep."

"Run PEX line?"

"Yep."

"Can you transition from copper to PEX?"

"With the right fittings and tools, yep."

Sean looked at the man. When he'd pulled into the Motel 6 parking lot, eight o'clock on the nose, Dan Young had been standing right about where he'd left him, not a thing to suggest he'd gone into the motel at all—his hair in the same windy disarray, his clothes unchanged, or seemingly unchanged; he might carry duplicates, as did Sean: your man of the trades found his dress code and did not much deviate.

"Got a list?" Dan Young said, and Sean pulled a square of paper from his hip pocket. It was a schematic he'd drawn and he stood beside the plumber, pointing things out with his forefinger. Dan Young said nothing until Sean was finished, then he studied the drawing a minute longer and said, "Do you have everything we need for sweating copper?"

"Everything but the copper."

"How about for PEX?"

"I don't have a darn thing for PEX."

"We'll need some tools."

"Grab everything you need. But do me a favor. I'm not getting rich on this job, so don't go top-shelf on me."

"Maybe you're paying too much for help."

"Shoot, I just found out the guy I hired off the street is a plumber. I think I hit the jackpot."

"I hope so."

"Me too. Let's move."

When they pulled up to the Devereaux house just after nine o'clock, the old shepherd came limping but stopped short when she saw the shape of the other man, or perhaps caught his scent. Her hair stiffened along her spine and she dipped her head and growled.

"That's old Bonnie," said Sean. "She's a vicious killer."

Dan Young ignored the dog except to say "Hey, girl," and she followed and snuffled at his knees as they carried supplies to the back door, then followed them to the truck for their second load. When they returned, the old man stood in the open door with his knobby cane, and Sean wished him a good morning.

"This is the man I told you about," he said. "Dan Young. Dan, this is Mr. Devereaux, the boss."

Devereaux gripped his cane in his right hand and Sean saw Dan Young watch to see if the hand would free itself in some way. When it didn't, Young nodded and said, "Good to meet you, Mr. Devereaux. I appreciate the work."

"Wasn't me who hired you, it was this man here."

Sean had warned the plumber. Young nodded and held the old man's gaze and said, "Yes, sir. I'm gonna help him as best I can."

"That's between you and him," said Devereaux. "End of the day, he's the one has to answer for the work."

"Yes, sir."

"Dan's one hell of a plumber," Sean said. "We're lucky to get him."

Devereaux did not look away from Young. "This one likes to fight." Jerking his head toward Sean. "Didn't know that about him when I hired him."

Sean looked down. The old man's boots were black and shineless. Maybe the only pair he'd ever owned. "I don't like to fight, Mr. Devereaux."

Devereaux said to Young, "I guess he already told you to use the toilet down there and not the one up here."

"Yes, sir, he did."

"And the sink down there for washing up. I don't know any reason you should be going anywhere in the house but down there and up to the new wash-machine room."

"No, sir, I don't either."

Devereaux renewed his grip on the cane and shifted his weight and looked beyond them at the trees, or perhaps the sky. Then again at Young. "What'd he say your name was?"

"Dan. Dan Young."

"Where you from?"

"Minnesota."

"Minnesota."

"Yes, sir."

"They run outta work in Minnesota?"

"No, sir. Not that I know of."

Devereaux grunted. He studied Young with those blue eyes.

"Like I told him," he said, "I don't want that dog down there with you. She's got bad hips and she can't be going up and down those stairs."

"No, sir. She won't."

"Well, go on, then," he said, and moved away into the house, and the two younger men carried in the supplies. Sean showed Dan Young the new small room he'd framed and where the machines would sit and where the valves needed to go and how the drain would run in the stud wall and where it would feed into the existing waste pipe.

At the top of the stairs he pushed a button in the old switch plate and they descended the steep run of steps, each ducking under the header joist, and at the bottom they stood on the concrete in the dank, fusty air as Dan took in the layout of the basement. The thick and cobwebbed ceiling joists just overhead, the runs of old galvanized pipes and the less-old copper pipes with their cruds of green at the joints. The seep stains that began in the mortar of the wall and ran down blocks as old as any he'd seen and wormed along the floor to a cast-iron drain grate so corroded that several of its squares had caved in like teeth.

The green plastic tubs—a whole wall of them on sagging wooden racks, floor to ceiling, full of God knew what.

The calcified showerhead in the far corner above another drain, its pipes and wheel valves fixed to the wall by clips and crusted screws. The toilet next to this that was not as old or foul-looking as it might've been.

The washer and dryer—a matching pair more than twenty years old and beset at their bases by a creeping rust. Next to them on rusted iron legs stood a porcelain farm sink, where laundry had once been washed by hand, and by a shorter race of people, or children, to judge by its height from the floor.

Through an opening in another wall came the roaring of the old furnace, and in that room, illuminated by nothing but the jetted flames, the squat little windows just below the ceiling joists were either black with dirt or else had been brushed with paint or stain to keep the daylight out. As had the windows in the main room where he and Sean stood. There were other rooms darker than the furnace room, and Dan would have stepped into each to see how the plumbing ran—to see the entire structure of block walls on which the house had been built—but Sean had gone to the washer and dryer and he was talking now, and Dan joined him there to see where he would cut into the copper and make the transition to the flexible PEX lines and how he would run them to the floor above. When Sean was done talking they both stood looking at the old copper running up the wall, and as they stood there the furnace shut itself down with a great shudder and in the new silence they heard a soft whimpering.

It was the shepherd, at the top of the stairs, out of view but for two forepaws hung over the threshold.

"He doesn't have to worry about that dog coming down here," Sean said.

"He doesn't?"

"You couldn't drag her down here. One time she started following me down, got halfway and stopped and just stood there, staring at me with those eyes, and then she flat-out howled and hauled ass back up the stairs. Now when I come down here she just lies there whimpering."

Dan looked around the room again. As if to see what it was the dog didn't like. He looked up into the ceiling joists and he looked for a while.

"What?" said Sean, looking with him.

"Nothing."

"You're not getting spooky on me too, are you?"

"No. I've worked in worse spaces. A lot worse."

"Me too," said Sean.

They stood there. The clicking sounds of the cooling furnace. The quiet whimpering of the dog.

"It won't be so bad with a work light down here," Sean said, and Dan nodded.

"At some point I'll have to shut off the main valve and drain the pipes."

"Right. He told me where it's at but we'll have to track it down. Let me go get that light."

As Sean climbed the steps Dan began pulling materials and tools from the plastic bags and arranging them on the surfaces of the washer and dryer and he didn't turn to look at the joists again, nor at anything else that didn't matter in some way to the job Sean was paying him to do.

BY NOON DAN had cut into the copper lines, hot and cold, and sweated new shutoff valves, and now he opened up the main valve slowly. Pipes rattled all through the house, and the long-necked spigot at the farm sink bucked and spat rusty water like blood on the yellowed porcelain, and he watched until it ran clear again and then shut off those faucets. Upstairs he heard Sean cross the floor and shut off the faucets at the kitchen sink and cross back again, and lastly he checked his joints and there were no leaks.

Sean came down for a look.

"Beautiful," he said. "Shutoff valves right here. I didn't even think of that."

"We can connect the PEX lines directly into these and we don't have to shut off the main valve again."

"Smart." He stood admiring the new joints. There was no excess solder, no drips.

"It's very clean work, Dan."

"Well," said Dan. "It's just how it's done."

"Not by everyone." He clapped the plumber once on the shoulder. "Hungry?"

They hunched over the farm sink passing a cracked cake of soap and drying their hands on the thin old bath towel the old man had provided. Sean named the available sandwiches and sides he could think of, and after they'd decided he found the number in his phone and handed the phone to Dan and asked him to place the order for pickup, in his own name, while he himself went back upstairs to tidy up for the inspection he knew Devereaux would make once they'd left the house.

Dan waited until they were in the truck and pulling onto the blacktop before he said, "Interesting old man."

"That's one word for him."

Dan was quiet. Then he said, "How do you reckon he got that way?"

"How'd he get so interesting?"

"Yeah."

"I don't know. Maybe that's what living in the woods by yourself does to you. Why don't you ask him?"

"Maybe I will."

"Good. But let's get paid first."

They took the winding road back through the bluffs toward town and Sean pulled once again into the parking lot behind the Wheelhouse Tavern. He got out his wallet and handed Dan a twenty. "You mind going in and grabbing it? I'm gonna have a smoke."

They stepped out of the truck and Sean said across the hood, "If it's Denise gives you the food, give her the whole twenty. In fact whoever it is, give 'em the whole twenty."

"How will I know if it's Denise?"

"She'll be the one with the black eye."

Dan looked at him. "Do you want me to say anything?"

Sean drew a cigarette from the pack with his lips. "To who?"

"To Denise."

"Hell no. I mean—thanks, but no. Just get the food."

"All right."

Dan pushed through the glass door and when it had shut again Sean saw the image of himself leaning against the truck. He knew from the times he'd come out here to smoke that there was no direct sight line from the bar to this door; you'd have to go to the back of the tavern to see him.

A train blew its horn, warning bells began clanging and Sean watched the engine plow at low speed past the tavern. The boxcars said BNSF and he remembered the firewood man, Lyle, whose father had stopped on the tracks with a load of apples. Was it these tracks here—this very intersection? Had the tavern been here in, what—1988? Its patrons spilling out to see the wreckage. The dead man.

The train was not long and it had passed on when the glass door swung and Dan stood in the opening with a white paper bag in each hand, and behind him the waitress. Denise. Dan held the door with his forearm so she could pass but she said something to him and he stepped out and she caught the door and remained standing in the opening. She was wearing red sneakers and a black sweater. Her hair in a ponytail.

Sean dropped his cigarette butt and ground it out with his boot toe. He caught Dan's eye as he crossed to him, and Dan shrugged.

"I didn't say a thing," Dan said. He stopped and glanced back at Denise. "I'll be in the truck."

Sean went to her and she watched him coming. He was dressed much as he'd been the day before. A little cleaner maybe. Smell of smoke and sawdust on him. He'd shaved. His eyes were half shaded by the bill of the dirty cap, and it crossed her mind that she could've just thrown it away, he'd have never known the difference.

He stood before her with his hands in his jacket pockets.

"Who's your gofer?" she said.

"That's Dan. I met him at breakfast the other day. After breakfast. He was there when our friend showed up."

"And he still wanted to work with you?"

"I don't know if I'd say wanted. But he took the job." He stood looking at her. "Your eye looks better," he said.

"Does it?"

"Definitely."

"Maybe it's Maybelline."

He stared at her. He didn't get it. Which, actually, she liked.

"I knew he was with you," she said.

"How?"

"He just had that look to him. Plus the big tip. And the sandwich. We don't get a lot of orders for the Big Turkey with no mayo, no tomato."

"Ah," said Sean Courtland. She watched him. She already knew, from the day before and the other times he'd come in, that he had no idea what he was doing flirtwise. She liked that too.

"What if I hadn't come out here?" she said.

"I guess I'd have come in."

"Why?"

"Why?"

"Yes, why."

"To see you."

"Why?" she said.

He laughed. He looked down—at her red kicks, maybe—and looking up again said, "I thought I might help you with something."

"What do I need help with?"

"I don't know. I thought I could do something for you. By way of making amends."

"You don't have to make amends."

"Yeah. I wanted to. I wanted to offer, anyway." He looked back at the truck—his gofer, Dan, sitting in the cab, pretending he wasn't watching.

When he turned back to her she said, "I had a visit from our friend the detective."

"Yeah, so did I. More of an ambush. Right here."

"She mentioned that. I don't think she used the word ambush, though. She wanted to know if you were bothering me."

"That's why she came here?"

"No. She was just following up with me. Seeing if I was all right."

"And what did you tell her?"

"You want me to tell you what I told the cop?"

"Yeah."

"I told her you weren't anything I couldn't handle."

Sean Courtland nodded. A small kind of smile. He stood there. She stood there.

She felt a laugh coming and said, "You're a carpenter."

"I am. Do you need a carpenter?"

"I might. I mean, I wouldn't want to take advantage."

"You wouldn't be."

"It's not a big job, I don't think. It has to do with a bathroom door. Is that in your wheelhouse, so to speak?"

"Totally in my wheelhouse. When's a good time?"

"I don't know. How's tonight?"

"Tonight?"

"Yeah."

"Tonight works for me."

"Do you have a phone?"

They traded numbers and when that was done she said "Gotta go, I'll text you," and turned and walked back toward the glass door. Before she pushed through she looked back. He was still there. Still watching. And she liked that too.

12.

THE HOUSE WAS on a quiet side street off West Avenue on the south side of town, a Midwestern two-story on a corner lot with big trees that must have provided good shade in the summer. Tall windows to either side of the front door cast light onto the large, open front porch, onto its steps and the geometry of a wheelchair ramp—two opposing runs that ran parallel to the porch with a switchback turn. Care had been taken that the ramp not look merely tacked on, but from the street Sean saw that the porchsteps had once been twice as wide, proportional to a porch of that size, and that one of the columns had been moved, throwing off their symmetry.

He took the steps up and she met him at the door.

"You found us," she said.

"Sorry I'm late."

"Bah. We don't fixate on time around here."

She wore the same red sneakers but had changed sweaters. This one green like her eyes and showing her collar bones. Her hair still in a ponytail.

"Did you eat dinner?" she said.

"No, I came straight from work. As you can see." He'd left his cap in the truck and had combed his fingers through his hair. The best he could do. He had dropped Dan at the Motel 6 and had not had time to go all the way back to the stone cottage to clean himself up. Dan had offered the facilities of his room; Sean had said no thanks—why would he clean up to go fix a door?—and Dan just shook his head.

"Are you hungry?" Denise said.

"I'm gettin there."

"Good. Come on in and meet the gang."

Stepping past her there was the clean smell of her and then the smells of the house, of the heated indoors and human life. Firewood burning and a tomato sauce bubbling and seasoned meat sizzling in a pan. She'd said meet the gang but the only other person he saw was a man in a wheelchair, his hands resting on the wheels, a glass of wine in reach. Reading glasses hanging from his neck on a lanyard. Hardbound book in his lap. He had a good head of hair, dark with streaks of silver, and at a glance he looked as if he sat in the wheelchair by choice. As if he might rise from it and walk at any moment.

"This is my dad, Henry Givens," she said. "Dad, this is Sean Courtland, the carpenter."

The father did not move and Sean stepped over to him with his hand out. "Mr. Givens."

The older man held Sean's eyes and took his hand in a quick hard grip and released it. His eyes were green like hers but a darker, harder green. Something made Sean glance at the hand he'd shaken. It was the Band-Aids, on the knuckles and the back of the hand, several of them, one overlapping another, dark-blotted at the pads.

"The man who hit my daughter in the face," the father said.

"Dad," said the daughter. "You promised me not five minutes ago."

"That was before I saw him standing in my living room. Why don't you come a little closer so I can punch you in the face, see how you like it?" A faint southern twang to his menace.

Denise Givens laughed. "Pay no attention to the man in the wheelchair. He's a great kidder. Also a great pacifist."

"I'm really sorry about what happened, Mr. Givens. I feel terrible about it."

"He knows you do."

"Pacifist? No man is a pacifist when it comes to his daughter."

"All right, Dad. Bravo. Sean—can I take your jacket?"

He stood there, unwilling to break the father's gaze. He was looking for the sign that the man was kidding but he couldn't find it. "Sure," he said. "But maybe I'd better look at that door first, so I can bring in some tools."

As they passed him the father wheeled in place as an owl turns its head, watching them walk down the hallway.

"Sorry about that," she said. "He's just amusing himself."

"I didn't know I'd be meeting the father of the woman I punched."

"Didn't I mention that?"

"No."

"That's funny," she said. "So here's the situation. He can't go upstairs anymore so he's got his room down here and this bathroom. Only the bathroom door is, like, narrow, and he doesn't steer so great, especially in the middle of the night when he's gotta pee, and he keeps ripping up his knuckles going in and out, which bleed all over the place because of the blood thinners he's on."

She fell silent. Put her hands on her hips. "That's the situation."

Sean considered the doorjamb, and the bathroom within. Between the toilet and the shower stall stood an aluminum walker with tennis balls for front feet, and he wondered did she have to help—with the showering? With the going to the bathroom? He thought of his own father, what they'd do if it came to that. Sad as hell, but not impossible.

Helping his mother this way? He could not even imagine it.

"I took out the door," she was saying, "which helps a little. Privacy isn't the issue here. That ship has sailed."

She was standing close to him in the closeness of the hallway and he smelled the clean smell of her again. The red wine she'd been drinking.

"So are you talking about expanding the jamb?" he said. "A whole new door? I don't think there's room for it with this layout. I think that's why the door is as narrow as it is."

"Right. No. I was thinking of just taking out the whole darn doorframe."

"The whole jamb?"

"Yes. How much space would that get us?"

He put his tape measure in the opening, though this would not answer her question.

"Two or three inches," he said, "depending on the framing."

"On both sides or—?"

"Altogether."

"Still. That would help. Don't you think?" She turned to face him and after a moment he turned too. Utmost seriousness in those eyes. Utmost interest in what he would say.

"It won't be pretty," he said. "I mean, I could make it pretty but you'd lose space again."

"Hey, you know what? Pretty isn't the name of the game around here either."

It isn't? he nearly said. "Let me get some tools," he said.

"Do you want to eat first?"

"Is it ready?"

"No. But it can be in twenty minutes."

"This won't take long."

"All right. Can I get you a glass of wine?"

"No, thank you."

"No, you're a beer man. How about a beer?"

"After," he said, and they walked back down the hall and he nodded to the father, and the father wheeled again in place, tracking him as he went out the front door and onto the porch.

When he let himself back in, man and wheelchair were gone, and passing the kitchen he saw him parked before the stove, reaching to stir a large steaming pot. Denise was at the counter behind him and they were talking calmly, lightly, as if nothing had happened. As if the carpenter were not there at all.

He spread a dropcloth and buckled his toolbelt, and when he turned around, the father was sitting there, having rolled up behind him on silent wheels.

"You don't mind me watching, do you?"

"No sir."

The father sat watching as Sean worked. Skilled, methodical, stupidly self-conscious: How he held the shop knife as he sliced the paint seams where the molding met the walls. How he tapped the blade of his molding lifter under the wood and pried up a gap, then with his flatbar prized the wood gently. How he walked the flatbar all along the edges of the jamb, popping the molding free as he went.

"How old are you?" the father said. "If you don't mind me asking."

"I'm twenty-six."

"No you're not."

"I'm pretty sure I am."

"You look older."

"I've heard that before."

"How long have you been doing this work?"

"Since I was seventeen. My father was a contractor."

"Was."

"He still does some jobs, but not as a contractor."

"And where does he do that?"

"Madison area, mostly."

"That's where you're from?"

"Originally, yes."

"And you didn't want to work with him—father-and-son business?"

Sean said nothing. Then: "Things happened. I went off on my own."

"I see."

Sean began to pry the jamb itself from the framing, and soon enough he had it free, the two sides and the top, all of a piece. He set it aside and ran his fingertips over the exposed faces of the studs for spurs of wood, nailheads, anything that would snag and tear. Lastly he put his tape measure in the opening as before.

"What'd we get?" said the father.

"Three inches."

"Altogether?"

"Yep."

"Let me give her a spin."

Sean picked up his tools and the cloth and stood aside as the father rolled into the bathroom slowly, checking his clearance side to side like a careful motorist. Denise returned to stand beside Sean, bringing the smells of the kitchen with her.

The father spun around and came out again.

"Is it better, Dad?"

"It's better."

"How much room did we get?"

"Three inches," said the father.

"That's awesome."

He looked up at her. "Awesome would be a sauna and a live-in masseuse."

"Your birthday's coming up," she said, sliding Sean a look.

The father looked at them both. "Something's burning."

"No it's not."

He rolled down the hall toward the kitchen and they watched him go.

"It looks great," she said, turning back to the opening.

"It doesn't, but it should help."

"It will, trust me. Thank you." She looked at him. "Miller time?"

"Definitely. Is there someplace I can put this wood?"

When he came back from the garage he stopped at the fireplace and stood rubbing his hands before the fire and looking more closely at the framed pictures on the mantel. Viewed left to right they told the story of a young, happy couple and their infant son, a daughter added two or three years later. A sporty family on the slopes of what looked to him like the Rocky Mountains of Colorado. A son who won a medal on his skis, a daughter who won a trophy on the tennis court. Then a family whose mother smiled as before but whose recessed eyes and kerchiefed head told another story, and after that no more family pictures, or none of the whole family, just the son and daughter—he in a marine uniform, a young man, she in her high school gown and cap of deep red, smiling for the moment's sake—for memory's sake, at least; for this mantel.

To the right of the fireplace on an end table stood the official military portrait of the marine, sharing the space with a glass-fronted display case that was like a small house, its pyramid attic filled exactly by a folded flag, four white stars on blue, the compartment below arrayed with medals and insignia on a red cloth.

The wood was birds-eye maple and it was well joined.

At the table he handed her his dish and she tonged up noodles and dipped the ladle into the sauce and stopped—the ladle poised above the pasta.

"I just remembered you don't like tomatoes."

"Who doesn't like tomatoes?" said the father.

"Sean doesn't."

"What? Who doesn't like tomatoes?"

"He doesn't like them on his sandwiches."

"We're not eating sandwiches."

"I know, Dad."

The sauce steamed in the ladle. Sean's stomach chewed on itself. "Release the sauce," he said, and she did so. At his first taste he sagged and gave a grunt of pleasure.

"That's not necessary," she said.

"I'm not kidding. This is awesome."

The father smirked and shook his head.

"And these meatballs," Sean said.

"Awesome?" said the father. Peering over his glasses at the carpenter.

"Yes sir."

"My grandmother's recipe," said Denise. "I grew up on these buggers."

"Please don't call them buggers while we're eating them."

"Right, because you're so delicate."

"Perhaps I'm speaking for the company, daughter."

"He can speak for himself."

"Can he?" The father turned to Sean. "Did you always want to be a carpenter, Sean?"

"Did I always want to be a carpenter?" He took a sip of his beer. "I didn't give it a lot of thought, to be honest. It just kind of happened."

"Take another hunk of that garlic bread. Did you ever want to be something else?"

"Dad, seriously?"

"What? I just wonder. My daughter wanted to be a tennis pro," he told Sean. "My son wanted to be an Olympic downhill skier. I myself once dreamed of working for NASA. Instead I taught high school science for thirty years."

Sean dipped the garlic bread into the sauce on his dish and bit that off and chewed. "Did you like it? Teaching?"

"Sure, I liked it. Sometimes I wanted to put a bullet in my ear. But when I couldn't do it anymore, when they fired me—"

"They didn't fire you, Dad. You retired."

"Whatever you want to call it. I never knew until then that I loved it." He wound spaghetti onto his fork and studied it midair, as if the twitching noodles, registering a shakiness of hand that Sean had not noticed before, were a revelation to him too.

"Life is funny like that," he said. "Pardon the banality."

They ate. They drank. Sean said to Denise, "So, what happened to tennis? You still play?"

"Oh, no. I tore my ACL my first year at college. Then I got into painkillers. Then I got into other painkillers. Then I dropped out of college. Then I got off the painkillers and got a job."

"What she isn't saying is she also thought she needed to take care of her disintegrating father."

"And save money living at home, sponging off him."

"Sponging, please. Who bought this food we're eating?"

"Anyway," she said. "That's what happened to tennis."

"College is still there," said the father. "It doesn't care about your age. Or your past."

She gave Sean a look. As if he'd surely heard such things from his own father. Which he had. A man who'd dropped out of college to be a carpenter.

"I assume you have other jobs that don't pay in pasta," said her father.

"Yes. I'm working on a house out in the bluffs."

"Doing?"

He described the job and the reason for it: a man who'd grown too old to go up and down the stairs to do laundry.

"I can't imagine," said Henry Givens. "Name?"

"Sorry?" Sean said. Poking at his noodles.

"Of the homeowner."

"Devereaux."

"Devereaux," said Givens. "Marion Devereaux?"

"Yes."

Givens raised his glass for a sip and set it down again. "I wonder," he began, and his daughter said, "Dad, don't."

"He might like to know."

"Know what? Old-lady gossip from a hundred years ago?"

"He might already know," said Sean, and they both turned to him.

"Ah," said the father, vindicated. "You have heard the lore."

"Lore," said Denise.

"It didn't take long," said Sean.

"And still you took the job."

"I'd already agreed to do it."

"And?"

"Dad."

"Sir?" said Sean.

"Strange goings-on, out there in the bluffs? A pricking of the thumbs?"

"A pricking of the thumbs?"

"Something wicked this way comes—*Macbeth*?" he said. "Bradbury—?"

Sean shook his head. "It's been an ordinary job for an ordinary man."

Givens took this in. He frowned in a satisfied way. "Good enough. And good on you for being a man of your word."

Denise gave her father a long look. Then, turning to Sean: "Let me restock you. There's plenty of everything."

He thanked her no, he was stuffed. She offered ice cream, coffee, another beer. He agreed to the beer.

"And a smoke," she said. "I know you want a smoke."

"That can wait."

"Let's go out on the porch. Dad, you'll clean up?"

"What?"

"Kidding. Just leave everything and I'll do it later."

"I'll clear this table, but then I'm going to my room to read my book. And I'm going to put my headphones on, so you all can talk as loud as you want." He began to gather dishes. "Sean Courtland," he said, "thank you for the extra clearance. My knuckles thank you."

Outside, she went to the far end of the porch and sat down, and until she did so he'd not seen the porch swing, hung there on its chains beyond the lightfall from the window. She sat to one side and snugged her denim jacket about her.

Sean stepped to the railing to light his cigarette.

"I like this ramp," he said.

"What?"

"The ramp. I could've used one of these when I was fifteen."

"What happened when you were fifteen?" she said.

"I was a hit by a car and had my knee all busted up. I was in a wheelchair for two months."

"Holy shit. Who hit you?"

"A man in the woods," he said.

She watched him. "A man in the woods?"

He flicked his ash. "Just some idiot up in the mountains."

"What mountains?"

"The Rockies. Colorado."

"What were you doing there?"

"Family vacation."

"Some vacation."

"Right?"

"That explains the limp," she said.

He nodded.

She waited for him to go on—he felt her waiting, giving him the space, but there was no air in that space, and his mind emptied. Finally he said, "I like the use of treads instead of plywood."

"Sorry?"

"The ramp."

"Ah," she said. "Good. I'll tell Dad."

"Who built it?"

"Dad."

He looked at her.

"Before he needed it. He built it for himself."

Sean looked again at the ramp. "He never mentioned he was a carpenter."

"Hey, Sean Courtland," she said, and he looked at her again. "Come take a load off."

He mashed the cigarette on the sole of his boot and looked around.

"Just leave it on the rail," she said, and he did so.

He sat with care, doubting the swing's capacity to hold them both. The wood creaked, the chains creaked. He leaned back and they swung a moment, then settled.

Across the street on the opposite corner of the intersection was a small commercial building. Two large illuminated plastic beer signs mounted to the exterior: PABST BLUE RIBBON, BUDWEISER. Dark windows. A gray metal door with an assortment of dents at boot level. A handful of cars and trucks in the lot.

"That's Eddie's Place," she said. "Although Eddie is long gone. I worked there once for about a month. Convenient as hell. Too convenient, it turned out."

He thought about that. *Painkillers,* he thought.

"Not like that," she said. "Do I look like a boozer to you?" Raising her glass and sipping. Smacking her lips. He laughed and drank too.

She was watching him.

"What?" he said.

"I like how you laugh. Or sorta laugh."

"Thanks—?"

Her gaze was steady, unreasonably green in that light, and he had the uneasy sense that he might not speak again, or even move, until she let him.

"Too convenient for the clientele," she said, releasing him. "I ended up driving my car to work, driving around the block coming and going, just so those idiots wouldn't try to walk me home. But it didn't matter. They knew where I lived. One of them banged on the door one night—this was after I'd already quit—and he got a good look at Dad's shotgun and that was the end of that nonsense."

Sean said nothing.

"He wanted to have that thing in sight when you came over," she said. "Like, leaning against the fireplace. Just for kicks."

"Maybe you shouldn't have told him I was the one who punched you."

"I thought he'd find it amusing."

"Amusing."

"Yes. The whole . . . situation." She smiled. "Anyway, he's over it. He likes you. He likes to see people doing things well. And without showing off. Can I lean into you? I'm a little cold."

"Do you want my jacket?"

"No, just lift your wing."

He raised his arm and she settled against him and he rested his arm on her shoulder.

"I probably don't smell too great," he said. His heart was thudding.

"You smell like work."

"That's what I'm afraid of."

She tucked her feet up under her. He pushed with his legs and they rocked awhile in silence.

"I saw the picture of your brother," he said.

"You saw the shrine."

"I did. I'm sorry—that you lost him."

She nodded; he felt it on his shoulder. "He could've been a professional skier," she said. "He was that good. But he decided to be a soldier instead. Don't ask me why."

He wanted to ask her why.

"Watching our mother die changed him, I think. It changed us all."

He rubbed her shoulder. Lightly, briefly.

"Are yours alive?"

The question surprised him—it seemed like something you ask an older person. Someone already old themselves. But if you'd lost one of yours, or both, maybe it was what you wanted to know.

"Yes," he said. "But not together."

"Siblings?"

"An older sister."

"Are you close?"

Sean straightened out his bad knee, bent it again. "Not like we were when we were younger."

"That's too bad."

"Were you close with your brother?" he said.

"Yes. He could be shitty to me when we were kids, but I adored him. He was my big brother."

"What was his name?"

She was silent. Then she said, "Adam."

Sean stared off toward the bar across the street.

"What is it?"

"Nothing."

She waited.

"I was thinking," he said, "that this place is not so kind to its sons."

"How so?"

"Well, your brother. And the people I'm renting from, they lost a son when he was fifteen. A suicide."

"That's awful."

"And those three boys, missing all these years."

"Yes." She was quiet. Then: "Do you think we're cursed? As a people?"

"I don't know. I never thought about it."

"It is stolen land."

"True."

"Stolen by choice," she said. "By . . . decision. By genocide in broad daylight." She seemed to look out over the wintry yard, the trees, her own plot of American land. "Maybe all these dead white boys," she said, but did not finish the thought. Or not aloud.

"Would you do me a favor?" she said.

"Sure."

"Would you stop us swinging? It's making me woozy."

He stilled the swing.

"And would you set my glass down?"

He leaned and set it on the floorboards, and his bottle next to it.

"And would you kiss me?"

He kissed her—and she pulled back.

"Your lip," she said. "Sorry—"

"It's fine," he said, and kissed her again.

Some minutes later, perhaps half an hour, coming up from under his arm and putting her feet on the floor, she rubbed her forehead and said, "You gotta be kidding me." She was looking across the street at the bar, and he looked with her.

"What is it?"

"It's our buddy."

It took him a few seconds to understand. "Where?" he said.

"In the black Monte Carlo. Can you believe he drives a black Monte Carlo?" They sat watching the car.

"He thinks we can't see him but there's light behind him, the idiot," she said. "He doesn't understand the concept of backlighting."

"Or maybe he does." Sean leaned forward, his elbows on his knees. His senses were still full of her: The heat and softness and wetness of her mouth. The winey taste. Her hand in his hair, on his neck.

"Has he done this before?" he said.

"Yes."

"I'll go talk to him."

She put her hand on his arm. "Hold on, cowboy. Ten to one he's got a pistol in the glovebox." She began patting herself down. "Crap," she said. "Do you have your phone?"

He got it out and handed it to her.

"Don't worry, I won't look at your private stuff."

"There isn't any to look at."

"I know."

She stood from the swing and walked into the light at the top of the steps and tapped the face of his phone until it lit up, then tapped at it three more times and put it to her ear. She began to talk and gesture but she made no sound. She nodded, pretended to talk again and then tapped the phone and crossed her arms at the chest and looked to her left, toward West Avenue. Nothing happened.

Then, across the street, a motor came to life. Headlights flared, and the black Monte Carlo rolled forward. It pulled out of the lot and went prowling off down the street, the red taillights, the grumbling engine, the huffing exhaust receding slowly, like a creature backing away into darkness.

She turned and smiled at Sean, who had stood up but had not come toward her. He came to her now and she handed him back his phone.

"Have you done that before? With him?"

"No. Last time I just ignored it and went to bed."

"Maybe I should stick around awhile."

She was looking up the street. "The thing is," she said, and did not go on.

He waited. Listening to her breathing.

"The thing is, he was nice, when we first met. He was nice and he was kind."

Sean didn't know what to say to that. It was hard enough to believe Mattis had been kind. Harder to believe she'd cared about him at all.

Maybe they'd stood together here, just like this. Had sat on that swing.

"I guess they all are at first," she said. "I guess that's how it works." She turned to look at him. Searching his eyes in the windowlight.

"You're nice," she said. "You're kind."

"Am I?"

"Don't you know?"

"I did hit you in the face."

"True," she said. "But it was in the act of kindness."

She shivered and he put his arm around her. She rested her head on his shoulder as before.

"How do you know?" he said.

"What—that you're kind?"

"No. That I don't have private stuff on my phone."

"Because you keep it someplace else."

He thought about that. "Where do I keep it?"

"I don't know," she said. "That's private too."

13.

June 1977

THE LONG WINTER *ends, the last dirty mounds of snow melt away, and the next day there are dandelions, bright as little suns on the school lawn. The last bell of the last day rings, the bedroom window is left open all night and in the morning the brightness falls on slow-opening eyes—*

Bil-leeee! *she is singing downstairs.* BillyBillyBilly. *A pause—then:* Let's go, Billy Goat!

Saturday morning, thinks the boy. Summer—what's the big rush?

Then he remembers: Swim lessons.

Bill-E! *she sings, less prettily, and is answered by a deeper call from down the hallway, in their bathroom:* Billy! Get your butt up!

Dad. No more fooling around.

The boy goes down the steps and into the smoky kitchen and into his chair. Three crispy-edged pancakes waiting, a pat of sliding butter, bacon strips.

Eat up, she says, kissing his hair. It's eight o'clock already.

You're not supposed to eat before you swim, he says.

She drops more butter hissing in the skillet. That's for afternoon swimming. You show me one kid who goes to swim lessons on Saturday morning without breakfast.

Who's going to swim lessons on Saturday morning without breakfast? His dad has come into the kitchen. He kisses her on the back of the neck and turns to stare at the boy over his coffee mug.

Billy does not look up. Absorbed in the slow-mo sinking of fork tines into the stack. I don't feel good, he says.

His dad sits down. Puts his elbows on the table. It's not a school day, Billy.

I know it.

It's swimming. You love swimming.

Not in the morning, he says. Not when the water is freezing cold.

It's only cold when you first get in, says his dad. Once you get moving, get the blood flowing . . .

It's freezing and it stays freezing.

The father—William Ross—pours syrup on the boy's pancakes. Take another bite, he says, and watches as Billy does as told, as he chews and swallows.

What if we go up to the lake this summer? he says. Up to Grandpa Bill's cabin? Don't you want to swim?

I swim.

I mean swim *swim, like your mom and me. We can swim out to that dock together, the three of us, and no smelly lifejacket. Wouldn't you like to do that?*

The boy picks up a strip of bacon and bites off the end and puts it down again.

I like the lifejacket, he says.

Billy—

Will, Mary says.

What?

Here's your eggs.

They eat, leaving the boy to his silence; maybe if they leave him alone he'll forget he's not eating and eat. But he doesn't, and finally Mary says, OK, time's up. Go get your trunks on. Travis will be here any second.

While he's upstairs stomping around there's the sound of a bike braking into a skid on the sidewalk, and Ross goes to the door and opens up and says, Morning.

Morning, the kid says.

He's coming, Ross says, and the kid, Travis, nods and sits spraddle-legged on his bike. A Schwinn Sting-Ray, identical to Billy's except in color: Travis's green, Billy's purple.

Two doors down Travis's dad stands on the porch, watching. He raises his mug and Ross raises his.

Ross sips—and here's Billy, pushing past him with his towel around his neck, going to his bike where it lies in the grass.

He's wearing pale-blue swim trunks, a white Brewers T-shirt with the beer-barrel man swinging his bat, the red Twins cap with the blue bill—he's been to both ballparks—dirty white Keds and no socks.

The towel is his favorite: Star Wars, with Darth Vader standing tall as the boy himself.

Billy swings one leg over the banana seat and says to his friend, Ready? and they're pushing off when Ross calls out, Hey, buddy, and Billy looks back. Blue-eyed. Freckles across his nose and cheeks.

You're a good kid. I'm proud of you.

The boy nods—that's all—and rides off.

From the front door Ross can watch them all the way down the hill, watch them traverse the park on the winding sidewalk to the outdoor pool, see them dump their bikes in front of the building and walk toward the entrance. Small as they are at that distance, he can see if they turn and look back, and one of them does—Travis, waving to his dad—and he can watch them disappear together into the building.

Later—two hours from that moment—this same boy, Travis, will stand under his father's hands with a trembling chin and tell Ross for a second time that Billy said he forgot something, he'd be right back. And Ross will have to tell the boy, a great rock in his throat, It's OK, Travis, it's not your fault. This after he's waited. After he's walked over to Travis's house the first time—only annoyed, that first time, until he saw the green Schwinn lying alone in the grass.

This after he's driven down to the pool and looked for the purple Sting-Ray, after he's gone inside without paying, passed through the small locker room and walked all around the pool, empty at that hour, to see for himself that the boy wasn't lying on the bottom. After he's tracked down the young instructor and heard her confirm what Travis has said—that Billy wasn't there, that he never got in the pool.

Then, leaving Travis's house the second time, he will drive all around the park and through the neighborhood and into the bluffs, his heart pounding, thinking all the time that he must get back home, back to Mary, who has stayed there in case

Billy returns—maybe he already has—and tell her it's all right, he's just out on his bike somewhere.

First, a boy named Teddy Felt, two years ago. Then Duane Milner last spring.

But Ross will not think of those other boys. That's another world where such things happen, where other parents go through something impossible. He doesn't live in that world. His boy is not one of those boys. He is not one of those fathers.

14.

In the morning Dan stood outside the motel and they drove again to McDonald's and back across town in the workday traffic, chewing their breakfast sandwiches in silence. From the buzzy old speakers a low and steady recital of the world's goings-on, while between the two men there buzzed the unspoken errand of last night, the waitress's unspoken name.

Her eyes. The softness of her mouth. The surprising lightness of her body and the heat just beneath her clothes—thoughts so primary in Sean's mind that he wondered did they transmit, like radio, until Dan could not help but receive them?

"Any news on your truck?" he said, and Dan shook his head.

"No good news," he said.

"It's not a goner, is it?"

"I don't think so. I mean, they're working on it. They say."

"They didn't have a loaner for you?"

"It was already loaned out." Dan studied his sandwich a moment. "Listen," he said, "if this drive is too far, it's all right, I can just . . ."

"No," said Sean. "That's not what I was saying."

"You don't have to feel—"

"I don't. I was just curious. Seriously. I'm actually saving time by not going to that diner in the morning. And money." He raised his coffee as proof, and perhaps in cheers, and they fell silent again.

They were stopped now in the turning lane on West Avenue, each watching the signal and not the man who stood on the median with his square of cardboard: *Veteran. Homeless. Will Work. God Bless.* Shadowed eyes in a creased

face. Gray-black beard lifting in the wind. Old green army jacket with his name, or someone's, still stitched to it, still legible: *Blake.*

The image of a marine in dress blues returned to Sean—her brother, Adam—and he took out his wallet. The light changed. He sorted out a few singles and cranked down his window and the man came forward.

"Thank you, God bless," said the man.

"Thank you for your service," said Sean.

The man nodded and stepped away again. No one honked.

Sean turned left onto Main. Sipped his coffee. "I always wonder if they're really veterans," he said.

Dan sat watching the passing buildings. "He's a veteran of something."

They did not speak again until they'd crossed the tracks near the Wheelhouse Tavern, closed at that hour, and Dan said, "Did you get that door fixed?"

"Yes, I did," said Sean. "It was more of a widening job than a fix."

"A widening job?"

Sean told him about the father in the wheelchair, the daughter's return home—you wouldn't call it caretaking, exactly, the man seemed able enough—the removal of the jamb.

"No mother?" said Dan.

"No mother. Cancer. An older brother gone too. A soldier."

"Damn," said Dan.

"Yeah."

Dan watched the road ahead. Then he said, "Did he know you were the one who . . . ?"

"The father? Yeah. He offered to return the favor."

"Ah."

"Yeah," said Sean. "Thirty minutes later we're all sitting around the dinner table. The three of us."

"And how was that?"

"It was . . . ," Sean said. "Pretty damn good."

They watched the road, sipping their coffees, until Sean, pursuing some arc of conversation they'd not spoken aloud, said, "What about you? Family?"

"You mean wife and kids?" Dan shook his head. "No, not me. You?"

"No. None of that."

"Folks? Siblings?" said Dan.

"Yeah, in the Madison area. You?"

"Mother and brother, back in Minnesota. My dad died when I was a kid."

"Oof," said Sean. "That's rough."

"Yeah."

"What of? If you don't mind me asking."

"Cancer. Lung cancer."

"Smoker?"

"Yep."

Sean nodded. "What about your brother?" he said.

"He doesn't smoke."

"I meant what's he do."

"He's a mechanic."

"Working man."

"Yeah, but a genius one. He could tell you every last thing about this truck just by looking at it. He could tell you what size socket you need for the oil plug."

"Maybe he should be working on yours."

Dan laughed—a true out-loud laugh that took Sean by surprise.

"Yeah," Dan said. "I could really use that big doofus right about now."

"Is he older?"

"No. We're twins."

"No kidding?"

"No kidding."

"Identical?"

"We used to be."

"What's that mean?"

"He's bigger."

Sean glanced at him again, recalibrating a world in which there were two Dan Youngs. "What's his name?"

"Mark, but we call him Marky." Dan smiled and shook his head. "Twenty-nine-year-old man and we still call him Marky."

AT MIDMORNING DAN stood listening to Sean's drill and watching the spot in the underside of the subfloor where he expected the point of the spade bit to appear. A dirty snow sifted down from the joists, then the spinning point appeared exactly where it should and Dan yelled "Ho!" and the point halted. Sean backed the bit all the way out to clear the woodchips and dropped it in again, the bit coming more slowly now so as not to create a ragged hole. A one-inch circle appeared, the last thin disk of wood spun in place and the bit dropped through, and when it withdrew again a neat beam of light cored the cloud of sawdust. Dan heard Sean set the drill on the floor and he stepped toward the beam of light, and just then it dimmed out and Sean blew into the barrel of the hole and sawdust gusted down on Dan's face. He stepped away spitting and blinking.

"Hey," said Sean, "I think there's somebody down there. Is somebody down there—?"

"What took you so long?" said Dan. Batting sawdust from his ears.

"Don't be an ingrate. How's it look?"

"Bullseye."

"All right. Let me do the other one."

Sean resumed drilling and had not gone very far into the sill plate when he called Dan's name—*Danny*, he called—and Dan was startled. Having not used this version of his name since he'd met Sean. Since he'd crossed the river into Wisconsin. Since his head wound.

"What?" he called back, but Sean did not reply that he could hear over the drill motor, over the bit chewing away in the wood.

He heard it again: *Danny*. But not from Sean.

Coldness climbed the back of his neck, the back of his skull.

He turned around.

Nothing there. The wooden stairs. The far wall with its yellow-brown seep stains. The darkened windows.

He followed the ribs of the ceiling joists with his eyes, where they crossed overhead from the wall of the stairs to the opposite wall—or presumably did; you could not see the wall itself for the green plastic tubs, stowed floor to ceiling on the sagging wooden racks. He would not have been surprised, in a house this old, to see cellar stairs, a shaft leading up to the hatch on the outside of the house.

There were no cellar stairs. And there was no light at all coming in above the top row of tubs, which was—it took him a second—the southern-facing wall, where the daylight would be brightest.

Sean's bit broke through in a second beam of light. Dan heard the drill set aside, waited for Sean to blow, and stepped up again.

"You never said ho," Sean said into the holes.

"Sorry. I got distracted. It's clean, though."

Dan stepped up on the aluminum stepladder and reached to feed the blue PEX hose into the hole on the right, pushing until he felt Sean's tug and then paying out the line as it rose. The other end was already attached to the new cold-water valve and he called "That's it" when Sean had taken up the slack.

A moment later, hearing Sean say something, he said, "What—?"

"I said beautiful," said Sean.

Dan got ready with the red line. "Did you say my name, earlier?"

"What?"

"Did you say my name—when you were drilling the second hole."

"Nope."

"All right. I'm hearing things down here."

"You just hang on, pardner, we're gonna get you outta there."

"Here comes the red line."

"I'm ready for it."

SHE DIDN'T TAKE their order when Sean called, and she didn't appear at the door when Dan came back out with the sandwiches and sodas.

"Ready to roll?" said Dan.

When they were moving again he pulled the Cokes from the bag and handed one to Sean and they cracked them open and drank.

"By the way," said Dan, working to free a small belch. "The ban is lifted."

Sean looked at him. Dan sitting there, watching the road ahead. "What?" he said.

"I said the ban is lifted."

"Says who?"

"Says her. Denise."

"She was there?"

"She brought out the sandwiches."

"And she said what, exactly?"

"She said tell him the ban is lifted." Dan raised the can again and halted, holding it midair, like an actor. "Also we should come in later. After work. If we feel like it."

Sean banked into a turn. "Anything else?"

"Nope. That was it."

Sean said nothing.

"I think she likes me," Dan said, and Sean shook his head.

"I'm gonna put you back where I found you," he said.

"Yeah," said Dan. "That's probably for the best."

At the Devereaux house Sean backed into his space and they sat on the tailgate in the sun with their legs hanging over and the shepherd sitting at attention, watching them with her clouded eyes, sorting out their sandwiches with her fine nose.

Devereaux's truck was in its spot but no sign of the old man himself. The wheelbarrow stood on end against the south side of the house, well clear of the sagging gutter and the icicles dripping there. Sunlit drops falling like little bombs on a small body of water trapped on the frozen ground and dammed up against the foundation between two dirty windows.

After a while Dan said, "That's funny."

"What?"

"Those windows in the foundation."

"What about them."

"They aren't there in the basement."

Sean, chewing, looked at the windows. "Whattaya mean?"

"I mean they aren't there. There's no light coming in above those tubs. That's where the windows would be."

"They must be as black as the others."

Dan picked at his teeth with a fingernail. "I don't think they're there."

"Maybe they got bricked in from the inside."

"Why would he do that?"

"Maybe they were leaking. Look at all that water. And there's all those seep stains in the walls down there."

"Yeah," Dan said. He took another bite of his sandwich and looked at the house again, at the space between the two windows where the pool of water was widest. The water blue like the sky and spitting up little drops with each drip from above.

When they'd finished eating and were heading back in Sean said, "I suppose you want me to go down there and show you where he bricked in those windows."

"I can look for myself."

"Well, Dan," Sean said. "Now you've got me curious."

They descended and stood before the racks of green tubs. They could hear the soft whistling sound in the shepherd's nose where she lay on her belly at the top of the stairs. Sean raised up on his toes for a better view, but it wasn't enough. He carried over the stepladder and unclamped his work lamp from it and trained the light on the space above the tubs.

"Well," he said. "We were both right."

"How so?"

"The windows aren't here and they've been bricked in. Or bricked over. There's a whole new wall of cinderblock back here. Newer than the original, anyway."

"That explains the joists," said Dan.

"What about the joists?"

"They didn't look right."

"Yeah," said Sean. "The blocks go on up into the spaces between the joists. The old wall must've been leaking pretty bad. All that water collecting right there."

Dan stepped forward and reached past the tubs at shoulder height to touch the cinderblock, to feel the mortar in the joints: clean, cool, but no dampness. Which there likely wouldn't be, this time of year, even on the original wall. Spring—true spring, the thaw, the rains—then you'd know.

Sean stepped off the ladder and reclamped the work lamp and stood there. The dog ceased its whistling and in that silence Devereaux's scraping bootsteps, the knock of his cane, sounded in the hollows between the joists as if he were walking on their heads. He progressed to the middle of the floor and stopped.

Sean and Dan looked at each other. They looked up at the dog, whose head was raised, her great pointed ears erect. Silent.

"Yeah," Sean said loudly, "That looks good, Dan." He rattled the stepladder and moved it back across the room and set it noisily down again. "Grab your tools and let's go on up."

Above them the boots scraped, the cane knocked, and the old man made his way to another part of the house where there was carpeting, or rugs, or someplace for him to sit, and they did not see or hear him again the rest of that day.

15.

SEAN HELD THE door for Dan and followed him into the bar and they stood a minute like two men adjusting to the darkness, though they'd come in from the dusk.

Smell of hay chaff, smell of fried food. Colored string lights swagged about. Low beat of an old rock song and the genial noise of the crowd. Little Jeff stood behind the bar mixing a drink. Sean gave him a nod and he went on mixing, then turned to serve the drink to a man in white shirtsleeves at the end of the bar. The two older men, Bonner and Bergman, were nowhere in sight.

Sean and Dan seated themselves at a four-top, and before long she emerged from the kitchen with plastic baskets of food in her arms. She came toward them, smiling. "Gentlemen . . ."

"Miss," said Sean.

"Right back," she said, and passed on, taking the food to a table of men in business suits, one man to each side of the table. The men came to life at her return, bantering, gesturing, clearing space, chiding one another for uncouthness as she placed the baskets before them, Denise smiling, laughing, then standing with her hands on the back side of her hips, elbows out, making sure they had all they needed—they needed more drinks—before turning away and pulling a face, a kind of hanged-woman's face with uprolled eyes and protruding tongue, so quick you needed to be watching to see it and they'd been watching, Sean and Dan, and she smiled at them and raised her forefinger and swung back to the bar to place the businessmen's drink order with Little Jeff.

"Sorry," she said, standing before them at last. "Stupid busy for a Wednesday. Plus Ann-Louise was supposed to be here at six and it's what"—she checked her watch—"half past you suck, Ann-Louise. Are you all ready for a beer?"

"We should've sat at the bar," Sean said.

"Yeah, that worked out so well for you last time."

Sean half smiled.

"Sorry," she said. "I shouldn't make fun of you in front of your friend."

"This is Dan."

"I know. We met." She set her hands on her hips again, and they ordered pints of Budweiser. Sean asked for a basket of fries.

"Two Buds and a basket of fries," she said. "Breakfast of champions."

They watched her go, then sat looking around. First time they'd sat together indoors, in an establishment, since the morning at the diner, what—two days ago.

Sean swiped his hand over the damp tabletop. "Did you want to check on your truck? You can use my phone."

Dan shook his head. "They close at six."

Sean nodded. "Well, anytime you want to borrow the phone, for any reason, just say the word."

"Thanks. I appreciate it."

"I don't know how the hell you can live without a phone."

"It takes some getting used to. But then you get used to it."

They watched Denise come back to them with the beers, a basket of hot, glistening fries, two small plates, a squirt bottle of ketchup. The salt and pepper shakers were already on the table.

She stood there, hands on hips.

No one spoke. Finally Sean said, "How's that door working out?"

"Great. Hasn't banged his hands once since you did your magic."

"Magic," Sean said.

She turned to Dan. "When you help someone out, that's magic. Don't you think?"

"Absolutely."

"Thank you." She moved on again, and Sean picked up the pepper shaker.

"I'm gonna pepper the hell outta these puppies unless you stop me."

"I won't stop you."

They sat chomping on the fries and drinking their beers. After a while Dan said, "Are you looking for someone?"

"Looking for someone? No. Why?"

"I just thought maybe you were."

Sean shook his head. He chewed on a fry. "I guess I wouldn't be surprised if a certain dumb-ass walked in here."

Dan looked toward the glass door. "You think his ban is lifted too?"

"I doubt it. His ban was a little more legal around the edges."

"Meaning?"

"She got a restraining order on him."

"Ah," said Dan. "Ex-boyfriend?"

Sean looked around. Denise was at a far booth, taking a couple's order. "I wouldn't say that," he said. "I don't think she'd say that."

"Would he?"

"He might say any damn thing."

"What'd he say to make you punch him?"

Sean shook his head.

"Sorry," said Dan. "Dumb thing to ask. Especially here. I haven't drunk a beer in a while."

"What's a while?"

Dan thought back. "Three weeks?"

"Maybe you better get some actual food in you."

"I'll be all right."

Three men in winter gear and yellow safety vests came in and crossed to the bar, their muddied treads lifting boot-shaped mats of hay chaff from the floor as they went. They'd not sat down before Little Jeff began drawing their beers.

"Listen," said Dan. "I gotta say something."

"OK."

"I like the work and I like making money and I like working with you."

"Uh-oh."

"No, it's not that."

"Good."

"The thing is," said Dan.

Sean waited.

"The thing is, there is no truck."

Sean watched him. "There is no truck. What's that mean?"

"It means there was a truck. There is a truck, somewhere. But I can't get to it."

"Where is it?"

"I expect it's sitting in the impound lot, back in Minnesota."

"Impound lot," said Sean. "As in the police impound lot."

"Yeah."

"What's it doing there?"

Dan rocked the base of his glass on the table. "I had to leave that truck on the side of the road," he said. "On the other side of the bridge."

"Because it broke down."

"No. Because I had to leave it behind."

Sean thought about that. "Was it your truck?"

"What? Yes, it was my truck. Did you think I was saying it was stolen?"

"I'm trying to figure out what you're saying."

"I know. Sorry."

Sean watched him. Then he said, "Hell, you don't have to explain yourself to me, Dan. I once took off in a truck that wasn't mine. It was my dad's and I flat-out stole it and I was gone a long time before he got it back."

"Where'd you go?"

Sean shook his head. "Nowhere special."

"Getting out of Dodge."

"Yeah."

Other voices, music, filled the silence. Then Dan said again, "It was my truck."

"OK," said Sean. "But if you're in trouble with the police I think you might want to say so. In fact I seem to remember asking you that before."

"You did. And the truth is they might be looking for me. The sheriff, anyway. But not because I did anything wrong."

"Wrong?"

"Illegal. I want to be clear about that."

"OK," Sean said.

Dan took a good swallow of his beer and set it down with care. As if he did not want to hear the sound of the glass making contact with the tabletop. Sean lifted his, watching Dan over the rim.

Dan said, "I guess I hope it's enough to say I needed to get away from there for a while, and I couldn't get away while I was driving that truck. So I gave it up. I gave it to them, and I walked."

The bar had become more crowded. Someone had turned up the music. The four men in business suits laughed uproariously. Something about the men, about Dan Young, the talk of stolen trucks, made Sean think of another bar in another time. College football players and two drunk girls and the reek of a men's room.

He swept his hand through the air and said, "Listen, Dan, it's OK. I've been getting away for a long while now and I don't want to explain that to anyone." He raised his glass and drank. "At least now I can stop asking you about your truck."

Dan smiled. He turned his glass in his hands. "I'm sorry I didn't tell you sooner. I didn't think we'd—" He stopped. "I didn't think you needed to know," he said.

"I don't," Sean said. "It's all good."

He looked around. Denise stood at the bar loading a tray. He turned back to Dan.

"So what was your plan? Just live out your days in the Motel 6?"

"No. I was thinking about getting on the train. Or buying a truck."

"You have the money for that—for a new truck?"

"Not a new one. But I could make it work."

Sean picked up a fry—limp, cold—put it back. "What about your family? Your mom and your brother, the genius mechanic."

"What about them?"

"Do they know where you are?"

"No. And I can't exactly tell them without putting them in a bind."

"Because—?"

"Because I'd have to ask them not to tell the sheriff."

Sean studied him. "And they'd want to tell the sheriff because he could bring you home."

"Correct."

Sean nodded. He scratched at his jaw. "OK, but—"

"What?"

"I don't know. Wouldn't that truck on the side of the road kinda freak them out?"

Dan looked into his beer—what was left of it. "Maybe," he said. "I tell myself they'd understand why I did it."

Sean watched him. "Did you lose your phone when you lost your truck?"

"Yes."

"So they can't try to call you. Or track you."

"Yes."

Sean nodded. He sat looking at Dan.

"What?" said Dan.

"Are you gonna split on me?"

"I'm not gonna split on you."

"Good."

"What's the story here?" Denise had come back to them. "Food, no food? More beer . . . ?"

Sean looked at Dan, and Dan shook his head. "Not for me."

"I guess we're gonna scoot along," Sean said.

"Seriously? I get off in ten minutes. I was going to join you."

"You do that," said Dan. "You join. I'll let myself out."

"No," said Sean.

"Yeah."

Denise looked from one to the other. "I'm gonna make a last round and check back with you two."

They watched her go.

"Take my truck," said Sean, and Dan laughed.

"After what I just told you."

"Especially after that. I know you ain't no truck thief like me."

"How will you get home?"

"I'll call a cab."

"No, I'll call a cab," Dan said.

"You got no phone."

"Can I borrow your phone?"

"Just take the damn truck."

Dan studied him, then turned toward the bar. He seemed to track her as she moved efficiently about. Sean sitting there impassively. Dan turned back to him.

"OK, I'll take the truck. What about the morning?"

"We'll figure it out." Sean got his keys from his jacket pocket and handed them over.

"I believe I'll hit the head before I go," Dan said, and Sean gestured with the flat of his hand: straight ahead, then left.

"Roger that."

She came back while he was in there and sat down at one of the other two chairs. She looked at his jacket on the chairback. "Is he staying?"

"No, he's taking my truck."

"And why's he doing that?"

"Because he doesn't have one."

"He doesn't have one?"

"No ma'am."

"He has no vehicle."

"No ma'am."

"And how are you getting home?"

"I don't know. I'll call a taxi."

"A taxi," she said. She smiled. "Shall I bring you a Tom Collins? Pimm's Cup?"

Dan came back and lifted his jacket from the chairback.

"You won't stay and have a beer?" she said.

"No, but thank you. Here, let me leave some money."

"Keep your money," said Sean.

"All right. Well." He stood looking at them, some bleariness in his eyes.

"You all right to drive, pardner?"

"Hell yes. One beer."

"Don't go wrecking my truck."

"I won't."

"I'll talk to you in the morning."

"All right. Denise," he said. "A pleasure."

"Likewise, Dan. Be safe."

He turned away and they watched him until he'd stepped out through the glass door and the door had swung shut behind him.

"A working man with no vehicle," she said. She didn't move to Dan's vacated chair but stayed where she was, on Sean's left.

"It's a long story and I don't even know it," he said.

"Then let's not talk about it."

"All right."

"Let's talk about something else."

"All right."

"As soon as I get us some beers."

"You sit," he said, rising. "I'll get the beers."

THE OLD CHEVY was just warming up when Dan pulled over on Jay Street and cut the engine.

He sat there.

The station across the street was a modern building with old-fashioned details meant to evoke, perhaps, the sounds of a steam engine at rest: its restless hissing, the clanging of bells, the call of a conductor. But there were no trains. No tracks. No one waited in the light of the glass-globe lampposts. The large round clockface on the brick facade with its roman numerals read ten after eight.

A kind of alley went through the middle of the building and a bus was parked there, idling. CHICAGO in its pale, irradiated banner. No one on board that he could see, but then a man came from the building and by some means opened the bus door, the forward compartment bloomed with light, and taking his seat behind the wheel he began to push buttons on his instrument panel. In a moment CHICAGO blinked out and was replaced by MNPLS-STPAUL.

Dan drummed his thumbs on the wheel. He could leave the keys on top of the tire, call Sean at the first stop.

"Yeah," he said, "after you just told the man you wouldn't split on him."

The headlights came on and the bus rolled out of the alley and turned left. He'd seen no one in the windows, but the windows were dark-tinted and you couldn't say if there were passengers in there or not. It could be full, or it could be on its way to MNPLS-STPAUL with not a soul on board save the driver. A ghost bus.

He got out of the truck and went walking the way the bus had gone, hands in his jacket pockets, jostling the keys loosely in his fist. Cold, river-smelling wind blowing the hair back from his hairline and coldly constricting the new thin scar there. He crossed Fourth, then Third, and he was halfway to Second when headlights came up behind him. Slow, prowling lights and he knew what it would be and it was—a white SUV sheriff's cruiser. He looked over, as any normal person would, saw that it was local, and looked casually away. The cruiser braked at the corner and sat there. Dan kept walking, no slower, no faster. "You dumb bastard," he said under his breath, and not to whoever was behind the wheel. He was just on the cruiser's tail when it signaled and turned left and was gone.

He walked on, his heart slowly quieting.

The street he followed came to its end and he passed through a courtyard between the last buildings and stood at the railing looking out over the dark emptiness of the river, head-on to the wind. Directly to his right: the sparkling interior of a restaurant, couples at their meals, faint notes of a piano. On a warmer night the couples would've been out on the patio under the pergola beams and the strung lights, nothing beyond them but the great river, the far summer trees of Minnesota.

Below where he stood was a kind of dock, or deck, and he took the stone steps down to it. It was maybe twenty by twenty and its forward pilings stood in the river. He took hold of the guardrail and looked at the black water below. No lapping, no sluicing, no sound to it at all. He leaned and landed a foamy dime of spit on the surface, and the spit lay there. Then slowly it moved to his left, downstream, in the direction of the bridge.

Out in the dark the bridge hung eerily in its own lamplight. Between the piers on the dark spans, the lights of travelers crossed in slow exchange, headlights for taillights, one shore for the other.

This time of night, his mother and his brother would be watching televi-
sion. A movie, maybe. They'd already watched the evening news—his mother
tense for the first fifteen minutes, when they reported on local deaths and
crimes, relaxing a little after that. A little.

He couldn't think about that—about what his absence, his silence, must
be doing to her. The latest in a long line of her griefs, going back to his father's
death. More beyond that he didn't even know of.

The news was over and they'd eaten dinner and now they'd settled in for
the movie. In an hour or so Big Man would be hungry again, and he'd get up
and make popcorn on the stove, using Crisco for the popping, and butter after.
Pretty much the greasiest popcorn on the planet but Marky loved it. And Dan
would give anything for a bowl of it right now.

"Easy on the salt, Marky."

After a few seconds he looked around, as if someone else might've spoken.
Or as if someone else were there to hear. But there was no one. He was alone on
the deck. On the river.

He saw it on the driver's-side window as he came around the front end of
the truck and he knew what it was before he got up close. It had come at some
speed from the opposite direction and had not yet begun to freeze to the glass.
He looked up the street the way the car would've gone and then he looked the
other way, back toward the river. Nothing moved anywhere.

He remembered the sheriff's cruiser. Where was it now? Had it been anywhere near when the spitter made his hit?

Dan grabbed a handful of dirty curb snow and smeared away at the spit
until there was nothing left but meltwater and bits of snow draining slowly
down the glass, then he found the keys with cold fingers and unlocked the door
and climbed in and started the truck and pulled out into the street.

"Ignorant dumb-ass," he said.

16.

June 1977

THE OLD WOMAN *did not look up when he walked in, nor otherwise mark his arrival in the cramped and heated kitchen.*

She sat sideways to the table, elbows on her spread knees, skipping her peeler over the curve of a potato and the peelings leaping like little flatfish into the mouth of the paper bag that stood between her stout black shoes, between stockings of such thickness and color her lower legs had the look of molded plastic—swollen, lumpy with clotting—as of some granny-legged mannequin so seated in a store window.

Devereaux slid the two grocery bags onto the counter, displacing a number of small pots and tin measuring cups, and began stowing the groceries in the cupboards, in the refrigerator.

Wan late daylight lay over the counter, the sink, the unwashed cookware, while in the air there buzzed a terrible fly. Or not a fly but a voice, droning and droning in the grille of the old plastic radio on the table, an alien transmission understood by none but the old woman, she and the radio having declined together year by year, hour by hour.

They didn't have the brand of milk you like, Devereaux said.

She seemed not to hear, but then she said, What does that mean?

It means they didn't have it.

Didn't have it, she said. Did you—don't put that away, leave that out—did you ask them?

Ask who?

Them. The store people. The stocking manager. Oftentimes they have things in the back they ain't got to putting out yet. You gotta ask.

She plopped a potato in a pot of water there on the table and began peeling another.

In the open sash above the sink, in a rusty square of screen, a man walked into view toting a posthole digger over his shoulder, and behind him came a boy, half carrying, half dragging a four-by-four barn post of some length. Boy of thirteen or fourteen in cutoff jeans and T-shirt, head of bright copper hair.

The man stopped and stood looking at the grass and weeds around him. The boy had stopped too, holding the post. Finally the man spoke to the boy and the boy let the post whump to the ground. The man spoke again and the boy looked around the area, took a few steps and pointed, and the man went to the spot and unshouldered the posthole digger. He set his feet and, having marked the spot with a few turns of the curved blades, raised and brought the tool smartly down. Spread the hafts, lifted, released grass and dirt off to the side.

The boy standing by with hands on hips, like a small foreman.

What's Uncle Frankie doing? Devereaux said.

Say what?

I said what's Uncle Frankie doing.

What's it look like he's doing?

Looks like he's putting in a post.

Well it's a wild guess but I'd say he's puttin in a post.

What for?

The old woman stopped peeling. Devereaux didn't turn around. Then he did.

Boy, are you done puttin my groceries away?

Yes, ma'am.

Then would you mind getting your hiney outta my kitchen so I can get dinner made?

Yes, ma'am.

He pushed out through the screen door and stepped down into the yard and ambled over to his uncle and the boy.

Uncle Frankie drove the digger into the hole, raised it, emptied it, and held the shafts out to the boy. OK, your turn.

The boy was not paying attention. He'd seen Devereaux coming toward them. Uncle Frankie followed his gaze.

Look what the cat drug in. Where you been?

Grocery store.

You put gas in that truck?

Yep.

Good. We're goin into town later for a bag of cement.

Devereaux looked from Uncle Frankie to the boy, and then he looked down. What's gonna go here?

I give you one guess.

A post.

Yeah. Or you, you go on standin there like that. He slid a wink to the boy, who was looking elsewhere. Hands sunk in his front pockets.

This here is Davy, said Uncle Frankie. Lives across those woods. Been helping me out around the place.

They looked at the boy. He was turned from them and squinting at something in the distance, in the treetops.

Found him a few days ago crawling around that garage and I said Boy, what're you doin and he says Nothin and I say Well, I'll pay you a dollar an hour to do somethin instead of nothin and he looks at me and guess what he says. Says Dollar fifty.

Uncle Frankie looked at Devereaux. How do you like that?

Devereaux made no reply.

Uncle Frankie watched him.

Davy, he said, this here chatterbox is my nephew, Marion.

The boy nodded and looked around. Looked at his own sneakers. Looked at the house.

I gotta go, he said.

Go? I thought we were gonna put this post in the ground.

I forgot I gotta do something for my mom.

Uncle Frankie sighed. All right. I know how that is. Well, here, don't run off till I pay you.

That's OK, I didn't do anything.

Sure you did. You lugged that post out here, and that sumbuck is heavy. Now here. Here's two bucks. Come back when you can and we'll finish the job.

The boy took the rumpled bills and stuffed them in his pocket. He took one last look at Devereaux, then turned and walked off, moving in the manner of a boy who knows he's being watched. When he was a few steps away he leaned to one side and spat—or made the sound of spitting, a boy unaccustomed to spitting—and then he sauntered into the woods and was gone.

You done scared him off, Marion.

Devereaux said nothing.

You ever seen such red hair before?

Devereaux seemed to be studying the hole in the ground.

Uncle Frankie said, I says to him Do you care if I call you Red? and know what he says?

Devereaux didn't.

Says Do you care if I call you Old 'n Bald?

Uncle Frankie laughed and ran his hand over his high pink forehead. He raised the digger and sank it in the hole, but with less force. His face had begun to shine.

What for? said Devereaux.

What for what?

What's the post for?

Uncle Frankie rested. Can't a man put a post in the ground, his own ground, without he's got to explain himself?

Devereaux shrugged. He began to turn away.

Basketball goal.

He turned back. A what?

Basketball goal. I found one out at that old Rickland farm, in all that trash and shit. Backboard and everything. Except the net. Me and Red there—Davy— we're gonna throw this barn post in here, a bag a concrete, and bolt that ol' goal right on up there at ten foot, not one inch more, not one inch less.

Devereaux looked up, as if to judge ten feet with his eyes, or to imagine the goal fixed at that height with the blue sky beyond. Then he turned toward the garage. A simple clapboard outbuilding with lesions of gray-white paint on the gray wood, its bay door out of square and biased to the north as if the entire structure were trained that way by steady gales.

Why don't you put it up on that garage? Devereaux said.

Uncle Frankie sank the digger in the hole again. Did they have a gymnasium at that junior high? he said. The one that fired you?

When Devereaux failed to answer he looked up from the hole, the shafts in his fists.

They did, said Devereaux.

With basketball goals?

Yep.

And what did those kids dribble those basketballs on?

Every weekday afternoon Devereaux the janitor had paced off the glossy hardwood floor, pushing the six-foot dry mop before him. On Fridays the mop was to be dampened with a water and Zep's solution.

Was it gravel? said Uncle Frankie.

Devereaux's gaze fell groundward. Around the dark cylinder of the hole in every direction grew a bristling miscellany of crabgrass and weeds, flourishing with the spring rains.

Uncle Frankie looked too, then passed his open hand over such verdancy in a slow scything. We're gonna clear-cut this all down to dirt and tamp her with that old tamper, hard and smooth and level as any goddam wood floor you ever saw.

Devereaux, to all appearances listening, considering, at last said, What about when it rains? and his uncle's hand, still scything, halted, and his face came slowly back to Devereaux.

Son, do I look like the kind of man who would shoot basketballs in the rain?

Uncle Frankie standing there in his undershirt and ill-fitting jeans, in boots so far gone the steel was bared at the toes like strange scalpings. His sunburned high forehead where hair once grew. In what derelict corner of his brain did he look like a man who would have the least idea what to do with a basketball?

That's not what I meant, Devereaux said. I meant—

I know what you meant, Marion. He lifted the digger and emptied it. Sank it in the hole again.

Devereaux turned to go.

By the way, Uncle Frankie said, and Devereaux turned back. Uncle Frankie kept going through the motions of digging, bringing up little dirt.

Saw someone you know at the VFW yesterday. Man by the name of Wilby?
Kind of a wiry little jug-eared guy? Kind of a talker?

He's on that crew with me.

So I gathered. Uncle Frankie turned the blades in the hole. Want to know how
I gathered?

All right.

I'm sitting there, having a drink at the bar, minding my own business, and I
hear my name. The family name. Devereaux. So I turn and here's this jug-eared
little gomer at the billiards table with his buddies and he keeps saying Devereaux.
Dev-ro, he says. So after a while I pick up my beer and I walk on back there and
I'm standing there and he looks at me and goes right on talking. Saying Dev-ro.
Saying Marion.

Devereaux said nothing.

Now if there's one thing I can't abide, it's people talking about the family. I just
can't abide it. So I say to this guy Hey, buddy, and he says Hey, buddy, and I say
Do I know you? and he says I don't think so, name's Wilby. Wilby, I say. Wilby,
I thought I must know you because you keep saying my name. Devereaux. And
this Wilby's jaw stops moving. He just looks at me. Damn, he says. You must be
the uncle. You were in the Corps. I was in the Corps, Wilby says. Like now we're
gonna be buddies and tell war stories and shit. I say First, I thought the Corps had
a height minimum, and second, if you were in the Corps I'd say you forgot what
you learned about respect. He looks at me and he says Hey, sorry if I offended you,
man. I like Dev-ro. I like your nephew. You got a funny way of showing it, I say.
Sorry, man, he says again, and I come in close to him and I say into his jug ear,
Wilby, I ever hear you talking about my nephew again, I'm gonna put my thumb
through your eye socket and scramble your little brains so you spend the rest of your
days shitting yourself in a diaper. I thought he'd wanna fight, a Corps man and
all. But he didn't wanna fight. He didn't say a word.

Uncle Frankie stood the posthole digger in the grass. He drew his wrist across
his forehead.

I don't know what business you had talking about me to this little gomer, he
said. *But I'll be God damned if I'll have the Devereaux name slandered.*

Devereaux crossed his arms and stood with his head bowed. As if in thought.

I won't abide it, Marion.

Another man might have pointed out to the elder Devereaux that he himself sometimes spoke cruelly of his nephew.

Another man, not Devereaux.

So you let me know, Marion—all right? You let me know if that little gomer gives you any grief. I promised him something and I keep my promises. All right?

All right, Uncle Frankie.

All we got is this house and this land and the Devereaux name, Marion.

I know, Uncle Frankie.

I hope you do. I hope you—He stopped, his eyes fixed on something beyond Devereaux, and Devereaux turned just as there arrived in the clearing the sound of car tires on gravel, a slow scud of gravel dust, the white-and-tan sheriff's cruiser.

Shit, Marion, said Uncle Frankie. What did you do now?

I didn't do anything.

The cruiser came to rest behind the Ford truck, and the driver got out, donning his stiff hat, peering casually into the bed of the truck, into the cab, as he walked by and then coming on across the yard. It was not the sheriff himself but one of his deputies, a young one. Younger than Devereaux by perhaps ten years. A boy in uniform and aviators, nodding at the two men and saying them a howdy.

Howdy yourself, Deputy—Uncle Frankie squinting at his breast pin—Veegus.

Viegas, said the young deputy. He removed his sunglasses and hung them in the V of his blouse. He set his hands on his utility belt and looked down at the hole, the mound of earth.

Digging a hole, are you?

Uncle Frankie looked with him, then up again. Actually, Deputy, I'm growin a hill.

Viegas gave a kind of smirk and looked toward the house. The old woman was at the kitchen window. She appeared to be washing something at the sink. He touched his hat brim but she did not gesture or nod or give any sign that she saw the deputy at all.

Viegas turned back. He looked from one Devereaux to the other, then with a studied air of sheriffing unsnapped a breast pocket on his blouse and fished up a square of paper.

Sheriff sent me to ask if any of you folks out here had seen this boy, he said, and held the paper up to their faces.

It was a color Xerox picture of a boy—his school picture. The deputy panning his arm so both men could get a good look. Blond little boy with a drift of freckles across his nose, buck teeth, spaces where the back teeth had not come in.

His name's Billy Ross, he said. Ten years old.

What's he gone and done? Uncle Frankie said.

Nothing. He's missing.

Missing?

Two days now.

Two days? Uncle Frankie sank a hand into a jeans pocket and came out with his smokes and lighter. He got a cigarette to his lips and flicked the Zippo open, lit the cigarette and snapped the lid to again. With the smoke he said Shoot, Deputy. He could be in Canada by now.

Have you seen him, Mr. Devereaux?

Uncle Frankie shook his head. Not me. You, Marion?

Devereaux took a good look at the picture. He shook his head. No, me neither.

You're sure—both of you?

Deputy, said Uncle Frankie. Don't you think we'd know if we saw a little blond-headed kid running around out here? Be like seeing a elephant.

Viegas lowered the picture. He looked toward the house. The old woman still at the window. Unchanged in stance or expression.

No point in bothering her, said Uncle Frankie. She can't see the end of her own arm and she never leaves that house anyway with those feet of hers.

She looks like she sees just fine from here.

That's just how she looks.

Viegas shook his head very slightly, but made no move.

Go on and ask her then, Uncle Frankie said.

The young deputy stared at the window. After a minute he looked away, off toward the woods. He slipped the picture back into his pocket and resnapped the button.

If you haven't seen him, you haven't seen him.

We'll keep an eye out, Deputy, said Uncle Frankie, and indeed began to skim his gaze about the property.

Viegas took up his aviators and put them on, and stood there. He seemed to be studying the dark neat hole in the grass. Finally he looked up again. You all take care, he said, and walked back to the cruiser. He got the car turned around, spun his tires briefly in the gravel and pulled away down the drive.

Uncle Frankie walked to the corner of the house, the posthole digger clunking alongside him like some odd chieftain's staff. Devereaux following.

Frankie! came the old woman's voice. She was at another window, watching through the screen.

What, Ma?

What did that sheriff want?

That wasn't no sheriff.

What was that he showed you?

Picture.

Say what?

I said a picture.

Picture a what?

Some little snot-nose gone missing.

The old woman drew in her breath. Billy Ross, she said. I heard it on the radio. Ten years old. She clucked her tongue. That makes three.

That makes nothin, Ma. Kid's probably hiding in the goddam attic or something.

What'd he come here for?

Who?

That sheriff.

That wasn't no sheriff, I said.

I don't like it, Frankie. I don't like him coming around here. It ain't respectable.

I don't like it either, Ma.

She clucked her tongue again. It ain't respectable, coming out here like that.

Uncle Frankie rubbed at his forehead.

You boys come inside now. Get washed up for dinner.

All right, Ma, we're coming. Here, Marion. He handed the posthole digger to Devereaux.

What do you want me to do with this?

I don't know, put it up somewheres. I'm hungry and my head is killing me.

Uncle Frankie walked away and Devereaux looked about him. Finally he stood the tool against the side of the house next to the cellar bulkhead, and there it stayed a long while before it slid of its own will to the ground. Blades rusting in the rains that came to wash away the small mound of earth Uncle Frankie had made, much of the dirt returning in muddy currents to the hole from which it had come, and in time, in years, no trace of hole or mound but a faint dip and rise in the weedy, grown-over ground.

17.

THE DETECTIVE, CORRINE Viegas, was staring at her computer screen when the sheriff across the river called her back, fifteen minutes after she'd left him a message. Sheriff Halsey. She apologized for calling him after hours and he said it was all right, he didn't even know what office hours meant in a job like this, and she said, "Tell me about it."

It was just after ten on a Wednesday night and she sat alone among the desks, Samuels having gone out to smoke a cigarette, Sergeant Russo having stepped into the break room, or the men's room.

"How can I help you, Detective?"

"Sheriff, I'm sitting here looking at a picture of Daniel Paul Young that your office posted a couple of weeks ago, and the reason I'm looking at the picture is because I received a call about an hour ago from a man who said he'd talked to a man named Dan Young in a bar here in town."

"Dan Young?" said Halsey. "Not Danny?"

"No, sir. He said Dan. I wrote it down."

"All right. Go on."

"The caller said he thought this Dan Young might be in some kind of trouble and wanted to know was he wanted or missing or anything like that."

"I take it the caller didn't identify himself."

"No, he wouldn't give me his name. Said he just had a feeling he should mention it to somebody."

"Caller ID?"

"No caller ID. I think he star-sixty-sevened me."

"Like any concerned citizen." There was a riffling sound on the sheriff's end, as of sheets of a writing pad being brushed away for a clean page. "And he called you—you in particular?"

"He called my cell phone."

"And he got that number how?"

"I don't know. He wouldn't say."

"Did he say why you?"

"He did not."

"All right. Go on."

"I told him I'd never heard the name Dan Young but I'd see if there was anything in the system and call him back, and he said he'd wait, and I said I couldn't tie up my phone that long, and he said he'd call back and hung up."

"But he never called back."

"Not so far."

"Well," said Halsey, "I'm guessing you're thinking what I'm thinking."

"Probably."

"You didn't happen to record the call."

"No, sir. Would you know his voice if you heard it?"

"I wouldn't, but I know some folks who would."

"His family?"

"Yes. I imagine they'd sure like to hear that voice about now."

"Wife-and-kids family or . . . ?"

"Mother and brother. Twin brother."

"He's a twin?"

"Yep."

"Do they sound alike?"

The sheriff seemed to think on it. "I couldn't say," he said finally. "I haven't heard either one of their voices in a long while."

Viegas was silent, replaying the earlier call in her mind, her eyes on Daniel Young's face on the screen—an outdoor shot from some spring or summer day, sunlight in his blue eyes, in his good head of brown hair. Some mother's cherished son, as were they all. Did the voice she'd heard match this face?

"How about his phone?" she said. "His voice message. Maybe if I heard that. Or a message he left on someone else's phone."

"Yeah," said Halsey. "I've called his cell once a day since he went missing two weeks ago and it's the same recorded message every time saying the box is all filled up. As for a message on someone else's phone, I'd have to say I'd as soon not bother those folks without something a little more solid to stand on."

"I understand," said Viegas. She tapped the point of her pen on her pad, inking a random configuration of dots. "Sheriff, I could help you track down this call, but I don't see any warrant here, and without an investigation, without a suspect . . ."

"I know," he said. "I've got the same issue with his cell phone records. And nobody gets paper bills anymore, especially if they move around as much as he has the last ten years."

"Right," said Viegas. She drew straight lines from one dot to another. "Ten years," she said.

"Yes, ma'am," said the sheriff.

"But he hasn't been missing for ten years."

"No, ma'am. That's just when he—I'd guess you'd say flew the nest."

"After the Holly Burke murder."

Halsey didn't hesitate. "After the Holly Burke murder, correct. I figured you'd read about that."

"Yes, sir. What there was online."

"Yeah, that's what I'd have done. Seeing how the microfiche is on the fritz."

"Right," Viegas said absently.

"That's a joke for us old-timers."

She clicked another window and looked at the girl. Young woman. Nineteen. Pretty. A certain intelligence, a certain wariness, in her gaze. As if she'd already seen, in one form or another, what the world held in store for her.

Or did Viegas see that in her because of what had in fact happened to her? The way she'd seen something in her own sister's eyes, but only after Mariana had told her about it five years later: A reeking sofa in a basement. A boy who would go on to be a dentist in New Orleans.

"Detective?" said Halsey.

"He was never charged," said Viegas. "Dan Young."

"No, he wasn't."

"No one ever was."

"No, ma'am."

Viegas sat looking at Holly Burke. At Daniel Paul Young, whose image was cropped from a photo in which he was not alone; in which he had his arm around another man's shoulder and the other man's arm around his. The brother, perhaps. The twin. Who perhaps had the same half-hearted, cooperative smile on his face, the mother having just said "Smile."

"Ten years," said the sheriff. "This kid—well, he's not a kid anymore—he's been mostly gone, like I said. He'd come home for a few days here and there, see his family, and go away again. And to tell you the truth I wouldn't give one flying hoot about him except this last time he came home I found his truck just short of the Mississippi with a bullet hole in it. Rifle round. Fresh. No blood, no other sign of foul play, but no Danny Young either. Looked to me like he just got out of the truck and walked across the bridge in the dark of night. Or else went into the river."

"What bridge was that?"

"Over here we call it the West Channel Bridge."

"The Highway 14 Bridge?"

"Yes, ma'am."

Viegas wrote *14* on her sheet of paper.

"And this was two weeks ago you found the truck."

"Yes, ma'am. Morning of"—he shuffled papers—"February twenty-sixth, around two a.m. That was a Monday. His mother says he'd been back since the eighteenth, two Sundays before."

Viegas drew slow circles around the *14*. Back in the '70s, in her father's day, they'd found one of the missing boys' bikes by that bridge, in the shallow water on the Wisconsin side. It hadn't been ridden or pushed there, but dropped from above. State police had dragged the river, they'd sent in divers, but found no boy. That was the third boy's bike. Billy Ross.

"Detective?"

"Yes," said Viegas, returning to the present. To Dan Young. "You think he might've jumped?"

"I think it less now than I did twenty minutes ago."

"And the abandoned truck and the bullet hole," said Viegas. "You don't think that's connected to the Holly Burke case?"

"Might be. Might not be. Ten years isn't very long in a town like this."

"Somebody was sending him a message with that rifle round?"

"Could be. Could be he got the message and decided to disappear again. Really disappear. Just park the truck and walk away."

Samuels had returned from his smoke and he stood glancing around the room. She pointed with her pen and he gave her the thumbs-up and walked off toward the break room.

"But, Sheriff," she said. "If you're trying to walk away, to disappear, calling up the police to ask about yourself may not be your brightest move."

"No, I'd say not. If I had to guess—if this was in fact Danny Young and not some concerned citizen—I'd say he figured by calling you, over there in Wisconsin, he could find out what he needed to know without it getting back to me."

"But he had to figure I would make this call."

"Well," said Halsey, "it's what you or I would figure."

"And that you would tell his family," she said. "And maybe that was the whole point."

Halsey was silent. Then: "He called you so you'd call me so I'd call his mother."

Viegas gave a quiet laugh. "I'm just trying to imagine the thought process of someone who doesn't want to talk to you but wants to let his family know he's alive and doesn't want to ask them to lie to you about hearing from him."

Now Halsey laughed. "I can't tell if you're giving him too much credit or not enough, Detective."

"Yeah, me neither." She stirred her pen in a bowl of bite-size candies in their foils, as if she would dredge up the one she wanted.

"But you won't make that call, will you," she said.

"No, ma'am. It's a bit slender to get their hopes up on. We'll have to sit on this awhile."

"I understand," she said, and in the silence that followed she heard Samuels and the sergeant talking in low tones in the break room. Something they didn't want her to hear. Cop gossip. A dirty joke.

Viegas stared at her screen. Those two young faces.

"Can I ask you one more question, Sheriff?"

He moved in some way and she heard the squawk of an old swivel chair. "You want to know do I think Danny Young had anything to do with that girl's death ten years ago."

"Yes, sir."

"Ten years ago I wasn't the sheriff," Halsey said. "I was just a deputy. But I'll say this, and I'm guessing you'll understand: Sometimes you want the man to be your man so badly it gets in you like a sickness. Like a disease."

"Yes, sir."

"Well, it wasn't like that with this kid. I hated to let him go. We all did. But I haven't spent the last ten years grinding my teeth over it, and I can't even tell you for sure why. Of course I might be in the minority, around here. Other than his mother. His brother."

"I understand, Sheriff. Thank you."

"All right. You know where to find me, Detective."

"Yes, sir, I do."

After they hung up she thought too late that she should've asked the sheriff for the full photograph—so she could see the brother, the twin, who was not missing. Who'd not been held in connection with the death of a young woman ten years ago. So she could see those effects, that difference, in the two men's eyes.

She sent the images of Dan Young and Holly Burke to herself, picked up her phone to make sure they were there, then cleared them from her computer screen. When she left, Samuels and Russo were still talking, still laughing in the break room.

18.

IT WAS TWENTY past five when Andrews came in, and he headed for the back room without a glance at Mattis behind the counter.

"Hey, Vince," said Mattis, and Andrews stopped, took one step back from the doorway and looked at him. Mattis already had his jacket on.

"Hey, what."

"You said you'd be here ten minutes ago."

"I know. I'm running a little late. Just gimme five, man. I gotta piss like a racehorse."

Mattis shook his head and came around the counter. "I don't have five, man."

"Are you serious right now?" said Andrews. "You gonna do me like that?" he said, but Mattis was already gone.

He gunned the Monte Carlo through two yellows, found a parking space out front, and took the stairs to the third floor and swept into the front office breathing hard. The receptionist was in her coat, standing there tapping at her cell phone.

"Blaine Mattis," said Mattis. "Here to see Mr. Grady."

"Yes, Mr. Mattis. He's been waiting for you."

"Yeah, sorry about that."

She dropped her phone into her coat pocket and picked up the handset and pushed a button. "Mr. Mattis is here," she said. "All right," she said, "you too," and replaced the handset. "He says to go on back. You know which door?"

"Yeah. Thanks. Have a nice night."

"You too," she said again, walking away.

The door was open and Grady was at his desk in his shirt and tie, staring into his computer screen. He looked up and waved Mattis in and turned back to the screen.

Mattis sat in one of the two matching chairs facing the desk.

"Just give me one sec," said Grady.

Mattis looked around the office. Diplomas. Law degree. Pictures of family. Pictures of a yellow dog. Three white golf balls lay together on the carpet in a triangle, and a putter of some elaborate design had been left leaning against the sofa.

Grady gave a single tap to his keyboard and shot his cuff for a look at his watch. "I'm sorry, but I've only got a few minutes, Blaine. One of my girls has a recital tonight."

"A recital?"

"Piano. She's in middle school. I can't be late."

"Yeah, I'm sorry. I got here as fast as I could."

"Are you still working at the rental car place?"

"Yeah."

"Good." The lawyer composed his hands on the desk. "So what can I help you with? Please tell me you didn't get pulled over again."

"No, sir. Nothing like that. Well, I got in a kind of a fight the other night."

"I thought maybe you had, by the look of you. What happened?"

"Some guy took a swing at me."

"Where?"

"At the Wheelhouse Tavern."

"And why did he take a swing at you?"

Mattis told him the story of the fight. His version of it. The lawyer sat listening, and when Mattis stopped and did not go on, Grady said, "But you weren't arrested."

"They put the cuffs on me."

"But no charges."

"No charges. Not against me. But next day, Sunday, the sheriff comes banging on my door and serves me with a restraining order. Denise, the waitress— she gets a restraining order on *me*. Not on the other guy, who hit her. On me."

"Ah," said Grady, and he leaned back in his chair and laced his fingers before him like a man who has just understood, or solved, some puzzle. He rocked slightly in the chair and its creaking was the only sound. "What was in the order?"

"What was in it? Besides bullshit?"

Grady straightened his fingers and clasped them again. "Were there allegations beyond what happened at the bar?"

"I don't remember."

"You don't remember?"

"I tore it up."

"I see." The chair creaked. "Did you go to the hearing?"

"No."

Grady nodded. He leaned forward and planted his forearms on the desk, on folders and yellow writing pads.

"So what is it you're looking for, Blaine?"

"Looking for?"

"Yes. Why are you here?"

"Because you're my lawyer."

"Yes. I represented you for your DUI."

"Yeah. So now I want you to represent me for this. For this restraining order thing."

"Represent you how?"

"What do you mean?"

"I mean what is it you want me to do?"

"I want you to get it—" Mattis's eyes made a kind of mad search of the wall behind the lawyer. "Revoked."

"Revoked."

"Revoked. Overruled. Whatever you call it."

"And why do you want to do that?"

"Because it's bullshit. I never touched her. And now it's on my record. What if my boss finds out?"

"And the girl?"

"What about her?"

"Are you still interested in her? Do you have feelings for her?"

"Feelings? What feelings? I don't want anything to do with that little—" Mattis shifted in the chair. He rubbed at his forehead with one hand and lowered the hand again. The lawyer watching him.

Grady looked at his watch again.

"I've really got to go, Blaine, I'm sorry. The bottom line is, I can't help you with this."

Mattis stared at him. "Why not?"

"For one thing, I'm a public defender. This is a civil matter. You need a private-sector lawyer."

"What's the difference?"

"The difference is I only handle cases appointed to me by the court. Like your previous case."

"I thought that was because I couldn't afford a lawyer."

"Yes. But again, this is a civil matter. The county is not bringing the case, there's no trial, and the restraining order has already been granted. Contesting it would mean filing a motion, and for that you would need to hire a private attorney."

"What if I want to sue for damages?"

"What damages?"

"Damages to my reputation. To my record."

Grady watched him. Then he fixed his eyes on something on his desk. Somewhere in the building someone locked a door with a rattling of keys, and a woman's heels rapped briskly down the empty hallway. Grady looked up again and said, "In that case you would also need to hire a private attorney. I can give you some names, if you like. They generally won't charge for an initial consultation."

Mattis sat staring at him.

"Do you want me to give you some names?" said Grady.

"No," said Mattis. "I don't want any names."

Grady watched him. Then he pushed back from the desk and stood and sank his hands into his trouser pockets. "I'm sorry, Blaine. I could've told you all this over the phone."

"Yeah. I guess so." Mattis leaned forward and pushed up from the chair, blowing air with the effort. He stood looking at Grady's desk. "I guess I thought a lawyer was a lawyer."

Grady shrugged. "Not in this case." He came around the desk. "I'll show you out."

"That's all right. I know the way."

"I have to go with you. Lisa will have locked the door when she left."

Grady followed him to the front office and turned the bolt and held open the glass door.

"Thanks," said Mattis. "Sorry to waste your time."

"You didn't."

Mattis had taken a few steps when Grady said his name. He turned back. The lawyer stood holding the glass door in one hand. "A restraining order is serious business," he said. "My advice is that you honor it."

The lawyer standing there in his white sleeves. His blue tie. His polished shoes.

"Your advice?" said Mattis.

"Yes."

Mattis nodded. He smiled crookedly. "All right. Well. Thanks for the advice, Counselor."

Two hours later he was sitting at a bar near the university with a pint of beer before him, staring at the game on the flat-screen. He was one of seven customers at that hour on a Wednesday night, before Raney came in and made it eight.

Raney took the stool to his right and ordered a pint from the young woman tending bar and they said nothing while she drew it. The athletes on the flat-screen moved up and down the court with no sounds other than the muted squeaks of their shoes. The ref's whistle. Some rock tune or other played from speakers connected to the jukebox.

When the young woman came back Raney thanked her and laid down a dollar tip and took his first sip and licked the foam from his upper lip.

"So did you talk to him?" he said.

"Yeah, I talked to him."

"And?"

"And nothing. He can't represent me."

"Why not?"

"Because he's not a regular lawyer."

Raney sat thinking about that. "This the same guy who represented you on the DUI?"

"Yeah."

"And he's not a regular lawyer?"

"He's a public defender. They're different from private lawyers."

"What's the difference?"

"Who pays them. The county paid him for the DUI but I would have to pay a private lawyer for this."

"Shit," said Raney. "That sucks, man."

"Yeah it does."

"So will you do it?"

"Do what?"

"Hire a private lawyer?"

"I can't afford a private lawyer. You know that."

"You never know. Maybe they'd do it—what do you call it, pro . . ."

"Pro bono? Yeah, I doubt it."

Raney sat thinking. "I think they all do some cases pro bono. I think it's required by law."

Mattis turned to look at him. "Did you go to law school since I last saw you?"

"No. I just remember hearing that somewhere."

Mattis looked away.

They drank. They watched the game.

Raney said, "You should've gone to that hearing, man. The judge might've thrown the whole thing out if he'd heard your side."

Mattis stared at the TV. Then he turned again to Raney.

"What?" said Raney.

"I wasted my time talking to that lawyer. I should've just come straight here."

"Hey, man. Just trying to be helpful."

"Telling me what I should've done is your idea of being helpful?"

"That's not what I meant."

"Sure it isn't. God damn. I wonder who else around here wants to give me some free advice." He looked about him, landed his eyes on the bartender. "Hey, miss. Miss," he said.

"Man, don't," said Raney.

The young woman came over. "Yes?"

"Where do you stand on the whole hearing-attendance question?"

"The what?"

"Pay no attention to him, miss. He's just messing with you."

Mattis turned to him again, and Raney looked away. The young woman stood waiting. White tank top, black bra straps. Tattoos up and down her lean arms. Mattis crossed his arms on the bar and smiled at her and she frowned and began wiping the bar with her rag.

"I like your tats," said Mattis.

She stopped wiping. "What did you say?"

"I said I like your tats."

She turned her look on Raney. "Are you guys ordering or what? I got things to do."

"We'll have two more," said Raney, "when you get a chance."

She went away and Mattis looked once again at Raney.

"What?" said Raney.

Mattis raised his glass and said into it, "When you get a chance."

"She doesn't need us bothering her. She's working."

Mattis tilted the glass empty and set it down again. "Was I bothering her?"

"You weren't helping her."

"I was complimenting her on her tattoos. Call the sheriff. Call the National fucking Guard."

Raney shook his head.

"What are you shaking your head about?"

"Nothing."

"Bullshit nothing."

"You just don't get it, man."

"What don't I get?"

Raney sat looking at him.

"What don't I get?"

"This," said Raney, indicating with his open hand Mattis, the bar, the bartender.

"What about this?"

"For one, you don't hit on the bartender. She's just trying to do her job."

"I wasn't hitting on her, you idiot. I was just messing with her."

"Yeah, that's better."

Mattis stared at him. "You know what? Fuck you, man. I don't need a lecture from a guy who lives in his mother's basement."

Raney smiled and turned away. After a minute he tilted back his glass and set it down empty. He lifted a five from his stack of bills and floated it to the bar and stood down from the stool.

"Where you going?" said Mattis.

"I gotta go. I got shit to do."

"No you don't. Sit down. I was just fucking with you, man."

"I'll catch you later."

"Seriously? All right, go, fuck it. Be a pussy."

"Yeah, I'm a pussy. See you around."

Mattis drank his beer and then he drank Raney's. After a while two young women came in and stood looking around the bar. One dark-haired, one blond. The dark-haired one walked back to the pool table and the blond stepped up to the bar and ordered two vodka cranberries. She smelled of the outdoors and perfume and breath mints. She stared straight ahead while she waited. She fussed with her hair in the backbar mirror. Finally she looked over at Mattis and he raised a hand in hello. She gave him a quick smile and turned back to the mirror.

"Students?" he said.

She looked at him again. "Sorry?"

"Students," he said. "You and your friend."

"Yep," she said. She faced forward and tapped her nails on the wood.

"What are you studying?"

She didn't look at him. Then she did. "What am I studying?"

"Yeah."

She stared at him with her pretty eyes. "Indifference."

The drinks came, cherry red with a lime wedge afloat in the ice, and the bartender, taking the young woman's money, gave Mattis a look. When she turned away he said to the student: "Indifference. That's funny. That's a good one," and he rotated on his stool to watch her walk away. He watched her all the way back to the pool table, to her friend with the dark hair, then came round again to his beer. He sat staring at his image in the mirror. His bruised face. He smiled broadly and raised his glass in toast and drank.

19.

THE NEXT MORNING, Thursday morning, some nine or ten hours after speaking with Sheriff Halsey in Minnesota, Viegas was in her Prius heading west toward the Highway 14 Bridge, the sunrise burning orange in her mirrors. She ascended above the streets, then above the Wisconsin-side bank where the Billy Ross bike had been found forty—no, forty-one years ago. Purple Schwinn Sting-Ray. Three summers, three missing boys and it was their first piece of evidence, her father had told her. They'd tried to keep it under wraps, but the parents themselves had told the press, to keep the police searching the river.

But the police didn't think the boy—any of the boys—was in the river. They thought the bike had either been found by someone, kids maybe, and thrown there from the bridge. Or else had been thrown there to make them think the missing boy, or boys, must be in the river too.

A diversion.

As were such thoughts. Belonging to an era before she was born.

It wasn't even the same bridge; in 1977, you'd have been throwing the bike from a two-lane trestle bridge built in the 1930s, not this wide, humming expressway—two lanes for each direction, two full miles shore to shore, including a brief landing on Barron Island between the channels. A long cold walk for Dan Young in the dead of winter, two a.m.

Near the end of the bridge on the Minnesota side the concrete divider gave way to a length of galvanized guardrail, and beyond that lay a median of mounded dirty snow, and where the snow ended she banked a U-turn and drove back toward the river and pulled over on the shoulder and put the car in park, fifty, sixty yards from the bridge.

She sat looking down the long straightaway before her, the morning commuters rushing back toward Wisconsin, the rising sun in their eyes, as it was in hers.

Halsey had not said exactly where he'd found the abandoned truck with the bullet hole in it but she knew it would have been in sight of where she sat, either behind or ahead. Unless she'd parked on the very spot of its abandonment. On the bridge itself there was shoulder enough to walk on, but there was also a walkway that ran the length of the bridge, as if the builders had foreseen considerable foot traffic in this remote place—adventurers come to walk across the great river and back before hopping into their cars again and returning home.

She checked her watch. 7:35. A good half hour, forty-five minutes before she ought to get to the station.

"Just a quick look around," she said. And got out of the car.

She walked west along the shoulder, away from the bridge, her eyes on the ground. The sheriff had gone over the same area at least once, and it didn't matter, as it would not have mattered to him if she'd gone first. If ten of her had gone first.

She walked until she thought she'd walked too far and then she turned and walked back, passing her car, and left the shoulder for the walkway—a blacktop footbridge contained on the river side by a backstop of cyclone fencing perhaps six feet in height. She walked out to the middle of the channel where a stronger wind harried the water, and there she stopped. Strands of loosened hair lashing about her, the traffic rushing by and no sign of anyone having been here.

Two weeks. Weather and wind. What signs could there be?

She hooked her fingers in the diamond shapes of the fence and looked out over the water to the south. Power cables spanned the channel in one great swoop from utility pole to utility pole, like guitar strings between distant frets, and if the strings did indeed play a song in that wind the tune was carried away downriver before she heard it.

Holly Burke, unlike the missing boys, had been found in the river. Not this one—the Upper Black Root. Which fed into the Mississippi some five miles south of where Viegas now stood. Another thousand miles south of that and the Mississippi fed into the Gulf of Mexico and was a river no longer.

She reached up and took hold of the top crossbar of the fence and there was nothing there to discourage her from doing so, no barbs, no nastily snipped fencing, just the smooth-nosed top row of diamonds. Two or three moves and she could be over the fence and on her way down the other side. A quick drop to the water fifteen, twenty feet below, though the distance would be hard to judge at night—the black and glinting surface in the darkness, the ungodly cold of it. But no ice to crash through, at least. Not this far out.

She walked back and stepped around the fence and stood looking down the snowy bank. Fresh tracks of animals, muskrat or beaver, a pair of slow-moving deer, and, less recently, a solitary man, judging by the wells in the snow: old bootshapes enlarged and blurred by days of sunshine. The sheriff, or one of his men.

She took one testing sidestep and her boot did not hold. She'd end up sliding down the bank on her ass.

She checked her watch. 8:05.

From where she stood she could see the shadowed space under the bridge span, the riprap of quarry rock along the shore, the shelf of ice. And what she couldn't see she could imagine: The cold, river-smelling cavern where the tires of cars passing overhead moaned. The slope of the concrete abutment with its ledges and cavities in its heights. Places to spend a hard, lonesome night.

The sheriff had been down there. He and his deputies. It was his side of the river.

She stood looking across the water toward hers, and she thought again of the purple Sting-Ray. On certain summer mornings, it was said, drivers crossing east into Wisconsin could see a figure downriver from the bridge—a solitary man walking in the fog that seethed along the river's edge, and the fog so thick that it could not be said the man wasn't knee-deep in the water. Ten, twenty years on, a father still searching for his boy. An old wives' tale, surely. Or ghost story. As any such story must be.

Viegas returned to her car and clicked her turn signal. Crawling along the shoulder, the traffic whizzing by. Finally she hit her strobes, the lane cleared, and she pulled nimbly out and got the Prius up to speed on the bridge, heading east.

THERE WAS NO record of a Dan or Danny or Daniel Young in the registry, and neither did the charge nurse recognize the picture Viegas showed her, but she was happy to pull up the records from Monday, February 26, and after that the 27th, and she was moving on to the 28th when she said hold on, and clacked at her keyboard, watching the screen.

In fact a man of Young's age and race had signed in for emergency care on Tuesday, February 27, at 1:10 a.m. A prolonged riffling of folders yielded his paper form and Viegas stood reading it. For his date of birth the man had written the current date, then crossed that out and corrected it. There was no photocopy of his driver's license, and a note in someone else's hand said "No ID." He'd sought care for a laceration to his forehead. His name was J. G. Tierney.

The doctor who had provided this care, Dr. Waller, was not currently in the hospital, but by chance the nurse who'd assisted him was, and while Viegas waited to talk to her she typed *JG Tierney* into her phone and clicked a link and read about the man who'd been among the first to perish in the construction of the Hoover Dam some hundred years ago, and about his son, who was the last. Father and son dying fourteen years apart to the day, which was December 20.

She checked her photocopy of Tierney's admitting form, his date of birth, and smiled.

The nurse came up to her in blue scrubs and yellow Nikes. Her name was Megan and she had the look of a young ghost: dark eye wells in a moonlit face. She looked emptily at the detective's badge and at the image of Daniel Young on the phone. Then she focused her eyes and said yes, she remembered him.

"You helped the doctor treat him?"

"I assisted, yes."

"So you got a good look at his injury."

"Front-row seat."

"And did it look to you like a . . ." Viegas checked the admitting form again "Like he'd slipped and fallen against the corner of a building?"

"It looked to me like a gash he could've gotten that way or about a hundred other ways. I mean, I work in the ER. People are . . ." She shook her head. "You know."

"Yes, I do," said Viegas.

The nurse sniffled and passed a knuckle under her nose. "Dr. Waller said he thought it looked like a graze wound," she said.

"Graze wound," said Viegas. "As in a bullet?"

"Yeah."

Viegas waited. "And what did *he* say to that—Tierney?"

"He said it wasn't. He said he slipped and hit his head on the corner of a building."

"And that was the end of it?"

"What do you mean?"

"I mean the doctor didn't pursue his . . . observation?"

Megan shrugged. "There's not much you can do. You can't exactly make a report on what a wound looks like. Especially when the patient is saying something different."

Viegas stood watching the young nurse. "But it didn't look like a graze wound to you," she said.

"No. It looked like a gash to me. Then again, I haven't seen too many graze wounds."

"Really? I would think in the ER . . ."

"Yeah, no. Usually the bullet goes right on in. And sometimes right on out again. And usually it's an accident." She shrugged again.

"Was he drunk?" said Viegas. "Tierney."

"Not that I could tell."

"Disoriented? Confused?"

"He knew the date and the president. They talked about his memory."

"His memory?"

"Dr. Waller told him how with a head injury you could remember historical facts and not your own name."

"Did he not remember his own name?"

"Not that I know of. I mean—it was there on the chart."

"But Dr. Waller was concerned about his memory?"

The nurse put her fingertips to her own forehead and moved the skin around. "I think he was just, you know, following the script with a head injury? To be honest I might've zoned out a little bit."

"I understand." Viegas was patient. She was sympathetic. "Just a couple more questions, Megan. Did he say where he was going, after the hospital?"

"I don't think so."

"Was someone waiting for him? Or picking him up?"

"I have no idea. It wasn't required for his release."

"Did he have a cell phone?"

"I don't remember seeing one. But who notices phones anymore?"

"Is there anything else he said that you remember? Anything at all?"

The nurse stood thinking. She drew her hand over her hair to the base of her ponytail and adjusted the hair tie. Finally, no, she could think of nothing else. She said Dr. Waller would probably remember better than she did.

"All right. Thank you very much, Megan." Viegas raised her phone by way of taking her leave, turned, and turned back—her hand, the phone, still raised.

"One more quick question."

"Sure."

She waggled the phone. "Has anyone else, any other authorities, talked to you about him—about Tierney?"

The nurse watched the phone, as though it were the prop of a hypnotist, before blinking once and saying, "Nope, not to me."

"All right." Viegas turned once more to go.

"Can I ask why you're looking for him—this guy?"

Viegas turned back. "You can. He's not in any trouble. He just went missing and his family would like to know that he's all right."

"Well," said Megan. "He left here better than when he came in, I can tell you that much. That wound was a mess. We cleaned the heck out of it and Dr. Waller shot him up with antibiotics and sewed him up beautifully."

Viegas stood nodding, staring at the young nurse distantly.

"How long do laceration stitches need to stay in, typically?"

"It depends where it is on the body. I think the doctor said ten days? It would say on his chart."

"You didn't see him again, though?"

"No, I didn't. Someone else might've."

"All right. You've been very helpful."

"I doubt it, but thanks."

Viegas went back to the desk and asked if Tierney had returned to get his stitches out and the woman clacked again at her keyboard and at last said no, not at that hospital he hadn't.

It was nine fifteen when she called Samuels.

"Nothing much happening here," he said. "Where are you?"

"I got a slow start this morning."

"Big night?"

"Oh yeah. Insane."

In the silence she could hear the wheels turning as he considered what he might say, and she knew he would say nothing. Boundaries.

"Well, it's a graveyard here," he said finally. "Take your time."

"Thanks, Victor. Call if you need me."

"Roger that."

She crossed town again, then took Rose up to where the franchise motels clustered along the river on the business strip, all in sight of the I-90 bridge: A ten-minute drive from the hospital. On foot—a good hour.

Unless he got himself a cab, or some other ride. A city bus.

The motels were a long shot at best but, grouped as they were, she would waste the least amount of her time satisfying herself that Young was not biding his time in a room there. That he would not be so easily found.

The first motel she tried, the woman's eyes widened like a cat's at the sight of the shiny badge, then narrowed to study the image on the phone, but in the end she shook her head—she didn't recognize him. But she was only at the desk three mornings a week, so. Then, with no word from Viegas, at her own discretion, or lack of it, the woman turned the screen so Viegas could see for herself that no one had checked in under the name J. G. Tierney, or Daniel—Dan, Danny—Young, or John Smith since the morning of February 26.

At the next motel a young man with a bright tattooed gecko climbing up from the collar of his T-shirt asked to see her ID and then took his time looking from the ID to her badge to her face and to the ID again, before at last consulting his screen for the names she provided and reporting his findings.

He stood looking at her. She at him.

"Do you mind if I take a quick peek myself?" she said at last, and he said did she not trust him, and she said it was not a matter of trust but that she might not know what she was looking for until she saw it, and to that the young man said nothing but only stood there, a slow caginess coming over him, as of one on whom it is dawning that one does not just give such favors away. A student of the TV shows, the movies.

His cleverness met the look in Viegas's eye and died. He turned the screen and stood back. Scratching at the gecko—in fact it was a tiny Spider-Man—as she scanned the entries and confirmed what he'd said.

She had nearly reached the end of the business drag when she stepped into the small lobby of the Motel 6. The young man behind the desk closed his book and stood to meet her.

"Yes, ma'am," he said, looking at the picture. "I checked him in a while back . . . Like a week ago?"

"You're sure?"

"I mean, ninety-six percent sure."

"Was there anything unusual about him? About his appearance?"

"Are you talking about the bandage?"

"Bandage—?"

"This guy had a bandage on his forehead."

"Yes," said Viegas. "What name did he use, do you remember?"

"That I don't."

Viegas was downcast. "Shoot," she said.

"Do you want me to pull up his registration?"

"That would be very helpful. Thank you."

He rolled a grubby USB mouse on the desktop behind the counter, clicked. Rolled it and clicked again. "OK, got it."

A printer wheezed awake out of view and began to grind and the young man retrieved the sheet of paper and handed it to her.

She sighed and shook her head. He'd used the same name he'd used at the hospital ER.

Of course, with his injury, with whatever had happened to him that night—mishap with a building, near miss with a bullet—he might not have been thinking too clearly.

Which might explain the decision to call a cop to find out if the cops were looking for him. But did not explain his calling her. Or how he'd gotten her number.

"He's been here more than a week," she said.

"Yes, ma'am. I guess so."

"He keeps rebooking the room."

"Yeah. I'm not always here."

"And you didn't rebook it for him for today?"

"Not me, no, ma'am. He might've done it last night."

"No ID?" she said. "No driver's license?"

"We don't require it, strictly speaking."

"There's a space for it here."

"I know," said the clerk, with an air of resignation.

"And how about this car," Viegas said, "this green Subaru Outback. Did you happen to see it?"

"No, ma'am. Sometimes they just take a parking spot and walk in. I mean, they don't always park right in front there like you did."

Viegas looked at the plate number he'd written down and knew it would not match the Subaru, or any car, except by random chance.

She stood staring at the sheet. The young clerk standing there.

"Do you want me to ring his room?"

Viegas looked up. "Do you mind?"

"What should I say if he answers?"

"Nothing. Just hang up. Please."

He picked up the handset and pushed three buttons. He listened awhile and then turned the handset so the detective could hear the little chirrup sounds for herself.

"Thank you," she said. "You can hang up."

He did, and stood by, hands at his sides.

"What are you reading?" said Viegas.

He glanced at the book on the desktop. "*One Hundred Years of Solitude*, by Gabriel García Márquez," he said.

"Is it good?"

"Yes. Very. You should read it."

"I did. In college."

"Oh." He turned his head to give her a kind of sidelong look. She smiled, and a few minutes later she was standing on the second-floor walkway looking out over the parking lot while the housekeeping woman knocked on the door and called out. There was no Subaru of any color in the lot.

The woman used her passkey and opened the door, then hesitated, her hand on the latch.

"It's all right," Viegas said. "I'm just going to take a quick peek."

The woman's eyes darted to the badge at Viegas's hip and she stood aside. Viegas thanked her and stepped in, then stepped out again.

"May I ask, do you clean this room every day?"

"No every day, ma'am. They say at the front."

"Today—hoy día?"

"Sí, señora, pero todavía no. Not yet."

"OK, solo necesito un minuto, por favor."

"Sí, señora."

Viegas stepped in and let the door shut behind her. The heavy drapes were pulled aside and there was plenty of light. No particular odor to the air: a clean, lightly used motel-room smell. The bedcovers made up carelessly over the pillows. A water bottle on the nightstand, half-full, the plastic cap lying there. On the dressertop next to the TV some pennies and nickels, a thin Motel 6 notepad, a Motel 6 retractable pen. Several one-dollar bills had been left on a sheet of the notepad paper with the words *Housekeeping / Thank You / Gracias*. She picked up the pad and held the clean top sheet slantwise to the light—the impression there of the note for housekeeping, but also, more faintly, a phone number. She tore off the sheet and folded it and put it in her pocket.

She saw no travel bag, no clothes. She opened the drawers and they were all empty.

In the bathroom the shower rod was hung with a damp white T-shirt, two pairs of white socks, a pair of boxer shorts. On the sink: The little bar of soap, bonded to the counter by its own lather. A tube of toothpaste. A toothbrush standing in a plastic cup. Also some small and new-looking scissors with sharp little curved blades—cuticle scissors—and tweezers.

She took up the tweezers and looked at the sharp, angled tips and set them back down. Then took them up again and with them poked about in the trash. A few crumpled tissues. No gauze or tape or bandages. No sutures. She returned the tweezers to their place and flicked off the light.

She opened the closet door and, after a second, closed it again.

There was a small writing table in the corner, small trashcan below. She scooted out the trashcan with her foot. Two cardboard coffee cups with the plastic lids still on. She took these up and set them on the tabletop and retrieved from the bottom of the can several crumpled, coffee-stained receipts, then stood at the desk uncrumpling and smoothing them on the desktop. One was from a restaurant nearby, around dinnertime—Jessica, his server. He'd paid in cash. Another was from the Walgreens on Rose, where he'd bought the scissors and tweezers, a bag of pretzels and three bottles of water, also cash. The third receipt was from the Wheelhouse Tavern—cash again for two sandwiches, two Cokes, served the day before, Wednesday, at 1:20 p.m. by Denise.

Viegas stared at the receipt. All the way over there. About as far from the motel as you could get and still be in the same town. Two sandwiches. Two Cokes. Denise Givens.

Someone had driven Dan Young there. Someone he knew well enough to have lunch with. Maybe it was this person who'd called her, and not Dan Young.

She folded the receipts like money and put them in her jacket pocket and dropped the two coffee cups back into the trashcan and scooted the can back into place with her foot, then stood taking a last look around. Finally she pulled some bills from her pocket and laid three more singles on top of those already on the dressertop. She was out the door, and the door had all but shut behind her when she turned and halted it.

She stepped once more to the writing desk and scooted out the trashcan again and dropped onto her heels and looked under the desk. Back a ways, upright on its edge against the baseboard, stood a white business card. A trashcan overshot, overlooked by housekeeping, barely registering in her own consciousness. She reached back and picked up the card and sat staring at it. An *X* had been drawn corner to corner through her name and her numbers.

She turned the card over and read the name and the phone number written there in blue ink.

Sean Courtland.

"What in the actual hell," she said.

She stared at the name. Then she stood and fished the sheet of notepad paper from her pocket and unfolded it, held it to the light. Same number, not the same handwriting.

Dan Young the missing. Sean Courtland the bar fighter. Defender of women.

She looked about the room once more. At the poorly made bed.

She drew back the covers and looked at the sheets, the pillows. Flipped the pillows over. Everything white and clean.

Outside, she stood at the railing looking out over the lot, clicking her nails on the top bar, a mindless tapping that raised in her mind the words *Tempo, Corrine, tempo,* and she realized she was playing a tune from her girlhood, from those Saturday afternoon lessons at Ms. Wheeler's, and the moment she realized it her fingers stopped, the chord progression lost, and what remained was the smell of the house, of the woman herself on the hard bench beside her—old to a ten-year-old but likely still in her forties at the time—the smell of her perfume or whatever it was, her hand lotion, her faint scent of sweat in the summertime, her peppermint-candy breath as she told you *Tempo, Corrine, tempo . . .*

20.

"You're sure this is going to work?" said Sean, and Dan said, "Yes, I'm sure."

They were standing in the new laundry room, staring at the old cast-iron waste stack where it ran floor to ceiling in the open wall. Sean had Sheetrocked all but this last section of original wall and they'd reached the point where they must now connect the new drain to the old stack, and to do this they must remove a section of the four-inch waste pipe and splice in a new tee joint. The old iron pipe and elbow joints for the drains in the bathroom on the other side of the wall had not been touched by human hands since they'd been assembled by men long gone from the world. Heavy. Thick. Unmovable. Iron fused to iron in the stillness of the years, in the sealed darkness of the wall.

The pipe cutter Sean had rented that morning lay at their feet, an unlikely looking tool that somehow used a length of motorcycle chain with small cutting wheels in the links not to cleanly cut but to snap the cast iron. To break it. He'd wanted to use the Sawzall with a cast-iron-cutting blade but it could not be done, Dan said, without slicing into the other side of the wall and probably cracking the hell out of the old plaster.

"What if the pipe just shatters?" Sean now said. The days, the money lost to repairing—even replacing—the destroyed old stack, all those joints.

"I've never seen one shatter."

Sean was silent. Looking at the stack.

"We can use the Sawzall if you want," said Dan. "It's your call." He toed the length of heavy chain where it lay at their feet like a black snake. "But this is what's called for."

Sean nodded. He picked up the cutter. "OK," he said. "Enough of your stalling. How does this thing work?"

Dan fed the chain around the pipe, hooked it into the cutter and cinched it tight.

"All right," he said. "Say your prayers." He fit the ratchet to the cutter and levered the handle. The chain tightened; the wheel blades bit into the iron, and bit again, deeper. He cranked and there was a popping sound and the stack shifted and debris drizzled down. Dan loosened the chain and drew it away and they stood looking at the break in the pipe—level and clean.

"That's it?" said Sean.

"That's it. One more cut and we're off to the races."

Sean looked up to where the stack disappeared in the top plate, beyond which it rose up through the rest of the house and through the roof to vent sewer gas into the open air. "What's gonna keep this whole stack from dropping when we take a section out of it?" he said.

"The connections upstairs," said Dan. "You can see there's no pressure on this break." He took hold of the pipe above the cut and moved it so the two ends ground against each other like teeth, and no sooner had he done it than a ferric, stale fecal stink tainted the air. The shepherd, who lay watching from the doorway, raised her nose.

Sean looked to be sure the old man wasn't there too and said in a lower voice, "What about . . . matter?"

"What about it?"

"Is it gonna come raining down on us?"

"Did you tell him not to use the upstairs toilet for a while?"

"Yeah."

"Well, I haven't heard him up there, so we should be good."

"Should be."

Dan nodded and was silent. The TV was on somewhere in the house, a continuous yammering hum in the walls.

Dan held out the pipe cutter. "Want to try it?"

Sean looked at the tool. He looked at the thin seam of break in the old iron pipe. "You know what?" he said. "I think I'm gonna watch the master at work one more time."

"All right," said Dan. "Try to pay attention this time."

"Yessir, I'll try."

Two hours later Dan connected the fill hose and opened up the valve and they listened as water sloshed in the new P-trap, as it gurgled down the length of PVC pipe that ran now laterally through the studs, as it splashed into the tee at the stack and fell mutely down the darkness of the iron pipe on its way to the sewer line under the house. The water ran quickly and pleasingly and without leaks.

They moved all their materials and tools to the corner and swept up the sawdust and Sean made one last inspection. "All right," he said. "I'll go get him."

"Want me to make myself scarce?"

"Why?"

"Give him some room."

"No, I'd rather outnumber him."

"OK," said Dan. "But I still don't like our chances."

"Me neither." Sean stepped over the shepherd and went down the hallway and poked his head into the kitchen. "Mr. Devereaux?" Cramped small space smelling of old grease and burned coffee. A yellow refrigerator from the 1970s or '80s. Darkened oak table squared to the wall with three unmatched chairs where perhaps generations of Devereauxs had sat for meals, for coffee, talking about God knew what.

He moved on to the living room, a flattened carpeting underfoot: vague suggestion of a brocade pattern, a color once green or blue. The TV, boxy and deep with its glass-tube insides, played with poor sound and poor color to a dowdy room a grandmother had been last to decorate, her taste running to floral upholstery and scuffed Queen Anne's legs, handmade doilies and ceramic figurines of winged little children. A gloomy portrait of the Savior hanging in weird adjacency to the TV, eyes rolled ceilingward at all that poured forth from the strange and constant box. The one shaft of daylight that fell through a gap in the drapes was shaped by a vastness of motes suspended in almost perfect stillness, and there, in like stillness, a keeper of stillness, lay the old man in his recliner. Boots in the air, hands folded on his stomach, his jaw fallen.

Sean watched the closed eyelids. Watched to see if the hands would rise with the stomach.

"Mr. Devereaux—?"

Didn't want to shake him awake. Didn't want to touch him. He looked at the knobby cane where it lay across the soiled arms of the chair like a safety bar. Poke the man with his own cane?

"Mr. Devereaux," he said again, and the eyes opened and began to roll and the mouth clapped shut. Devereaux fixed his roving eyes on Sean's face and grabbed up his cane and waved it like some maddened wizard who would banish the carpenter from sight. As if he were no carpenter at all but something more dire, more loathsome, heaved up from his dreams.

"What do you want?" said the old man.

"Sorry to wake you—"

"You didn't wake me."

"You said you wanted to see it before we closed up the wall."

"Why didn't you just yell for me?"

"I did."

"If you'd of yelled I'd of heard you." He jerked at the chair's lever and his boots dropped to the floor. He clutched at the arms of the chair and pushed himself up onto his feet, took one step forward with the cane and stopped and looked at Sean again.

"Go on, then," he said. "I'm coming."

The shepherd was gone when Sean returned and Dan, waiting the while, moved aside as he stepped in and then both men stood aside to give the old man his berth.

Devereaux entered and took up his bent stance in the center of the room. He stood staring at the plumbing awhile and then cast his gaze about the room from wall to wall and from ceiling to floor.

"What's that thing there?"

"That's the soil pipe cutter," said Sean. "It's what we used to cut into the old stack."

"You own that?"

"No sir, we rented it this morning."

"Rented it?"

"Yes sir. It's about a four-hundred-dollar tool."

The old man grunted. He studied the plumbing again. "Where's the vent for that drain?"

"It doesn't require a vent," said Sean.

"What do you mean it doesn't require a vent?"

"It's within five feet of the stack," Dan put in. "So you don't have to vent it."

Devereaux stepped forward and took hold of the new tee joint in the stack and jerked on it. It barely moved. He tried to shake the drain but Dan had wedged it tight with wood shims at the holes in the studs through which it passed.

"What's to keep those shims from wiggling loose?"

"They're glued in, sir," said Dan.

Devereaux rapped a knuckle on one of the small metal plates tacked onto the edges of the studs wherever the pipes or PEX lines ran through them, then turned his attention to the fill hose, still connected to the cold-water valve.

"We ran water through it, but we can run some more if you want," Sean said.

"How long'd you run it for?"

Sean looked at Dan. "A good minute?"

"Two minutes," said Dan. "And at full volume."

"Full volume," said the old man.

"With the valve wide open."

"I know what full volume means." Devereaux snuffled at the air, then leaned toward the drain in the laundry box and snuffled at that and stood back again.

"Well," he said, waving the cane, "you best get your wallboard up, then."

"It looks good?" said Sean.

"Yeah, it looks good. When are you going to be finished?"

"Once we get the wallboard up there's the taping and mudding, the sanding, the priming and painting." He looked again at Dan.

"And getting the machines up here."

"And getting the machines up here," said Sean. "This is what, Thursday? We might get her all wrapped up by Saturday. Monday, I think, at the latest."

"What about the trimwork?" said the old man. "What about the door?"

"The trimwork and the door," Sean said. "Yes sir, those too."

"Saturday," said Devereaux. "That's pretty much what you said at the beginning, before you brought in your hired man."

"Yes sir. I never could've kept to that schedule without him."

"No, I don't reckon you could of." The old man turned about on the axis of
one leg and said, "All right, Bonnie girl, let's let 'em get back to work," and he
stepped from the little room, out of view. They listened to his progress down
the hall, across the kitchen floor and on toward the distant TV. They watched
to see if the shepherd would reappear and follow but she did not.

"I know what you're thinking," Dan said.

"What am I thinking?"

"You're thinking you never saw the old guy so happy."

"Yeah," said Sean. "That's exactly what I'm thinking."

Some hours later Dan was in the basement washing mud knives and pans
in the old farm sink when he heard Sean call to him from above and he shut off
the faucets. He opened his mouth—and closed it again. Listening. Sean was
scraping mud droppings from the covered floor with one joint knife and shav-
ing them off into the trash bucket with another. A sound like a chef sharpening
his blades. He kept at it without pause and did not call out.

Dan turned, mud knife still in hand, and saw the boy.

Blond little boy, standing beside the toilet. Blue T-shirt and jeans. White
sneakers. Large blue eyes. Thin pale arms at his sides.

The blood dropped out of Dan's heart.

The boy stood staring at him. Dan watched him. He looked at the stairs and
back again. The boy still there.

"Where did you come from?" he said. Believed he said.

One of the boy's arms reached across his stomach to scratch at the other
forearm and then returned to his side.

"How did you get down here?" said Dan. His voice so strange in that space.
The space so strange with the boy. "What's your name?"

"What—?"

It was Sean, upstairs. Dan laid the mud knife in the sink, his eyes on the
boy. Unthinkingly he felt out the raised welt of scar on his forehead, then lowered his hand again.

The boy watching him.

"Are you OK?" Dan said more quietly. He made the smallest move forward and the boy backstepped and Dan stopped. "I won't hurt you."

"Are you talking to me?" Sean's voice again—close and loud. He was at the head of the stairs, from which vantage, Dan knew, he could see only the steps and a section of concrete floor.

"It's all right," Dan said to the boy, more quietly still. "That's just my friend."

The steps creaked with Sean's weight and were silent again and, without turning, Dan knew he was stooping to see beneath the header joist.

"What's up, pardner?" said Sean.

Dan did not look away from the boy. Then he did, turning to look at Sean's face, nearly upside-down in the wedge of space between the steps and the joists.

"Everything all right down here?"

Dan nodded. He picked up the mud knife and scraped at the drying mud with his thumbnail. He didn't look back to where the boy had been.

"Just talking to myself," he said. "I do that sometimes."

"Yeah, I do too." Sean stood watching him. Behind him, at the top of the stairs, the dog began to whine.

"Ready to roll?" Sean said finally, and Dan said, "Yeah, I'm ready."

THEY WERE CLIMBING into the truck when Sean's phone buzzed. He shut his door and got the phone from his jacket pocket and looked at the screen, then set the phone facedown on the bench seat between them. He turned the key and put his foot on the brake and took hold of the shift lever—and held it. The truck idling.

"Bad news?" said Dan.

"What? No." He lifted the phone and set it down again. "It's her. Denise."

Dan waited. "Is she at the bar?"

"No. She's home, I think."

Dan nodded. "You don't have to drive me to the motel," he said. "You can let me out wherever."

"Yeah," said Sean absently.

"What'd she say? Not that it's any of my business."

"It's more of a visual."

"Oh," said Dan.

"I mean, nothing like that," Sean said. "But still."

Dan was silent. He glanced at the phone where it lay under Sean's right hand.

"I'm no expert," he said." But I think you're supposed to reply. The sooner the better."

"Yeah. Gimme one second."

"Take your time."

Sean thumbed in a reply and set the phone down on his thigh. In a few seconds it buzzed again. He looked at the screen. Thumbed in another reply and returned the phone to his thigh. It buzzed and he made a last quick reply and set the phone down on the bench seat and dropped the truck into gear.

"I'm going over there," he said. "In a little while."

"Seriously, you can just drop me anywhere."

"Actually, efficiencywise, I wonder if you'd mind going to my place for a minute while I clean up? Then I can drop you off on the way."

They took the blacktop road south through the woods, turned into the private drive among the trees and pulled up to the small stone cottage. Sean killed the engine and opened his door. Looked back at Dan.

"You want to come in, or—?"

Dan sat looking at the little house. When you opened the front door you'd see the bed. A reading chair, perhaps, a small table. The kitchenette in one corner. A bathroom with the door ajar.

"Think I'll just wait here," he said, and Sean said, "Ten minutes, tops."

Dan sat. Then he got out of the truck and shut the door and stood taking deep breaths: cold March dusk, pines and old snow in the pines' shadows, woodsmoke from a fireplace. He looked at the larger, modern stone house where Sean's landlords lived, the ground-floor windows just faintly alight at that hour, then took a seat on Sean's steps.

Perhaps a minute later a silver SUV pulled into the clearing and rolled into its place near the larger house. The driver cut the motor and busied himself with something in the passenger seat until, glancing toward the stone cottage,

he saw Dan and stopped what he was doing. Staring at Dan where he sat on the steps. Dan lifted one hand from his knees in a kind of greeting but the man made no sign that he'd seen it. He seemed content to sit in his car staring.

Finally he got out and shut the door and began to walk toward Dan.

Dan got to his feet.

The man was older than he'd looked behind the wheel and as he made his way across the clearing in the last brindled light of day, Dan recognized him as the old man who'd patted down his wife's hair in the restaurant, who'd hung her coat with such care.

The old man stopped short of Dan and said howdy and there was no sign of recognition in his eyes, only the wary question as to what the younger man was doing sitting on those steps.

"Howdy," Dan answered, and the old man gestured with his chin at the green Chevy.

"Are you with Sean?"

"Yes, sir. I'm just waiting for him. He's getting cleaned up."

"Ah," said the old man. He studied Dan's face, his hair. "You his brother?"

"No, sir. I didn't know he had a brother."

"I didn't either. But I thought you might be one."

"No, I just work with him. I work for him."

"I see. Over at the Devereaux house?"

"Yep."

"I didn't know he was hiring."

"Mr. Devereaux?"

"Sean."

"I don't think he was, but we ran into each other and it just kind of worked out."

"Are you a carpenter?"

"More of a plumber. On this job, anyway."

"I see. Well, I own this place. That's why I came over."

"Yes, sir. It's a beautiful property."

"This here was the original house. I raised my family here." The old man was looking at the cottage now. The light from the window reflecting in his eyes.

"Then my wife and me, we built this other house. That was 1970. Forty-eight years ago."

"You've lived here a long time."

"I won't ever live anywhere else and neither will she."

Dan said nothing. He turned and looked at the cottage door. As if Sean might be standing there, ready to go.

"What's your name?"

Dan turned back to the old man. "Dan Young."

"Niles Parnell." He put out his hand and Dan shook it.

"How do you like working on that house?" Parnell said.

"The Devereaux house?"

"Yes."

"I like it fine. We're just about done."

Parnell nodded, looking into Dan's eyes. As though to read something there that Dan wasn't saying.

"You from around here?"

"No, sir. I'm from across the river originally. Minnesota."

"You got family there?"

"Some. Yes."

Parnell nodded again. "Well," he said. "I guess it was good luck you and Sean ran into each other."

"Yes, sir, I think it was."

"OK, Dan," said Parnell. "You take care."

"You too, Mr. Parnell."

The old man turned and walked back to the car, to the passenger side, where he collected two plastic grocery bags, one for each hand, gave a final nod to Dan and went up the steps and on into the house.

Sean came out and stood in the open doorway buttoning his shirt.

"Did you meet the landlord?" The warmth of the room spilling around him. Smell of soap, of Colgate shave cream. His hair thrown wetly back. His jaw gleaming.

"Yes, I did," said Dan. "He came over to see who I was."

"Kind of a strange old guy. I mean, not as strange as Devereaux."

Dan stood staring at the house. "I bought him pie. Him and his wife."

"Say again?"

"I bought them each a slice of pie. A few days ago, at that restaurant by the motel."

"Why'd you do that?"

"I don't know."

"Did you talk to them?"

"No. I had the waitress take it to them after I left."

"Did he recognize you?"

"No. I don't think he ever saw me—at the restaurant."

They both stood looking at the house. "They lost a son, years ago," Sean said. "Fifteen years old. Hung himself."

Dan shook his head. "He said he raised a family."

"Yeah. That was the family."

WHEN HE STEPPED into his motel room some fifteen minutes later, Dan saw that the bed had been made, the carpet vacuumed, the dollar bills collected from the dressertop. His plastic water bottle stood on the night table where he'd left it, and the plastic cap too.

The loose change he'd left separate from the bills lay there still, and to these he added more coins from his pocket, the cardkey, the crumpled receipt from lunch, then stood looking at the notepad.

On the topmost sheet someone had written a single word in a small, neat hand: *Señor.*

The note he'd left with the singles was gone, as it had been each time. Today, though, this single word. Like a gracious nod of thanks—*Señor.*

He pressed his fingertip to the ink and pressed it again to a clean place on the paper and it left no print.

In the bathroom there were fresh white towels, a fresh bar of soap in its little box. His T-shirt and socks and boxers where he'd left them on the shower rod. The scissors and tweezers as he'd left them, though the sink had been wiped down. He stared at the scissors and tweezers. Then he walked back to the dresser and turned back the top sheet of the notepad and saw the rest of

the message on the next page—three lines centered on the page in that same compact hand:

There is a lady in you room this morning. A lady policía.
They say at the desk I have let her in.
I say you so you know. OK, gracias.

He read the lines over several times, his heart pounding.

He looked around the room again, to see what she'd seen, the lady policía.

He stepped over to the little writing table and pulled out the trashcan but of course it was empty. He took a breath and let it out slow.

After a minute he returned to the dresser and peeled off the two sheets of notepaper and folded them and put them in his pocket with the coins and placed a five-dollar bill on the notepad. Then he gathered all his clothes into a tight roll tucked under his arm and took a last look around. He thought about calling the desk to get a refund for the night but in the end he left the keycard behind and stepped out and shut the door behind him.

He stood at the railing, looking over the parking lot. No policía cars that he could see. No lady policía—no one of any kind sitting in the cars and trucks in the lot. He went down the concrete steps and from there out to the service road, where the illuminated signs of other motels, of gas stations, of the restaurant where he'd bought pie for the Parnells hung bright in the darkened sky. He turned from the lights and sought out darker streets, darker routes by which to go.

21.

June 1977

DEVEREAUX SAT AT *the old woman's bedside as she slept, and he'd been sitting there the better part of an hour while on the other side of the curtain some unseen roommate, man or woman, lay in apneic distress, wakened every ten or eleven minutes by sudden gagging, a dry-throated gasping, a clacking of gums, before lapsing again with a wheeze into unconsciousness.*

Who's there? said the old woman, his grandmother, raising her near hand abruptly, as though to fend him off—the dark-spotted hand with its great black bruise where the needle entered the vein, the strips of cloth tape holding the needle in place puckered up with the thin stuff of her skin.

It's me again, Gramma.

Marion?

Yes, ma'am.

Where's my glasses . . .

They're just right here, he said picking up the loose-hinged frames. He fitted them to her lifted face, her eyes blinking large and wet and blue in the lenses, and she lay her head back in the pillow, in a flattened nest of her own gray hair. She looked about the room, or the half room, until her gaze came to rest on the lidded cup of water, and she groped toward it. He picked it up and guided the flexible straw to the seam in her face that was her empty, caved-in mouth, the dentures gone away to some place only the nurses knew and returning only with her meals. Lest they slip in her sleep and become lodged in her throat, perhaps.

She gummed the straw and swallowed and moved her head aside when she was done, trailing a rope of spittle that swung between mouth and straw before breaking of its own weight. Devereaux looked around and finally took up the hem of the blanket and daubed at her chin.

She worked her lower jaw and said, I guess I ain't dead yet.

No, ma'am.

I dreamed I was. I dreamed I was a little girl looking at my old dead self in a coffin, a wood coffin down in a dirt grave, and I was standin there holdin on to my daddy's hand and when I looked up I saw he was dead too. Everybody was dead but me. So then I thought I must be dead too. Old me and young me both, one just as dead as the other.

A tear slipped loose and vanished into the creases of her face.

I hope that ain't what it's like, she said.

You just had a dream, Gramma.

Say what?

I said you just had a dream.

I know I did, I just told you. She let out her breath. You see where they took my foot?

Where they took it . . . ?

I mean you see they took it.

Yes, ma'am.

The bandaged stump lay exposed and resting on a pillow, the wrappings so thick there was no sign of blood or other seepage, not one spot, amidst the white.

Said they'd most like take the other one too, she said. I said Take it, I don't care, I already can't walk. Just set me in a wheelchair and roll me back on home.

Devereaux unfolded his hands and folded them the opposite way.

Why ain't you at work? she said.

I was. I came directly from there.

They ain't fired you?

No, ma'am.

Frankie says they fired you.

Devereaux looked toward the dividing curtain. He looked toward the open doorway. No, ma'am, he said. You're thinking of the school, and I wasn't fired, I quit. I got a new job laying block.

Fired, I says—fired! How do you get fired from pushing a broom at a school?

I quit that job, Gramma.

What are people gonna say?

The body in the other bed began to gasp. It smacked its gums, sighed, and resumed its troubled rest.

The old woman breathed her own heavy sigh. I guess this is the room you go to afore the morgue.

No, ma'am. It's just a hospital room. The doctor said you'll go home in a few days.

Mm-hmm. He would say that. She closed her eyes, as if she would sleep. You ain't got to stay here, she said.

I haven't got anyplace else to be.

Where's Frankie at?

I guess he's home.

Was he here?

I don't know. He might've come while I was at work.

I don't recollect it.

You might've been asleep.

I know it.

You want me to turn on that TV?

No. She opened her eyes. I can't hear a word they say on that thing.

Devereaux looked around the room. Where'd your radio go?

They took it away. Said it didn't work and was too loud. Didn't work. Too loud. Explain that one to me.

I'll get it back.

It don't matter. Nothing good ever comes out of it anyhow.

It wasn't theirs to take.

Don't tell Frankie. She closed her eyes again. He's like to get himself into a state over it. Like to get himself into a state over just about anything. She shook her head, a dry rustling in the gray mat of hair.

He was borned in this same hospital, she said. Same one.

Devereaux was quiet. Sitting bedside.

He was borned bottom-first. Not feet-first, bottom-first. The frank position, they call that.

Frank—? said Devereaux.

Don't ask me why.

She moved her hands to her stomach. Lord's way of saying You are too old for having babies, woman. Like to have killed me. I asked him to. Prayed for it. But he said No, you are gonna have this baby and you are gonna raise him same as you did his sister. Virginia, your mother, was already ten years old by then. Sweet girl. Good girl. Married a great big dummy of a man. But who hasn't?

She cracked one eye at her grandson sitting there. No offense, she said, and shut the eye again.

She sighed.

Good, sweet girl, she said.

How she and little Frankie come from the same pair a folks has been one of the confoundments of my life. Same way he come out hiney-first, I guess, which was me being too old.

Ginnie says to me one time, after she married that dummy and moved away, she come home one time says Momma, you ought to send Frankie to military school or some such, afore he gets any worse.

He was at the high school then. Or supposed to be. One time downtown shopping I thought I seen him drive by in a big yella car. But it wasn't him. Couldn't of been him.

Few years later the draft come along and off he goes. I says to Ginnie they'll either shape him up over there or ship him home in a box. Ship shape. But they did neither. They shot him and they half blowed him up and then they shipped him home. Give him the disability and told him there you go, son, you on your own and best a luck to you.

She sighed and moved her untubed hand, her right hand, to her chest. As if in allegiance, or to push down her heart.

People staring on the street, she went on. Talking, thinking I can't hear 'em. Just like when you come to live with us. After that fire. Just like that all over again.

Devereaux was silent.

After I'm gone, Marion. After I'm in the ground there won't be no one to watch him but you.

Watch him, Gramma?

Watch him. Watch out for him. He's like a little child, someways. Can't keep a thought in his head. And them headaches he gets . . . You can't listen to him when the headache comes on. You can't believe a word he says. You understand? It's just the devil talking. It's them little Viet Nams tryin a blow him up all over again.

She opened her eyes and turned toward Devereaux.

Do you understand what I'm telling you?

Yes, Gramma.

Her gaze remained on his face, the magnified eyes roving in a tight circuit, as though finding something amiss among his features but unable to say what.

You got to keep folks away from him, Marion. I can't abide folks talking about him. Folks talking, sheriff coming round—it just ain't respectable. I just die of shame.

She began to smack her jaw, a dry popping sound.

Do you want another drink, Gramma?

No, I don't want another drink. She fumbled at her glasses and he reached and she swatted feebly at his hand. She lowered the glasses, jiggling, to her stomach and closed her eyes.

He sat watching her awhile, then began to stand.

Marion, she said, and he halted in a kind of stoop.

I'm here.

Did they find that boy yet?

Which boy? said Devereaux.

The one they come out asking about. Billy Ross.

Devereaux stood the rest of the way. No, ma'am, I don't believe they have.

They took my radio. She shook her head slowly—that dry rustling. Sheriff coming around . . . I just die of shame.

He stood watching. She didn't open her eyes. Her breathing became heavy.

At the foot of the bed he turned back as if to say something but he did not. He stood there. Then he stepped over to the curtain and found the seam and parted it with his forefinger and put his eye to the opening.

A skull lay on its side, as if had turned at that instant, at that small distur-bance: dark cave of a laboring mouth, eyes dead white in the darks of their sock-ets, eyes without iris or pupil, like the eyes of something born blind. In fact the eyes were rolled up into half-fallen lids, staring into whatever dreamscape or black immensity the old thing's brain conjured in sleep, or whatever you called the place it went to when not awake.

Sir—?

He dropped his hand and turned. Like a boy from a rip in a peep-show tent. A nurse had come in, a tiny paper cup in her fingers. Young, pretty, not happy.

Sir, can I help you?

No, ma'am. I—

You must not disturb the other patient, sir.

No, ma'am, I was just . . . Devereaux gesturing vaguely. I thought—

Marion, what have you done now?

Nothing, Gramma, I was just—

Sir, said the nurse.

His eyes downcast now, Devereaux stepping toward the pretty young nurse, turning to get past her, the nurse turning with him all in white, dance-like, a chaste little waltz, and then he was out the door and gone.

22.

VIEGAS PULLED UP in front of the house and shut down the car and sat a minute in the dark, watching the downstairs windows. The curtains were not drawn and she could see the play of firelight on the far wall of the living room, on the paintings hung there, but no other movement.

Lights had been turned on in the dining room and kitchen but no movement there either. No preparations for dinner. No sitting down to it.

She sent a text and waited. The reply came, and by the time she reached the stone steps he was standing in the open door.

"Detective," said her father.

"Counselor."

He was out of his tie and jacket but still wore his good pressed shirt, his suit pants, the nice black belt she'd given him for Father's Day. The sight of his black Gold Toe socks made her smile, as they always did—a little shiver of childhood, days of starched khaki blouses and the wide-brimmed hat and the black utility belt with its pouches and snaps, the holster that smelled of leather and gun oil. He'd worn the same socks then.

He kissed her cheek and shut the door. "Your face is cold—how long have you been out there?"

"Not long."

"Come warm up by the fire."

She preceded him into the living room. The fire crackling in the fireplace. Piano music playing on the stereo, a concerto. On the big coffee table next to his newspaper sat the one bottle of beer. No glass of wine.

"Is he on call?" she said.

"Is who on call?"

"The butler," she said. "Who do you think?"

"You mean the good doctor. No, they beeped him three hours ago."

"So you haven't eaten."

"I had some peanuts with my beer. Would you like some?"

"Peanuts, no. Beer, yes."

He continued on to the kitchen and she stood looking at the lineup of photos on the oak mantel: The more recent photos of her father and Martin in various beautiful lands with white sands and palm trees and scuba-diving gear, on skis on white mountaintops. The older pictures of herself and Mariana when they were girls, these earlier pictures taken by the girls' mother. But no images of the mother herself, who lived now in Chicago with her husband.

She got out of her coat and sat on the big, deep sofa. After a moment she leaned forward to pull off her boots, then sank back again and put her insoles to the edge of the heavy table and pressed them there, one then the other, as a cat kneads her paws.

From that vantage she made a review of the art on the walls, all originals, all familiar to her, all beautiful. The piano notes slowed . . . *Andante, lento.* She closed her eyes and was sinking into a deeper, altered version of the room, or some other room, when the floorboards creaked and she opened her eyes and smiled up at him and took the bottle of beer he handed her.

He sat beside her and likewise raised his sockfeet to the table and they touched the bottle necks and took a swig.

She sat listening a minute. "Brahms?"

He shrugged.

"Don't act like you don't know."

"It's whatever he left on the turntable."

"Uh-huh," she said.

"Are you playing?"

"Not much. Not in a while, to be honest."

"I used to love listening to you girls play. Even when you were just learning."

"You're being nostalgic."

"Possibly." He studied her. "You look tired, Corrie."

"I am tired. But what's new."

He would not generally ask about her work and she would not generally ask about his, as each could well imagine without asking. But when she remained silent he said, "Is there anything I can help you with? In any way."

She shook her head. Then: "I spent half my day today looking for someone I have no business looking for."

"Who was that?"

"A man who called me trying to find out if anyone was looking for him."

"Clever."

"He claimed to be someone else, a concerned citizen. But I think it was him."

"And was anyone looking for him—other than you?"

"Yes," she said, and she told him about her talk with Halsey, the Minnesota sheriff. The dead girl ten years ago. She showed him the two pictures on her phone. And seeing Holly Burke he shook his head.

"But he was never charged," he said. "This Daniel Young."

"No."

"And there's no warrant, just the missing person."

"Just a worried family and a concerned sheriff, as far as I can tell."

"And why did he call you? You in particular?"

"That's what I wanted to know. He didn't say."

"So you decided to take a look around."

"Yes, I did."

"And what did you find?"

She brought out the business card from the pocket of her suit jacket and told him about the Motel 6.

"I won't ask you how you got access to his room," he said, taking the card.

She raised her bottle and sipped.

"This explains the call, but not how he got your card."

"Turn it over."

"The plot thickens." He put his feet down and took up his glasses and read the back side.

"Who is Sean Courtland?"

She told him: The Wheelhouse Tavern the previous Saturday night, the fight between the two men. The pretty waitress in the middle of it with a bloody nose and black eye.

Her father scrutinized the card, front and back. "What's the connection?"

"I have no idea. There shouldn't be one."

"They met somehow," he said. "Here in town. Is he gay?"

"Who?"

"Either one."

"That crossed my mind too. But I don't think that's what this is. For one thing, the pretty waitress."

Her father shrugged. "One does not exclude the other." He handed back the card. "I assume you haven't talked to Sean Courtland since you had him in custody."

"Not about this. I ran into him at the tavern when I went to check up on the waitress. He was coming out as I was going in."

"Returning to the scene."

"Yes."

"But you haven't called him."

"No. Not yet."

"You don't want to spook Daniel Young into running."

"Correct." She brushed at her knee. "I've driven by the place he's renting—Courtland—but he hasn't been there. Or his truck hasn't."

Her father set down his glasses and put up his feet. "It's a strange set of circumstances, Corrie, but no actual crime that I'm seeing. Other than the girl ten years ago."

"I know. I don't know why I'm wasting my time."

"Well, he called you. So he did involve you, to a degree."

"Yes."

"And you are helping a fellow officer—"

"Who didn't ask for my help."

"Not to mention a worried family."

She said nothing.

"But it's more than that," he said. "Maybe you think he did it." He watched her. "Maybe you want to look into his eyes and see if you see a man who killed a young woman ten years ago and got away with it."

"Maybe," she said.

They fell silent. Watching the fire. Listening to the piano. The pureness and complexity, the rightness of the notes. Then the strings, the woodwinds. Difficult to believe it was all made by human hands when you did not see the hands in motion.

"Have you talked to your sister recently?" he said.

"No, why? Is she all right?"

"As far as I know. I was hoping you'd know."

"We don't talk as much as we used to."

"We don't either. She and I."

Viegas put her hand on his and gave it a squeeze and let it go. "Daughters," she said.

"Fathers," he said.

She sat looking at the photos from afar. In one of them he was kneeling with an arm around each girl, and she, Corrine, was wearing his wide-brimmed deputy's hat, her face in shadow but for a child's cheesy smile, the missing front teeth. "Do you ever miss it?" she said. "Being a cop."

"Not for one minute."

"Did you hate it?"

"No. But I got . . . disheartened. Too many kids in car wrecks. The meanness of my fellow citizens. The violence. The lack of resolution, too often, to that violence. The lack of justice."

"Those three little boys."

"Those three little boys, yes. That was a tough one." He looked at her. "In the end I think I just wanted a different kind of life for myself and my family."

"So we wouldn't worry about you getting shot."

"Yes. And so what does my youngest do?"

"She becomes a cop." She patted his hand. "You don't have to worry, Dad. I'm almost never in a shoot-out."

"Oh, good. Very comforting."

They were silent. She was about to say she should get going when he spoke again.

"Did you know about the fourth boy?"

She looked at him. "I never heard about a fourth boy."

"No, probably because he wasn't actually a fourth boy. We just thought he was at the time. Or thought he might've been."

"He went missing?"

"Yes. Briefly. His parents had put him to bed and locked up the house and gone to bed themselves, and then around midnight they heard someone come in the front door. The father came down, and there's the boy he thought was upstairs in bed. Dressed in shorts and T-shirt, sneakers, and scratches just all over him. Shaking like a rabbit."

Viegas waited.

"This was the summer of '77," her father went on. "At that time there'd been three boys, spaced about a year apart, and the last one had been just that spring—"

"Billy Ross."

"Yes, so the timing was off."

"That happens. The intervals tend to get shorter."

"Yes. Well. Suffice to say the parents were on edge—everyone was on edge—and they called the police, the police called us, and we descended on that house like locusts, middle of the night. Which in retrospect was the exact wrong thing to do. I didn't go in, I was searching around the house, the woods, but the sheriff told us later the kid wouldn't talk. Terrified of all those men. They were all men in those days—as you well know."

"Yes," said Viegas. "And—?"

"And so we wrapped it up and went home, and it wasn't until the next day that the mother said the boy told her he'd gone out to get his toy—his G.I. Joe—that was all. He'd forgotten it in the woods and he'd gone out to get it, got lost, got scared, started running around, finally found his way back home. Which explained the scratches."

Viegas watched him. "But you didn't believe it."

Her father tapped his fingertips on the bottle, pinky to forefinger, a soft arpeggio. "Some other summer, in some other town, his parents wouldn't have called us in the first place."

"You thought he was the fourth boy," Viegas said. "Or almost the fourth. You thought he was too traumatized, or terrified, to say what had happened to him."

Her father shook his head. "It's hard to know what I thought back then."

"Why?"

He scratched at his cheek, the day's dark stubble. "Because that was the same night the Parnell boy hung himself," he said.

She stared at him. "The Parnell boy."

"Yes. David Parnell." He turned to her. "You know that story."

She looked at him without really seeing him. She had the feeling of waking, or trying to wake, from a drugged sleep.

"Did I mention that?" she said. "Earlier?"

"What?"

"The Parnells."

"No. Why would you?"

"Because that's where Sean Courtland is living. He's renting from the Parnells."

Her father gave his head a quick shake. As one does when one doubts what he's just heard. "Niles Parnell—out in the bluffs?"

"Yes."

"That's . . . remarkable."

She tapped her forefinger slowly at her temple. "Why didn't I make that connection?"

"Well, for one thing, you weren't even born yet."

"But I knew the name. I knew the story." She sat thinking. Trying to remember.

"But you didn't tell me," she said.

"No, I didn't."

He was watching the fire. What else had he never told her, or Mariana, to spare them?

Perhaps less than they'd never told him for the same reason.

"So, the Parnell boy," she said. "That was the same night as the other boy?"

Her father's brow bunched. He was finding his way back through his thoughts. At last he told her yes—on that same night, or early the next morning, the Parnells had reported their son missing. David. Their only child. He was older than the others, fifteen, but with the scare they'd just had, the entire force went right back out to those woods. Flashlight beams everywhere you looked. When the sun came up they saw they'd walked right under him. He had bright red hair, this boy, and in the morning sun . . . at first you thought it was something copper up there, like a saucepot, caught somehow in the branches. Then you saw the rest.

He fell silent, and Viegas waited.

"Luckily his folks were back at the house," he went on. "They didn't see him like that. Up in that tree. We got him down and there was no chance of resuscitation, he'd been there all night, so we just laid him out as best we could and another deputy on the force, Alan Chaska, pushed his tongue back in his mouth. With his thumb."

Viegas was silent.

"The rope wasn't long enough to be thrown up there from the ground," her father said. "He'd climbed up there with it."

He sipped his beer and did not go on.

"Did you think there was a connection?" she said. "Between Parnell and the other boy? Did you think he saw the Parnell boy in that tree?"

"It was something we wanted to ask. But his parents said he'd been through enough. And anyway it didn't seem likely. He'd've had to go an awful long way through the woods, and he never would've found his way back, not at night. Not even in daylight."

He sat staring into the fire.

"Why are you telling me all this?" she said.

"I'm not sure. You asked me about being a cop, and maybe that was the moment, seeing the Parnell boy up there, that I understood I wasn't meant to be one. That I should find another path in life." He turned to her and smiled faintly.

"I always thought it was the three boys. The ones you never found," she said. "Not you," she added. "Anyone."

"It was. It was. But as long as you didn't find them, you could go on thinking they might still be alive. The Parnell boy, up in that tree. Pulling him down, bringing his mother to him . . ."

"But you kept doing it." She gestured vaguely toward the photos on the mantel. "I was six or seven before you quit the force."

"Yes. I had to put myself through law school."

"Plus raise two girls."

"That was the easy part."

"Right."

They smiled. They sipped their beers.

"Why did he do it?" Viegas said. "The Parnell boy."

Her father shook his head. "His folks had no idea. No warning. Or none they'd recognized. No note or anything. He'd been picked on at school—bullied, they call it now. That was about all we could find out. They called him the flaming fairy, something along those lines. That red hair of his."

The room was quiet. The concerto had ended some while ago and Viegas did not remember hearing its ending—the final lingering chord, the hissing quiet of the empty groove.

"I drove over the 14 Bridge this morning," she said, and her father turned to her.

"Looking for Daniel Young," he said.

"Signs of him. Yes."

"And?"

"What ever happened to that bike, the Billy Ross bike? The purple Sting-Ray."

He studied her. "I assume it was returned to his parents. Why?"

"And that was the only piece of evidence—for any of them?"

"As far as I know."

She sat thinking. Her father waited.

"Three years apart," she said. "Three different places. Three different times of day. What did they have in common? Other than being nine-, ten-year-old boys?"

"I think that was the main thing. Don't you?"

"Yes. But."

"But what, Detective."

His smile was gentle.

"Why them?" she said. "Why . . . *them?*"

He shook his head. "I don't know. The only thing I could ever figure is they were all three alone, and should not have been. They'd all just . . . gone away from where they were supposed to be."

"All four," she said.

"Potentially four, yes."

Viegas sat watching him. "But not lured away," she said.

"No, not lured." In each case someone had seen the boy leave on his own, he told her. With Teddy Felt it was the school bus driver and a dozen kids—saw him get off the bus, the wrong stop, and go walking down the sidewalk alone. With Duane Milner it was the older brother, Joey. Said he saw Duane walk off toward home when he, Joey, wouldn't quit playing baseball. Billy Ross's best friend Travis saw him leave the swimming pool on his own.

Her father turned the bottle in his hands. "They may have been lured once they were on their own."

"Or they may have just been grabbed."

"Or that, yes."

Viegas and her father watched the fire. The silent, guttering flames.

"Who was the fourth boy?" she said.

"Who was he?"

"What was his name?"

"Harlan Olson."

"What happened to him?"

"Nothing, that I know of. The family moved away the next year. Texas, if I recall."

"And he never said anything else about that night in the woods?"

"If he did, we never heard about it. I never did, anyway. I've thought over the years that I might try to contact him, or his parents. But sometimes . . ."

"Yes?"

"Sometimes one must get on with one's own life, Corrie. One's own family."

He took her hand and squeezed, and she squeezed back. Then both let go.

At the door he helped her into her coat.

"You're going back there," he said. "Aren't you."

"Back where?"

He didn't bother answering.

"Just a quick drive-by," she said, turning to him.

He made an adjustment to her coat. "How about a slow and controlled drive-by?"

"Slow and controlled." She kissed his rough cheek. "You got it."

23.

BY THE TIME Sean got to the house the sun was well down and he saw from the truck that someone was out on the porch, sitting in silhouette against the lit, tall window, and before he reached the steps he saw it was her father, Henry Givens.

Sean stopped at the foot of the steps and raised his hand and said, "Evening."

"Evening. Can I help you?"

"It's Sean Courtland, Mr. Givens."

"Who?"

"Sean Courtland. The carpenter?"

"I know. I'm kidding around. Come on up, Sean Courtland."

He went up the steps and Givens put out his hand and Sean took it, mindful of the Band-Aids, but feeling none.

"What's that you're totin?"

Sean raised the bottle. "Bottle of wine. Red wine. I didn't bring anything the other night, so." He lowered the bottle again.

"Kind of you. You can set it inside when you go in."

"All right." He turned toward the door.

"Where are you going?"

"Inside?"

"Don't go in there yet. She's not ready. Just set it on the floor there by the door and have a seat."

Sean set down the bottle. The only seat was the porch swing, and he stepped around Givens in his wheelchair and lowered himself onto the bench, setting the chains to creaking. He rested a boot over his knee, his hands in his lap.

"Can I get you a beer?"

"No sir, I'm good."

"I'm having one." He held up his bottle.

"That's all right."

Givens leaned to one side and lifted a second bottle. "I got a spare right here. Icebox-cold. Never been opened. Free to a good home."

"In that case."

Givens dipped a finger into the breast pocket of his jacket and hooked forth a paint-can key of the kind you get free with your paint, and with its looped end popped off the bottlecap and then dropped both key and bottlecap back into his pocket and reached the bottle out to Sean.

"Cheers," said Givens, reaching again to touch bottle necks, Sean meeting the older man's eyes in such light as there was and then both upending the bottles for a swig.

"All's well at the house of Devereaux?"

"We're coming along. Another two or three days."

"I heard you got a helper."

"Yes sir. Turns out he's a plumber. A good one."

"That's the kind you want. I had this house replumbed the minute I bought it. Replumbed and rewired. Wish I'd had it reframed too. I don't know what people were thinking about back in the day but one thing it wasn't was wheelchairs."

"No, it sure wasn't."

"You need a door? I got one or two I'm not using."

"No, but thanks."

They lifted their beers and drank.

Sean said, "Denise told me you built this ramp."

"I did. With some help from her brother when I could nail him down on a Saturday. So to speak."

"It's very well-built."

"The treadboards are showing their age."

Sean was silent. Then he said, "I could help you with that."

Givens seemed to study his bottle, but did not lift it.

"In high school I worked summers for a contractor named Shorty Lovinsky," he said. "A friend of my father's. Shorty had no sons of his own—no daughters either, I should say—and he made a fair kind of carpenter out of me. I think he was hoping I'd come work for him when I graduated. But of course I had other plans." Givens looked off. "I don't know why they called him Shorty but it wasn't because he was short on words. Whenever I got to work he'd be talking, and he'd still be talking after I'd gone home for dinner. Stories about Korea, boys he'd known over there. Places he'd worked over the years. Characters he'd worked with."

He lifted his beer and drank.

"Do you remember the stories?"

"Some I do." Givens looked toward the bar across the street, Eddie's Place, and Sean looked too. A man had come out the metal door and was standing with his chin to his chest, intent upon his jacket zipper. At first Sean thought it was Mattis—but it wasn't.

Six or seven cars in the parking lot at that hour. No black Monte Carlo.

"Shorty told me one time about a young man named Randall Sprat. Pratt? Something like that. You go ahead and smoke if you want."

Sean had been touching the breast pocket of his jacket where he sometimes kept them. He waved away the offer. "No, I'm good."

"Go ahead," said Givens, and Sean reached under his jacket for the package and plastic lighter in his shirt pocket. He cupped the flame and turned his head to blow the smoke. Givens watching closely.

"You got another one in there?"

Sean looked at him. "Take this one."

"Thank you." He took the cigarette and drew on it and closed his eyes and blew the smoke out slowly. Sean lit up another for himself.

"What was I saying?"

"A young man named Randall Sprat, or Pratt."

"Right. Shorty was a young man himself in this story, him and this Randall both working on a crew building houses up here in Eau Claire. Well, Shorty and some of the other boys would tip one or two back after a day's work, and they'd invite Randall along and he'd always say he couldn't do it, he had to do

this or had to do that. They gave up asking. The job went on into the fall and one day in October here he comes, this Randall Sprat or whatever his name was, and they all order them some beers, then a round of whiskeys, and next thing you know they're making a proper night of it."

Givens took a puff and tipped the ash, though the ash had already fallen from the tremoring in his hand.

"Well," he went on, "one by one these old boys get up and wobble off toward home, until finally it's just Shorty and Randall, sipping on a last whiskey with a beer back, and Randall gets to talking and by and by he tells Shorty why he's drinking on that particular day, and it's because it was on that day two years ago that his house burned down."

Sean blew his smoke and shook his head.

"He'd built it himself, this little house way off in the woods, and there'd been a cold snap up there that year, that October, and he was working late, closing up some other house for the winter, and when he finally drove home he could see the flames two miles away in the woods, and he had to drive all that way knowing there wasn't anything would burn like that out there except one thing."

Givens seemed to watch the ember of his cigarette, the little jig of red it made before him, as a Fourth of July sparkler scribbles on a dark night.

"Randall didn't go on," Givens said, "and Shorty thought that was the end of it, and it was end enough for him: watching the house you built with your own two hands burn to the ground. Reason enough for a man to drink."

"But it wasn't the end," said Sean.

"It wasn't the end. Randall, he takes another swallow of whiskey and says how the firemen found the kerosene heater in the back bedroom of the house, where the two children slept. Two little girls. His wife had hauled it back there to keep the little ones warm and she hadn't set it up properly or the girls had messed with it or something. They found her back there too. The wife. The three of them all together in the ashes."

Sean sat motionless. In the smoke of his cigarette he smelled the kerosene. The charred studs. The little ones.

"I know," said Givens. "Why would I tell you such a story? Why would Shorty tell it to me?"

Sean waited.

"Well. After that, Shorty went out of his way to be kind to Randall. And who wouldn't? But Randall didn't change his ways toward Shorty one bit, and neither did he go out with the boys again. Finally on toward winter, Shorty and Randall got to talking off by themselves somehow, and Shorty says to him, 'Randall, I want to tell you I never told anyone what you told me. I know I'm a talker but I wouldn't tell anyone that. I just wanted you to know.' And Randall kind of rears back, as if to focus on him better, and says, 'Tell anyone what?' 'What you told me,' says Shorty. 'About your wife and your little girls. And that fire.' Randall stands there just staring at him. Like he was waiting for the punchline. Finally he says, 'What in the hell are you talking about, Shorty? I've never been married a day in my life.'"

Givens raised his beer and drank.

Sean sat watching him. Waiting for more.

"He never saw Randall drink another drop," Givens said, "and a month later he—Randall—left the crew for some other job and Shorty never saw the man again."

Sean said nothing. Watching him.

"Anyway," said Givens. "That's one Shorty Lovinsky story I remember. I never think of it but I hear Macduff: 'All my pretty ones? Did you say all? O hell-kite! All my pretty chickens and their dam at one fell swoop?'"

He took another swig and was silent. End of story.

Macduff, Sean sat thinking. Was that Shakespeare? *Pretty chickens.* Did the woman and those little girls burn up or didn't they?

Givens was watching him. "Are you looking for the point?"

Sean half smiled. "I guess so."

"Yeah, me too." He smoked thoughtfully. "Maybe it's the improbability of knowing anyone. Knowing their whole story."

Sean nodded. "Maybe it's don't believe what a man tells you when he's drunk."

"Yes," Givens said. "Or maybe when he's sober."

Sean studied him. "Which man are we talking about here?"

"Ah," said Givens, pointing his cigarette. "Now we're getting somewhere."

But they would not get there, not that night, for just then they heard the clock-clock of her heels coming down the stairs, and with the quick ease of habit Givens filliped his cigarette butt over the railing into the yard. Sean made to do the same but Givens raised his hand, "Keep yours a second."

She pushed open the stormdoor and stepped out and let the door wheeze shut behind her. She was wearing a dark-blue dress that showed her knees and lower legs. Dark little ankle boots. She set her hands on her hips.

Sean raised himself up from the creaking swing.

"How long have you been out here?"

"Me?" he said.

"Yes."

"A little while." He lifted one of his boots and ground the cigarette on the sole and lowered the boot again.

She looked at her father. Givens at her.

"You look very pretty, daughter."

Her hair was down. Sean had never seen it like that before.

"Why didn't you just send him up like I asked?" she said.

"Did you ask?"

"You know I did."

"Well. I guess it didn't feel proper. I guess I felt it my duty to keep the man until you were ready."

"Your duty."

"Yes."

"Mr. 1950s."

"Well," said Givens. He turned to Sean. "Why don't you go on in now, Sean?"

"Don't," she said. "I'm getting my jacket." She turned and went back inside.

Givens looked at Sean and shrugged his shoulders. "Sorry about that, Sean. I don't get many visitors. I don't know how to behave anymore."

IN THE CAB of the truck she leaned to him and they kissed a long moment before she settled back and drew the seatbelt around her.

The smell of her just dizzied him.

"Where to?" he said.

"Just take this all the way to Fourth and bang a right."

"Yes'm." He put the truck in gear and pulled away from the house.

"Good chat with Mr. Givens?"

"Good chat, yes."

"Good smoke?"

He checked his mirrors. "How do you mean?"

"Did he enjoy the cigarette you gave him?"

Sean cleared his throat.

"It's all right," she said. "He's got his own. He just wanted to see if you'd give him one."

"I'm sitting there on the man's porch."

"I know. He knew it too."

At the restaurant the waiter showed them the label, then opened the bottle and poured a small amount into Sean's glass. Sean rocked the wine about and stuck his nose in the bowl of the glass and shut his eyes, and finally he tossed back the entire pour in one swallow. She had her fingers over her lips and her shoulders were shaking. They listened to the night's specials and placed their orders and when they were alone again they touched glasses and sipped the wine. In the soft light of the dining room he could see little trace of the bruise under her eye. A faint darkness, maybe.

Sounds of couples at their meals. Silverware on china. A woman in a spangled black gown playing a black baby grand. Great blond beams of heartwood traversing the whole of the high ceiling, and in the spaces between the beams the black fans silently churning the air above the diners. One side of the room was a canted wall of glass and from where they sat, from wherever you sat in the room, you could see the distant lights of the bridge over the Mississippi and those lights slurring again in the black water. Beyond that you could not see the sky, the stars, only the far, depthless dark of Minnesota.

They drank the wine. They dipped small hunks of bread in olive oil and talked. The woman finished the tune she was playing and they clapped lightly with the others and she began a new one. They sat as if listening but then Denise looked at him. The light playing in her green eyes.

He waited.

"Did you keep it?" she said.

"Keep what?"

"You know what." Holding his gaze.

"Oh, that." He sipped his wine. "Yes." Then: "Shouldn't I have?"

She shrugged. "You can't tell it's me."

"I can tell."

She smiled. "I hope it came at a very inopportune moment."

Sean looked to his left and right. No one was paying the least attention to them. "I wasn't exactly alone," he said.

"Dan Young?"

"Yes."

"Did you show it to him?"

"No." He gave her a sidelong look. "Did you want me to?"

"No. But I wouldn't have minded if you did."

"Why not?"

She shrugged again. "It's not even that racy. And if you were just like, 'Damn, look at this,' I'd forgive you."

He thought about that. Then he said, "No, I wouldn't do that."

She smiled and raised her glass to her lips. "Good. It was just for you anyway."

"Am I supposed to delete it?"

She studied him. "Have you never gotten one before?"

"No."

"Seriously?"

"Yes."

She sat thinking that over.

He sipped his wine and set the glass down in the same impression on the white cloth. "Is it something you do . . . regularly?"

"Uh-oh. Are you gonna shame me now?"

"No," he said. "I was just curious what you . . . what your . . ."

She waited him out with a raised eyebrow.

"Hell, I was just curious, that's all."

She laughed. "No," she said. "I don't do it regularly. I mean I've done it. Most of us under the age of like fifty probably have. I was just thinking about you and I remembered you said you had no private stuff, so." It may have been the lighting, or the wine, but color had come to her face. "I thought it might shock you a little," she said. "Among other things."

"Mission accomplished."

"You were shocked?"

"I meant the other things."

"Good," she said, and more than anything he wanted to kiss her.

He turned the glass stem in his fingers. "And if I'd come upstairs?"

"How do you mean?"

"If he'd sent me on upstairs instead of keeping me on the porch?"

"Yes?"

"Would you have been . . ."

She waited.

"Dressed?" he said.

Her shoulders dropped, and he said, "What?"

"I was hoping you'd say decent."

"Decent, then."

"Would I have been decent," she mused. Tapping her lips with two fingertips. "That," she said, "we will never know."

Later they went down the steps outside and stood on the deck looking out over the water. Festive white lights were strung along the iron rail. Another couple was standing there but after a minute they went up the steps holding hands.

"Are you cold?" he asked her. They'd left their jackets inside.

"No. It feels good. I drank too much wine before the food arrived."

They looked out at the lamplights of the bridge. The lights of the cars crossing from one shore to the other. She rested her head on his shoulder. There was wind enough to lift her hair, and strands of it brushed his face like scented webs.

"What were you talking about when I came down?" she said.

"When?"

"*When*," she said. "When you weren't coming upstairs."

"He was telling me a story about a man who got drunk and told another man about his house burning down. His own house, not the other man's."

"Was it a Shorty Lovinsky story?"

"Yes."

She shook her head.

"What?" he said.

"Nothing." She lifted his hand and ducked under his arm and rested the hand on her far shoulder. He felt her shaking.

"You're cold. Let's go in."

"No, I'm laughing."

"Oh," he said. "Why?"

"I shouldn't tell you but I'm going to tell you."

"All right."

"All right," she said. "Once, when I was eleven, maybe twelve, I asked him what Shorty Lovinsky looked like. He said he had bright red hair and weighed two hundred fifty pounds. A few months later I asked him again and he said Shorty was bald as a doorknob and skinny as a yardstick. I asked him what Shorty's real name was and he said Shorty never said."

"Did you Google him?"

"I asked Jeeves. Yeah. That's how old I am."

Sean laughed. "I remember Jeeves."

"Anyway, there was someone going by Shorty Lovinsky in Santa Monica. He liked Bob Marley and catching waves. He was the only one."

"Did you tell him—your dad?"

"No. I couldn't have found him online either, back then. And he would've just blamed the descriptions on his memory."

"He remembered the story pretty good."

"Right? Or he didn't have to remember it at all."

Sean recalled how vividly he'd smelled the kerosene, the charred wood—how completely he'd believed Randall Sprat's story. Shorty's story. Givens's.

"I know two old dudes at the Wheelhouse Tavern your dad would love," he said, and she laughed.

"Plus he actually knows French," she said.

"Perfect."

They fell silent. They watched the lights of the bridge on the water, and as the silence went on, there was time and space enough for a thought to rise and take hold of his heart.

"Jeeves," he said.

"Yeah."

"Did you ask him about me?"

"Jeeves?" She looked up at him. "No. Should I?"

He blew a puff of air. "He'd be like, *who*?"

"You'd be surprised," she said. Then: "Did you—about me?"

"No. Why would I?"

"Exactly," she said, and tucked back into him. "Fuck Jeeves," she said. "If you want to know anything, ask Denise."

Sean looked out over the river. "Same here," he said.

HE THOUGHT SHE'D be quiet coming home but she went on up the porch-steps in her hard little boots and crossed the floorboards and hauled open the stormdoor and put her shoulder to the wooden door and swept into the house, all to the purpose of confounding his notions of caution and discretion. Or so it seemed to him.

A lamp had been left on in the living room. She slipped out of her jacket and waited for his and then draped both over the arm of the sofa.

"Do you want a drink?"

"No, I think I've had enough," he said quietly.

"Water?"

"Yes."

"I have glasses upstairs."

She took hold of his arm with one hand and raised one of her boots to her knee and unzipped it and slipped it from her foot and set it down on the floor, then the other, and stood straight again, shorter, and looked up at him. "Now you." He bent and undid the laces on both boots and got them off, and as he stood again she turned with her boots in one hand and started in her

bare feet up the stairs. He picked up his boots and followed. Pale, smooth flex of her calves in the shadow-stripes of the balusters. Whisper of her dress at the hips.

She led him to the threshold of the dark room and left him there. He heard her moving, and after a moment she appeared again bedside in an amber half-light, her hand coming out from under the scarf or kerchief or whatever the colored cloth was that she'd put over the shade. From that same nightstand she picked up two clear glasses and came back to him.

"Across the hall," she said. "Rinse, fill, repeat, return."

He crossed the hall and flicked on the light. A spacious, bright bathroom. Enlarged from the original, though a cast-iron clawfoot tub remained. A tiled walk-in shower had been added, glass door and stainless steel racks in the corners full of plastic bottles and squeeze tubes and soaps. Her towels all different sizes, all shades of blue. More bottles and tubes standing on the sink counter like a little city. Pumice soap in an antique saucer that had once been her mother's, perhaps, or grandmother's.

When he came back to the bedroom with the water, she was sitting in the amber light with her back to him, watching him in the oval mirror. He recognized the mirror, its wooden scrollwork frame, from the image she'd sent him.

"Set those down by the lamp," she said, and he crossed the room and did so and then went to stand behind her. From that vantage he could not see his own face, only hers, her eyes holding his in the glass. He saw his hands as they appeared on her shoulders. No sound in the room but her breathing. She bowed her head and swept her hair to one side, baring the back of her neck to him. The pale skin. The finest hairs. A dark little mole. He moved his hands to the back of her dress and raised the tiny zipper pull from the fabric and drew it downward, the slow buzzing sound of the teeth uncoupling—how slow was too slow?—and the dress parting on more pale skin, no bra strap, the slow, singing zipper falling along the tender steps of her spine and the dress parting down to her hips and to a black lacy waistband, just, and no farther.

He placed his hands on the slopes of muscle to either side of her neck, his fingertips resting lightly, as if to make notes on the flutes of her collarbones. She pressed her bare back against him. She placed her hands over his and they both

watched in the mirror as these four hands descended, hers like pale, small riders on the backs of his, as hands slipped beneath the slackened collar of the dress and, continuing, took the bodice down with them, and all at once filled with the softness of her breasts. The warmth of them. Her hands pressing his hands that they press too, that he feel in his palms the push of her nipples.

She caught her breath and released it again.

"Breathe," she said. Or seemed to say.

"What?"

"Breathe, Sean Courtland."

He did, finally. He breathed.

24.

WHEN HE CAME down the stairs again it was after midnight and the house was silent but for the creaking treads.

He raised his jacket out from under hers on the sofa arm and let himself out and closed the doors quietly behind him. The cold popping of the porchboards, the coldness leaching through his socks before he sat on the steps and got into his boots. He turned to look at the ground-floor windows, but the only light was from the lamp in the living room. He became aware of music, a muted beat, and turned back.

Eddie's Place. No black Monte Carlo in the lot.

He shut the truck door as quietly as he could and looked at the house again. You could not start an old truck quietly. It just could not be done.

"You might've thought of that earlier," he said.

"And what, parked at the corner? Smooth."

He picked up his phone and blinked at its brightness. 12:15. No new texts. A missed call from a number he didn't know, a voicemail. He played it on speakerphone and it was Dan Young, calling to let him know he'd changed motels, the Fairfield down on Third, a shorter drive for Sean, should've done it sooner . . . anyway, see him in the morning.

Sean set down the phone and looked a last time at the house. He started the truck and dropped it quickly into gear and pulled away from the curb. Farther on he gave it gas and got up to speed; slow, residential speed though it was. Dark quiet street of houses where people slept and had no idea, just no idea. The smoothness of her. The naked pressing coolness—then the heat. Her whispered breath in his ear. A few days ago he'd punched her in the face. That was what,

Saturday night—five nights ago. He shook his head. You could not predict a thing in this world.

He glanced in his rearview mirror, then looked again. Headlights, a block back.

At that hour, on that street, it had to be someone leaving the bar. Or a cop, thinking Sean had just left the bar. Easy pickings for a DUI.

At the intersection he came to a full stop, signaled, turned right, watching the mirror. The headlights came around.

He drove on and signaled left and turned. The headlights followed.

"You cannot be serious," he said. He made one more left and watched. Nothing in the mirror at first, darkness. Then the headlights, sweeping around.

"Come on, then," he said. He signaled once more and turned right and headed north, the direction he needed to go, and took the headlights with him. He drove one more block, then pulled over to the curb and put the truck in park and left it running.

The headlights came up behind him and stopped. Forty, fifty feet back. He waited to see the flashing colored lights but there were none.

He sat watching the mirror. Nothing moved. He shook his head again. He laughed. Then he got out of the truck and walked back to the other car. It was the Monte Carlo. Of course it was.

The window powered down and Mattis looked up at him. As though Sean were the cop and he the wondering, complying motorist. A humid pungency of beer and body odor rose from the open window.

"Can I help you?" Sean said.

"If it isn't funny man," said Mattis. "What brings you down here, funny man?"

"Did you have something to say to me?"

"Something to say?"

"Yeah."

"No, I was just heading home."

"Heading home riding my ass," said Sean.

As he spoke he saw the gun lying on the passenger seat. Black and old-looking, the black worn away from some of its edges. It looked like someone's old service pistol. Or a replica of one.

"Look who's talking," said Mattis.

"What?"

"Riding asses. How did you like it?"

Sean stared at him. Mattis staring back, not a thing in his eyes but dumb, drunken misery.

"What is the matter with you?" said Sean. "Are you just this stupid?"

"First he gets out of his vehicle and approaches mine, then he insults me."

"Is that thing real?"

"What thing?"

"You know what."

Mattis looked around the car. "I don't know what you're talking about."

"Tough guy."

"That's right. Why don't you get back in your shitshow truck before you find out."

"You keep following me, I'm going to back this truck into your front end."

"Sure you are. Assault with a deadly weapon, they call that."

"Genius." Sean shook his head. "Have a good night."

He'd turned away when he heard the door open behind him. When he turned back Mattis was standing and Sean booted the door with everything he had. Mattis was thrown back against the car and Sean side-stepped the rebounding door and grabbed him by his jacket front and hauled him around, big as he was, and threw him rolling to the concrete and it was only then that he saw he wasn't holding the gun, or fake gun.

He stood back and watched Mattis get to his feet. Watched him brush off his palms and turn and grin.

"All right, funny man," Mattis said. "Let's see how you do against a man who ain't drunk." He put up his fists. Like some old-time pugilist. Drunk, but not so drunk Sean didn't watch the fists carefully.

He stood with his own hands at his sides. He thought he had one chance, and he waited to see if Mattis would give it to him. The bigger man stepped forward and swung with his right, and Sean turned his head in time that the blow did not land square and yet it rocked his entire skull, red bombs of light reeling through his vision, the street gone to tilt. But now Mattis was in tight and off-balance from the swing and Sean came in tighter still, and with his weight and strength under him he drove his fist up into the other man's neck and underjaw. There was a loud popping of teeth and he felt the hard knuckle of Adam's apple under his own knuckles, and Mattis gagged and fell away clutching at his throat. Sean booted him at belt level as he'd booted the car door and Mattis took two steps backwards and sat down in the road.

"Just sit there," he said to the choking man.

He went to the Monte Carlo and got in behind the wheel. The dome light was on and he found the latch and popped the trunk. He hit the door-lock buttons, turned off the engine, the lights, pulled the keys from the ignition and picked up the gun and stepped out again and shut the door and checked that it was locked. The gun heavy in his grip. The gun real. He stepped around to try the passenger door and then he walked back toward Mattis, and when he looked at him again Mattis had one hand on his throat and the other in the air and he was shaking his head.

"Don't," he croaked up at Sean. "Don't shoot me."

"I'm not gonna shoot you, you dumb-ass, though I probably should."

Mattis did not lower his hand. Watching Sean. Sean caught a whiff of something foreign to the cold night, to the street, like ammonia. Like piss. He squatted before Mattis, ignoring the blade of pain this drove into his left knee. He set his elbows on his knees, the gun hanging loosely between, and worked his throbbing jaw. His head likewise pounding, and both in time to the beating of his heart.

"What I'd like you to do," he said, "is leave that woman alone. Her and me both. Now and forever. Do you think you can do that?"

Something changed in Mattis. Fear drained away and in its place was a dull-eyed disregard. For Sean. For his own situation.

"Fuck off," he said.

"What?"

"I said fuck off. You ain't got the balls to shoot a man."

"And you do."

"Give it here."

Sean looked at the gun. He thought about firing into the sky but thought better of it.

"It's loaded," said Mattis. "Not much good otherwise. Go ahead. Put it right here and just squeeze." He was tapping at the space between his eyebrows. "Quick and clean."

Beyond him a light came on in an upstairs window. A curtain stirred.

Sean looked at Mattis. Then he stood and walked back to the Monte Carlo and raised the trunk lid and pitched in the keys and the gun and shut the lid and checked that it locked.

He stepped back to Mattis. A second light had come on in the house.

"How far away do you live?"

Mattis shook his head.

"Come on, get up," Sean said. "I'll give you a lift."

"I don't want a fucking lift."

Sean looked up and down the street. Not a thing moved. No headlights anywhere. He walked back to the Chevy and got in and shut the door. He looked once more at Mattis sitting there, then dropped the truck into gear and drove on.

At the next block he turned right and the last thing he saw before the view was lost was Mattis, or some projection of Mattis, risen from the street and reared up now behind the black Monte Carlo and beset upon it like a crazed shadow, a dark thing kicking and raging soundlessly in the dark.

25.

HE PULLED INTO his spot in front of the cottage and cut the engine, the lights, and sat staring at where the cottage had been until it raised again out of the dark, ghostly against the black deep woods. As if it were not lit by ambient sources—the snow, the stars—but gave off its own light, as if there were some element in the stones that soaked up light and dispensed it again at the lowest wattage, like the little stars and planets that had once burned above his bed long after the light had gone out. The boy he'd been, lying there certain he could see them pulsing, keeping himself awake so he could witness the fading, the moment of blinking out, and he would not remember closing his eyes but he'd open them and the sky would be empty and it was like the ceiling itself was gone and nothing up there but a great void for his eyes, for himself, to fall into.

Now as then something changed in the light, or seemed to. As though the stones had dimmed all at once and brightened again. There was the sound of the creaking stormdoor, sound of boots on the steps, and he turned toward the big house and saw the shape of a man against the light of the kitchen window, coming toward him. Niles Parnell. Up at that hour. Dressed for the cold.

Sean pursed his lips and blew. "Now what," he said. His jaw, his head, still ached from Mattis's swing.

He got out of the truck and said, "Evening, Mr. Parnell," and the old man made no reply, raised no hand, but came up to the passenger side and stopped there, the truck's front end between himself and Sean.

"Saw you pull in," he said. "Thought I'd catch you if I could."

"Yes sir. Everything all right?"

The light was in Parnell's favor and the old man moved his head as if to get a better look. "Something happen to you?"

Sean touched his jaw. It stung under his fingertips, but no blood that he could feel, no stickiness. "I was in a bit of a scrap," he said.

"Yeah, she mentioned that."

Sean stared at Parnell across the hood. "She—?"

"The detective."

His heart slid.

"She said her name but I forgot it. I got her card here." He already had the card in his gloved hand and he reached it across the hood and Sean picked it up. Too dark to read but he didn't need to read it.

"Viegas," he said.

"Viegas. When she pulled in with that little car, I'd already seen her drive by the house twice. I guess she was waiting to see your truck."

Sean looked at the card. The black print on white. He turned it over, turned it back. He didn't think Mattis would've called the police but someone else might've. Might have gotten his license. But so quickly?

"This was tonight?" he said.

"Earlier," said Parnell. "About an hour after you left. You and the man you got working with you."

Sean shook his head. "Did she say what she wanted?"

"Said she wanted to talk to you. Said she was looking for another man and thought you might know where he was."

Sean's mind all at once corrected course. Coldness pumped into his gut. "Another man," he said.

"By the name of Dan Young," said Parnell. "That's his real name, anyway."

"His real name?"

"She said another name he might be going by but I don't remember it."

Sean was silent. Then: "Did she say why she's looking for him?"

"Said she just wanted to talk to him. Said he wasn't in any trouble—standing there with her badge and her gun. Showing me his picture. Not in any trouble," said the old man.

Sean looked toward the road.

"I asked her how she knew you were here," said Parnell, "and she told me about that fight of yours at the bar. Hitting that waitress. I guess you gave this address at the police station."

Sean held the old man's gaze, what he could see of it. "I hope she also said that that was an accident, what happened with the waitress."

Parnell snugged up his gloves, one hand in the grip of the other.

Sean looked again at the card. "What made her think Dan Young was with me?"

"Asked her that too. Said she found your name written down in the man's motel room. Name and number."

Sean stood shaking his head. Finally he flicked the card onto the hood. As if to return it to Parnell. There it sat.

"This is just a series of coincidences, Mr. Parnell. I met Dan by chance at the diner the other day. He looked like he might be looking for work, so I asked him and he said he was and I wrote down my number on the first thing I found, which was her card. That's all there is to it. I don't have any idea why she's looking for him."

Parnell looked down and scuffed at something with his boot and shook his head. Sean knew what was coming and he didn't much feel like fighting it.

"If she just wants to talk to him," Sean said, "then I'll tell him. Tomorrow morning. He can call her and talk to her."

He remembered then the voice message from Dan—the change of motels—and he thought it entirely possible he might never see the man again. Though he owed him money. Then he had another thought that made him shut his eyes. Opening them again he said, "Mr. Parnell . . ."

The old man looked up.

"Did you," Sean began. "Did she ask you where we were working?"

Viegas, the detective, knocking on Devereaux's front door. With her badge and her gun. With her picture of Dan Young.

"She asked," said Parnell. "I told her I didn't know where you were working, just that you were working, and that you'd paid the rent and been a good tenant, so far."

Sean nodded. "Thank you for that."

"Don't thank me. I let her into that cottage to see for herself he wasn't hiding in there. She didn't touch anything. She hardly looked. But I can't say I liked doing it. Letting her in there."

"I appreciate that."

"Not for your sake. For mine. For Mrs. Parnell's, sitting up in the house right now, wide awake."

"I understand."

"I'd have to say I'm not sure you do. Truth is, we never wanted to rent this place out, but we had to. And we've been lucky. We've considered ourselves good judges of character, and we've been lucky. But we're old and I guess we don't trust all that easy. There's a lot of bad folks out loose in the world. They may seem all right—they've got their credentials and they say all the right things and you trust your instincts about them. But when your instincts let you down, when you find out they aren't who you thought they were, that they've not been honest with you. When a detective comes around looking for them, well." He shook his head. "You feel a fool. You feel like you've opened up the door and let it right into your home."

Sean said nothing.

Parnell cocked a thumb over his shoulder. "She's sitting up there in the bedroom window, in the dark, with the phone in her hand."

Sean did not look at the house. "I'm sorry, Mr. Parnell. I really am. It was just a series of accidents. It was just chance I met this guy at all."

"I know that's how it seems to you, son. But to Mrs. Parnell, it all looks connected to something. It all seems a little south of what she'd call honest. Of what she'd call trustworthy."

"Is that how it looks to you?"

"Does it matter?"

"It does to me."

Parnell shook his head. Glints of light in his eyes. "I can't separate what she thinks from what I think. We've been married too long."

Sean stood there. "What do you want me to do?" he said, and Parnell scratched at the cap on his head and dropped his hand again. He glanced back at the house, the upstairs windows, and turned back to Sean.

"I'm not gonna kick you out tonight. Not gonna do that. But I think you'd best not plan on staying here past the weekend. That ought to give you time to work something else out."

"All right. I appreciate that."

"I'm sorry to do it."

"It's all right."

Parnell seemed to study the hood of the truck. Or perhaps the detective's card lying there. "I won't keep you any longer," he said.

"I'm sorry she came over here like she did," said Sean. "I wish I'd been here. But she won't come again, Mr. Parnell. She won't have any reason to."

The old man stood in silence, his breaths pale and slow. Finally he turned and began his walk back to the house, back to his wife, who would come down now from the bedroom to meet him in the light of the kitchen, in her robe. To make tea, or coffee. To sit and listen to all he said and to tell him he'd done the right thing, they were doing the right thing. Or perhaps just to lay her hand on top of his in the silence of the house.

PART II

26.

THEY BURIED THE *old woman at the end of June, a Thursday, and the follow-ing Saturday night a full moon shone brightly on the south side of the house, filling its windows with light enough to give shape to the things within the rooms: the few mean pieces of furniture in an upstairs bedroom, the dingy walls, an open closet door, Marion Devereaux lying in boxer shorts on the narrow bed, on his back, his eyes open. Like a man just awakened.*

Sounds of night insects pouring in through the screen with the moonlight, that drowsing rise and fall, and nothing more.

Devereaux shut his eyes—and opened them again. Sometimes the old woman would sit up talking with her son in the kitchen, but the old woman was dead.

He got out of bed and stepped into coveralls and fastened the bib snaps over his bare chest and descended the staircase in his bare feet. At the foot of the stairs he held still, then continued on toward the kitchen, toward a weak yellow light in the open doorway. A quiet voice or voices talking within—Uncle Frankie saying, And this one here I got at Ia Drang. Mortar round blew up two other guys forty feet in front of me, and son—

A floorboard popped and Uncle Frankie stopped.

Devereaux stopped too, poised on burglar's toes.

A chair creaked, the sound of someone rising. In a moment Uncle Frankie resumed and so did Devereaux. He reached the doorway and eased his face into the light.

Uncle Frankie sat at the table with his back to him. Bare-shouldered as Devereaux, altogether bare-backed. Bone and muscle. Scars gleaming dully in the light of the ceiling fixture, within which the last of three forty-watt bulbs still

burned. He was leaned forward on the table, muttering to some invisible listener in the chair opposite, but abruptly he stopped and grew still; muscles rolled, and he sat erectly in the chair.

Devereaux had not made a sound or moved. Had not blinked.

Do it, said Uncle Frankie. Do it or damn you to hell for a chickenshit.

When he received no answer he turned slowly in the chair and looked behind him. Empty-eyed and slack-faced. The look of madness. But in the next moment his eyes snapped to and a prankish grin transformed him.

Messing with you, Marion.

Devereaux half smiled, looking around.

Uncle Frankie followed his gaze. What're you looking for?

I thought maybe you had company.

Company? It's just you and me and the old gal's ghost, nephew. Come on in here.

Devereaux stepped into the kitchen.

Have a seat there, said Uncle Frankie.

The chair was out from the table, and Devereaux sat.

Uncle Frankie scooped up his T-shirt and pulled it over his head and fussed with his thin hair. His cigarettes and lighter lay at hand. The dirty glass ashtray. A brass-knuckled knife with a blade like a long, sharp mirror. He looked at Devereaux and he looked at the knife.

Can't be too careful, Marion. You never know who might be creepin around.

Devereaux scratched himself under the jaw. Maybe I'd best make us some coffee, he said.

Too warm, said Uncle Frankie. Too late for coffee besides.

I'll get us some water.

Yes, by God, said Uncle Frankie. By God, go fetch us some water.

Devereaux stepped to the sink and held one glass and then another under the tap. In the window square the backyard weeds and grass lay in a ghostly icing, pale as frost in the moonlight but for a darker, bisecting line that ran from the woods to the kitchen's screen door, or the other way. It was two lines, in fact: the parallel tracks of a single person, moving recently and at speed through the grass and weeds.

At the treeline where the tracks ended, something orange caught the moonlight and dropped away.

Devereaux set the second glass on the counter and picked up a vial of pills from the small pharmacy arrayed there and held it to the light. He set that down and held another to the light and then returned to the table with the two glasses and the pills, Uncle Frankie watching him all the while.

Think you're pretty clever, don't you.

No, sir. Devereaux lifted his glass and drank.

Uncle Frankie took up the knife and passed the blade through the air on the hinge of his elbow—the bright liquid gleam of it—and with the point of the blade slid the vial of pills to his side of the table. He picked up the vial with fingers that wore the brass grip like rings and read the label at some distance from his face.

What the hell are these?

They're your pills, uncle. I think you forgot to take one.

Is that what you think?

Devereaux shrugged. When did you last take one?

When did you?

They aren't my pills, Uncle.

Uncle Frankie slid the vial to his free hand and thumb-popped the lid, and the lid hopped and took a coin's turn about the table before keeling over with a soft rattle.

Hold out your hand, he said.

What?

You heard me.

Devereaux sat there. Then he placed his hand palm-up on the table. Uncle Frankie tilted the vial and tapped at it until a white pill dropped into Devereaux's palm, and Devereaux sat as if weighing the pill.

Uncle Frankie bobbed the knife blade at him. Go on.

Devereaux tossed back the pill and took a drink of water and set the glass down again.

Show me your hand, said Uncle Frankie, and Devereaux did so. Open your mouth.

Devereaux did so and Uncle Frankie leaned forward, and when he leaned back again Devereaux shut his mouth.

Your turn, said Devereaux, and the elder Devereaux studied him. One corner of his mouth twitched upward. He shook his head.

All right you little bastard. He took up the vial again and tipped a slide of pills into his palm and slid them back all but one. You sly bastard son of a bitch. He clapped his hand to his face and raised the glass of water and drank, then opened his mouth hugely and stuck out his tongue and bugged his eyes, and in the downcast light of the bulb he looked a stone gargoyle before he clopped his jaw shut and sat back in his chair. Observing Devereaux coolly from that greater distance.

Creepin around, he said.

He slipped the knife from his fingers and slid it to the edge of the table near the wall.

The Creep, creepin around.

He grabbed up the cigarettes and drew one out with his teeth, lit it and set the lighter aside again. He blew the smoke and looked at Devereaux.

Devereaux lifted his glass and drank.

Easy on the agua, son. You don't want to have a accident.

Devereaux returned the glass to the table.

You remember that? said Uncle Frankie.

Remember what?

Remember what. You and Ma thought you could hide it but you couldn't hide that smell.

Devereaux rolled the bottom edge of the glass on the tabletop, absorbed, it seemed, by the movement. Well, he said. That was a long time ago.

That was 1959, said Uncle Frankie. I remember because it was the year you came to live with us. After your folks burned up in that house fire.

He took a drag and blew the smoke.

In 1959 I was sixteen, he said, so you were what, eleven?

I was eleven when I came here.

Eleven, said Uncle Frankie. Tad bit old to be soakin the ol' sheets. Weren't it.

Devereaux folded his hands on the table. The insects droned in the window screens.

Don't worry, Marion. No one but us Devereauxs ever knew it. I never told no one and Ma sure as hell didn't. She'd sooner burn the house down herself.

Devereaux said nothing.

In fact, Marion, I'ma tell you something not another living soul knows now but me. He looked craftily over his shoulder and back again. Just between us. All right?

All right.

I did it too.

He rolled his cigarette once in the air in two fingers and put it to his lips and pulled it away with a pop and sat back again to blow the smoke thinly, altogether like some pleased raconteur. Then, gesturing with the cigarette: Granted I was eight years old, not eleven, and it was just that one winter, but still.

He sat studying Devereaux. Devereaux sitting there studying, it seemed, his own hands on the table.

Eight years old, eleven years old, said Uncle Frankie, you never forget that smell. That feeling of waking up in it. That . . . He looked away to tip his ash in the ashtray. Shame.

Devereaux said nothing.

Do you remember your grandfather, my dear old daddy?

I don't have much memory of him. I only saw him a time or two before he passed.

That was 1952, when he passed, as you say. I was nine years old. Ginnie, your mom, had gone off and married your daddy, and I come home one day from school and Ma says Daddy's at the hospital, let's go. But when we got there they wouldn't let me see him. I found out later from Ma it was because he'd fallen at the quarry. Fallen, she said. He'd been standing up high on a rock wall and he'd had a heart attack, she said. I couldn't see him at the hospital and she wouldn't have the coffin open either. Must've been some fall.

Uncle Frankie smoked.

Thing is, he said, she knew he was dead when she told me he was in the hospital. He was there all right, but he was already deader'n dead.

Uncle Frankie tipped his ash. Kid one time at school says There's that Devereaux kid whose old man took a gainer off the quarry wall, and I pushed that

kid's face against the brick wall of the school and broke his front tooth. Ma had to pay the dentist bill, but when we were alone she says Frankie, your Daddy's gone and we ain't got nothing now but his name, you hear?

I heard. And no kid ever said nothin like that again. Not to my face he didn't.

He squinted at Devereaux through the smoke.

Did you know he was over there in France, your old grandad, fighting those Nazis?

I think I've seen some pictures of him in uniform.

Day after Pearl Harbor he drove to the recruiting station up in Onalaska and signed on the dotted line. Thirty-three years old. He wanted to fight the Japs but they sent him to France. He was on those beaches, survived that, only to jump off a goddam quarry rock.

Uncle Frankie shifted in the creaking chair and settled himself forward on his elbows.

Anyway, he came home from the war and got him a job at the quarry, and everything's hunky-dory until I'm eight years old and I start having these nightmares—the same one, night after night, where I'm being hunted by this little man. Weird little man in shiny black boots. I can see him to this day clear as I see you, his black eyes and his big white teeth, and he's got this big ol' silver sword like no kind of sword I'd ever seen or have seen since, and he's swinging away and hacking up everyone in sight—all my family, all my friends, my teachers at school, trying to get at me with that sword and grinning with those teeth.

Uncle Frankie smiled crookedly.

But that wasn't the worst of it. If it'd just been that I'd of been all right. What did it was I'd open my eyes. I mean my eyes were open, I was awake, and there he was. The little man. Right on top of me in those boots. Squatting on me like he was takin a dump—he wasn't—and looking down on me and just grinning. Just grinning with those teeth. Those black eyes. And I could not move. I could not move a finger. I could not scream. All I could do was lie there with the weight of him on my chest. And that's what did it. That's when I pissed myself. Not because I slept through the urge to do it, to get up and piss. But because I could not. Get. Up. And because I was terrified. I pissed myself because I had a weird murdering little man with black eyes squatting on my chest in my bedroom. Eight-year-old boy. Night after night.

He smiled his crooked smile and shook his head.

Ma tried to hide it. The wet sheets. Ginnie knew and she tried to hide it. They wouldn't let me drink anything after dinner. They'd wake me up at midnight to make me pee. Didn't matter. The little man came back, and come morning I'd wake up in that cold wet stink. Ma said I'd grow out of it, but she took me to the doctor anyway. Old dude with more hairs up his nose than any man I ever seen. Listened to my heart and made me cough and asked me a lot of goddam questions about how I was feeling, how things were at home, at the house. He talked to Ma in private a long while and told her I have no idea what. This was 1951— if there were shrinks for kids in those days she sure as hell wasn't sending hers to one.

And so on it went, on into that winter, and I don't know how he finally found out. In fact I don't know how he couldn't of known all along, all that washing of bedsheets and PJs—pee jays. All that ammonia stink in the house. But anyway he found out or he decided to take an interest and one midnight instead of Ma or Ginnie, in comes the old man into my room and he jerks me awake and he's just this great big shadow standing over me and he jerks the covers down and starts feeling around the bed with his big paw, feeling my PJs, and he says Good, you ain't done it yet, now get up.

Get up, he says and he pulls me by the arm and marches me into the bathroom and stands there behind me a good five minutes till finally I piss, then takes my arm again and down the stairs we go and out the front door in nothing but my PJs, my bare feet, and he sets me out there, and this was December, a week or so before Christmas, and, son, it was cold. He says You don't move from this spot till I come get you, and he shuts the door and throws the bolt and there I stand. Shivering. Crying after a while. Tears and snot freezing on my face. I can hear Ma inside, bawling about the neighbors—what neighbors, I ask you? I can hear Ginnie just about screaming at him. Then they stop too. It's quiet as a graveyard. I think they've all gone to bed. I think they've forgotten about me.

I don't how long I was out there. Ten minutes. An hour. But I was just about to run down the road to the old Widow Rickland place in my bare feet—eight years old in the God damn middle of December. But then I hear that bolt in the door, and the door swings open and he's standing there looking down on me shaking and dancing on my numb feet, and he says All right, get your butt in here and get on up to bed. Ma and Ginnie sitting on the sofa watching me go by blubbering and half-froze, watching me go up the stairs. I crawled deep, deep under those covers, curling up hard as a baseball under there, had to be a good hour before I stopped shaking enough to go back to sleep, and then bang—

He bounced the heel of his fist on the table.

In he comes again to feel those sheets, my PJs. Dry as a bone, he says. That's good. See you in an hour.

Uncle Frankie fell silent. He reached and fit his fingertips into the four holes of the brass grip of the knife and dragged the knife a short ways across the wood. Sat looking at it.

He only did it that one night, he said, but three things never happened again.

He turned back to Devereaux, who sat as before. I never saw the little man with the black boots again, he said, raising the first of three fingers from the knife. I never pissed the bed again. And I never slept more than an hour at a time. To this day I don't.

Anyway. Uncle Frankie looked at his cigarette and mashed it in the glass ash-tray. The next year he took his gainer off the quarry wall, and that was all she wrote for the great child psychologist your grandaddy, my daddy.

Devereaux put his hands under the table and there was the sound of his palms running along the worn denim of his coveralls.

I'd best get on back to bed, he said.

Uncle Frankie said nothing. Then he said, I always wondered something, Marion. I always wondered why you let her change your name after that fire. After you came to live with us. Didn't you want your daddy's name? I mean, I wouldn't blame you if you didn't. He was something of a perfect idiot, you want my opinion.

Devereaux shrugged. She seemed to want it that way, he said. Gramma did. I guess I didn't much care one way or another. Anyway I don't remember caring.

What do you remember?

I remember my mother was very pretty.

Yes, she was. She was. Why she went and married that big dummy I will never understand. Why she ever went out with him at all.

I remember coming here, said Devereaux.

Yeah? Me too. It was right after my big sister burned up in a house fire that you walked out of without a scratch.

Devereaux seemed to stare at the tabletop. I couldn't get to them, he said. That fire was already too far gone. I had to climb out a basement window.

I know you did. We all know it.

They sat there.

Well, said Devereaux.

Well, said Uncle Frankie dully. I don't guess she hated getting those government checks for your care and welfare. Ma, I'm talking about.

I never knew about any checks, Devereaux said.

No, of course not. But she got 'em, till the day you turned eighteen. Along with her other government checks—the old man's army money. His social security on top of hers. Disability. Hell, if she'd had the decency to die at home and not at that goddam hospital, come the first of the month we'd have us a whole stack of checks.

Uncle Frankie smiled but his eyes were on the tabletop. The darkened patterns of grain beneath the years of grease and smoke.

The night insects droned on in the screens.

After a while Devereaux stood from the chair.

See you in the morning, Uncle Frankie, he said.

Uncle Frankie neither looked up nor answered. As if Devereaux were no more commanding a presence, and perhaps a far lesser one, than whoever he'd been speaking to earlier.

But then he did speak, and Devereaux, crossing the floor in his bare feet, paused.

We're both orphans now, said Uncle Frankie. Ain't we.

Devereaux looked back.

Uncle Frankie sat as before, staring at the table.

Devereaux nodded. Then continued on.

27.

Sean didn't sleep—he knew he wouldn't—and finally he got up and got dressed and sat on the porchsteps watching the new day rise up through the woods, watching the mist slowly disperse like ghosts going home.

What new day—? Friday.

The night's events reeled in his mind, vivid as a fever dream: Denise, watching him in her mirror, her hands resting on his.

Mattis leering up at him from the Monte Carlo.

Parnell coming over to talk, the white card bright on the hood of the truck.

He moved his jaw around until it clicked, and shook his head. Behind every good, the bad waited its turn. You thought you knew it but then you forgot.

Forty-five minutes later he was parked in the back lot of the Fairfield Inn, watching the identical doors upstairs and down.

"It is closer," he said. "I'll give you that."

The sun was up in a blue sky and it cast the building's shadow over the lot. A few other cars and trucks there. No blue Prius.

He checked his phone—eight a.m. on the button—and when he looked up again Dan Young was on the second-floor walkway, shutting his door behind him. He raised a hand to Sean, and Sean watched him come down the stairs and cross the lot to the truck. The truck rocked with his weight and the door swung shut.

"You got my message," said Dan.

"I got it," said Sean. He didn't start the truck. He was staring at the motel. "How is this place?" he said.

"How is it?"

"Yeah."

"It's about what you'd expect." He looked at Sean. "Why?"

Sean turned to look at him. To see if there was something he'd missed before. As Parnell had missed something in him.

Dan endured the scrutiny calmly. Mild confusion, perhaps. Trying to figure out what he'd done wrong. After a moment he tapped his own cheek with his finger.

"What's this?"

"Nothing," said Sean. "Just a little touch-up work from our friend the brawler."

"You're kidding me. Last night?"

"Yep."

"Jesus. What happened?"

"Oh, we had us a little chat is all. Got some things cleared up."

"Was she there?"

"No. This was after I left her house."

Dan shook his head. "I can't believe this guy."

"Yeah," said Sean. "Wait till you hear what happened next," he said—and he told Dan about the visit from Detective Viegas. Her talk with Parnell, Parnell's talk with him. The business card she said she'd found in Dan's motel room. The picture she'd shown the old man.

When he'd finished, Dan Young was silent a long while. Then he said, "Shit."

"Shit," he said again. "I'm really sorry, Sean."

"Well," said Sean. "I was the genius who gave you her card with my name on it."

"Which I know I threw away."

"You threw away my number?"

"I threw away her card. I wrote your number down on another piece of paper."

"Because you have no phone."

"Because I have no phone."

"And you threw the card away . . . why?"

"I don't know. I guess it felt like bad luck. But why is he kicking you out? It has nothing to do with you."

"He doesn't see it that way," said Sean. "And I guess I don't either."

"What do you mean?"

"I mean I didn't just find her card lying in the street. She gave it to me."

"After that fight," said Dan. "That first fight, at the bar."

"Yeah. Which is how she knew where to find me. I was already in the books."

Dan sat as if thinking about that.

"It doesn't matter how you got her card," he said. "It's all just coincidence."

Sean tapped his fingers on the wheel. "I asked you if the cops were looking for you," he said. "Twice. The first time you said they weren't and the second time you said you didn't know, they might be."

"I know. I'm sorry about that. But the truth is, I didn't know if they were or not. That's why I called her. I was just trying to find out."

Sean stopped tapping the wheel. He turned to Dan. "You called her?"

"Yes. To find out if anyone was looking."

Sean said nothing.

"I was trying to avoid something exactly like this," Dan said. "I didn't tell her it was me calling, obviously."

"Did you use your alias?"

"My what?"

"Your alias."

Dan held his gaze, then turned and looked out the windshield. He put fingertips to his hairline and rubbed there briefly. "That was just in case anyone was looking. And no. I didn't use it when I called her. I didn't give a name."

"Except when you asked about yourself."

Dan did not reply. After a while he said, "Did Mr. Parnell tell her where you were working?"

"I asked him that. He said he didn't." And to Dan's expression Sean said, "I believe him. I don't see how she could show up there."

"I wouldn't have thought she'd show up at Mr. Parnell's."

"Yeah. It's almost like she's a detective or something."

"She's not trying to arrest me, Sean. I promise you."

"I know it. She told Mr. Parnell she just wants to talk to you. I told him I'd make sure you called her, so she wouldn't come back. Although obviously I can't do that. Make you call her."

Dan shook his head again. "Christ," he said. "What the hell business is it of hers, anyway?"

Sean watched him, and for a moment he thought he'd known him for years—since they were boys. That he'd been hearing that voice since the days when they rode bikes and read comic books and talked about girls, and sometimes they got pissed at each other but always they made up and nothing changed except that they became young men, and then, before they knew it, men. He would know Dan's voice anywhere and Dan would know his.

Sean looked away, not to break the feeling but to live in it a little longer.

"I'd like to say it's none of my business, Dan," he said finally. "But now it kinda is."

Dan exhaled, heavily. As if he'd been expecting just these words.

"All right," he said. "OK."

TEN YEARS AGO, when he was nineteen, Dan told Sean, he'd been in a park where a young woman had been found dead. Big park on the Upper Black Root River, in Minnesota, in the town where he'd grown up. He'd gone into the park to let his dog out of the truck to piss, and as he was leaving he'd been pulled over by a sheriff's deputy—for driving through the park after dark. Which was how they'd placed him in the park around the time of the young woman's death.

Worse, he'd been driving home from the bar where she'd last been seen alive.

Worse yet, he'd known the young woman all his life. Holly Burke. Her father and his had been in business together—plumbing supplies. Holly and Dan and his twin had all been born the same year, had played together as kids, and after their father's death when Dan and Marky were twelve, Holly's father, Gordon Burke, had taken the boys under his wing, given them jobs at the store. He was teaching Dan the trade.

The friendship with Holly Burke was a childhood thing, Dan said, nothing more; by the time of her death he hadn't said a word to her in years. Nor had he seen who she'd left the bar with that night, if anyone.

Sean was silent a good while. Then he said, "Let me get this straight. You took your dog to the bar?"

"What? No. He was in the truck. In the cab. I took him places with me."

"Ah," said Sean, and was silent again. Then he said, "So they hadn't found her yet. The body. When the deputy pulled you over."

"No. Not till the next morning."

"And cause of death?"

"They thought she'd been hit by a car and then thrown in the river."

"Jesus Christ." Sean straightened his left leg under the dash and bent it again.

"A car?" he said.

"Or a truck. A moving vehicle."

Sean nodded. "Go on," he said, but there wasn't much more: Hours of questioning before they let Dan go. No evidence on his truck or his person. No arrest, no charges. And no more job with Gordon Burke either—for him or Marky. A rock through the living room window one night as his mother sat watching the news. Headlights another night in his rearview, right up on his ass. The whole town watching him.

Nineteen and his life was over. Same as if he'd done it. Same as hers.

Or not the same, because he could leave. He could go away and start over someplace else—try to, anyway. And he did. He'd been trying for ten years, coming back home from time to time to see his mother, his brother, and leaving again before anyone else noticed.

And then this last time—almost a month ago now—he'd not been home a day before someone put a rifle round in the side of his truck, before the deputy who'd pulled him over that night ten years ago—a full sheriff now down in Iowa—came poking around again, harassing him, harassing his mother and his brother.

It was all too much. They weren't ever going to let him be. Let his family be. Not as long as he was around.

He fell silent. Staring out the windshield.

"So you left your truck on the side of the road, across the river," Sean said.

"Yeah."

"With a bullet hole in it."

"Yeah."

Sean watched him. "What about your mom? Your brother?"

"What about them?"

"What do they think about it, I guess?"

Dan looked at him. "You mean do they think I killed her?"

"That's not what I was asking."

Dan looked away.

"Marky would never think anything like that in his life," he said. "My mother . . ." He seemed to consider. "I used to wonder if she had her doubts. But that was just my own brain. She's my mother. I'm her son. She has no doubts."

Sean tapped at the wheel. "So you called the detective here to find out if the sheriff there was looking for you."

"Yeah."

"And now you know he is, because why else would she be looking for you."

"Right."

"You figure after you called her—asking about yourself—she typed your name into her computer and got a big fat hit."

"Yeah. Missing persons."

"Not a wanted," Sean said.

"No, not a wanted."

Sean got out his cigarettes. "Tell you what, pardner," he said.

"What."

"You make a terrible outlaw."

"I know it. I can't outlaw for shit." He looked at Sean. "I'd ask for one of those, only I'd probably light the wrong end."

"I wouldn't give you one. I've got enough on my conscience."

Dan said nothing. Then he said, "You haven't done anything, Sean. Other than give a man a ride. Give him work. Let him borrow your truck."

"No good deed," said Sean. He lit the cigarette and cranked down the window.

"Maybe if I talked to him," Dan said.

"Who?"

"Mr. Parnell. If I explained it to him from my side, maybe he'd let you stay."

"Thanks. But I don't want to be bothering those folks anymore. And that's not even the main issue here."

"What's the main issue?"

"Viegas. I can't be looking over my shoulder for her everywhere I go. I'm looking for her right now. And if she shows up at Devereaux's . . ."

"Yeah," said Dan. "All right. So I just won't go back there—to Devereaux's. I'll move on. And if she bothers you again you can say you have no idea where I went and you won't be lying."

"If she shows up at Devereaux's it won't matter what I know or where you are, I'll never see a dime of what he owes me." Sean took a drag and blew. "You were right about one thing," he said.

"What's that?"

"I should stop giving rides."

Dan had to think. "Because last time you ended up in jail."

"Yeah."

Dan looked at him. "How'd you end up in jail?"

Sean tipped his ash out the window and shook his head as if he would not go into it. Then he said, "The man I gave a ride to, turned out he was wanted back in Lincoln, Nebraska for attacking one of his professors."

Dan sat watching him. "Did he have a gun?"

Sean looked at him.

"You asked me if I had one," Dan said. "Before you gave me a ride."

"Yeah," said Sean. "He had a gun. He left it behind at the first sign of the cops. A little going-away present. He vanishes into the night and I get the gun and a night in jail."

"Because of the gun?"

"It didn't help," Sean said. And said no more.

"I don't have a gun," Dan said. "I didn't assault anyone, and there's not gonna be any cops."

"There's a detective."

"I know it. Some genius called her."

They were silent.

"Anyway," Sean said, "she's got a positive ID on you now, from Parnell. She could report that to the sheriff, and he'll tell your mother and your brother, and maybe that'll be the end of it. They'll know you're alive, at least."

"That won't be the end of it."

"No, probably not." He looked over at Dan. "What do you want to do? Do you want to vanish into the night?"

"Is that what you want?" said Dan. "If that's what you want, I'll do it. I'll do it right now."

"Vanish into the morning?"

"Yeah."

Sean frowned. "No, I'd just as soon keep an eye on you." He watched Dan a minute, then said, "Before the cops got there, the man with the gun ended up saving my ass. And I mean literally."

Dan waited. "What happened?" he said.

"What happened? We ran into a winter storm is what happened." Then he told Dan about the bar just outside Omaha where he and the man had stopped to get off the road. Where the man had drunk himself stupid and Sean, in the men's room, had heard the college football players going past the door.

Earlier he'd watched four of them in their red-and-white jerseys making friends with two girls at the bar. Buying them shots. But then one of the girls had wanted to leave and the other had not, and finally the first girl had gotten up and left, and the boys had huddled around the one who stayed.

The reek of the men's room was strong in Sean's memory. The sound of the boys jostling by on their way to the back door.

He'd finished up and gone outside by the same door. For the cold air, for a smoke, and there he'd seen the tiretracks in the snow. Fresh tracks leading not to the exit but toward the alley that ran between the bar and the building next to it.

And then he'd seen the boy at the corner. Or had seen his breath, the boy himself standing just out of view. That was enough.

He went back to the men's room and he unscrewed the stick from a plumber's helper and went back out with the stick up his jacket sleeve, and when he saw what was going on in the alley he hit the boy at the corner, the lookout, with the stick and down he went. A big linebacker of a boy.

He walked into the alley and hit the next one across his bare ass and down he went. The other two holding her on the tailgate took off running. The girl started to slide and he dropped the stick to catch her and that's when the first one, the lookout, got him in a choke hold. Big kid. Strong. He had to let go of her and she just—

Sean coughed once, lightly. "Slid to the ground like a doll."

Dan looked off.

Sean sat staring into the darkness, the falling snow, of that alley.

The big one had lifted him off his feet. He couldn't breathe. The other one, the one he'd hit across the ass, was buckling up and he told the big one to let him breathe. Told him to hold him over the tailgate, like they'd held her. Sean fought but the football player was on him like a bear—that heavy, that strong. The other one got Sean's jeans down and he showed him the stick and he told him what he was going to do with it, and Sean braced himself for that—for a thing he could not imagine and could not stop.

He was silent. Dan was silent.

"That's when my hitchhiker buddy showed up with his gun," Sean said. "Cleared that alley of football players in two seconds flat. Half an hour later he was on the run and I was in custody."

He mashed his cigarette in the tray. "I never told anyone that before," he said.

Dan sat watching him, then faced forward again.

"Course if I'd never given that dude a ride," Sean said, "he wouldn't have had to save my ass. And if I'd never gotten a flat tire I never would've given him a ride, so."

"The flat wasn't a choice you made," Dan said. "It was just a random . . ."

"Act."

"No. Event. It just happened. No one made it happen."

"And now, here, we're in the territory of choices. Is that what you're saying?"

"I didn't set out to, but yeah, I guess I am."

Sean watched the motel. There seemed to be no more guests in all those rooms, upstairs or down, end to end, and never would be again.

"Well," he said, "I got to get to work. I guess that's a choice now too."

"Yeah."

"And yours is to come with me or not. But I think you should come."

"What about Viegas?"

"I don't know," said Sean. "But my next choice is to shut down this phone." He scooped it up and thumbed the screen. "God knows what consequences will come of that."

He turned the key and gave the Chevy gas. He buckled up and looked at Dan.

Dan buckled up. "Can I just say one more thing?"

"Why not? We're on a roll here."

Dan rubbed at his forehead. "So, I wasn't in the best shape when you found me."

"Yeah, I kinda got that feeling."

"Yeah, I was not . . . great. But this job, working with you. It's helped. A lot. And I just wanted you to know it, in case you didn't."

Sean looked at him briefly. "OK, glad to hear it. But let's not get carried away. You helped me more'n I helped you, trust me."

"I doubt it, but I'm not gonna argue with you."

"Good." He dropped the truck into gear but kept his foot on the brake. "I just have one more question," he said.

Dan looked at him. "I had nothing to do with that girl's death," he said.

Sean stared at him. "That wasn't the question. But thanks for clarifying."

"What was the question?"

"Forget it." He pulled out of the lot and into the street, heading east toward Devereaux's.

"What was the question?" said Dan.

Sean flipped down his sun visor. "I was gonna ask what your alias was."

Dan was quiet a minute. Then he told Sean about the Tierneys of the Hoover Dam: The father who'd been among the first to die in the great dam's construction, and the son who'd been the last, ten years later to the day.

"To the day?"

"Yep."

"Damn," said Sean.

"Funny," said Dan.

"What are the odds?"

Dan was looking out his window, watching the world go by. "Three hundred sixty-five to one," he said.

28.

THEY GOT A late start but they worked fast and by noon they'd finished the mudwork and begun installing the door. It was a prehung louvered door already in its jamb and they stood it in the framing with the door shut, Dan on the inside and Sean on the outside and each with a sheaf of cedarwood shims in his hip pocket. As Sean slid a shim in behind the jamb Dan did the same from the opposite side until the two shims were tightly paired and would not slip. They fixed the hinge side with finish nails, then shimmed out the rest of the jamb, squaring it up as they went. They were just setting the last pair of shims when Devereaux came around the corner and stood watching.

Sean stepped back from the door. "How's that look, Mr. Devereaux?"

Devereaux stood looking the door up and down.

Sean put his fingers into the hole for the knob and swung open the door, revealing Dan standing in a mirror image of himself.

Dan moved aside and the old man, leaning on his cane, looked into the new room.

"What do you think of those machines?" Devereaux said, and Sean said, "I think if they work all right for you—"

"Not you," said Devereaux. "Him. The plumber."

Sean looked at Dan. Devereaux did not. Dan said, "I agree with Sean. They've got some rust on them, but if they still work for you, then you can keep on using them. New machines would be more cost-efficient in the long run, but they're not cheap."

Devereaux said nothing.

"In any case," Dan went on, "it'll be a whole lot easier replacing them from up here, if you decide to replace them. Or we could replace them now, while everything is ready for them."

"And just leave the old ones down there, I suppose."

"We could haul those up and take them away," said Sean.

Devereaux cocked one eye briefly at Sean and shook his head. "Just bring 'em up here and be done with it," he said.

"OK."

"There's a handtruck out in that garage if you need it."

"OK. Good. Thank you."

"You going to finish today, then?"

"We'd sure like to," Sean said. "But I might have to come back tomorrow to finish the trimwork."

The old man grunted. "Day gets short when you don't start till after nine."

"Yes sir. But we're moving right along here."

He grunted again and turned and hunched away into the house. Sean looked at Dan and Dan looked at Sean. "Don't laugh," Sean said.

"You either," said Dan. But one of them sputtered—it didn't matter which—and both turned away and stood huffing into their fists, the harder for the effort not to. Like boys at a funeral.

They worked through lunch and by three o'clock they'd rolled a coat of primer on the walls and with nothing left to do while the paint dried they decided to bring up the machines. Dan went to the garage for the handtruck, Sean to the basement to clean his paintbrush and disconnect the machines.

The garage was as old as the house and it had once had a single bay door, but the door was gone and in the darkness of the opening the building's tilt could be seen, its keeling to one side like a ship. One good nudge and the whole thing would come crashing down.

But it had stood this long, and Dan figured it would likely keep standing until he got out of there.

Inside was all darkness and dust and the oil-soaked smell of ages. Ruinous and nameless pieces of farm equipment, engine parts and the wheel rims of cars from the forties and the decades since. Black stains in a dirt floor packed hard

and level but for two parallel depressions leading in and out, and in the wells of these ruts at the rear of the garage, a small antique tractor, cemented in its own corrosion despite the roof over its head, despite open ceiling joists where sheets of ancient plywood lay in a rancid attic dust.

The handtruck was not in plain sight, and Dan began rooting through a cobwebbed pile of tools: shovel and rake and hoe and posthole digger and pitchfork leaning all together like the surrendered weapons of an army, the wooden hafts dark-stained and worn away by years of handling and some of them fractured like bone in some final and violent overuse. He was picking his way through the tools, rummaging deeper into the past, when the flesh on his shoulders drew tight with cold and his heart slid in his chest. He let go the tools and turned around.

No one there. No movement whatsoever but a slow-wheeling cloud of dust motes that he himself, his own entrance into the garage, had set in motion.

He watched. He listened.

"Are you in here—?" he said.

The stillness and silence. Watching. Listening. Not breathing. "Where are you?"

Nothing. His own pumping heart.

It passed. It had been something but now it was gone. He released his breath and shook his head. "Spooky son of a bitch."

He found the handtruck finally and it turned out to be a sturdy model of welded round tubing and black paint, little rust, good rubber tires that, spongy though they were, held air enough for the task. He wheeled it to the bay door and looked at the muddy way and picked up the cart and had not gone far when he saw the old man. Devereaux had come out the door on that side of the house and he stood on the stoop watching him.

Dan nodded to him and walked on with the cart in his hands. He'd intended to carry it in the back door, but when he reached the house he stood it on its wheels and turned and walked over to the old man. The old man watching him come.

He stopped short of the steps, and the old man spoke.

"Got a flat?"

"Sir?"

"That handtruck."

Dan looked back at it, and back at Devereaux. "No, sir. There's air in the tires. Enough, anyway."

"Then why you carrying it?"

"So I don't track mud into the house."

Devereaux said nothing. Leaning on his cane, looking down at Dan.

"I just came over to thank you for the work, Mr. Devereaux."

"Told you before, I didn't hire you."

"Yes, sir. But you hired Sean and that makes you the boss. So I just wanted to thank the boss before I go."

Devereaux grunted. He was looking at something beyond Dan. The garage, perhaps. "Going back to Minnesota, are you?"

Dan didn't answer, and Devereaux looked at him. Waiting.

"I can't say for sure, sir. It's kind of complicated."

"Complicated."

"Yes, sir."

"You in trouble over there?"

Dan stood thinking. "No, sir," he said. "Not real trouble."

"What's the other kind?"

"I don't know. The kind that other people decide, I guess."

Devereaux was silent. Looking down at him. Then he said, "Decide about you, you mean."

"Yes, sir."

"That's why you hightailed it outta there."

"Yes, sir."

He thought Devereaux would ask what it was that people had decided about him but he didn't. The old man's lips were tight and he was chewing on something he hadn't been chewing on a moment ago. He looked beyond Dan again.

"Well," said Dan, "I better get back to it."

"I know something about that," said Devereaux, and Dan stood where he was.

"People deciding," said the old man. "People have been deciding about me my whole life. Since I came to live here, anyways. Eleven years old. My grandma took me in after my folks died in a house fire."

Dan stood watching the old man. The old man staring off.

"People decided about that," said Devereaux. "Said I set it myself. Eleven years old."

Dan said nothing.

"I lived here with her and my uncle Frankie, who was in the Vietnam War, and people decided about him too. Said he wasn't right in the head. Said he got his bell rung over there."

Devereaux changed his grip in some way on the knobby cane; Dan heard it more than saw it.

"Boy goes over there, twenty years old, fights those commie bastards in the jungle. Gets himself shot up, blowed up, and they want to talk about him? Not the commie bastards. Him?"

The old man stared at Dan with his bright, burrowed eyes.

"Folks gotta have somebody to look down on," said the old man. "And some folks around here got it in their minds to look down on the Devereauxs. My grandma knew it. Who never hurt a fly in her life. Who took me in and gave me a home. Gave me a name. It ate her away till she just didn't want to live anymore. My uncle Frankie knew it, and it deviled him worse than any commie bastard ever did. Like to drive him crazy."

The old man appeared to choke on whatever it was he'd been chewing—he coughed and hawked and leaned and spat over the wooden railing. He drew the back of his wrist slowly over his mouth.

"They wanna take your home," he went on. "Wanna take your land. But mostly they wanna take your name. Wanna take it and put it on whatever it is they got no other name for. Whatever it is keeps 'em awake at night. And if you let 'em do that," said Devereaux, his eyes fixed on Dan's, "if you let 'em take your name, well. Then you might as well be what they say you are."

Dan said nothing. He had no idea what it was that "they" wanted to put the Devereaux name on, but under the old man's gaze the words worked their way deeper into him, until he felt certain they'd been chosen deliberately for him.

As if Devereaux had somehow recognized him as someone who would understand. And the old man wasn't wrong.

Devereaux turned aside to cough, and turning back said, "I'm an old man. I ain't used to talking. I guess I never really was."

Dan stood there. "I best get back to it," he said.

"Go on," said Devereaux. "But one thing."

"Yes, sir."

"He didn't know you, did he."

"Sir?"

"Man who hired you. Courtland. He didn't know you."

"No, sir. We'd just met the day before."

Devereaux did not nod. Did not smile or shake his head. "That's what I figured."

"He knows me now."

"You mean he knows your work."

Dan didn't correct him, and Devereaux almost smiled. "He got lucky."

Dan did smile.

"Go on," said Devereaux. "Go help your buddy finish his job."

"Yes, sir," said Dan.

THE SHEPHERD LAY at the top of the stairs with her great ears cocked, and Dan stood over her, likewise listening. Sean, in the basement, was talking. Dan's heart kicked. He set down the handtruck and stepped over the shepherd and took a few steps down and stopped, bending from there to see.

Sean stood on the stepladder, his hands up in the ceiling joists connecting the new dryer-exhaust tube to the collar they'd set in the subfloor. He was muttering to himself and then he said clearly, "What goes up must come down, by God."

Dan carried the handtruck down the steps and set it on the concrete.

"Dang," Sean said. "That looks like it was made in this century."

"I know. There must be some mistake." Dan walked over and they both stood studying the new exhaust tube, neatly clamped to the old duct connection in the wall and to the new collar overhead.

"This is gonna work, right?" said Sean. "Venting downward like this."

Dan nodded. "It's my understanding that there's less chance of lint clogging this way."

"Gravity," said Sean.

"Gravity."

Sean stepped down from the ladder. "OK. Which one you wanna do first?"

The machines had not moved in more than a decade and they groaned at their rusted footings and broke free with a sudden jerk and a scream of the leveling legs on concrete. Sean and Dan pulled the dryer away from the wall and Sean squatted down behind it to disconnect the old exhaust tube and toss it aside. It came away easily and took with it a floating top layer of webbing and lint from off a more substantial base of lint and dust and God knew what all that lay on the floor and on the wall and on the back side of the machine itself.

"Christ," said Sean.

"What?"

"There is some serious filth back here. It looks like they never even bothered to sweep when they put in these machines. Hand me that broom there."

He swept the lint and the blackened webs from the back of the dryer and stood the broom against the wall and they pivoted the machine about and strapped it to the handtruck with a ratchet tie-down, and Sean tilted it back and wheeled it to the steps. He went up backwards a step at a time while Dan assisted from below, or gave the appearance of assisting, so light was the load.

"We might as well have just carried this one up," Sean said.

"Yeah. But this way we look like professionals."

"Hell, we are professionals."

"Don't trip over that dog."

They off-loaded the dryer in the new room and went back down for the washer, many times heavier, and when that was done they returned to the basement with a black garbage bag and the dustpan. Sean broomed the lint and dust and webbings from the wall and he broomed what he could from the floor but there remained a square of ancient grunge, and before he could ask for it Dan handed him one of the mud knives from the sink and he set to scraping the layer of filth up.

"Oh, man—what is that?"

Something stiff and flat had popped up. Flat and gray and possessed of a fuzzy coating all its own, like fungus.

"Is that a rat?" said Dan.

Sean poked at it with the corner of the mud knife. "I don't see any feet. Or tail. Or little . . . rat teeth." He flipped it over carefully with the blade. The underside was less fuzzed, paler in color. They were both hunched and trying to see it in their own shadows.

Sean stood and unclamped the work lamp from the stepladder and bent again with the light.

"That's a sock," Dan said. "A little kid's sock. See the stripes?"

Sean nodded.

They both stood up. Each had seen it before, or one just like it, in their own dresser drawers, when they were boys.

Dan looked up at the joists. There was no sound in the house but the distant mumbling of the TV.

In a lower voice he said, "I just assumed he didn't have kids. I mean . . ."

"Yeah," said Sean. "Same." He poked the sock again with the mud knife. "This thing is so old it might've been his when he was a kid."

"I doubt there were machines down here then," said Dan. "These water lines aren't that old. And anyway he didn't live here until he was eleven years old."

Sean looked at him.

"And how the hell do you know that?"

"He told me."

"He told you?"

"Yeah."

"When?"

"Earlier, when I was bringing the handtruck. He came out that other door, the kitchen door, and we talked."

"You talked."

"Yeah."

"He talked to you?"

"Yeah."

"What about?"

Dan looked up at the ceiling joists again. Sean looked too. The rough old timbers, the swags of dusty webbing in the spaces between.

"I'll tell you later," said Dan.

Sean looked at Dan, who stood following the length of the joists with his eyes. Sean did the same.

"What're you looking at?"

"Nothing," Dan said. "I don't know." He rubbed at the back of his neck. He wasn't looking at the racks of green tubs, the cinderblock wall they obscured, though you could not say what other thing he was looking at instead. Finally he turned and picked up the garbage bag again. "I'll scrape up the rest if you want to hold the bag."

Sean looked at the broken cake of grunge on the floor and the stiff little figure of the sock. "Naw," he said. He clamped the lamp once again to the ladder. "Who knows what else I'm gonna dig up here. You just hold the bag and hold your nose and we'll have you outta here quicker'n you can say Jack Robinson."

Dan held the bag. "Who's Jack Robinson?"

"I don't know. Ask Jeeves."

Dan said nothing. Then: "You know that isn't a thing anymore, right?"

"What isn't?"

"Ask Jeeves. Not since like—"

Sean looked up at him. "Yeah, Dan, I know."

Dan held the bag and Sean pitched the scrapings into it. The edge of the mud knife loud on the concrete. When Sean paused Dan said, "What will you do next?"

"How do you mean?"

"Workwise. Placewise."

"I don't know. I was thinking we might find another gig together. If that interests you."

"It interests me."

Sean nodded. "Good." He resumed scraping.

"You mean around here?"

"Sure. Why not?"

Neither said her name, though they might as well have: Denise Givens.

"I can think of one reason," Dan said, and Sean stopped scraping and looked up at him. He wasn't talking about Denise.

"You mean Viegas."

"Yeah," Dan said.

"Yeah," said Sean. "I've been thinking about that. And I have an idea."

"Let's hear it."

"You're not gonna like it."

"Let's hear it."

"I think you gotta go home."

Dan stared at him.

Sean glanced at the joists overhead, and in a lower voice said, "I think you gotta walk right into that sheriff's office and say Sheriff, here I am. I'm alive, I'm not missing, I'm not wanted, so you can quit looking for me now—and by the way can you tell that detective in Wisconsin to quit looking too? She's about to cost a buddy of mine a crapload of money."

Dan said nothing.

"After the sheriff, you go see your mom, your brother. Then you come back and we finish this job."

Dan said nothing, holding the black garbage bag.

Sean nodded. "I know," he said. "But he can't keep you there. He has no cause. Unless abandoning your vehicle is a crime in Minnesota, I don't know. Failure to call home."

Dan's expression did not change—not through any of it. He seemed to be in a kind of trance of listening.

"Dan," said Sean, and Dan looked at him.

"Yeah?"

"You called her. Viegas. I think you knew this would happen. Or something like it. I think you wanted something to happen. I think you don't want to keep running from this thing. I think you want to be able to go home and see your family."

Dan looked at him. "That's a lot of thinking."

"I know it."

They were silent. Then Dan said, "You're right."

"What about?"

"I don't like your idea."

Sean shrugged and resumed scraping at the floor. "I told you you wouldn't."

"But I'll think about it," Dan said.

29.

THAT EVENING A dark head of weather brought early dusk and thunder, cracking lightning, a blowing downpour that lashed equally at the houses of Devereaux and Parnell in the bluffs before sweeping on toward the Great Lakes and the cities to the east.

Behind the front came a calmer, quieter rain, and it was this rain, landing in a steady din on the tin roof of the porch, that Henry Givens watched from just inside the stormdoor. Watching the water spill over the edges of gutters full of rotting leaves and curl to the underside of the fascia board that had not been scraped and painted and where the raw wood had begun to rot, the water leaching even as he sat there into the basement where cracks in the mortar had not been addressed. A man could not keep on top of it all even when he could climb a ladder, even when he could carry bags of mortar mix down a flight of stairs, when his hands did not shake, some days, like madmen at some palsied jig. He had put so much of it off awaiting his son's return—Adam, who had rebelled against such work as a boy but had become as a young man the more ready, the more insistent of the two of them. *Dad, if we don't get started on that upstairs bathroom it's never gonna get done. Dad, if we don't repair those porch posts the whole roof's gonna cave in.* In those days his sister did not seem likely to need or want the house, and Givens would have been happy to see it pass on to his son and his family, once the boy was back from the war.

Back from the war.

Back from the war.

Even now it did not seem possible. Especially now. His son, his boy, gone off to the far side of the world. Trained and armed to defend but also to attack when necessary and to kill. To take the lives of other men by nothing more than raising his weapon and flexing his finger. And if he'd come home from that place—that sunblasted, dustblown, tripwired, godforsaken place—alive, what kind of man would he have been? Missing his legs. His hands. Part of his skull. His original self. Would they have rolled around the house, the two of them in their chairs, cared for by Denise or a hired nurse, a host of nurses? The house meanwhile falling to pieces around them.

"The world is full of carpenters," said Givens aloud.

Sean Courtland, for one. And she likes him.

She has liked them before. Those you met and many more you didn't.

Carpenters?

Men.

But she likes him. And he's a good carpenter. Not a deadbeat or a user or an abusive type.

Except for hitting her in the face.

Defending her. Hitting that other one—the one who never got out of his car. Who'd picked her up and dropped her off, or met her somewhere. Who'd never stepped foot on this porch. But Sean Courtland, the carpenter . . . him she brought right in.

To fix that door.

And make him dinner. And sit with him on the porch. Not to mention her clothes, her hair. Makeup.

Not to mention the last two nights.

Well. He could be a help to her. If he stays good. Could help her with the house. Help her make it the home it once was.

She hardly knows the man.

But you know good when you see it, like you know bad.

Is he good, though? Is a man good if he isn't bad?

Givens leaned to one side and lifted the glass of wine from the floor and sipped and lowered it again. The rain was letting up, a thinner scrim drifting through the halo of the streetlamp and through the light of the beer signs on Eddie's Place across the way and through the headlights of the car that came up out of the darkness down the street. Headlights coming along slow and then slower still as they approached, and Givens's heart caught in his chest because he knew the car—a black Monte Carlo—and had not expected to see it again pulling up in front his house.

The Monte Carlo stopped and sat with the headlights burning, chugging pale exhaust.

Givens rolled to his room and when he came back the exhaust had stopped and the lights were dark. He pushed through the stormdoor and rolled to the shadows of the porch and leaned the shotgun against the side of the house.

He lit a cigarette, that the driver know he was there. That his home had not been left undefended.

The driver stood from the car, dark figure against the dark car, his breaths clouding, until at last he separated from the car's shape and came up the sidewalk. Hands sunk in jacket pockets, a good-size man, watching Givens, it seemed. Watching the house, the windows, as he came.

"Can I help you?" said Givens, and the man stopped just short of the steps. A casual stopping, as of some neighbor pausing to exchange pleasantries. He looked toward Givens, his face wet and half-lit, and Givens saw an absence, an emptiness he'd seen too many times from the front of the classroom. Blaine Mattis.

Mattis looked at the stormdoor. "Is Denise home?" he said. Like some playmate, come round on a summer day.

"I know you," said Givens. He flicked the cigarette over the railing.

Mattis leaned to improve his view into the house. "You do?"

"I don't forget former students, Blaine. Especially the ones who've been court-ordered to stay away from my daughter. Which includes staying away from her home."

Mattis shook his head, droplets of water flying from the tips of his hair. "That was a mistake, Mr. G. I wasn't the one who hit her."

"I know that. And I know why the other man fought you. I know all about it." Givens stopped himself from looking to his left. He didn't think Mattis could see the shotgun leaning there in the shadows, but maybe he could. His heart was thudding.

Mattis took a step back and looked up toward the upstairs windows. Her bedroom was on the corner and one of her two windows was on this side. "Is she here?" said Mattis, squinting in the rain.

"It doesn't matter if she is or not."

"Why's that?"

"Because you're leaving."

"I just need to talk to her a minute."

"No you don't. You need to go now. You need to go and calm yourself down."

"I am calm. I'm just standing here."

"It's that or the police," said Givens. "And they'll throw you in jail this time. I guarantee it."

Mattis turned to him. His hands in his pockets. "Is he in there?"

"No one's in there."

Mattis looked up again. He drew a breath and yelled, "Are you up there, funny man?"

"That's enough," said Givens.

"Denise!" called Mattis. "Denise! I just want to talk to you one God damn second!"

He stood blinking up into the rain. Then he dropped his gaze to the storm-door again and stood breathing smoky, open-mouthed breaths. He shook his head. "All right," he said. "Well, fuck it," and he turned and took two steps away from the house—then swung around again and strode toward the steps and up he came.

"Hold it," said Givens, and Mattis stopped at the top of the steps, one foot on the porch floorboards and the other on the step below, gutter water spatting on his shoulders, and looked at Givens. Givens held the shotgun in his lap, leveled at Mattis. Mattis stared at it, then raised his eyes to Givens's. He grinned crookedly.

"So this is what you do now? Sit out here in your wheelchair with a shotgun?"

Givens held the gun. The barrels did not shake. "The first thing you're going to do," he said, "is take your hands out of your pockets. Slowly, please."

"Am I?"

"Yes, you are."

"You expect me to believe that thing's loaded?"

"That's up to you. It's either loaded or it isn't."

Mattis lowered his raised foot to the step below so that he was out from under the dripping gutter and he stood looking at Givens. Some strange light in his eyes. "And if I don't take my hands out of my pockets—slowly," he said, "you're going to shoot me. Is that the situation?"

"I've got the legal right to shoot you either way, but I might be less inclined to do so if I could see your hands."

Mattis looked at Givens and he looked at the wheelchair and he narrowed his eyes at something in the rainy distance beyond. Givens didn't take his eyes off him.

Mattis looked at him again.

"No," he said. "I don't think you'll do it, Mr. G. I don't think you can pull that trigger on one of your students. One of your former students."

Givens stared at him and Mattis stared back—in those eyes both the boy he'd been and the grown man he now was.

Givens reset his grip on the gun. "You need to understand this, Blaine. If you don't do as I ask, I will have no choice but to pull the trigger. Because if I believe it's a matter of you or my daughter, that's no decision at all. And it won't matter what happens to me afterwards. What happens to me is the least of my concerns."

Mattis shook his head. "But it isn't a matter of me or your daughter, Mr. G. I'm not gonna hurt her. I just want to talk to her."

"That's why she took out a restraining order on you."

"I don't know why she did that. I guess to punish me somehow."

"She did it because she considers you a threat. And if she does, then I sure as hell do too."

"It won't hurt her to talk to me."

"You're just not getting this, son. You won't even get the chance to talk to her."

"I won't?"

"Do you think I'm going to let you walk away from here now? So you can ambush my daughter elsewhere? Do you think I would allow that?"

Mattis watched him. "So now even if I try to walk away, calmly and reasonably, you're going to shoot me?"

Givens had thought it through: The call to his daughter, wherever she was, who sometimes did not answer. The police who would have no idea where to find her.

"What I would prefer," he said, "is that you take your hands out of your pockets and sit here quietly until the police come and talk to you."

"If the police were coming they'd be here by now. And I haven't seen you call them since I got here, so."

"No. My phone is in the house, unfortunately. Why don't you toss me yours?"

"You want my phone so you can call the cops?"

"Yes."

Mattis stood thinking. "It's in the car," he said. "I'll have to go get it." He waited. "You want me to go get it?"

"No, I don't." Givens cleared his throat. He held Mattis's gaze but all his attention, his beating heart, was on the younger man's hands in his jacket pockets.

Mattis stood there. Staring at Givens. And then with a shrug: "Well, it's been nice catching up with you, Mr. G, but I gotta be moving on now. If you're gonna shoot me, I guess you're gonna shoot me."

He began to turn and Givens said, "Do you know what kind of gun this is, Blaine?" and Mattis turned back.

"What kind of gun?"

"Yes."

"It's a goddam shotgun."

"It's what they called a scattergun, back in my grandfather's day. He said they called it that because when men saw it they scattered. Maybe so. But it also scatters a lot of shot rather than a single bullet. Meaning a far greater radius of impact."

Mattis stared at him.

"More to the point," said Givens, "it's got two barrels and two triggers. Which means I can fire one barrel into that oak tree there to get someone's attention, and I'll still have a second barrel. It's important you understand that. Because if you move before the police get here, I will fire the second barrel into your lower leg. It might not take the leg off but at this range maybe it will, I don't know. In either case you will bleed an awful lot and I won't be able to help you with that, sitting in this chair."

Mattis said nothing.

"Do you understand what I'm saying?"

"I understand that if you fire that thing in that chair you're gonna end up flat on your back."

Givens almost smiled. "Then you understand Newton's third law of motion."

"Newton's what?"

"Nothing. The point is," Givens said, and there was a sudden muffled bang and something slammed into his right shoulder and Mattis's jacket pocket on his right side ballooned and tore open as if a small bomb had gone off and it all happened in the same instant and it was a long time, or seemed a long time, before Givens understood what it all meant. The impact had turned him, turned the chair, and when he swung the shotgun back toward Mattis it moved strangely and he looked down to see the stock lying at his hip and his right hand fallen to his thigh, no longer holding the grip. And neither would it do so—it would not do so. His shoulder jerked and began to burn with a deep throbbing fire and he watched his sweater arm change color in a dark soaking he could not feel. Nausea rolled through him and he fumbled to take up the shotgun grip in his left hand but the gun wrenched free and he watched it go.

Mattis stood over him, holding the shotgun. Givens reached for it and Mattis raised it. Like a toy out of the reach of a child. He stepped back and breached the gun and looked at the bores. "Shit," he said. "You weren't bluffing."

He looked at Givens. Looked at the gun. Finally he pitched it over the railing behind the porch swing, into the boxwood hedges there, and turned once more to Givens.

"You should've shot me when you had the chance. Instead you sat there talking. Like you were back in that classroom." Mattis shook his head. "All those brains and look where it's gotten you."

Givens stared at him. The pain in his shoulder was just incredible, but his mind, all his brains, as Mattis said, were tuned to the younger man's face. The shine of his eyes in the shadows of his skull. He made a kind of lunge with his left hand and Mattis swatted down his arm. Givens gripped his wheel and tried to roll forward to block him or ram him or he didn't know what but his chair only rolled farther to the right. As if it too had been shot on that side. He heard a ragged, desperate breathing and understood it was his own. His heart had moved to his shoulder, the better to pump the blood directly from the wound. He let go the wheelchair tire and clutched his shoulder to stanch the blood.

Mattis had stepped away. He stood now looking into the house through the glass of the stormdoor. He watched a minute and then he turned once more to Givens.

"I gotta go now, Mr. G."

"You stay here, you son of a bitch."

"Can't, Mr. G. Gotta go." He turned and trod down the ramp, first one run, then the other, and then down the walkway.

"You come back here, you son of a bitch," Givens called. Struggling with the chair. Shoving at the wheel instinctively on the left and then reaching across himself to turn the wheel on his right and finally pushing himself up one-handed from the chair, fully expecting his legs to support him, to carry him forward across the porch. But they did not and he fell hard to the floorboards and there he lay, bleeding. The smell and the taste of blood smeared about with the smell and taste of flaking paint and the worn-down wood and Mattis's wet bootprints.

30.

THE STORM HAD come while they were in the restaurant and it had still been raining hard when they'd made a dash for her car, and now, hunkered at the stone fireplace with one hand up the sooty chimney, Sean could smell the clean, dampened scent of her on the air drafting past him. The flue was open.

"Have you had a fire in there before?" she said.

She was standing behind him, and turning to look at her he tottered on the balls of his feet.

The wine. The sight of her there, in the cottage, holding herself for warmth. The rain on the roof and the fire that would soon warm her. No Mr. Givens downstairs.

"Nope," he said, turning back to the firebox. His heart was going but his movements were deliberate: a man of patience, of sobriety, building his fire. He put his lighter to the newspaper and watched as the flames guttered and licked and climbed up through the logs.

He turned to her again, still in his crouch.

"What?" she said.

"Nothing. You looked . . . absorbed."

"Did I?"

"Maybe it was the fire."

"Maybe," she said. "Maybe it was your hands."

He turned his hands this way and that. The blackened palms and fingers. "Yeah," he said. "Filthy."

She shook her head, smiling down on him with pity. "Come over here," she said.

He followed her to the sink and stood watching as she ran the tap over her fingers, adjusting one faucet handle and then the other. She opened her hands to him and he gave her his and she placed them under the water and turned them slowly. Sooty water darkened the white basin and when it ran more clearly she took up the rounded cake of soap and worked it in her palms to a good lather, then took one of his hands, the left, between hers—warm and slick. She kneaded the flesh of his palm with her thumb and combed her fingertips between his knuckles and in the Vs of his fingers, and in such small and handsome hands as hers it did not seem his own hand she washed but the paw of a great oaf fallen by chance into her care, and he thought to close his eyes for the sensation alone but he didn't, he watched, and soon, too soon, she set down the soap and drew the lather from his hand in the tight sleeve of hers and turned his hand under the tap again and he did not look away, and it was all for one hand. And now she was working up a fresh lather, now she was holding her hands open for the other.

THE SOUND OF the rain on the roof had all but ceased. The logs hissed and popped with bursts of sparks, some small number of which flew from the firebox to hop brightly on the stone hearth and darken. Sean and Denise were sitting at the small oak table where the Parnells had once eaten their meals, talked about their plans, watched their little boy play with his food.

After a silence she said, "So where will you go now?" and Sean shrugged. He took a drink of water.

"Motel, I guess. We've only got a couple more days on that job anyway."

"Then what?"

"I don't know," he said. "Dan and I talked about finding another job together."

"He could save up for his own truck."

"Right?"

"Around here?" she said.

"Yeah. If he can get his shit straightened out."

"What about Madison?"

"What about it?"

She gave him the slightest of looks. "You won't go see them?"

He shrugged. "I could do that on a weekend."

She nodded. She seemed to study their two jackets where they hung on the back of the third chair, one on each vertical post and facing each other. Like a man and woman met in the street in the rain and standing close. He tried to guess what she might be thinking, and when he realized what he was doing he said, "What are you thinking?"

"I was thinking you could stay at the house, save your money."

She let the words hang—to see the effect on him, he thought. He tried not to have one. Which itself was an effect.

"But I don't think Mr. Givens would go for it," she went on. "Even though there's a perfectly good bedroom—two perfectly good bedrooms—nobody's using."

"Thanks for thinking of it," he said. "But if I were him I wouldn't go for it either."

"You wouldn't?"

He thought a moment. "I don't know. I never had a daughter."

She lifted her glass and said into it, watching him over the rim, "Pray you never do."

It was a joke and he smiled, but the thought raised the image of his own father and the nature of his love for his daughter, Sean's sister. It was not the same love as his love for his son, and if you were lucky, as a son—or a daughter—you might never have to understand that.

"Anyway it's not about his daughter," Denise said.

"It's not?"

"No. It's about him not wanting anybody—or more accurately, somebody like you—to see him in his . . . natural state. Not that he would ever say such a thing out loud."

"I can understand that."

"I'm sure you can."

He half smiled. "Meaning?"

"Oh, you know. The nature of men."

"Yeah," he said.

She reached for his hand and he gave it to her. "It's OK," she said. "I'm not so great at it myself."

"What?"

"You know. *Feelings.*"

"You seem pretty good at it to me."

She looked at him with something like wariness. "In what way?"

The room was getting warm. He should probably open a window. "Your dad, for instance," he said. "The way you take care of each other. The way you are together. It's really . . ." He searched for the word. "Beautiful."

She nodded slowly. "Yeah." Her eyes shone and after a moment she wiped at them.

"I'm going to watch him die," she said.

Sean said nothing. His heart had fallen. He held her hand more firmly.

She gave a kind of choking laugh and shook her head. "Holy shit, what did you put in my drink?" She took a good swallow of water and set the glass down again. "Let's talk about something else."

"OK," he said. But where did you go from there—from Denise watching her father die?

"What's her name?" she said.

He stared at her. "Who?"

"Your sister. You never said her name."

"I didn't?"

"Nope."

"I thought I did."

"Nope. I can play back the tape if you want."

She gave his hand a squeeze and he smiled. Silent. Then he said, "Caitlin."

"How old is she?"

"Three years older than me."

She sat staring at him. "And how old are you?"

"Twenty-six."

"Twenty-six?"

"Yep."

"I thought you were older."

"I get that sometimes."

She said nothing for a good while. Then: "Don't you want to know how old I am?"

"Sure."

"Thirty-two. I'm six years older than you."

"It doesn't matter," he said. "Does it?"

She shrugged. "Not to me."

He held her eyes, and after a moment he saw that she had another question and he thought he knew what it was.

"You said you used to be close when you were younger," she said. "Did something happen? Or was it just . . . time?"

"Some of both," he said.

He looked at the fire. The flames were struggling and would not last.

Denise was silent.

"When I was fifteen," he said. "After the age of fifteen, I didn't see her for two years. More than two years."

"She went away."

"Yeah."

"I can relate to that," she said.

He turned back to her. "Your brother?"

"Yes. But me too. I went away too, in my own way."

They were silent. Finally she said, "So—then what happened?"

He stared at her hand in his. Her thumb playing lightly over his knuckles.

"You don't want to talk about it," she said. "I shouldn't have asked in the first place. It's none of my business."

He shook his head. "It's not that." He let go her hand and got up and crossed the room to the fire. Squatted once more and took up a chunk of cordwood from the hearth and used it to poke at the crumbling logs.

"I'll tell you sometime, Denise," he said. "Sometime when I haven't been drinking. When I can tell it right."

She didn't answer, and he turned to look at her. She sat watching him from the table.

"Is that all right?" he said.

"Of course it's all right. We can talk about something else. Or we don't have to talk at all. We can just stare drunkenly into each other's eyes."

She smiled and he did too.

He placed the unburned cordwood onto the embers, waited for the flames to climb, and stood and went back to her.

It was her phone that woke them, playing its muffled tune in her jacket pocket across the room. They looked at each other in the almost dark, waiting for it to stop. At last it did and she smiled and closed her eyes, and he lay watching the last of the firelight play over her face, her bare shoulder.

The phone started up again, and she sighed.

"I'd better check. It might be Dad."

He lifted the bedding and she slid over him and went quickly to her jacket and brought the ringing phone quickly back and slid over him again, and Sean thought he'd never seen anything so beautiful.

She lay back and squinted at the phone's light and frowned. Not her Dad. Not a caller she knew. She swiped the screen and put the phone to her ear and Sean could hear the caller's voice, a woman's—direct, informational—but not what the woman said, and so he watched the effect on Denise's face: first the eyes, then the mouth. She sat up. She found his hand and gripped it. He sat up too. Her grip tightened.

"When?" she said. She was staring at him but not as though to convey some meaning. Not as though she recognized his face in any way but had fixed on it because she must fix on something as she listened. "Oh my God," she said. "Oh my God." She closed her eyes. "Is he going to be all right?" She opened her eyes again and brought them into focus. "OK," she said. "OK. Thank you. I'm leaving right now. I'll be right there. Thank you."

She held the phone and stared at Sean, her face pale in the dark.

"What's happened?"

"It's Dad. He's been shot."

Sean's heart dropped through space. "What?"

"He's been fucking *shot*," she said. "He's at the hospital. I have to go." She threw back the bedding and crawled over him.

"I'll drive you," he said.

"Yes," she said, grabbing up her clothes. "Please. Thank you."

31.

VIEGAS WAS OUT in the bluffs, taking the wet curves with care, when her phone began to ring in the car's speakers, and her first thought was Sean Courtland, finally calling her back. After her talk with Niles Parnell the night before, she knew she'd tipped her hand, and today she'd called the number Courtland had written on the back of her card—voicemail, both times.

But it wasn't Courtland calling. It was Samuels.

"Are you home?" he said.

"No, I'm driving. What's happening?" She began to slow for the Parnells' driveway—one more pass, just to see if the truck was there.

"There's been an incident out near the Highway 14 Bridge," Samuels said. "A pickup truck down the bank, this side of the river. One dead on the scene."

She understood at once. Why else call her? She pulled into the drive hoping to see the Chevy truck, but she didn't. The cottage was dark.

"You there?" said Samuels.

"I'm here."

"Yeah," he said. "I thought you'd want to know that the plate they called in matches your man from last weekend. The tough guy who punched the waitress."

She'd already backed out of the drive, turned around, heading toward town. "He went off the road?" she said.

"Yeah. But that's not what killed him."

Viegas watched her headlights on the wet pavement. "What killed him?"

"A bullet. Either before he went off the road or after."

She was silent again and Samuels said, "You there?"

"I'm here."

"Could be self-inflicted," he said, anticipating her question. "But they haven't found a weapon yet, last I heard."

"All right," she said. "I'm going to go take a look. Can you do me a favor?"

"Find the waitress," said Samuels.

"Yes. Thank you. And let me know when you do."

"I'm on it," he said. "Highway 14 Bridge," he said again.

"Thanks, Victor."

Five units were on the scene—two city police, two county sheriff, one county ambulance—all splashing their lights silently over the bridge and the trees and the fog that lay over the water. She parked to the rear of the vehicles and left her own blue strobes going and walked up the road looking for tire-tracks, skid marks, but the road was wet and black and flashing with too many lights. Up ahead, out on the bridge, a lone officer walked the westbound walk-way, sweeping the beam of his flashlight before him.

She pulled her coat and jacket aside to show her badge but the sheriff's deputy posted there to keep the traffic moving let her go by without looking at it.

The truck had gone down the embankment short of the guardrail, and its tracks through the mud and old grass were not erratic or helical, as in a spinout, but more indicative of an asleep-at-the-wheel incident or even an intentional nosedive. But if he'd been aiming for the water he'd come up far short, the truck having bogged down in the narrow lane of earth that ran between the embankment on one side and the trees on the other. At least four officers were down there, slashing flashlight beams in the fog coming in off the river. Two EMTs stood a little ways from the open passenger door, faintly lit by the cab's dome light. Staying with the body, as was their duty.

She switched on her own Mini Maglite and began to make her way down the slick bank, and one of the officers, seeing her coming, put his big Mag beam on the ground before her. Some half dozen or more pairs of boots had gone slipping up and down the bank and now she'd added hers to the party.

"Thank you," she said, reaching the truck. She unclipped and raised her badge and the officer, another sheriff's deputy, put his beam on it briefly and tipped his brim to her.

She looked at the other officers, three of them, all men, all busy with their flashlights, then turned back to the deputy. A lean young man in his brown sheriff's jacket, his face in shadow under the hatbrim but a jaw so smooth and clean it shone with the blue and red of the units. It might have been her own young father she was meeting, summoned by some weird misfiring of the ordinary world.

She put her beam on the truck and the deputy did the same with his brighter beam, lighting up the old green Chevy, rusted and dented, the Knaack job box sitting square and tight to the front wall of the truck bed, behind the cab—it must have been bolted down. Someone had shut off the engine, or it had shut itself off, and the lights were dark but for the dome light. The windows were up and unbroken.

"We got one dead in the cab," said the deputy. "Probably the driver, but he's in the passenger seat now, slumped over. You can see the damage to the driver's-side door where he sideswiped something or got sideswiped. The door won't budge."

Viegas played her beam over the door. It was dished in and streaked with black paint. "Were you first on the scene?" she said.

"Yes, ma'am."

"Was the passenger door open when you arrived?"

"Yes, ma'am."

She probed her beam in the grass around the truck, then up the slope. "A lot of foot traffic," she said.

"Yes, ma'am. We were trying to get down here as quick as we could."

"I understand, Deputy."

"Do you know the truck?" he said.

"Yes. Did you find ID?"

"No, ma'am, but the plates are registered to a Sean Courtland. Colorado plates. Same name on the documents in the glovebox. The repair receipts too."

"He didn't have ID on him?"

"Not that we've found."

She stood looking at the truck. She put her beam on the Knaack box. "What's in the box?"

"Just a few tools. A level. A pry bar. A maul."

"Was it locked?"

"Yes, ma'am, but the key was on the ring in the ignition."

Viegas said nothing, and the deputy gave the latex glove of his flashlight hand a snap at the wrist. "I wanted to make sure there wasn't another body in there," he said. "I put the key back in the ignition."

Viegas nodded. "And no weapon," she said.

"No, ma'am, not so far."

"All right," she said. "I'll look at him now."

"Yes, ma'am."

They went around to the passenger side of the truck. The other three officers, city cops, had walked deeper into the fog, stirring it before them with their beams like first men on a new planet.

The body was indeed on the passenger side of the bench seat, slumped away toward the driver's side. No seatbelt. If he was the driver he'd either been thrown there or was trying to get out or had moved for some other reason. Or he was a passenger all along. In which case the driver would've had to crawl over him to get out.

The blood spray on the ceiling of the cab and the windshield indicated a shot from his right-hand side, which might account for the slumping to his left.

"Any attempt to resuscitate?" she said.

"No, ma'am," said one of the EMTs. "No heart activity, no breath. Some rigor mortis. That wound. He'd been down here awhile. Our assessment was DOS."

Dead on scene. Viegas had brought latex gloves from her glovebox and she pulled them on. "You can douse your light, Deputy," she said, and the deputy, behind her, lowered his beam. She leaned in over the body.

"Is it your man?" said the deputy.

Viegas stood back again. "I can't tell from this angle. With the blood." She placed her left hand carefully behind the headrest and her right boot on the sill plate and stepped partway up into the cab. She reached carefully into her pocket for the Maglite and put its beam on the face and kept it there a long while. No sound but her own breathing, her pumping heart. The smell was of an old truck cab that had been freshly splashed with blood.

She stepped down from the cab.

The deputy waited.

"It's not him," she said. "It's not Sean Courtland."

"Are you sure?"

"I'm sure, Deputy."

The deputy stood looking in at the body. "Then who is he?"

Viegas peeled off the latex gloves and dropped them in her coat pocket. She dried her damp hands on her coat, then took out her phone and stood looking at the dark screen. Not swiping, not tapping.

"Detective?" the deputy said.

She turned to him. "Yes?"

"We got a John Doe here?"

Viegas looked toward the river, the bridge, but could see neither for the fog.

Just the day before, she'd stood on the walkway looking down into the water. Forty-one years ago a boy's bicycle had been found not far from where she stood now.

She turned back to the deputy, intending to ask him to keep looking for the weapon, and to keep anyone else away from the cab until the homicide detectives arrived, but before she could speak his shoulder radio crackled and he picked it up.

"This is Deputy Allen. Go ahead, Louisa."

The dispatcher advised him that another vehicle had been located, another shooting victim inside. This one an apparent suicide. Black Monte Carlo, said Louisa, near the Highway 14 Bridge on the Minnesota side.

32.

SEAN RAN THE yellows when he could, jumped hard on the greens and pushed the speed limit at every stretch, banking the car through the slick turns with the control, the proficiency, of sudden sobriety, of adrenaline. Of the strangeness of the unfamiliar car and the silence of the woman he must deliver quickly and safely to the hospital.

There was nothing more to ask her that he didn't know from her responses to the phone call and from what he'd seen in her eyes and what she'd told him: Her father was shot. He was alive. She didn't know or even care in that moment how it had happened, and as long as she did not know the rest Sean could hope that he himself did not know either. Or that he was wrong. But in the silence of the car he couldn't shake the memory of Mattis, rearing up behind the Monte Carlo and flailing his arms in soundless rage.

The first thing Sean saw in the emergency parking lot was the police cruiser. Unattended. He kept stride with Denise from the car to the ER lobby and only then fell back, letting her go on alone to the desk. He'd not looked directly at the two cops where they stood, hands in their jacket pockets, but had seen them as plainly as if he had. One of them, the female, stepped up to the desk and stood by as Denise gave her father's name, her own name, and only when the man behind the desk had turned to his screen and begun his search did the cop speak.

"Ms. Givens?"

"Yes?"

"I'm Officer Bowen and that is Officer Kawata."

"OK," said Denise.

"I know you just want to see your father right now, but I'd like to ask you a question or two if you don't mind."

"Actually I do," said Denise. "I'm trying to find out if he's alive."

"Yes, ma'am. He's alive. But we haven't been able to ask him what happened."

"Neither have I. I don't know any more than you do."

"Yes, ma'am. But the sooner we talk to you and your father, the sooner we can locate who did this before he harms anyone else."

"Maybe you could just give her a minute?" Sean said, and the other cop, Kawata, came forward with his hand up.

"Sir, step away," he said.

Sean looked at him. "What?"

"I said step away from the officer."

Sean looked at the other officer—Bowen—a good six feet from where he stood. He raised his own hands and took a step back.

"And who are you?" said Kawata.

"He's with me," Denise said. "He drove me here."

"Yes, ma'am," said Kawata. "Your name, sir?"

"My name is Sean Courtland."

"And what is your relationship here?"

"My relationship?"

"Yes, sir. How do you know these folks?"

"I'm just a friend. I drove her here."

Kawata looked at Denise, who met his gaze with a kind of withering disregard, as she might look upon some tiresome drunk at the bar. He turned back to Sean. "May I see some ID, Mr. Courtland?"

"What for?"

"Because I asked you, sir."

Sean got out his wallet and slid the license from the window sleeve and handed it over and stood by as Kawata flipped open his pad and began to take down the information.

The man behind the desk finished his search and turned back to Denise. "Your father is out of surgery and in the ICU. You can't see him yet, but you can go there and the doctor will come out and talk to you." He gave her directions and she began to walk away—but stopped, looked back at Sean, at Kawata.

"Can he come with me?"

"We'll be right behind you, ma'am," said Kawata.

She looked at Sean.

"I'll find you there," he said.

She went on, with Officer Bowen at her side.

After Kawata had taken down, it seemed, every last detail of the license, he handed it back and Sean returned it to his wallet, and the wallet to his jacket. He began to move away and Kawata raised his hand again.

"Hold on a minute, sir."

"She'd like me to be with her."

"Yes, sir. Just give me one more minute here."

Sean turned back to him.

"How do you know Mr. Givens?"

"Through his daughter."

"And how do you know her?"

"As a friend."

"You're dating?"

Sean thought a moment. "We've been spending a little time together."

"For how long?"

"Is that relevant?"

"How long, sir?"

Sean thought again. "Not long. Less than a week."

"And you were with her tonight?"

Sean looked more carefully at Kawata. A living manifestation of a thousand procedures and protocols, including the authority to detain and question. Including the skills and arsenal to subdue and restrain and tase and shoot and one way or another end his ability to take another free step in the world.

"Yes," Sean said. "I was with her tonight."

"Since what time?"

"Since she came to pick me up. Around seven thirty."

"And she picked you up where?"

Sean told him about the cottage he rented from Niles Parnell.

"And where did you and Ms. Givens go?"

He told the officer where they'd gone to dinner, how long they'd stayed, and where they'd gone after, which was back to the cottage.

"Do you own a firearm, sir?"

"No, I don't."

Kawata consulted his notes. "Do you know a Mr. Blaine Mattis?"

Sean said nothing. Then he said, "I know who he is."

Kawata watched him. "Ms. Givens took out a restraining order against Mr. Mattis Monday morning," he said. "Following a fight in which you were involved."

"Yes, I'm aware."

"Have you seen Mr. Mattis since then?"

Sean said nothing.

"Mr. Courtland?"

"Yes. I saw him last night."

"Last night," said the officer. "You mean a few hours ago?"

Sean had to think. "No, the night before," he said. "Thursday night. Or early Friday morning, technically. We got into another fight, of sorts."

"Where was this?"

"A few blocks from her house."

"Ms. Givens's house?"

"Yes."

"Mr. Mattis was at her house?"

"He was in the area. When I left the house he followed me, in his car, then I stopped and we both got out and we had a fight. A second fight. I locked his keys in his car and left him there."

"What was the fight about?"

Sean shook his head. "You'd have to ask him."

"What time did this happen?"

"It was twelve-fifteen when I noticed his headlights."

Kawata wrote it all down and looked up at Sean, and Sean knew what was coming.

"Mr. Courtland, does Mr. Mattis own a firearm?"

Sean held Kawata's gaze. "I don't know if he owns it," he said, "but he had one. It was in his car, on the passenger seat."

"Did he threaten you with it?"

"No. He never touched it that I saw."

"Did you touch it?"

"Yes. I picked it up and threw it in the trunk with his car keys, after the fight."

"What kind of a gun was it?"

"I have no idea. A handgun."

Kawata wrote in his pad and looked up at Sean again. "You didn't call the police about this incident with Mr. Mattis?"

"No sir."

"Even though you knew Ms. Givens had taken out a restraining order against him."

Sean held the cop's gaze. "That's correct," he said. "He was following me, not her, and I wasn't worried about me. Not as far as he was concerned."

Kawata watched his face. His eyes. "And did you tell Ms. Givens about it?"

"No. I didn't want to worry her."

"I see." Kawata wrote once more in his pad, then flipped it shut and pocketed it like a wallet inside his winter cop jacket. "I'm going out to my unit now," he said, "and then I'll come find Officer Bowen."

But he didn't go out to his unit. He didn't go anywhere.

Sean waited.

"You can tell Ms. Givens about Mr. Mattis and the handgun," Kawata said, "or I can tell her."

"I'll tell her," Sean said.

"Good. I appreciate your cooperation."

Sean stared at Kawata. Then he turned away. And turned back once more. Kawata hadn't moved.

"I would have told her," Sean said.

"Yes, sir."

"I didn't need to be given a choice."

"All right."

"Cooperation," said Sean.

Kawata dipped his head. "Do we have a problem, Mr. Courtland?"

"No sir, Officer. No problem."

He found her in the wide hallway outside the double doors of the ICU, standing with Officer Bowen at some remove from the only other people in the hallway, a family of three, or what appeared to be a family of three, seated together and looking up at Sean's arrival: mom and dad in their late thirties, paper coffee cups in their hands, daughter in her early teens with her feet up on the chair, her knees a backstop for her hands and phone. Sean stopped and stood apart and all three looked away again.

Denise, beyond them, looked at him. Bowen looked too, then both turned back to each other.

Sean stood looking at nothing, hands in his jacket pockets. When he glanced again the officer had her hand on Denise's upper arm and Denise was nodding her thanks.

The officer came down the hallway toward him.

"Mr. Courtland," she said.

"Officer," he said.

"I don't suppose you've seen my partner," she said without stopping.

"Last I saw he was on his way to the car. The unit."

"Copy that," she said, and turned the corner and was gone.

Sean went to Denise. "Are you all right?"

She smiled thinly and touched his arm. "I'm all right. I'm glad to see you weren't arrested."

"Could've gone either way. How's your dad?"

"He's still here—in the ICU. But the doctor came out and said he was sta-ble. Out of danger. Said I should be able to see him in a little while."

Sean nodded. He watched her. "Do you want me to wait with you?"

"Do you mind?"

"Of course not. Do you want to sit down?"

They got out of their jackets and sat in the two chairs at the end of the row. They sat staring at the empty chairs across from them, at the white wall. Denise took a deep breath and let it out slowly.

"The officer said he was out on the porch," she said, "and that he crawled from his chair back into the house, or partway into the house, before he lost consciousness. A neighbor out walking his dog saw the open door, saw him lying there. That's the only reason he didn't bleed to death."

Sean didn't know what to say. He shook his head.

"I told the officer I had no idea who would shoot him," she said. "Then she told me about my restraining order on you-know-who. But I don't know why that idiot would want to shoot my dad. It makes no sense."

Sean sat staring at the wall. She turned to him.

"What did you and the other cop talk about?"

"The same. He wanted to know if I'd seen him—Mattis—since that night at the bar. At the Wheelhouse."

"Did you tell him about the diner?"

"No. I forgot about that. I told him about last night. Thursday night."

She said nothing. Watching him. Then: "Thursday night?"

"Friday morning, technically. I didn't tell you. I didn't want you to worry about it."

"What happened Friday morning technically?"

He heard himself, his voice. As if he'd gotten up and taken a seat on the other side of the hall and was listening—watching—from that distance: Telling her about Mattis following him. The fight in the street. The handgun he'd locked in the trunk.

She sat staring at him a long while and he did not look away. He saw the comprehension, the confusion behind the comprehension, and then the pain.

She was silent.

"I'm sorry, Denise. I should've told you. I should've told the police. But I thought it was about me, about him wanting to get back at me. I didn't want to go running to the cops. And I didn't want you to worry about it. I thought I could handle it. I thought I had handled it." He shook his head again. "I made a mistake. A bad one. I'm sorry."

She put her face in her hands and rubbed at it roughly.

"Fuck," she said into her hands. "I mean, just—fuck."

She dropped her hands and shook her head. She wouldn't look at him, and he felt sick to his stomach. He thought there must be something else he could say, something to make her look at him, but just then one of the ICU doors swung mechanically inward and a tall man in green scrubs and surgeon's cap stepped out into the hallway. He stood before the two of them and said warmly to Sean, "Hello, I'm Dr. Felderman."

Sean looked at him. His white mask had been pulled down under his chin and though he'd not shaved in some hours his mustache was neatly shaped. Middle fifties, early sixties. Gray-frame glasses with red accents but otherwise not a drop of red on him.

"Hello, Doctor. I'm Sean Courtland."

"He drove me here," said Denise.

"Ah," said the doctor. "Well, you can see your father now, Ms. Givens, but I'm afraid it's family only."

"All right," she said, and stood. Sean stood too.

"You don't have to wait," she said. She caught his eye briefly.

"I can wait."

She shook her head. "Just . . . take my car. We'll figure it out later."

She followed the doctor and did not look back.

He'd walked clear of the emergency entrance and was ordering a ride on his phone when a woman coming from the parking lot stepped up to him in her bootheels, in her dark winter coat. He looked up from the phone and met her eyes.

"Sean Courtland," she said.

"Detective Viegas."

"Are you here with Denise Givens?"

"Yes ma'am. I drove her here. She's with her dad. Who I guess you know all about by now."

"Yes. Are you leaving?"

"Yes ma'am. She kind of insisted."

"Where's your truck?"

"We drove her car. I was just setting up a ride."

"Where's your truck?" she said again, and he looked at her. This was not about Henry Givens. Or not only about him.

"My truck is in Minnesota," he said finally.

Viegas studied his face. "Did you loan it to him?"

"Yes. For the weekend. He decided he'd go home and see if he could straighten things out himself."

"You didn't return my calls," she said plainly. Factually.

"No ma'am. I didn't want to interfere with his business if I could help it. Other than helping him get home."

"He didn't get home, Sean."

Sean looked at her. "What does that mean?"

"It means he didn't get home. It means your truck is out by the Highway 14 Bridge, down at the bottom of the embankment."

"What?"

"It looks like he was forced off the road."

Sean was shaking his head.

"And then he was shot," said the detective.

"No—"

"I've just come from seeing him," she said. "I'm sorry to tell you he didn't survive, Sean."

Sean opened his mouth but said nothing. A terrible wind was blowing in his inner ears. Like the roar of the sea in a conch.

"I think I'm gonna be sick," he said.

"Come over here. There's a trashcan."

He didn't move.

Viegas watched him. "Are you all right?"

"No."

"Can you answer a question for me?"

"I don't know."

She took something from her pocket and handed it to him and he took it in fingers that were not his own and stared at it. It was her business card. The one she'd given him that he'd given to Dan.

"Why did he have this?" she said.

"Because I wrote my number on it."

"Why did you do that?"

"Because," he began—and came up empty.

Dead—?

Dan Young is dead?

Some days ago he'd seen him for the first time in the diner. Seen him again outside the diner. Had given him a ride . . .

"He was going to help me on this job," he said.

"Did you know him?"

"Did I know him?"

"Before that?"

"No. We just . . . met."

"How did you meet?"

"What?"

"How did you meet?"

"At the diner. The . . ." He shook his head. "He looked like somebody who might be looking for work. I gave him a ride to his motel. I wrote my number on this card."

"When was this?"

He had to think. "Monday?"

"This Monday?"

"This Monday," he said. "Jesus," he said. "Dead—?"

She watched him. "Do you know who might have done it?"

Reflexively he shook his head—who would do such a thing?

Unless he'd not told you everything. Unless it wasn't just the police or his family looking for him.

But then, looking into the detective's eyes, Sean saw the beginning of the truth, and his mind fled away from it. Would not allow it. "Oh God," he said.

She nodded very slightly. "We found him too, Sean. On the other side of the river, in his car, with a service pistol in his hand."

Sean stood helpless as she went on. He didn't think he could hear her over the noise in his ears and he was watching her lips as she said, *He shot Henry Givens, Sean. Then he saw your truck and ran it off the road and shot Dan Young. And then he drove across the river and shot himself.*

PART III

33.

JULY AND AUGUST *were never easy in that house. There was no central air and there were no window units and only the rattling box fans to move the hot air in and out of the rooms, and on some nights the only relief to be found was in the cellar. But spiders and mice and even a snake or two had discovered the same thing and among the three people still living in the house, and then among the two after the old woman died, only one would make his bed down there at night, lying in his underwear on the mold-freckled canvas of the old US Army cot, the doors of the cellar bulkhead thrown open that the bats and other small creatures might freely enter and move about him where he lay smoking in the dark.*

On this morning in mid-July it was no small creature who emerged from the cellar, returning to the wild, and neither was it the man who sometimes slept among them as he might once have done in the jungles of Asia; it was a man fully dressed for work in long sleeves and indeed already at it, already sweating as he stepped to the rear of the pickup truck and dragged from the dusty jumble in its bed another three cinderblocks, stacked them on the tailgate and, with the stack tipped against his chest, turned and carried the blocks down the four wooden steps into the darkness. Within a few seconds of his descent the man emerged again and returned to the tailgate, stacked another three cinderblocks, hefted them, descended once more into the cellar, and he was still down there when the sheriff's cruiser pulled into the drive and the same deputy who'd been out a few weeks before, in June, stepped from the car and came around it through a haze of gravel dust.

The young deputy, Tomás Viegas, stopped and stood in the early light, the early quiet, his gaze taking in the pickup truck, its load of cinderblock, then the open cellar bulkhead.

He waited. At last the man in the cellar rose in four gritty steps into the light and stood looking at the deputy. Like a man waiting to be told what to do next.

Viegas nodded and said, Mr. Devereaux.

Deputy, said Devereaux.

Getting an early start, looks like, said Viegas. And though the same could be said of Viegas, Devereaux did not say it. When the deputy tipped back his hatbrim and looked at the sky and said it was gonna be a hot one, Devereaux looked too. He took hold of his own forearm and rolled the denim sleeve back and forth. As if nagged by something there. Then he moved to the truck and dragged a cinderblock grinding over the bed onto the tailgate.

Viegas stepped up to the truck and rested one arm on the side panel, as though to take his ease. Whatever the impression this made on Devereaux, if any, the deputy was in fact tired; he'd not slept and he was up at that hour because of it.

Looks like you're building you a wall down there, he said after a minute.

Devereaux selected a second block, stacked it and squared it to the first. I got a wall that's leaking pretty bad, he said.

Leaking? said Viegas. He raised his face to the sky again. It hasn't rained in weeks.

Yep, said Devereaux. That's when you do it, when it's dry down there.

Ah, said Viegas.

Devereaux stood holding the third block. As though contemplating some optimal placement of it.

You doing this all by yourself? said Viegas. All these blocks?

Yes, sir. It's not that hard, once you get going.

Viegas unleaned himself from the truck and moved to the cellar bulkhead. Cool, dank air rose from the opening. A good amount of fresh dirt seemed to have been tracked, or even spilled, on the wooden steps. Fresh dirt all around the bulkhead too. No bootprints anywhere but Devereaux's own, going up and down.

I thought maybe your uncle might be helping you out, he said, and when there was no reply he turned back to the truck.

Devereaux stood there, holding the cinderblock in his hands, something faraway and dumb in his face, in his blue eyes. Something childlike. Or like a dog who has come to expect to be kicked for no reason at all.

No? said Viegas.

Devereaux stood there. No, what?

He's not helping you?

No, sir. He's not around.

Ah, said Viegas. I was hoping to catch him. Have a word with him. He looked toward the bulkhead again. And back to Devereaux, who stood as before, holding the cinderblock.

We haven't seen that boy around here, Devereaux said.

What boy?

Devereaux stared at him. The one you had that picture of.

Why don't you go on and set that block down? Viegas said. Take a break.

Devereaux didn't move at first. Then he turned and placed the cinderblock on the stack and squared it carefully.

Where's he at? said Viegas.

Devereaux turned back to him.

Your uncle, said Viegas.

Devereaux turned the sleeve on his forearm. No idea, Deputy. He just up and goes off sometimes.

Where's he go off to?

No idea.

How long's he been gone?

Devereaux appeared to give this some thought. He let go his forearm and scratched at his jaw.

Four—no, five days.

Viegas stood with his hands on his belt, nodding slowly.

What's it about, Deputy?

How's that?

What's it about?

Viegas looked toward the bulkhead. I expect it'll keep, he said.

I could give him a message. When he gets back.

That's all right. He turned back to Devereaux. But since I'm here, maybe I could ask you something else.

Devereaux leaned into the bed and dragged another block over the metal. He aligned it on the tailgate, stared at it. Then he turned toward Viegas.

All right, he said.

I understand you used to work at the junior high. Harding Junior High.

Yes, sir. I was on the maintenance crew.

Did you know, or do you remember, a boy by the name of David Parnell?

Parnell?

Yes. David Parnell.

Devereaux seemed to concentrate. Was he a kind of redheaded boy?

Yes. Bright red hair.

Yeah, I remember that boy.

The deputy looked at the ground a minute, the dry and faded weeds, then looked up again. *That boy hanged himself last night in a tree,* he said.

Devereaux said nothing. Then finally: Dead?

Yes.

Devereaux looked off toward the woods. Whereabouts?

Whereabouts?

Where'd he do it?

On his folks' property, said Viegas. *Didn't leave a note or anything like that, and his parents, they were just—He shook his head. We talked to some folks at the school. The principal there. The boy's teachers. One of them, a Ms. Wheeler, mentioned a certain incident she witnessed, back in April, out on the ballfield after school.*

Viegas stood watching Devereaux. Devereaux staring back.

Some older boys were picking on the Parnell boy, Viegas said. *Calling him names, and she said you came out and broke it up.*

He watched Devereaux. You remember that?

Devereaux nodded. I remember. They were pushing him around and I came on out and told 'em to knock it off and get on home.

That was it?

That was it. The boys went on home. Or went away, anyway.

You didn't say anything to the boy—to Parnell?

I might've asked him was he all right.

And what did he say?

Devereaux shrugged. I don't recall he said much of anything. Just kind of turned and walked away.

Viegas nodded. So he didn't say anything to you? Didn't stop and yell anything?

Devereaux frowned. No, sir. Not to my memory he didn't.

And then what happened?

Devereaux looked down at something and looked up again. If you're talking about me leaving that job, well, I left that job.

You were let go.

If you want to put it that way.

Viegas watched him. And you didn't have any other interactions with the Parnell boy?

No, sir.

Did your uncle?

Devereaux's head jerked back, as if from a passing bee. His hands remained in his pockets. My uncle? he said. He frowned and shook his head. I don't know why he would, he said. He didn't have interactions with much of anyone except me and my grandma, and she's gone now.

Yes, I was sorry to hear about that. I'm sorry for your loss.

Devereaux nodded, and that was all.

Anyway, Mr. Devereaux. The crux of it is, the reason I wanted to talk to your uncle, is this.

He reached into his trouser pocket and pulled something forth and held it up between thumb and forefinger. It shone dully in the sun.

Devereaux leaned and squinted.

Here, take it, said Viegas, and Devereaux unpocketed one hand and took the lighter from Viegas's fingers.

Do you recognize it?

It's a Zippo lighter.

Yes. With the Marine Corps emblem on it. It was in the boy's bedroom, in one of his dresser drawers.

Devereaux studied the lighter where it lay in the palm of his hand. Or seemed to study it.

We figured he got it from some other boy, said Viegas. Or maybe stole it somewhere. Then I remembered I'd seen one just like it pretty recently.

Yeah, said Devereaux. I have too. Seen one like it pretty recently.

Viegas waited. Then he said, And where was that?

At a bar called Eddie's Place. This man I work with named Wilby had one just like it, sitting on the table there.

Viegas watched him. Did your uncle have his? Last time you saw him?

I believe he did. He smokes a lot of cigarettes. It's not something you notice, after a while.

No, said Viegas, I expect not. He turned and looked toward the garage—and looked a second time, confirming, perhaps, that the structure was indeed leaning to one side: the skewed geometry of the opening.

And that was four days ago, he said, still looking, that you last saw him?

I'd say more like five.

He turned back to Devereaux and nodded at the lighter. So it's not your uncle's.

Couldn't swear to it, Deputy. Like I said, I've seen others just like it.

Viegas nodded again. Well, he said. He held out his hand and Devereaux placed the lighter in the center of his palm. Viegas weighed it there, then slipped it back into his pocket. I appreciate you answering my questions, Mr. Devereaux.

I didn't help you much.

I didn't expect you to. I was casting my fly blindfold in the stream, as my granddad used to say.

Devereaux stood there.

Well, Viegas said. I'll let you get back to it, Mr. Devereaux.

All right, said Devereaux. I sure am sorry to hear about that boy. He shook his head. It doesn't seem like he'd know what he was doing, a boy that age.

Viegas was silent, giving these words, the consecutive, the unsolicited sentences, their due.

It sure doesn't, does it, he said. And then he turned and walked back to his cruiser, his bootheels scuffing clouds of dust from a gravel bed white as bone in the climbing sun.

34.

SATURDAY DAWNED COLD and icy in the bluffside woods, the rain from the previous day's storm having hardened overnight into a bright glaze that lay over the bare branches and the needled boughs, over the old, flattened grass of the clearing and over the boards of the little porch where Sean stood smoking. By noon when he came out again the glaze was gone and wisps of steam wandered the ground like little spirits where the sun poured into the clearing, and when he stepped out a third time, in the dusk, there was no sign that there'd been ice that morning and little sign of the storm itself. The air smelled of pine needles, that heated turpentine scent that always raised in his mind the mountains of Colorado at midsummer. Pine trees upon pine trees. The high, breathless trails with their soft, rust-colored carpets of needles. His burning lungs as he tried to keep pace with his sister on the strange and random path.

He sat on the edge of the porch with his feet on the step below, the damp and cold seeping into his socks. Watching distractedly his hands where they hung between his knees in the last pink light of the day. Distantly he heard a large, windy rustling, as of a new storm front coming on through the woods, but there was no wind and still the sound grew more distinct, more expansive. The twilight abruptly deepened and he looked up to behold a moving blackness in the sky—liquid and undulate and faintly iridescent like oil, a great roiling cloud, convulsing in waves of darker and lighter black as it swept from west to east. His first thought was bats, disgorging by the thousands—millions—from a cave in the bluffs. But the sound, enormous and constant though it was, distorted by mass replication though it was, was unmistakably the sound of birds in flight. A great feathery chittering sky of little black birds, twisting and thickening and thinning all together as schools of fish do in the sea.

He thought the birds would pass in a few seconds but they didn't. They kept coming, dark, thick, rushing, morphing, innumerable and singular.

He'd heard the stormdoor open and shut but had not connected it to the movements of another human being until Parnell was standing beside him, likewise craning at the sky. And neither had he realized, until then, that he himself had left the porch and was standing in his socks on the cold ground.

He and the old man were silent, watching. At last Sean said, "What are they?"

"Starlings."

"That is one hell of a lot of birds."

"It's a murmuration."

"A what?"

"A murmuration. Like a murder of crows. When it's starlings it's a murmuration."

They watched. Listening. A windy susurrant chittering, on and on.

"They can also be called a constellation," said Parnell. "Also a scourge."

"A scourge of starlings."

"Mostly it's people who hate them who use that one."

"Why do they hate them?"

"Because they are nasty little bastards, every last one of them. They come into a nesting area and wait till some other bird has made a nest and then they attack the bird and drive it out. They take up other birds' eggs and drop them on the ground. I knew a watcher one time saw a starling dangle a string in front of a redheaded woodpecker's nesting hole, and when the woodpecker poked its head out the starling killed it with one jab of its beak."

They watched the birds.

"There must be millions," Sean said.

"Maybe. A creature that lets other creatures do all the work and then runs them off is a pretty successful kind of creature, I guess."

The words pushed Dan Young into his mind again. The day before—Friday—they'd been finishing up at Devereaux's. Hauling those machines up the stairs. Scraping up that crud. The kid's sock.

Dan had said something about Devereaux. What was it—?

The blackness of the birds grew thinner across the sky and then fell to tatters. The last few individuals passed over and were gone, and the two men stood looking at the quiet and empty sky, at a twilight the brighter and bluer for the dark passing of the starlings.

"All those birds you just saw," said Parnell, "plus many millions more, all came from eighty birds set loose in Central Park in 1890."

Sean turned to Parnell, who still watched the sky. "How do you know?"

"Because they didn't exist in this country before then. Before that they were Europe's problem. Then this one fella in New York had eighty of them shipped over, and he set them loose in Central Park."

"Why'd he do that?"

"Shakespeare."

"Shakespeare?"

Parnell turned his attention from the sky to the shadowed woods. "This fella got it into his head to introduce all the birds Shakespeare ever mentioned into Central Park, and that's what he did. And them little devils have been multiplying and killing off native populations ever since."

"All my pretty ones," said Sean.

"How's that?"

Sean shook his head.

"Thing is," said Parnell, "you look at just one of them and it is a pretty bird. Very pretty. Not black at all but a dark, dark blue with little white spots on it like stars, and other colors bright and iridescent like a hummingbird. Whipsmart, too. A starling can imitate better than a mockingbird, and not just other birds but anything it hears on a regular basis. Cows. Sheep. Barking dogs. Sounds of city traffic. Honking horns and the like. But then again," the old man mused, "you have to consider that a less clever bird might not be so good at being so nasty."

Sean remembered he was holding a cigarette. When he lifted it the long ash dropped and there was nothing left to smoke. He bent down and turned the butt in the wet grass and stood again holding it in his fingers.

"You forgot your boots," said Parnell.

"I know it. I had to get a better look at those birds."

"Same here."

They both looked up again, the sky still empty, already a deeper shade of blue. Or not quite empty, the points of the constellations beginning to surface in the blue heights.

"You seem to know a lot about birds," Sean said, and Parnell shrugged. He and Mrs. Parnell used to go out and look at them with the binoculars, he said. Back when there were more of them to see in those woods.

The mention of Parnell's wife drew a silence behind it. Sean lifted one foot and looked at it. The sagging, darkened sock. He set it down again.

"You haven't got your truck back yet, I see," Parnell said.

"No sir. Not yet."

"But you'll get it back."

Sean nodded. "Once they've gotten what they need from it. And cleaned it up."

"They clean it up?"

"So they say. Some kind of special biohazard cleaning. I don't know. I don't know that I even want it back."

Parnell cleared his throat. He rubbed at the back of his neck.

"I don't need it to move out, though," Sean said. "I can fit what I've got here in a car. I'll just have someone come and pick me up."

"I wasn't worried about that," Parnell said. "In fact, I wanted to let you know you could take longer if you needed it. Under the circumstances."

"Thanks. I appreciate that," said Sean. "But it's probably best if I stick to the schedule."

"All right. I can give you a lift myself, if that makes it easier."

"It's no trouble to get a ride. Thank you, though."

"Well."

Sean looked at the sky once more, the stars, and let out his breath.

"How was it he was driving your truck?" Parnell said. "If you don't mind me asking," he added, and Sean turned and met his gaze. Sadness in those eyes but not for Sean, and not for Dan Young even, but a deep old private sadness, a sorrow that no one could comprehend unless it was Mrs. Parnell, who must have the same or even greater sorrow in her eyes.

"I loaned it to him so he could drive home and see his family," Sean said, "over in Minnesota. He was going to do that and come back tomorrow. He was going to talk to the sheriff over there and get him to call that detective and tell her she could stop looking for him."

Parnell watched him as he spoke, then looked off toward the woods.

"That was generous of you," said the old man.

Sean stood a long while. "It wasn't generous," he said. "I wanted to stop her from coming back here. I wanted to stop her from showing up at the Devereaux house."

"If that were strictly true," Parnell said, "you might've just called the detective yourself. Or had him—Dan—call her."

Sean lifted the cigarette butt, looked at it and lowered it again. "I don't see how putting him in that situation can be considered generous. By any stretch."

"You loaned the man your truck," said Parnell. "You didn't put him in a situation."

"I should've driven him over there myself."

"Then maybe you'd both be dead."

Sean said nothing.

"Anyhow," said Parnell. "I'm sorry about it. He seemed like a nice young man."

Sean nodded absently. "He bought you pie once. You and Mrs. Parnell."

"Pie . . . ?" Parnell searched his memory. "That was him?"

"That was him. It was before he met you. Before he even knew you were my landlord."

"Why would he do that?"

"I asked him the same thing. I guess he just wanted to."

Parnell stood thinking. "Why didn't you tell me about that before?"

"Before what?"

"Before," said Parnell. "After the detective was here."

Before I gave you the boot, he was saying without saying it.

Sean shrugged. "It was kinda far from my mind at the time."

Parnell took a breath and let it out. Sean thought he would turn to go then, but he didn't.

"I could've told her where you were working," he said. "The detective. And maybe if she'd found you there, found the two of you, none of this would've happened. I've thought about that."

Sean said nothing. Then: "I gotta say I doubt it, Mr. Parnell. I doubt anything would've changed—except me not getting a dime out of Mr. Devereaux."

"Maybe," said Parnell.

Sean shook his head. "I think about it and I can't understand the progression of things," he said. "How one thing led to another. But I know it did, and what it all comes back to is me. If I'd never come to this town, none of it ever would've happened. And that's just a fact."

"You might be right about that," Parnell said. "It wouldn't have happened exactly the way it did. But you coming here didn't make it happen. Those other things, those other people, they were already here. Most likely it all would've led to some kind of trouble anyway. With or without you."

Sean gave no indication he'd heard this. He stood as if watching a beetle make its slow way across the ground, but he saw no beetle and not even the ground. He saw Blaine Mattis. Saw Denise. Henry Givens. Dan Young.

Dead.

Dan was dead.

Just yesterday they'd been finishing the job. In that basement. He'd said something about Devereaux.

"Anyhow," said Parnell. "I expect your feet are about froze by now." He shifted his weight but did not turn away. "I won't tell you things will look better in the morning," he said, "because they won't. Not in my experience. In my experience you wake up and it's still there and it's worse, because for a little while you forgot."

Devereaux had been eleven when he'd moved into the house, Dan had said.

And how the hell do you know that?

Because he told me.

You talked to him?

Yeah.

What about?

I'll tell you later.

Parnell sniffled and passed a knuckle under his nose. "What I was gonna say was, you are gonna think what you are gonna think about what you might've done different. But the fact is, all you did was try to give that man a way to go home to his family. The rest of it . . . hell, that was just bad luck."

"Yes sir. I wish I could see it that way."

"Saying it doesn't amount to much, does it?"

"No sir."

"All right then," said the old man, turning away. "You go on inside now."

"Yes sir," said Sean. And after a long minute alone under the stars he turned and walked back to the cottage in his wet, cold socks.

35.

THE DRIVER'S NAME was Amee, she was a student at the university, and she took Sean to the ER lot as instructed and he thanked her and got out of the car.

Denise's little red Honda was not there. Though she might have moved it to another lot when they'd transferred her father out of the ICU.

He took the elevator to the third floor and walked down the hallway and found the room and stood outside the open door, listening. No voices, no movement that he could hear. No TV. He looked in and rapped his knuckles lightly on the door. "Mr. Givens—?"

"Yop," said the man in the bed, "I'm awake."

Sean stepped into the room. Givens lay with his head and torso raised, and Sean would not have known it was him. His thick dark hair was in disarray and the silver in it seemed to have spread, until he looked, at first glance, like a man who'd been transformed by lightning, or a great fright. He'd not been shaved, and above the whiskers his face shone with a dull waxiness. Puffy, drowsing eyes looked out from darkened wells, unrecognizing at first, then brightening with something of the old intelligence, the old slyness. He raised his hand and beckoned and Sean stepped forward.

A rolling tray table on that side of the bed kept him from coming closer. On it lay a hardback book, reading glasses, a lidded plastic cup with an oversize bendy straw, a box of tissues.

"Mr. Givens, how are you doing?"

"Never better," he said, "as you can see." He looked down at himself and made some adjustment to the thin gown. Only one of his arms, the one he raised to make the adjustment, had been fed through the short sleeve; the other arm and shoulder were left exposed so that you could easily see, and access, the Ace bandages that wound about his upper chest and all about the bulging shoulder and upper arm. This same arm was bent at the elbow and bound to his stomach by still more wrappings.

"But never mind how I'm doing," said Givens, and he looked more soberly at Sean. "I can't tell you how sorry I am about that young man. Dan Young. I don't even know what to say. It's just a goddam hell of a sad thing."

"Yes sir," said Sean. "It could've been worse."

"Yes, it could've been you."

"I was thinking of you, actually. I was thinking of Denise."

Givens shook his head. "I'm not allowing myself to think about that. Nothing good can come of it. Can it?"

"No sir. How's your shoulder?"

"Shoulder? I'm here for the mummification package. In a day or two they start filling the viscera jars."

Sean worked up a smile. "I hope you don't mind me coming to see you," he said.

"Why would I mind?"

He thought about how to answer that and said nothing.

Givens watched him. "I gather she hasn't been in touch with you."

"No sir. Not since the other night."

"Since you told her about Mattis and his gun."

"Yes sir. I would've told you too if they'd have let me see you."

Givens raised his free hand and swatted mildly at the air. "Don't worry yourself about that."

"I should've told Denise about it. And you. I should've told the police. She has every right to be mad at me. You both do. If that's even the right word for it."

Givens watched him in silence. Then he said, "Did you know I taught that boy in high school?"

"No sir, I didn't."

"I did. Tried to. The lights were on but nobody was home. Not for science, anyway. He was bright enough, but it didn't come out in any productive kind of way. A talker. A swaggerer. If she'd ever told me she was seeing him, I'd have . . . Well, I don't know what I'd have done. I learned a long time ago that the less I say, the sooner she comes to her senses. When she was a little girl—" He stopped himself and shook his head. "If she knew I was telling stories about her as a little girl she'd punch me in the shoulder."

"The last thing I ever wanted to do was hurt her. Or you."

"I know that, Sean. She does too. She's just gone down into a bit of a bunker right now. She'll come up again before too long."

Sean was silent.

Givens reached across his chest to scratch at his bandages. "This straitjacket they've got me in reminds me of Shorty Lovinsky. Remember him?"

"Yes sir. The contractor you worked for."

"Yes. I think I told you he liked to tell stories."

"Yes sir."

"Yes. So this one time—sit down there, Sean."

"I'm all right."

"Sit. It's hurting my neck looking up at you. Just push that blanket and pil-low out of the way."

Sean scooted them to the back of the chair beside the bed and sat forward on the cushion. Where she had tried to sleep. If he were alone he would've held the pillow to his face.

This time it was the story of an old man named Garth Dickey who'd hired Shorty Lovinsky to repair his stairs, the old man one day telling Shorty a story about his mad uncle Ephraim, who'd gotten shell-shocked in the war, over in France, who'd fallen in love with an American nurse named Lillian and mar-ried her and brought her back to Wisconsin, but whose shell shock only got worse in the years to come—headaches so bad he couldn't get out of bed. The tremors. Worst of all the night terrors.

Givens coughed and reached for the lidded plastic cup on the tray and raised it slowly. The oversize bendy straw wagged about in the air until he seized it in his lips. He sipped a good while and returned the cup to the tray.

"Night after night," Givens went on, "Uncle Ephraim would scream about the gods trying to tear out his arms. Not God—*the gods*. Went on like that for years. Then one night he's thrashing around in the bed, yelling and swinging his arms, and Lillian tells him, 'Ephraim Dickey, quit that, you quit that right now or you'll wish it was just the gods.' And he wakes up and that very morning he goes to see his doctor, whose name was Grubbs."

"Dr. Grubbs," said Sean.

"Dr. Grubbs. So. Grubbs runs his tests and finds out it wasn't shell shock, all these years—or not entirely shell shock: Uncle Ephraim has a brain tumor on his right frontal lobe. The tumor might kill him, Grubbs says, but the surgery might kill him too. So Uncle Ephraim goes home and talks it over with Lillian. They talk all night and when the dawn comes she takes his head in her hands and says, 'Ephraim, we must get this bad thing out of you.' And so Ephraim goes back and tells the doctor what she said and Grubbs looks at him a long while and tells him, 'Ephraim, Lillian has been gone two years now, God rest her soul.'"

Givens fell silent. He lay without moving in the bed, without blinking, and Sean remembered the picture of the mother—Denise's mother, in her headkerchief. Her sunken eyes.

He waited for him to go on—he knew there was more—but Givens just lay back on his pillow and closed his eyes.

"I'm sorry, Sean. I just suddenly got very tired."

"It's all right," Sean said. He sat there—then got to his feet. Givens was silent. Breathing. Sean turned to go.

"Wasn't your fault, Sean."

"Sir?"

The older man's eyes were closed. "What happened to Dan Young," he said. "Wasn't your fault. It was just . . . the gods."

Sean waited, but Givens said no more.

36.

HE WAS AWAKE at dawn, but it was nine thirty before he got on the road. Cool, clean morning air with the smell of spring in it whistling in the near window and drawing coolly over his face and sucking from the cab the smell of bleach, or whatever it was they'd used to disinfect the interior.

He'd retrieved the truck from the impound lot on Friday afternoon, taking the keys from the gaunt old lot keeper as if they'd made a deal, *She's all yours, son,* and the keeper telling him *You cain't get in her that way, you got to get in her the other side,* and Sean going around and climbing in from the passenger side and pulling the door shut behind him and crabbing across the bench seat above the stains, washed out though they were, and his eyes beginning to burn almost at once. His window would not open more than a crack and he'd leaned back across the seat to crank down the passenger window, then driven away at speed for what breeze it gave, back to the Fairfield Inn, and parked the truck there with the one window down and the other gapped. And there it had sat all weekend, until eight thirty this morning when he'd gone at the driver's-side door with the flatbar and the maul that were in the Knaack box where he'd left them, managing finally to wrench the door open, then forcing it open and shut many times until he could do so without the tools.

Monday morning this was. One week and three days since the shootings. An entire week of not finishing the Devereaux job, close as he was to finishing. When he tried to call, the house line only rang and rang, no message service. And neither did the old man call him. His voicemails were from detectives. From Viegas. One from Denise Givens, calling to say she was sorry about Dan

Young, that she felt bad about how she'd reacted that night, at the hospital, she'd been somewhat out of her mind, that she was here if he wanted to talk . . . finally that she'd like to hear from him if for no other reason than to know he was all right. The message was accompanied by a text: *R U OK? Left a message. Call when u can.*

And he'd begun a reply, staring at the empty box a long time before typing *I'm OK. Just need a little time, but will call u.* He read the words and thought them true, thought them reasonable, until the moment he sent them, and then it was as if he'd stepped out onto stairs where there were no steps—no light, no railing, nothing but the drop.

He heard Dan Young's voice, two words: *Call her.*

But he didn't. He'd told her he needed a little time. And he did. She would understand—hadn't she needed time herself after he'd told her about Mattis and the gun?

Dan said nothing, and Sean looked over, fully expecting to see him sitting there in the passenger seat, shaking his head.

He was nearly to the bridge and he thought he would see some evidence or remnant of that night—yellow police tape, skidmarks, a guardrail twisted back on itself. But he saw none of these, and when he braked to pull over, a black SUV surged by with a blast of horn and he saw a man in a white shirt and tie thrusting a gun at him.

Not a gun, in fact, only his middle finger. The man's face contorted with anger.

Sean got out and stood looking down the bank, toward the bridge, and back the other way.

Dan wouldn't have known the Monte Carlo's headlights in the rearview, would not have known who was racing up alongside him in the black car, in the rain, who was forcing him off the road—the truck jostling down the embankment, Dan somehow not rolling her. Sitting down there in the Chevy, dazed, trying the door, moving to the passenger side. All the while someone coming down the embankment in the rain, in the dark.

One bridge away from Minnesota. From home.

Sean got back in the Chevy and drove on, crossing the river to the Minnesota side, where he saw no signs of the black Monte Carlo either, no traces of police or forensic activity of any kind. All he knew, from the Minnesota sheriff, was that the investigation had been straightforward, the autopsies without surprises, the firearm identification conclusive, the bodies released to the families.

Somewhere, even Mattis had a family. A mother who grieved him.

Sean drove due west on Route 16, a two-lane highway that kept a smaller river, the Upper Black Root, just off its right-hand side, mimicking its bends and loops, as if the road's builders simply went as the river went, deeper into the state on nature's own course, passing through the small Midwestern towns that lay cupped in the horseshoes of the river like little fiefdoms in their moats. It was just beyond one such town that he saw the sign and turned off from the highway into the countryside and there, surrounded on all sides by farmland glistening black with the thaw, lay the cemetery.

Go through the gate, the sheriff had said, and Sean walked through the gate. *At the fork in the path go right, north, and at about the third or fourth oak tree start looking to the left.* He didn't need to look long: the plot was new and the sod a darker shade of green than the surrounding grass, which had not come in yet and would not for some weeks. There was no stone, but Dan Young had been buried next to his father, who had died when Dan and his twin, Marky, had been boys.

The father's stone was black polished marble with veins of white running through the black. The inscription and dates chiseled simply.

ROGER WILLIAM YOUNG

BELOVED HUSBAND & FATHER

At the foot of the black stone stood two sets of flowers in square glass vases: fresh-looking arrangements of yellow lilies and orange roses, and one bright sunflower in one bouquet with its dark face turned to the sun itself—*son-flower.* And it was the brightness of the flowers that delayed his noticing the large blue coffee mug that sat on the ledge of the stone's plinth.

He stepped forward to see what might be inside, and there was something— a bolt. Thick hexagonal head and a half-inch or five-eighths thread, maybe an inch and a quarter in length. The brassy coloring of newness. An oily, automotive look to it.

He got down in a squat and turned the mug on the stone with a gritty sound. BIG DAM MUG printed on the mug's curvature in blocky white lettering. He stared at it, and turned the mug again to reveal the image of the Hoover Dam.

He laughed.

What day was that—that Dan had told him about the Tierneys of the Hoover Dam, the father and son who'd died ten years apart to the day? He and Dan had been talking in the parking lot of the Fairfield Inn. Then they'd gone back to Devereaux's to move the machines upstairs . . . They'd driven to the Parnells' and he'd watched Dan drive away in the truck, going home.

The same day. Jesus. All the same day.

He was quiet. Still in his squat. Bright nails of pain shooting through his knee.

At last he said, "Dan, I don't even know what to say. Except I'm sorry you ever met me."

He hung his head and stared at the grass between his boots—the individual blades that had been grown elsewhere and brought here in slabs of sod, and the slabs fitted so neatly into the shape of the grave.

"I'm going to go see your mom and your brother now," he said. "I wish like hell you were going with me." He looked up again. Then he took the mug by the handle and lifted it in a silent cheers. The bolt rolled about with a musical sound, strangely loud and bright in the silence of that place, and then he replaced the mug as he'd found it.

FROM PERHAPS A half mile away he saw the farmhouse, and as he came around the bend he saw the green wagon in the drive and the blue truck and he slowed for the turn. His heart was thudding and he wanted a cigarette but he could not light one now, it would have to wait.

He pulled up behind the blue truck, leaving room for the wagon to back out should it need to, and cut the engine. He sat looking at the house, the truck—and his thudding heart went cold. Would she know the Chevy? Would she know it was the truck her son had been driving?

And why would you bring this truck to the woman's house?

Panic rose in him and he thought to back out, drive down the road, ditch it somewhere and walk back. But then: "Relax," he said aloud. "She knows you're coming. She had to figure you would drive your own damn truck."

He got out and came forward in the crushed gravel to look at the blue truck. A Ford F-150 four-by-four. It had its dents and scrapes, and among these in the bed panel of the passenger's side was the bullet hole. The indented gray circle of primer paint and the smaller black circle of the hole itself. No sign of rust. A film of weather and gravel dust lay over the area, as it did the rest of the truck.

Sean stood staring at it. Trying to imagine how this bullet hole in this truck had led Dan Young to another truck and another gun. The two guns—the two shooters—as unconnected as they could possibly be.

But were they? Unconnected? Or had there been something in Dan Young that brought violence his way—or delivered him to it?

The same thing that's in you, he thought. The path that's not random at all, but the only path.

And was it all one path? He and Dan heading for each other from opposite directions?

If that were true, then why was Dan dead and not him? What god or gods decided that one?

A stormdoor creaked and he turned to watch the woman, Dan's mother, step out onto the porch in a yellow raincoat, jeans, rubberized boots. Like a woman accustomed to walking out into storms and not the calm, blue-skied day it was. She stood squinting at him, then at the Chevy parked behind her son's truck, at him again. Silvered shoulder-length hair and a roundish smooth face made her look both younger and older than she might have been: midforties on the young side, late fifties on the old.

She came down the porchsteps and he moved to meet her.

She stopped short of him, her hands in her jacket pockets, and he stopped and stood likewise. Holding her gaze, her mild blue eyes, as she took him in. His neck beating dully with heartbeat. His voice jammed up in his throat.

"You must be Sean," she said.

"Yes ma'am," he said. "I'm Sean Courtland."

"I'm Rachel Young." Her eyes searching his with a kind of benign intensity until he had to look down. When he looked up again she was watching him still.

"I'm sorry I missed his service," he said. "The sheriff said it would be better if I . . ."

She took her hands from her pockets and stepped up to him and he bent to her so that she might put her arms around him and pull him close. She held him, only that, and he held her too, and waited until she released him before he released her. She stood at arm's length with her hands on his upper arms, her thumbs in his biceps through the jacket.

"I know what happened, Sean," she said. "The sheriff told me everything. It wasn't your fault. It was just a terrible, random mistake."

"Yes ma'am. It was that. But I wouldn't call it exactly random."

"Why not?"

Because we were on the same path.

"Because I had the chance to call the police," he said. "Because I knew about that gun."

"Lots of people have guns. This is America."

"Yes, but not all of them are angry and jealous and stupid."

She stared at him. "Do you watch the news?"

He held her eyes. "Mrs. Young, no matter what you say, I'm still going to try to tell you how sorry I am. If Dan had never met me, he'd still be alive."

She sighed and looked at her son's truck. Or perhaps at Sean's. Or at something altogether invisible to him.

"Sean," she said at last. "Will you come inside for a cup of tea?"

IT WAS AN old farmhouse and it smelled of its years, a fustiness that emanated from the walls and floors, from the basement and attic. But also a clean lemon scent of waxed floors, polished wood.

She stood at the counter pouring hot water into two mugs.

"It was my grandfolks' house," she was saying. "They came here from Sweden. Then it was my dad's, and then Marky and I moved here after Danny went away. The first time he went away. Ten years ago."

She brought the two mugs to the table along with a small plate of store-bought cookies.

"And your people?" she said, sitting. "Where do they come from?"

"I think Ireland, originally," he said. "But since then Wisconsin, as far as I know. Grandparents. Great-grandparents."

"And your folks?"

"Still in Wisconsin."

"Brothers? Sisters?"

Sean sipped at the tea. "One sister."

"Older, younger?"

"Older by three years."

Mrs. Young smiled. "She must have doted on you."

"Doted," Sean said, as if trying out the word. He stirred the tea with the spoon.

"No?" said Mrs. Young. "Not so much?"

"Maybe when we were little. Mostly what I remember is a girl who was always going somewhere, and as fast as she could get there." He looked up at Mrs. Young. "She was an athlete. A track star."

Mrs. Young watched him. "And you were not?"

"Me? No."

She smiled. As though she'd understood something he hadn't said. Or didn't think he'd said.

"Danny and Marky are twins," she said. "Did he tell you that?"

Are.

Sean nodded. "Yes, he did."

"Before they were born the doctor said one of the babies had a bad heart, and we might lose them both if we let the pregnancy go on. He thought we should terminate one and give the other baby a chance. And we almost did it. We almost did that."

She put a hand on her chest and patted there softly.

"But then we went to another doctor," she went on, "got more tests, and we decided to go ahead and have them both. And Danny, he had a heart murmur, sure enough. They didn't think he'd make it but he did. He grew and he got strong, and it was Marky—" She looked at Sean. "Did he tell you about Marky?"

"Yes, he did. He said he was a genius mechanic."

She nodded, and her eyes shone the more brightly.

She gathered her tea bag in her spoon and wound the string and squeezed out the tea, and Sean did the same. They set the spoons and tea bags on the cookie plate.

He looked around at the kitchen woodwork: The rich old hand-planed Doug fir cabinetry. The wide cuts of trim and baseboard in the same darkened wood—perhaps the same tree, felled on that land by some long-ago Swede whose sense of dimension must have come from the size and abundance of his timber.

"And you," she said. "You're a carpenter."

"Yes ma'am."

"How did you get into that?"

"My father was a contractor. I just kind of fell into it."

"Danny was going to be an engineer. Did he tell you that?"

"An engineer? No, he never mentioned that."

"Dams and bridges. He was taking classes at the college."

She didn't say what happened to dams and bridges, and she didn't have to. The girl in the river ten years ago.

"Big Dam Mug," Sean said.

"Sorry?"

"Big Dam Mug. I saw it at his—on the stone."

"His father's stone." She smiled. "That was Marky's idea. Since we don't have Danny's yet."

Sean nodded. "He was one hell of a good plumber," he said.

"Yes. His father was a plumber. And after he died—after his father died—Danny was trained by his father's old business partner, Gordon Burke. Gordon took both boys under his wing, for a while."

"Yeah, Dan mentioned that," he said.

She smiled. "I notice you call him Dan."

"He introduced himself as Dan."

"We always called him Danny," she said. "Danny and Marky."

They sipped their tea. After a time Sean said he should probably get going, and she said, looking up again, "Do you want to see his room?" In her eyes he saw Dan's—the color, yes, the way they looked at you. But also the pain, which he understood to be the pain of the last ten years of her son's life.

"Yes," he said. "I'd like that."

He followed her up the old stairs and into the bedroom. The twin bed made up. A hockey stick leaning in the corner. A chest-high bookcase with all the books on one shelf. The old plaster walls, cracked and bare of posters or hangings of any kind.

"Of course he's hardly stayed here at all since we moved," she said, "so there's not much of his childhood, his . . . personality in here, but still." She made a humming sound and looked quietly about.

"He played hockey?" Sean said.

"Oh, yes. He was like a dream on the ice."

Sean kept looking around. "It's a good room," he said. "It would be a good room to come home to." And quickly added: "If it were me—I'd be happy to come home to a room like this."

She smiled. She sighed. "Well, that's it. I don't know what's keeping Marky, but I'll let you go," she said, and had no sooner said it than there was the sound of boots on the porchsteps, boots stomping on the welcome mat, the stormdoor rattling open, boots thudding about the first floor, a man's voice calling out, "Momma—?" And again, "Momma—?"

"Up here, sweetie," she called out. "In your brother's room."

The boots abruptly changed course and came thudding up the stairs two at a time and the man called out, "Momma I saw that Chevy pickup is that his pickup where is—" The hurrying man, a big man, came around the jamb into the room and stopped and said, "Oh!" He had a mouthful of something—a cookie, the whole thing.

"Marky, slow down," said Mrs. Young. "Finish eating that cookie."

The man worked his jaws, his eyes on Sean, taking him in head to foot, and Sean saw in an instant that this was Dan's identical twin brother. And that they were not at all identical. It was in Marky's speech, of course, and in his size, but mainly it was in his eyes, which looked upon Sean as though he were some marvelous being, or a character from a story he'd long adored.

"Marky, this is Sean Courtland. Sean, this is Marky."

"Hey, Marky." Sean put out his hand and Marky came forward to grab it and shake it once up and down and let it go again. It wasn't Dan's hand, but it was the closest thing to it on this earth.

"I saw your Chevy pickup," Marky said, "that's a 1994 Chevy Silverado 1500 four-by-four with a five-point-oh-liter V-8 engine."

Sean smiled and nodded. "Dan said you were a genius with cars."

"I know every kind of car and truck," he said, "this is Danny's room."

"Yeah, your mom was just showing me."

Marky stepped up to the bookshelf. "Did you see his college books?"

"I saw his books."

"Danny was in college."

"Your mom said."

"That was a long time ago," Marky said. He went to the dresser and took up a framed photograph and turned it for Sean to see. "That's me and Danny at the lake when we was boys and Poppa was still alive and I caught this perch fish and Momma took this picture."

"That's a good-looking fish."

Marky looked at the photo again and returned it to its place on the desk. "Are you gonna stay here Sean?"

"He can't stay here, Marky. He has to go back to Wisconsin."

"Danny died in Wisconsin," said Marky.

They were all silent. "He knows, Marky," said Mrs. Young.

Marky took a breath. "Hey Sean do you want me to look at your Chevy engine?"

Sean looked at Mrs. Young, who said nothing, who waited to see what he would say.

He said, "Do you have time, Marky?"

"Sure I got time I'm not working today, Mister Wabash said take some time off Marky but I told him I don't like not working Mister Wabash and he said take some time off anyway and so I did."

"Marky," said Mrs. Young, "go downstairs and have another cookie. Sean will be down in a minute."

Marky looked at his mother. Looked at Sean. Then without a word he turned and went, and Sean stared after him, listening to his calm descent, the creaking steps, until he knew he had to face her again.

"He's so happy you came, Sean," she said. "He's so happy to meet Danny's friend."

The word struck him in the heart. They had never used the word, he and Dan.

He held her eyes. "I wasn't much of one, Mrs. Young. I don't think I even know what it means."

"To be a friend?"

"Yes."

"Really? You're here, aren't you?"

"Of course," he said a little wildly. "How could I not be?"

"Stop," she said, and took hold of his arms. "Did he tell you why he left here?"

"Some of it, yes."

"And he told you why he wanted to come home?"

"Yes."

"And so you loaned him your truck."

"I did."

"Do you loan your truck to just anyone?"

"No."

"And do you think he would've told just anyone what he told you?"

Sean shook his head. "No ma'am."

She squeezed his arms. "There," she said. "That's what it means."

37.

HE PULLED INTO Devereaux's just after eight the next morning and got out of the truck and stood holding the door. The old shepherd did not come round limping, did not bark from inside the house. No sounds from inside the house at all.

He shut the truck door with the lift-and-slam technique he'd found worked best and stood a moment longer, then walked to the back door as was his routine and without knocking turned the knob and pushed. The door didn't move. He tried again.

"God damn it," he said. All his tools, or nearly all, were inside the house.

He'd turned to go around to the front door when he heard the old man's cane rapping on the floor and he turned back. The rapping came up to the door, the deadbolt clocked back and the door swung open. The old man standing there regarding Sean dully, no sign of recognition in his eyes.

"Morning, Mr. Devereaux," Sean said.

"Thought you were gone for good."

"No sir. I tried to call. No one answered."

"You gotta let her ring."

Sean stood there. The old man watching him. Finally he said, "I'm ready to wrap up this job, sir."

"That's what you said ten days ago Friday. Said finished Saturday, Monday at the latest. Ten days ago Friday."

"Yes sir. Some things happened that day."

"Things," said Devereaux.

"Yes sir."

"That's what you call two men shot dead and another in the hospital?"

Sean stared at him. "No sir. I just didn't know if you'd heard."

Devereaux's eyes went to the Chevy, lingered there and came back. "Did he steal that truck?"

"Sir?"

"Your buddy. The plumber. He steal that truck?"

"No. He borrowed it so he could go home for the weekend and see his family."

"That's what they said," said Devereaux. "On the TV."

"Yes," said Sean. "Because that's what happened. It was all just . . ." He took a breath. "It was all a big mix-up, Mr. Devereaux."

"That's one thing to call it."

Sean said nothing. Holding the old man's gaze. Finally he said, "If I can get to work I can finish up, clear out my tools. Then we can square up."

"Square up," said Devereaux.

"Yes sir."

"Man goes and disappears for ten days, no word of when he'll be back, leaves his tools behind. His buddy gets shot dead, then here he comes one day says, 'Here I am, Mr. Devereaux, I'm ready to square up.'"

Sean watched the old man carefully. "Are you saying you don't intend to pay me?"

The old man held his eyes, then looked down, perhaps at Sean's boots. He leaned out toward the railing and spat. "And there it all is on the TV for everyone to see," he said. "In the paper. Everybody talking."

Sean said nothing. If he had to he would push the old man aside and go get his tools and leave—to hell with the money. To hell with this old man. Jerk the door a little and he would topple over and break into pieces.

"The sooner I finish this job, the sooner I'll be moving on, Mr. Devereaux."

"Moving on where?"

"Just moving on."

Devereaux grunted. "You can move to the moon, it won't change what happened. Gonna follow you wherever you go, end of your days."

Sean looked down. And looking up again said, "I'm sorry, Mr. Devereaux, but I don't think you know a thing about me, or my days."

Devereaux seemed almost to smile—a thing Sean could not have imagined.

"Buddy," he said. "You think I haven't seen you before? You think I don't know exactly what you are?"

FIRST THING SEAN did, he put every tool he didn't need back into the Knaack box, all puzzled together tight and secure, and when he had finished the last of the trimwork he put those tools in the box too. By noon he'd swept the floor of the little room for the last time and he shimmied the two machines into their final places, ready for the days and months and years ahead of the old man's dirty clothes. He shut the louvered door and tested the latch a final time, then left the door open and stepped around the shepherd who lay in the hallway, and descended into the basement to gather up the last of the trash and wash up.

The old farm-sink spigot, when he turned the valve, kicked and spat blood over the basin. Rust, in fact, residual from their work, collecting here in the house's lowest extremities.

He unclamped the work lamp from the ladder and swept its light over the space where the machines had been and where Dan had done his good work. The clean new copper couplings with their neat rings of solder. The beautiful shutoff valves. The red and blue PEX lines so new and colorful against the rough old wood.

He stood looking at the floor awhile. Then he aimed the light up into the ceiling joists. The webs and white spider balls, the old porcelain wiring knobs from the early 1900s, the galvy pipes. His skin began to creep and he shook that off.

He clamped the lamp to the ladder again and gathered up the black garbage bag by its neck and gave it a good spin in the air, then watched while it slowly unspun, overspun by a half turn, and settled. Fat with lint and filth and saw-dust and old plumbing parts, stain and paint rags. He set it down and opened it up and went stirring around with his bare hand. He moved the bag into the lamplight and dug more deeply until he saw the sock. Child's sock, alone and weird in the sawdust and lint. He pinched it up and shook it in the bag and lifted it free, as one lifts a mouse by its tail, and he stood upright and laid it in the palm of his other hand.

"No," he said. "Don't be ridiculous."

He tilted his hand and watched the sock drop into the mouth of the bag, the small detonation of its landing.

He took the bag by the neck again and set it by the stairs and turned back to the ladder and picked it up and halted, holding ladder and lamp in midair. Then abruptly he set the ladder down in front of the wooden racks of green tubs and stepped up and looked back into the shadowed space between two ceiling joists, to where the joists dead-ended so strangely in the new cinder wall behind the tubs. He reached over the nearest tub and felt the coolness of the two blocks in the space between the two joists—a block and a half block, in fact. He thumped on them with the heel of his hand. Solid.

He shook his head.

"Shit," he said.

"All right," he said.

He got down from the ladder and went up the stairs and over the shepherd and out to the Chevy and he opened the passenger door and grabbed up the maul and the flatbar from the footwell and went back into the house, and when he stepped over the shepherd again she began to whine.

"Quiet," he said, starting down.

He climbed the ladder again and clamped the work lamp to the joist overhead and he reached back into the space between the joists with the maul and using only his wrist he knocked the maul lightly, testingly, against the half block. He did it a second time, harder, and held still. Listening. The dog paused at the noise, then resumed whining with greater volume, greater despair. No other sound that he could hear.

He looked at the half block. A small crack had opened up in the joint. He gave another knock with the maul and the half block shifted, minutely cockeyed to its fellow and to the joist, the mortar joint cracked all the way through.

The dog groaned low in her throat.

"This is it," he said, up in the dusty air of the joists. "You either hit this son of a bitch again or you leave it forever."

He turned and looked around the basement. As though someone were standing there, come to watch his next move.

Do it, said Dan Young.

He turned back and knocked the half block hard with the maul. It shifted, it ground and jammed in its space, and he hit it again—a hard, tough son of a bitch it was, it gouged into the dark wood of the joist, exposing the paler flesh below. He refreshed his grip on the handle and wristed the maul once more and the half block popped free and fell into the darkness behind the wall like a stone tumbling down a well before it landed with a dull boom and all was silent again. His heart thudding. The dog crying and yipping and up on its feet now when he turned to look at her, or what he could see of her, her forepaws, on the topmost step.

He listened for it—and there it was: movement, upstairs. A sudden stirring and a shifting of weight from one place to another. The cane on the hardwood. The hitched, unbalanced footfall, the muttering growl as he made his way across the rooms.

Sean struck the other block, the full block, and it shifted at once and sat crosswise to the course below it. He set the maul on the ladder top and took the block in both hands and stepped down with it and set it on the floor.

The shepherd, at the top of the stairs, barked at it as though it were some living thing. As though she could see it.

He climbed again and unclamped the lamp and there was just room to sidle it through the opening and he stepped up onto the next ladder step and braced himself on the lid of the tub and saw the old wall—the crumbling, stained, seeping clay blocks, perhaps eighteen inches back from the new wall. Just enough room for a man to move sideways, as perhaps he must under such circumstances—Sean didn't know, he was no stonemason; but there was not room enough for his head in the opening he'd made and he could not look down into the space.

The dog skittered its nails on the floor upstairs and went whimpering away and the old man called out, "What in the hell is going on down there?"

Sean yanked free the tub, moderately heavy, and set it on the floor with the cinderblock and the flatbar, then climbed again and took up the maul and drew it back and slammed it into the next row of blocks, directly on the joint. The two blocks there caved in together like front teeth and he struck them again until they tumbled each in turn over the ledge and went crashing down into the darkness.

"Stop it," said Devereaux. "Stop it." He pounded the floor with the tip of his cane. Then he pounded the top step with it. "God damn you," he said. He was coming down the stairs.

Beyond the old man, somewhere in the house, the dog was howling.

Sean set the maul aside and reached in with the lamp and, boosting himself forward on the top shelf, he plugged his head into the opening and looked down into that dank and narrow space. Dust swarming in the light. The pale shapes of the fallen blocks on the dark floor below. Nothing else on the floor.

But in the old wall—a darker space. An opening, a kind of passage. Squared and cornered with the old clay blocks. He shifted the lamp until the light raked into the space and he saw the wooden steps.

"You there," called Devereaux. "You there, God damn you, what are you doing?"

Sean plunged the lamp, his arm, into the space, the light climbed the steps, and he saw the boot. A man's boot. Hundred-, two-hundred-year-old boot, gray and dull as old dead skin and the leather worn away at the toe to reveal a smooth and rounded undersurface like a skull. A metal skull, thickly dusted over yet somehow gleaming in the light.

It was just a boot. Left there by the workmen, perhaps by Devereaux himself, a lone and random thing for future workmen to puzzle over. A kind of message in a bottle. Sean had one time found a Skoal tobacco can in a wall with two 1938 buffalo nickels rattling around inside—eighty bucks for the pair from the man at the pawn shop. A dust-haired doll one time, still in its dress. Old bottles and beer cans. A wooden-hafted hammer, dropped or forgotten in the haste of closing up.

He wished it were only that. Only a boot. But when he shifted the light again he saw the bare foot. Or what remained of it.

Shrunken though it was the foot was not a match for the little sock, the boot far too big, but there was some connection, there had to be, and the breath went out of him. The blood from his heart. The ladder began to pitch and he thought it was his own sense of balance, a wave of vertigo, but when he looked back it was the old man, hunched and gripping the ladder leg with one claw hand and pulling on it, grunting with the effort, and far more substance to him and strength than Sean would have imagined. Sean let go the lamp and the light tumbled down between the two walls and stopped dead and jerked about at the end of its cord. He held to the shelving and, with no other thought than to stay on the ladder, to not fall—to not come down to the same level as the old man—he dropped his boot on the old man's forearm and felt it give way not at the grip but at the bones first, then the grip, and the old man howling, and the dog howling, and the old man raising the forearm with its new, second elbow in the air. So posed, he brought his cane around in a whistling arc and struck Sean a stinging blow to the arm. He drew back to strike again and this time Sean grabbed the cane and held on. The old man jerked at it, strong. Insane. He would not relinquish it, not now, not in death itself, and when the old man jerked again Sean let go and he watched the surprise, the amazement in Devereaux's eyes as he overbalanced, as he rocked back on his heels and staggered and did not sit down but toppled backwards like a man whose joints had long ago ceased to bend. He clattered to the concrete and let go a woof of air and somehow did not shatter like pottery but instead lay gasping and writhing, his eyeballs rolling in their sockets. A great misshapen infant outraged on its back.

Sean stepped down from the ladder and stood over him. "You did it," he said. "You actually God damn did it."

Devereaux choked and gagged. He found his voice and said, "God damn you to hell. God damn you to hell." He tried to lift his cane but Sean was standing on it.

Sean shook his head. "He tried to tell me. He knew something was wrong down here but I didn't believe it."

The old man, working his mouth, spat up a white spittle that fell back to his face. He said something.

"What?" said Sean.

"Shouldayou."

"What?"

Devereaux swallowed. "Shoulda been you. Shoulda been you got his brains blowed out."

Sean said nothing. Looking at the old man on the concrete. Then he said, "Yeah, you crazy old fucker. It shoulda been me."

He stepped off the cane and turned to the stairs and had taken one step before he swung his shin into something incredibly hard and there was the ringing sound of metal and he cried out and dropped to his hands and his bad knee on the gritty concrete. "Fuck," he said. He looked to see what he'd walked into and what he saw instead was his flatbar, swinging through the air again. It struck him this time in the elbow and he rolled away from the blunt force, the immediate dull nothing of it, and got to his feet before the pain rushed in. The shin, the elbow, both jolting with the same hot live current.

"Fuck," he said again. "God damn it."

The old man swung once more but Sean was out of reach and when the old man tried to get up Sean gave him one to the face with his boot sole and Devereaux fell back and the flatbar dropped clanging to the concrete. Sean picked it up and raised it over the old man's head. The old man choking and his eyes rolling again and a watery blood leaking from his mouth.

Sean lowered the flatbar. "You ain't gonna get me to bash your head in, Mr. Devereaux. You just lie there. They're coming for you soon enough."

Devereaux gagged and tried to speak.

"What?" said Sean.

"Done," said Devereaux.

"Yeah, you're all done."

"You," said Devereaux. "You were done. You were done. Why din't you just go?"

Sean stood looking down on him. The twisted gargoyle body. The weeping eyes. "I don't know," he said. "I'm done now." Then he turned and taking the flatbar with him he climbed the steps—climbed them, as if they were far steeper than they were. As if they were in fact the cragged, uncertain hand and footholds of a mountainside.

38.

Samuels stood off by himself, smoking a cigarette, and when Viegas appeared beside him he looked at her and nodded and turned back to watch the small Cat backhoe where it was deployed to the south side of the house. Each time the machine clawed gingerly at the turf, as a living cat might with its forepaw, three men in yellow vests moved in to probe the new dark earth with their shovels. Cops and sheriff's deputies standing by watching, their shadows long in the setting sun. Detectives and K-9 shepherds pacing about, the forensics team pitching its camp. From inside the house, the dull booming of sledgehammers, the gritty tumbling of broken cinderblocks.

"What's the story?" Viegas said.

"One John Doe, so far," said Samuels. "A good 'n old one, behind a wall in the basement. Or a kind of false wall. They're digging here because of the dogs, but now they think it's probably the same body they were smelling, and somebody used the old cellar bulkhead as a tomb. Covered it over outside, walled it up inside."

"Just the one body?"

"Yeah, and he's full-grown. Although they did find a sock. A kid's sock."

Viegas looked at him. "Where was that?"

"In a garbage bag. Your man told them to look. Said he found it behind the dryer, or under it."

"Did you see it?"

"Negative. Franklin bagged it and locked it in his car."

"And the old man?" she said.

"At the hospital, along with your man."

"Is he talking?"

"Not that I'm aware of. Heavily sedated, from what I hear. Broken in several places."

Viegas said nothing. They watched the men with shovels.

"Your man's story is he knocked the old man over after the old man attacked him with his cane," Samuels said. "But then somehow the old man managed to whack him a couple good ones with some kind of crowbar." He shook his head. "If it's not women with this guy it's old men."

He took a drag and blew. "I've been trying to put it all together in my head—him punching the waitress in the face. Then those shootings last week. Now this. I can see the connection between the waitress and the shootings—but this here. How the hell does this connect with all that, other than your man? I mean, can it be he just has some kind of gift for falling ass over saddle into shit? Is he some kind of supernatural, I don't know"—the detective circled his cigarette in the air—"finder of shit?"

Viegas said nothing. Then she said, "What made him go looking behind that wall in the first place?"

"Exactly," said Samuels. *"Exactly."*

One of the men with shovels said something and the other two came around and all three worked at the earth and soon there was the sound of shovels scraping over wood. When one man tapped the wood with his shovel point, little clods of dirt danced as if on a drum top and there was the sound of emptiness below. In response a muffled voice called out, "We hear you!" like a miner awaiting rescue.

Viegas and Samuels and the others gathered round. Tossed among the dirt pile were faded rags of tar paper and threadbare once-green tarpaulin. The workmen cleared a square flat space and they got their shovel points under the lip and pried all together, and the rotting sheet of plywood bent away from the earth, then ripped and spun in the air. The men moved forward and pried again along the blackened framing. A greater slab of ply raised up before it too cracked, flipping back on itself like a lid, and daylight poured down into the cavity, that lightless place, for the first time in perhaps forty years.

Gray grinning mummy on the old wooden steps, arranged as if he'd sat himself down and fallen asleep. His head cocked back on the upper step, mouth agape, the dark pit of throat behind the teeth. Shirtless all these years, all these winters. Basket of ribs and sternum in a tight truss of hide, one withered arm resting on the bend of bones in his denim pants, the other stretched out along the step. The curled claws of his hands. One stringy bare foot out of its boot and the boot standing upright on the step below.

For all that, no smell other than the turned earth, the moldy wood, the dampened old concrete.

Down there, from the other side of the breached cinderblock wall, someone put his beam on the skull and lit up strands of dusty hair clinging to the scalp.

"Skull fracture," said the man with the beam, or perhaps another man near him. "Blunt force trauma."

"Folks, can I get a little space here?" a man said, topside, and Viegas and Samuels stepped back as the photographer began taking pictures of the body from above with his flash.

"Wasn't there a missing man back in the day?" said Samuels. "Back in your dad's day?"

"Yes," Viegas said. "The uncle. Devereaux's uncle. A Vietnam vet. Not altogether right in the head, apparently."

"You can say that again."

"Yeah," she said dryly, "I'm thinking he didn't get that fracture in Nam."

"Think it was the old man—when he was a younger man?"

Viegas shrugged. "Somebody had to put him in that . . . what's it called—?"

"Bulkhead."

"Bulkhead, and wall him up. Somebody who had time, and access, to do all that work."

Samuels was silent. He smoked.

"There's patricide," he said. "There's matricide and fratricide. What is it when it's your uncle?"

"Murder," said Viegas.

They stood looking at the opening in the earth. Samuels dropped his cigarette in the yellow grass and stepped on it. He stared at it, then stooped and picked it up.

"I'm gonna head out," Viegas said.

"You gonna go talk to him?"

"Who?"

"Your man."

Viegas looked at him. "Does it give you some kind of satisfaction, calling him that?"

"Courtland, then."

"No," she said, answering his question. "Why would I? It's not my case."

"It might be," said Samuels. "If he straight-up assaulted that old man. Crimes against the elderly," he said.

Somewhere a dog was barking. Officers had begun calling to each other. There was general movement away from the house and toward the garage. Viegas looked at Samuels, Samuels at Viegas, and they began to move with the others toward the listing old structure.

From the dark square of the bay door, or the leaning rhomboid of it, there issued the odor of age and decay and dereliction, and the barking of one of the K-9 dogs.

The handler held the shepherd back by the collar but it went on barking hoarsely at the ancient tractor that occupied the rear of the garage, that had sat there on the dirt floor, by the look of it, for a hundred years. Detectives were down on their haunches sweeping their beams underneath it. Franklin, the lead detective on the scene, cast about the garage and said, "Dusty—where the hell is Dusty?"

Another man standing in the open bay door turned and yelled toward the house, "Dusty!"

"What?" came the answer.

"Need you over here."

Viegas and Samuels turned to watch the big, out-of-shape man jog toward them in his yellow vest—jog past them, on into the garage.

Franklin looked up at him. "Dusty, I need you to haul this tractor out."

Dusty stood catching his breath. He looked critically at the tractor. "Gonna have to drag her out," he said. "She ain't gonna roll."

"So drag her out."

"Drag her out, you got it, boss."

Two of Dusty's men drove forward in four-by-four trucks and set about lashing long yellow tow straps to the rear tractor axle.

"Everybody out," said Dusty. "Go on, get back. One a these straps goes and snaps, she'll take your head off."

His men dropped the trucks into gear and backed away. The straps rose from the ground and grew tight and vibrated in the air. The tractor bucked once in place like an unwilling horse, hove forward a few inches, then came along more readily in the dirt, gouging along in the old ruts—out of the shadowed garage and into the slanting light of the dropping sun, the shadows of the trees.

The men with shovels trooped in and began chopping at the packed, oil-blackened dirt, until the shovels reached a deeper, softer dirt and the digging went easier. Franklin said, "Bring the dog," and the handler returned with the shepherd and gave it rein to jab its snout into the turned earth. The dog scrabbled at it and was pulled back again wheezing in its throat; shovels plunged and swung and emptied dirt at the detectives' feet and the detectives, squatting again, stirred the earth with bare fingers.

The men booted the shovels deeper, they widened the dig. Someone said they'd best bring in the Cat and in the next moment a shovel struck something, a hard grinding scrape, and everyone grew still. Grew silent.

"Slowly," said Franklin.

The man whose shovel had made contact choked up on the haft and began to spoon away the dirt with the shovel point. A yellow, dirty dome surfaced. Franklin produced a Maglite and put his beam on the object. "Stop," he said, and the digger withdrew his shovel. Franklin got down on his knees and began clearing dirt from the object with his fingers. It was the small, hard crown of a skull.

"Get the photographer," Franklin said, and the other detective hustled off and did not yell out. No one spoke. Franklin pulled latex gloves from his jacket pocket and stood tugging them on, looking around the garage. "Is there a . . ."

"Hand trowel?" another man said. One of Dusty's drivers. "I just saw one . . ."

He found the tool and passed it handle-first to the detective, who began mining a sort of trench all around the skull.

The photographer stepped up to the edge of the dig and Franklin said, "Start taking photos, Jerry. The camera might pick up something I can't see."

"You got it."

The camera, though digital, made the clacking sounds of shutter and mirror. Bursts of light flooded the site and blanched the exposed dirty bone. Cops and detectives and Dusty and his men loomed, bobbing their heads to improve their views. Viegas and Samuels stood just inside the bay door, watching the movements of the others, listening to what was said. From that vantage Franklin seemed to pause—surprised, perhaps, by something he saw. He resumed digging. Then dug with less caution.

"Jesus Christ," he said.

"Holy shit," someone said.

The flash bloomed and the shutter clacked. The shepherd barked and strained against its handler's grip.

"Is that—?" Franklin's fellow detective said.

The photographer aimed his lens. "What the hell is that?"

"Is that a . . . dog?" said a cop.

The shepherd bore his teeth at the long, fanged snout in the dirt.

"Tell you what that is," someone else said. It was Dusty. "That's a damn coyote."

Franklin stood with the trowel in his grip. With his free hand he spanked the knees of his slacks. To the handler he said, "Get that dog outta here, will you, Mike?"

Franklin stood looking at the skull. "Dig this thing up," he said, and the men with shovels stepped into the shallow grave.

The other detective said, "Who the hell would bury a dog here, in a garage, under a tractor?"

"Coyote," said Dusty.

"Mighta already been there," ventured one of the cops, looking on from an extension ladder that leaned between the open ceiling joists.

"Some son of a bitch," said Franklin. He handed the trowel off to the other detective and dusted his palms. "Some son of a bitch mighta put that thing there just so we wouldn't dig any deeper. So we'd think that was it."

The digging men paused and looked at him.

"Go on," he said. "Dig it up and let's see what's underneath."

Viegas turned away and walked back to the bulkhead site. The shirtless corpse sat on the steps as before, alone and waiting.

She let herself in the back door and stood at the head of the basement stairs listening. Silence down there now; they'd all followed the excitement to the garage.

As she listened she was looking at a door that stood open down the short hallway. Louvered door, newly varnished—you could smell it—new brushed-nickel hardware. Sean Courtland.

She walked to the door and looked into the darkness of the room, then hunted up a latex glove from her coat pocket and flicked the wall switch with it. Smooth, newly painted walls without a thing on them, not one nail hole, a bright and pristine effect that gave the two old machines, centered and squared to the back wall, the look of artifacts, or artwork. A statement of some kind. Whiff of mildew amidst the varnish and new wood and paint smells. Clean, pretty woodwork that matched the house's old woodwork. Better work than the old man could have hoped for when he first imagined bringing the machines up from the basement. When he imagined not having to go down those stairs again to do his laundry.

She flicked off the light and returned to the stairs and took the steep steps down.

Gloom and cobwebs lit only by two bare bulbs up in the joists; the workers had turned off their work lights. The broken, dismantled wall, or the section of it that had covered the bulkhead cavity, lay in a pile of blocks, and some safe distance from this rubble sat eight or ten green plastic tubs, off-loaded from a section of wooden racks that had itself been hauled from place and stood again out of the way. Several tub lids had been lifted and left standing alongside the tubs, others lifted and put insecurely back on. Those tubs that remained on the unmoved racks were likewise unlidded, or incompletely lidded.

She stood looking down into one of the tubs on the floor. A pile of old clothes—an old woman's clothes: flower-print dresses, knee-high tan-colored stockings, a pair of old black orthopedic shoes. In another tub, a great number of handmade doilies and other knitted things with a chipped porcelain statue of the Virgin Mary enswathed at the center.

She lifted the loose lid on another tub and looked down on a jumble of men's jeans and coveralls and flannel shirts, dingy old tube socks and boxer shorts, various old T-shirts, grimy billcaps. Other tubs held assortments of bric-a-brac and figurines, a lifetime's worth, wrapped up in newspaper from 1982. One was half-full of paperback romance novels and on top of these, weirdly, like a bird on its nest, sat a kid's black baseball mitt. Not black—blackened. As if it had been pulled from a fire. She could smell the stale smoke, the charred old leather, amidst the mildew of the books. It looked smaller even than a kid's mitt, as if it had shrunk when it was scorched, or with age, or both.

Franklin had bagged the sock and locked it in his car—why not the mitt?

Maybe because it was in a tub and the tubs themselves were evidence, and he wanted them as they were found.

In any case—not her crime scene.

Still, she'd ask her father: Had a boy's baseball mitt gone missing too?

She moved to the broken passageway the sledgehammers had made in the wall and stood looking in at the space between the false wall and the original. The strip of concrete floor, perhaps a foot and a half wide, that extended to either side of the bulkhead stairs, left and right of her the length of the room. Space enough for a thin or smallish man to move sidewise if he were so inclined. Though why he would be she couldn't imagine. Unless he were searching for a way out. And this man, whoever he was, had done no searching. Not with that skull.

She looked at him again from this new angle. His lonesome shrunken foot. The stringy dusty hair. The empty sockets and the ghoul's smile. And as she looked, something in him shifted—his hand, maybe his leg, loosened from ancient stasis by all the digging and pounding of his untombing—and coldness climbed the back of her neck. It was as if he'd stirred. As if he were trying to wake from his sleep and speak to her. Tell her what had happened to him.

He did not move again, and finally she turned and went back up the stairs, and from there out into the cool dusk, the earthy wet smell of spring in it, the last lacy shadows of the trees on the ground, her heart quieting, the dying light, the air.

39.

THE OLD MAN's hospital room could be identified from a distance by the officer posted at the door, and the officer, likewise pegging Viegas well before she reached him, closed his magazine and got to his feet. He'd been on the scene of the Daniel Young shooting and didn't need to see her badge. His name was O'Neal.

Viegas glanced into the room. "Is he awake?"

"No, ma'am. Well, he might be."

"Might be?"

"He's opened his eyes but then he shuts them again and won't speak. Won't eat or drink."

She stood looking in at Devereaux, his eyes indeed shut, and sunken in shadow. He was partially raised in the bed, his gray head deep in the pillow, his mouth open but not gaping. His nose was bandaged, his face discolored.

"I'll just say hello," she said, and O'Neal said, "Be my guest."

She stepped in and stood at the foot of the bed. No restfulness in his face even in sleep. Or fake sleep. A tenseness and a resentment somehow in the overgrown eyebrows. His right forearm was casted to the thumb in white plaster and the cast lay on his abdomen where it rode the rise and fall of his breaths like a toy boat. His right leg, in white plaster like his arm, lay on its own bed of pillows.

Night had fallen and the blinds were open and she could see her reflection in the glass: dark-haired figure in a dark coat standing at the foot of the bed like Death.

She studied his face and she thought of the story of the doctor, a French doctor of the early 1900s, who called out the name of a man whose freshly guillotined head lay in a basket at his feet. The head's eyes slowly opened, the doctor observed, fixed on his own for a few seconds, then slowly closed again. The doctor called out a second time and the eyes opened a second time, fixed on the doctor's again, and once more slowly closed, or half closed. To a third call, the eyes made no response at all.

"Mr. Devereaux?" Viegas said to the old man in his bed, and the old man's eyelids twitched faintly but did not open. She watched. Then said again, "Mr. Devereaux," and this time there was no twitch.

"Mr. Devereaux," she said a third time. "I'm Detective Viegas with the Investigative Services Bureau, and I just want to ask you a question or two. I understand you are sedated and may not be able to respond, but if you can blink, or raise a finger—any finger—to indicate yes to my questions, that will suffice for now. Can you do that?"

The eyes did not blink, and no fingers moved. On the monitor the colored graphs trekked across a black field toward like-colored numbers. The quiet beeping that communicated, somehow, that all was as it should be.

"Is that your uncle we found behind the wall at your house?" she said.

No blink. No movement of the fingers.

"Did you put him there?"

Nothing.

"Did you give him that skull fracture?"

Nothing. She watched the cardiac graph and saw no obvious change. His heart rate remained steady at 89 beats per minute.

"Did he know something?" she said. "Did he find out something you'd done, and you had a fight?"

Still nothing.

She came around and stood next to the bed. She reached into the tote bag at her hip and brought out the plastic bag and, holding it by the seal, let the rest of it unfold with a weighted snap.

"Mr. Devereaux," she said. "Do you recognize this burnt-up baseball mitt?"

The old man's eyes opened, already in focus—already focused on her, as if he'd been watching her through the veiny lids—and her own heart spiked, a single anomalous peak.

He closed his mouth. He looked at her and then he looked at the bag she held. Sealed evidence bag, the blackened mitt tagged, logged, and released to her by Sergeant Russo with the promise that she return it in an hour.

Devereaux stared at it. Cold, lucid blue eyes in shadowed wells.

"Who the hell are you?" he said thickly. Gunk in his throat, his sinuses packed.

With her free hand she unclipped her badge from her belt and likewise held it for him to see. "I'm Detective Viegas, Mr. Devereaux, with the Investigative Services Bureau."

"Viegas," he said.

"Yes, sir."

"There was a Deputy Viegas. Long time ago. Deputy sheriff."

"Yes, sir. That was my father." She held the mitt in the air. He wouldn't look at it again, and finally she slipped it back into the tote. Returned the badge to her belt.

Devereaux watched her. "Come around the place bothering folks. Asking questions. And him hardly old enough to shave."

"He's not a sheriff's deputy anymore."

"Not surprised," said the old man. "Don't believe he was cut out for it."

"Why do you say that?"

Devereaux shut his eyes and raised his chin, his Adam's apple working.

"Do you want your water, Mr. Devereaux?"

He opened his eyes and looked at her. "Where's my dog?"

"Your dog?" She watched him. "What dog? An old dog? A buried dog?"

"Buried dog? I'm talking about Bonnie. What'd you do with her?"

Viegas shook her head. "The only dog I know about is the one they dug up in that garage. Was that Bonnie?"

He stared dully at her for another few seconds, then closed his eyes. She watched as his face relaxed into sleep again. Or what he thought must be the face of sleep. Or what was in fact the face of sleep for a man who had murdered his uncle, and perhaps others. Perhaps three little boys. A monster's face of sleep.

"Mr. Devereaux," she said. "Are there more bodies on the property? Human bodies?"

Silence—nearly: the old man's breathing. The quietly beeping monitor. Her own beating heart.

SEAN COURTLAND'S ROOM was at the far end of the hall and there was no officer posted there and, when she looked in, no Sean Courtland.

"Corrine."

She turned to the voice—to a tall man in green scrubs and surgeon's cap and blue paper face mask. She wouldn't have known him but for the gray-frame glasses with red stems, the warm, smiling eyes behind the lenses.

"Martin," she said. "Is that you in there?"

He lowered the mask briefly—the mustache, the smile—and replaced it. "What are you doing here?" he said. "Is everything all right?"

"Oh, yes, I was just here to see . . ." She half turned to look down the hall, to O'Neal sitting there with his magazine.

"Ah," said Martin. "The Devereaux affair. Lord. What the heck happened out there?"

"I don't know. The old man isn't talking. I'm looking for the man who came in with him, Sean Courtland."

"The carpenter who smashed down the wall."

"Who first breached the wall, yes."

Martin stood nodding. "And no other—findings?" he said. "No . . ."

"Little boys? No. Not so far."

He nodded. "And why did he do that—why did he breach the wall?"

"That's what I wanted to ask him."

"Right." Martin sighed, puffing out the mask. "Well, you just missed him. He checked himself out about fifteen minutes ago."

Viegas shook her head at the tall, masked doctor. The good doctor. Her father's partner. "What kind of outfit are you running here, anyway?"

"I know. Very slipshod. But his injuries didn't require a longer stay and the detectives—the other detectives—were satisfied, it seemed, and he wished to discharge himself, so that's what he did."

"What were his injuries?"

"He suffered an olecranon fracture to the left elbow." The doctor cupped his own left elbow in his right hand. "That was the more serious injury. And then a good periosteal contusion to the left leg."

"Periosteal contusion," she said.

"A bone bruising of the tibia. The shinbone. He'll be limping on that a good while. The elbow will take even longer, since he opted out of surgery."

"He can do that?"

"Surgery was recommended, but not absolutely required."

"What is the—what did you call it?" She cupped her elbow.

"The olecranon. It's the pointy bone of your elbow that sticks out when you bend your arm like this, which is actually the end of the ulna."

"Ah. The funny bone."

"No, in fact the funny bone sensation comes from the main bone of the upper arm. Which is called . . . ?"

"The . . ." she had to think a minute. "Humerus."

He watched her. Finally she got it.

"Humerus. Funny bone." She shook her head. "All my life I never made that connection."

He shrugged. "Anyway, he opted out of surgery and limped away with his arm in a brace."

"I see."

They stood looking at each other. One of the few men she knew she could do that with and feel nothing but calm, nothing but love. One of the two men.

"I like your cap," she said finally, and he raised a hand to touch it. The cap was black with images of white bones, the pieces of the human skeleton in random and irreverent disarray. "Kind of makes you look like a pirate."

"Yes, very skull and crossbones. One guess who gave it to me."

"I'm sure he thought it was very humerus."

"Ha! He did. I sent him a picture but he thinks I staged it."

"I'll tell him I caught you in the act of wearing it as part of your whole . . . doctory, surgery thing."

"Ah, wonderful. I'm so glad I ran into you—grim though the circumstances."

"Me too."

"I've gotta run off now."

"OK. Just, quickly—"

"Yes?"

"Do you happen to know where he went—Courtland?"

"I don't, but if he's smart he went home and put that leg up and passed out."

"Yeah," she said. "I don't think we can count on him to do the smart thing."

He watched her a minute. "Funny thing," he said, "I remember him from what, a week ago? He was here with the daughter of a man who'd been shot."

"Henry Givens."

"Yes. He'd driven the daughter to the hospital." Martin stood nodding, recalling. "And it was his truck the other young man was found in?"

"Dan Young. Yes."

Martin puffed out his mask again. "He's got a certain knack, doesn't he? Courtland."

"You could say that."

The doctor shook his head. Abruptly he looked at his watch and said, "Boogers, I gotta run. Why don't you come for dinner tonight? I'm actually going to leave this place in about two hours. I'll make the duck."

"The duck!" she said. "God, yes, I'll bring a . . ."

Martin was staring past her, troubled, and she turned to look. Officer O'Neal was on his feet, keeping a man from pushing his way into Devereaux's room. An older man, seventies, the plaid flannel jacket he wore riding high on his shoulders with the struggle. Both his bare hands were visible, both empty.

"Don't tell me I can't go in there," the older man said.

"Sir," said O'Neal. "Sir—"

Viegas hustled down the hall and took hold of the man's upper arm—gently at first, then more firmly when she felt the strength, the hardness under the jacket.

"Sir," she said.

He looked at her. Pain and confusion and rage all at once in those eyes, all enlarged by the thick lenses of his glasses. "What do you want?" he said, jerking at her grip. "Let me go."

Viegas caught O'Neal's eye, and he understood. He turned the man's wrist so that he cried out and bent forward, then cocked the man's arm behind his back and guided him to the wall and stood him there, his face pressed to the painted cinderblock, puffing, grimacing, while O'Neal collected his other arm and held it likewise.

"You're not carrying a weapon, are you, sir?" said Viegas.

"No, I'm not carrying a weapon."

"I'm just going to pat you down quickly," she said, and did so. The flannel jacket, the baggy old jeans.

"You have him right there," the man said. "Right there, and I'm the criminal?"

"Sir, I'm Detective Viegas and this is Officer O'Neal. What can we help you with?"

"You can't help me with anything except let me go in there and talk to that man."

"Mr. Devereaux?"

"Yeah, Devereaux—who else?"

"What business do you have with Mr. Devereaux?"

"What business, she says!"

Viegas moved to where the man could see her. His glasses were pushed out of place and she said to O'Neal, "Ease up a little, please," and O'Neal eased up and she righted the man's glasses for him.

"Do you have some ID, sir?" she said.

"Yeah, I've got ID. Of course I've got ID."

"In your wallet?"

"Yeah, in my wallet."

She'd already felt it: inside jacket pocket. "I'm going to take it out. Is that all right?"

"Take it. I don't give a damn."

She reached in and took out the wallet, old and thin and creased, cracked it open, and studied the license. A gray, older man in the picture, nothing more. Weariness in the eyes behind the lenses.

"Mr. Ross?"

"Yeah, Mr. Ross. William Ross."

It had already come to her when he said, "Billy Ross was my son. Ten years old. Ten years old. And I came here to ask that man in there where's he at? Where's my son Billy?"

Billy Ross. The name raised two images in Viegas's mind, one she'd seen with her own eyes—the boy's school picture from 1977, blond, buck-toothed, freckles across his nose—and one she'd only imagined: the boy's bike, a purple Schwinn Sting-Ray, dragged from the muddy bank of the river by the Highway 14 Bridge.

"I'm sorry, Mr. Ross. I'm truly sorry, but you can't ask him that."

"Then you ask him!"

"I've tried, Mr. Ross."

"Well, try again. Go on. I want to see you try. You cops—will you look at what you're doing? Holding me here like I'm the criminal?"

"Mr. Ross," she said. "Mr. Ross—?"

"What?"

"If Officer O'Neal lets you go, can you stand here calmly?"

"Yeah, I can stand here calmly. I'm an old man, for Christ's sake."

O'Neal released him and stood again in front of the open door.

Ross turned and faced Viegas, rubbing his arms. He tugged at his jacket and stood looking into her eyes. As if he knew her. As if they'd met before, though she was sure they had not.

"Mr. Ross," she said. "May I ask you a question?"

"You want to ask me a question?"

"If you don't mind."

He looked around as if for a place to spit. "Go ahead and ask."

Viegas adjusted the tote-bag strap where it crossed her chest. "Did your son Billy have a baseball mitt?"

"He was a ten-year-old boy. Of course he had a baseball mitt."

"Yes, sir. Do you know what happened to it?"

He looked at her. "Nothing happened to it. My wife kept it with all his other things in his room. Why?"

"We found a mitt, a youth's mitt, out at the Devereaux house."

Ross watched her as if she were speaking a foreign language.

"Swim lesson," he said. "He was going to a swim lesson, not a baseball game." He shook his head. "We wanted him to be able to swim, Mary and me. So he wouldn't drown. But he didn't want to go. The water was too cold."

Viegas saw the thoughts, the decades-old agony, in the man's face. The idea that his boy might have spent his last moments in the cold, dark river.

"I'm sorry, Mr. Ross."

"Sorry," he said. "You know how many times I've heard that in forty-one years? I'd rather die than hear another cop tell me how sorry he—or she—is."

Viegas was silent. Then: "Mr. Ross?"

"Yeah."

"Did you drive yourself here?"

"Yeah, I drove myself."

"All right. Officer O'Neal is going to walk you back to your car and make sure you get home all right."

"I don't want any cops following me home."

"He won't follow you home. He'll just make sure you get on your way."

Ross looked at her. He looked at Officer O'Neal, or past O'Neal, and O'Neal watched him closely.

Ross looked at Viegas a last time.

"Home," he said. "What in the hell does that even mean?" Then he turned and began to make his way down the hall, favoring one leg.

She told O'Neal to go ahead—she'd stay here till he got back—and he set off after the older man, then slowed himself so that he remained a few steps behind.

"Are you all right?"

It was Martin. Still with her.

"Yes. Thank you."

He watched her.

"Go on," she said. "I know you got stuff to do."

"All right. We'll see you later tonight?"

"Yes."

"Excellent."

"Martin," she said, and he turned back.

"Let's not mention this to Dad? Mr. Ross."

He studied her, his intelligent eyes above the mask, and nodded. "You got it."

When he was gone she looked in at Devereaux in his bed. If he'd opened his eyes, if he'd heard any of it, she would never know.

40.

He took a booth along the wall, not too close and not too far, and he sat on the side of the table that gave him a view to the bar, and after he'd been sitting there awhile a man sitting alone on the stools turned and seemed to stare at him. An older man. He stared, then beckoned Sean with the fingers of one hand. As a king might some reluctant subject, or child: *Come. It's all right...*

It was a Tuesday—incredibly that same Tuesday in which he'd broken into the basement wall, seen the corpse, fought off Devereaux, gone to the hospital— now a little after six, and the bar was quiet, the music turned down low. They'd given him drugs at the hospital for his pain, and crossing the tavern he heard the hay crushing under his boots like cracking ice. All the various colored lights of the room bright and clean and primary. Little Jeff stood at the end of the bar near the gate, organizing, stocking, and but for the flat look of disregard he'd given Sean when he walked in the back door, paid him no mind.

The older man sat watching his progress, his limp not much more pronounced than before, Sean imagined, the same leg, and gaining the bar he saw it was one of the two men who'd told him the story of a family massacred on a rubber plantation. The names arrived slowly through the fog of drugs: Mr. Bonner, the one who spoke French, and his translator, Mr. Bergman.

It was the latter who smiled up at him now from the barstool.

"The man who tells the time," said Bergman.

"Mr. Bergman," said Sean.

"What on earth have you done to yourself, my friend?"

Sean raised the bent wing of his arm in its black brace. He thought a moment. His brain was humming nicely. He said: "I was walking along the road minding my own business when a little yellow car with flowers painted on it stopped. Three clowns, then three more, then another three piled out of the car and threw me down and kicked me all to hell with their big clown shoes. Then they all jumped back in the little yellow car and drove off again."

Bergman watched him. "A likely story," he said.

"Look who's talking. Where's your pal, the Frenchman?"

"Frenchman . . . ? Ah—you mean Mr. Bonner." Bergman looked into his glass. "You misremember, my dear. He wasn't French. His young wife was French. And her family."

Sean watched him: a man alone in a bar, daylight yet in the windows, staring into his glass. When Bergman looked up again there was nothing but kindness and history and sorrow in his eyes.

"One must forgive old men their tendency to tell their stories," he said. "It's often all they have, you know."

Sean nodded. "Yes sir."

Bergman studied him. "And yours precedes you. Building upon your notoriety."

"Not on purpose."

"No," said Bergman. "I don't imagine so. Are you going to have a drink?"

"I don't think one is going to be offered."

"Nonsense." Bergman began to raise his arm and Sean reached across with his right hand and stayed it.

"That's all right," he said. "I'm on pain meds anyway. Not supposed to mix."

"Ah, yes. Sensible," said Bergman. "A glass of water, then. A soda . . ."

Sean thanked him no and Bergman made him a silent toast and sipped from his own glass and set it down again and regarded the younger man anew. He drew a forefinger over a silvered eyebrow and Sean watched—believed he heard—the hairs springing up again behind the fingertip.

"Something was begun," the older man said. "It was set in motion. It ran its course. Most unfortunately. Most tragically."

"Yes sir."

Bergman watched him. "Was he a close friend? A dear friend—the young man who was in your truck?"

Sean was slow to answer. He'd met Dan Young on a Monday and that Friday he was dead. Yesterday he'd driven across the river and stood in his bedroom with his mother. His twin brother.

"We were on the same path," he said at last.

Bergman nodded. "I understand." He looked toward the aluminum door with the glass porthole, and Sean looked too. No movement in the door, none in the glass.

"And the father of our young friend?"

"Sir?"

"Miss Givens. How is her father?"

"I believe he's recovering well."

Bergman looked at Sean's arm in its brace, and his brows came together over his nose. "But you weren't in the truck, if I'm not mistaken. You weren't injured in those events."

"No, this was something more recent."

"And not a gang of clowns."

"No. But probably about as believable."

Bergman waited. "You don't wish to talk about it," he said.

Sean thought about that and said, "I don't think what I wish enters into it."

The older man nodded. "Understood."

"Anyway, you'll read about it."

"Oh dear."

"Yeah," said Sean.

Bergman took a drink, then sat observing Sean in the backbar mirror. With sympathy. Pity, perhaps. "She's not here, you know," he said.

"I was beginning to get that idea."

"Sometimes she's here when I leave and sometimes she's not. Of course I don't always leave at the same time, so the variables only compound. You see the trouble."

Sean nodded. "I just thought I'd take a chance on catching her."

Bergman looked down. He seemed to stare at Sean's good hand where it rested on the old worn wood. "I understand you are a carpenter."

"Yes sir."

"And you hired the other young man to help you on a job."

"Yes, I did."

"And did you finish the job?"

Sean nodded. "Finished it today."

"Today—? In this contraption?"

"No. This happened after I finished."

"Ah," said Bergman. Then, after another silence: "A job well done?"

"Sorry?"

"Was it a job well done?"

"Yes. I thought so."

"Then let's drink to that."

"All right."

"And to old friends. To old dear friends."

"Yes sir."

Bergman lifted his glass and Sean raised his empty hand shaped to a glass and rested his hand on the wood again.

"You take care, Mr. Bergman."

"I believe that's my line, young man."

"Yes sir. I'll try."

"You had better. Between you and the world, I put my money on the world. It has more practice."

"At what?"

Bergman's shoulders rose and fell. "At what else?"

THE RED HONDA was in the parking lot when he came out, and she was behind the wheel.

To the west the sun was setting in bright reefs of color, the air smelled richly of spring, and he crossed to her noticing only the slow, alien movements of his legs.

She got out and leaned on the car, hands in her jacket pockets, watching him.

"I thought I missed you," he said, stopping short of her.

"It was a close one," she said. Her eyes a golden-green in that light. Steady. Impassive.

"How's your dad doing?"

"Better. Thank you for going to see him."

Sean raised his arm to wave this away—tried to—and shut his eyes against the pain.

"Careful," she said. She looked him over. "He looks about like you, only the sitting version."

"He's back home?"

"Yes, he was only there another . . ." She shook her head and looked off toward the bluffs, then at him again. "Jesus, Sean. What happened out at that house?"

"How much do you know?"

"I know you found a body behind a wall—there's that. And you got into a fight with that old man that sent you both to the hospital, where you stayed about one hot second."

He stood in dumb silence, unable to figure it out. Then it came to him.

"Viegas," he said.

"Yes, Viegas. She came to the house looking for you. I said I hadn't seen you since the night of the shooting. Or heard from you."

He moved some gravel with his boot toe. "That's about all there is to know," he said. "I found that body, and the old man didn't appreciate it too much, so I got this and he got knocked down and broke some bones."

She took that in. "The body was there the whole time?" she said. "While you were working?"

"It had been there a lot longer than that. Years."

She shook her head again. "It's all just . . . too much."

"Yeah."

She watched him. "I called you. Again. After I talked to Viegas. Left you another message."

"I know."

"Texted you."

"I know. I'm sorry." He ran the fingers of the hand he could lift through his hair. "I didn't know how to talk about it."

"With me."

"With anyone."

She smiled. Not a smile of pleasure. "Be still my heart," she said.

He looked at his truck, parked a few spaces away. In the dusk he thought he saw the phantom shape of Dan Young sitting there, waiting.

"I guess I didn't take it very well," she said. "At the hospital."

"I don't know how you could take it well."

"I didn't hear about Dan, or Blaine Mattis, until later. After you were gone."

"Yeah, I know."

She stood watching him. Searching his face, his eyes. "I don't even know what to say, Sean. It's all just too incredibly . . . fucked-up."

"I know."

"You keep saying that."

He said nothing.

She took a breath and as she let it out a train, somewhere in the dusk, blew its lonesome horn—a strange concurrence.

"I need to get to work," she said.

He nodded. He looked off toward the east as if looking for the train.

She looked him over again. "Are you in pain?"

"I'm all right. I didn't come here so you could see me like this."

"I know."

"I came to say I'm sorry. For everything."

She waited. When he didn't speak again she pushed off from the car. "I'm sorry, but I gotta get in there. Maybe you can come by later."

He shook his head. "I don't think I can, Denise."

"Why not?" She looked at him. At the Chevy. At him again.

"Oh," she said. "A little slow on the uptake here."

His heart was thudding.

She watched him. "Where will you go?"

"I thought I might stay with my dad for a while."

"In Madison," she said. She nodded, then took a step nearer to him but kept her hands in her pockets. She seemed to be looking for something in his eyes she'd not seen before. Or that she'd seen and not recognized for what it was.

He thought she would say something but she didn't. He felt distinctly that she was waiting for him to tell her something. But he did not, and the longer he didn't, the more improbable it seemed that anything he said would be anything but pathetic, until finally he said the only thing he could think of that would not be, which was her name.

"Denise."

"Sean."

"I just don't know how I can stay."

"Oh, shoot, that's easy," she said with Tennessee in her voice. "You just *stay*. And to hell with everybody else."

"Easy to say."

She watched him. "Is it my dad? You know he doesn't blame you. You know he actually likes you—right?"

The train sounded its horn again and they both looked toward it, the faraway hulk of it, the three round eyes of headlights in the dusk.

He turned back to her and she smiled at him.

"If this was a movie, that would be your train and you'd be getting on it. The big good-bye scene."

He was about to speak and stopped himself. "Now anything I say is gonna sound like a line," he said.

"Try me."

You're not safe, he wanted to say. *Nobody I care about is.*

"Everything that's happened," he said. "Every bad thing—Mattis, your dad, Dan Young. None of it would've happened if I'd never come here."

She cocked her head. Taking that in. "You think Mattis shot my dad because of you?"

"Not directly, but—"

"Do you think you feel more responsible for that than I do?"

His mind turned, and he saw what he hadn't seen—that there was another world in which he was nothing more than someone else's bad luck. A minor but consequential player in a larger story that had begun long before he ever stepped foot in the Wheelhouse Tavern. Before she'd ever seen him as anything but another customer wanting a beer.

She watched him, and he believed his thoughts were obvious to her—more so when she smiled and shook her head.

"What about the good, Sean? What about the good that happened because you came here?"

"Yes," he said. "God, yes—I'm not saying there wasn't good. The good has been . . . I don't think I even knew what good was before I came here. Before—"

She waited. She wanted him to say it, he understood. And doubted that he would.

"Before I met you," he said.

She smiled. "God, that was a line."

He laughed. She laughed.

"Look," she said. "I know this is hard, everything that's happened. I know it feels like you're responsible for it all. I know. And I'm sure there's a lot more going on that you haven't even told me. I wish you had. I wish you'd told me when we had the time and the space to talk about it. But right now . . ." She looked at him and her eyes shone wetly.

"Right now we're out of time, Sean Courtland. Your train is here and I have to go."

Sean said nothing. What could he say? She had to go, she said.

And so he let her go.

41.

Viegas saw the truck first, parked across the street in the lamplight, and
then she saw Sean Courtland, the shape of him, sitting on the low stone wall
across from the police station, the old stone church risen up behind him in its
footlights as if for some dramatic effect. The arches and towers and turrets of
a fortress, or castle. The figure of Christ floating in stained glass, backlit from
within the church.

Courtland raised his hand to his face. Embers brightened, and the white
cloud of smoke drifted off.

She crossed the street and stopped and stood looking down at him.
Courtland looking up at her, his legs stretched out before him, boots crossed
at the ankles. He wore no jacket but only the same red flannel shirt he'd been
wearing the first time she saw him, or one just like it, as this one had no blood-
stains that she could see in that light. His left arm slung in a black brace that
kept his elbow at a right angle.

"Detective," he said.

"Mr. Courtland. Were you looking for me?" She glanced beyond him, at the
church. "Or someone else?"

Courtland looked over his shoulder and turned back. "I rang the bell but
nobody answered. I think he's gone home."

"I wouldn't be surprised."

"Yeah," he said. "Anyway I think it was you who was looking for me."

Viegas nodded. "You talked to Miss Givens, finally."

Courtland looked at her. "I talked to her."

"I thought maybe you'd left town."

"Not yet."

"Mind if I sit?"

"No ma'am."

She sat with her long coat under her but even so after a minute she felt the damp coldness of the capstone. There was little traffic at that hour and when a car did go by, east- or westbound, they watched it as if it might be someone they knew.

"Smoke?" Courtland said, reaching for his pack.

"No, thanks. I'm trying to quit." She looked at the green Chevy, parked facing west, its passenger side to the curb. The side where she'd looked in at the body she'd thought was his. The smell of blood so strong she'd tasted it like copper in her mouth.

"They cleaned it up," he said.

"I figured," she said. And after a moment: "You went to Minnesota."

He tipped his ash in the grass behind him. "I didn't intrude. They were expecting me. Did you know he had a twin brother?"

"Yes, I did."

Courtland nodded. "Yeah, so . . . I went. The sheriff had talked to them. They knew how it happened. They were awful nice to me, considering."

"Good people," she said.

"Good people."

"Did you know what happened to Dan Young over there—his history?"

"He told me some," Courtland said. "Enough to know why he was over here with no truck."

Viegas straightened her legs and crossed her ankles. "And his injury?"

"What injury?"

"The laceration—?" She tapped her own forehead.

Courtland's gaze lingered at her hairline, then he looked away. "I never saw any laceration," he said. "And he never mentioned it."

Courtland looked up at the sky and she looked too but there were only gray, thin clouds and no stars to see.

"How's the old man doing?" he said.

"You busted him up pretty good."

"He fell over on his own."

"He fell on his face?"

"No. I did have to boot him once, after he fell, just to get outta there. He was dead set on killing me."

"He didn't appreciate your sudden interest in archeology."

"I guess not."

He drew on his cigarette and blew away from her but the smoke came back and she breathed in the smell of it.

"Is he talking?" he said.

"Not in any useful way."

"The detectives," Courtland said, "the other detectives, said they thought it was his uncle. The body."

"That's how it's looking. A significant blow to the head. He was most likely dead before he got walled up."

Courtland said nothing. Then he said, "What about that sock?"

She looked at him. "So you knew about the rumors. Those three little boys."

"I knew about the rumors."

"Is that why you decided to bust into the wall—that sock?"

"It was . . ." he said. "In the mix."

"When did you find it?"

"About a week ago. When Dan and I were cleaning up."

"Why didn't you bust into the wall then?"

He tipped his ash. "I guess I had to think about it awhile."

"Why the wall?"

"What?"

"Why bust into the wall?"

"Dan noticed it," he said. "He saw there was something off about the ceiling joists. And the windows. Something didn't make sense to him. And when we looked we saw it wasn't the original wall."

"This was after you found the sock?"

"No, before. We decided it was just a wall to keep out the water."

She watched him.

"After that, though," he said, "Dan got kinda spooky."

"Spooky?"

"Yeah. I heard him talking down there. Not talking to himself, like I do when I'm working. He was talking to someone. And when I came down the steps he looked . . ."

"Spooked," she said.

"Yeah. Plus the dog."

"Dog?"

"Devereaux's old dog, Bonnie."

"Ah," said Viegas. "He asked about a dog named Bonnie, at the hospital."

"What happened to her?"

"No idea. They must've taken her away."

"Taken her where?"

"The animal shelter, I suppose. What about her?"

Courtland's thoughts had drifted and she watched them come slowly back.

"She wouldn't go down there," he said. "In the basement. And whenever we went down there she'd lie at the top of the stairs and just whimper until we came back up."

"No wonder Dan Young got spooked."

Courtland tipped his ash. "Anyway. After he—after what happened to him, I saw that sock again, in the garbage, and the next thing I know I'm fighting an old man in his basement."

They were silent. A city bus came groaning up and went groaning by, a cloud of diesel in its wake.

"So the sock—?" Courtland said.

"The sock," said Viegas. She got out her phone and showed him the image. Laid out and digitally cleaned, it was unmistakably a white sock with two stripes on the cuff, one red, one blue. A metallic ruler showing it to be almost eight inches, end to end.

Of the six parents, only three still lived in town, she told him: the first boy's parents, the Felts, still married, and William Ross, the third boy's father, a widower.

We wanted him to be able to swim, Mary and me. So he wouldn't drown.

The Felts couldn't say what socks Teddy was wearing but they didn't recognize the sock Courtland had found. Ross said his son wasn't wearing socks at all. It was summer. The second boy's parents, the Milners, divorced but both living in Salt Lake City, looked at the image on their phones, their computers, and said no—no memory of what socks Duane was wearing, and they did not recognize this one.

She slid her phone back into her pocket. "They'll run DNA tests, see if it matches family members. But God knows how much DNA was under that dryer. I don't even want to know."

"What was in those tubs?" Courtland said.

"You didn't look?"

"No."

She looked at him and he held her eyes.

"A lot of old household crap," she said. "Old clothes—adult clothes. Old books. Probably just to have something to put on the shelves." She brushed at something on the wing of her coat. At nothing. "A burnt-up old baseball mitt," she said.

He looked at her.

"Burnt-up old *kid's* baseball mitt," she rephrased, and he sat staring at her until at last she shook her head. "None of the parents had seen it before," she said. "Two of them still had the boys' old mitts. Forty-one years later."

Courtland faced forward again.

"It was too old anyway," she said. "By about twenty years."

"Do you think he did it?"

She took a while to answer. "There's a theory going around that the uncle found out about it and that's why Devereaux killed him."

"Is that what you think?"

"I think it's just as likely they got into a fight about something completely unrelated," she said. "I think it's just as likely Devereaux woke up one day and decided to bash his uncle's head in. Without a living, talking witness or other forensic evidence . . ."

They were quiet. A white pickup truck rumbled by with cordwood stacked high in the bed. When it had gone on Courtland said, "Can I ask you something?"

"Sure."

"Did you ever think about finding the man who did that to your sister?"

Viegas turned to him. Stared at him, her heart dropping. Courtland held her eyes.

"Of course I thought about it."

"After you became a cop?"

"Yes."

"That's how you know he's a dentist in New Orleans."

"Yes."

He watched her. He seemed about to ask another question but did not.

Viegas held two fingers toward him. "I'll take one hit before you kill that off if you don't mind." He passed her the cigarette and she drew on it and held the smoke in her lungs, her eyes shut, and let the smoke out slowly. Instantly the nicotine sped to her brain. She handed it back.

"And what about Dan Young?" Courtland said.

"What about him?"

"Why did you go looking for him?"

"Because he called me."

"How did you know it was him?"

"I didn't. It was just a feeling."

Courtland took a last drag and stubbed out the butt on the capstone. "And did you think he did it?"

"Did I think Dan Young killed that girl ten years ago?"

"Yeah."

"I thought there was a chance."

"So you went looking for him."

She narrowed her eyes. "If I hadn't gone looking for him, he wouldn't have been in your truck trying to get home—is that where this is going?"

"No," Courtland said. "But that doesn't mean it isn't true."

Viegas thought to point out that it was he, Courtland, who'd given Dan Young her card. Instead, after a silence, she said, "Where will you go now?"

He shrugged. "Madison, maybe."

"And Denise Givens?"

"What about her?"

"She won't keep you here?"

Courtland said nothing. He fished his cigarettes, his lighter, up from his breast pocket and sat holding them.

"Can I ask you something?" he said for the second time.

"Yes."

"What's it like going into that station every day, doing the work you do, and coming out and seeing something like this across the street?"

"Something like you?"

He smiled. "Something like this building."

She looked at the church. The stained-glass Christ with his open hands. "Are you asking me if I believe in God?"

"I'm just asking what you think when you look at this building."

"I guess I don't think much." She considered. "I suppose at some level I like seeing it. A sign of good in the world. Or a sign of the belief in that good."

"A sign of belief," he said. "But not belief itself."

"The word doesn't have a lot of meaning for me personally. That doesn't mean I don't understand the value of it for other people. Or that I don't appreciate its influence on their behavior." She looked at him. "What about you?"

"Do I believe in God?"

"Yes."

He sat as if thinking it over. "When I was a kid my parents were split on the subject," he said. "My mother was a believer and my father wasn't. How that worked I don't know. But the message was I had to make up my own mind."

"And did you?"

"No. I was raised in a state of doubt and it kind of stuck."

Viegas looked at her hands where they lay in her lap, her fingers twined and pale against the darkness of the coat.

"You can never get them all," she said, and Courtland looked at her. She at him. "These men," she said. "For every one of them you manage to catch and put away, or punish, or kill . . . there's ten more right behind him. You know this."

He watched her. Then he looked away.

"One of them found my sister, Mariana," Viegas said. "Dumb-ass college-boy rapist. And another kind, a far worse kind, found your sister, Caitlin.

Up in those mountains. But they were the same kind of man in the end. A taker. A destroyer." She felt the hardness in her jaw, her mouth, and said, "No, screw that. They are nothing but weaklings and cowards."

Courtland made no reply, and she watched him in profile. Somehow he looked younger.

"He wasn't even looking for her," he said. "Not her in particular. We just happened to be there."

"Yes," said Viegas. "It seems like a hell of a long shot. But trust me, it isn't. The longer shot is that you go your whole life—a woman does—without one of them finding you. And more likely more than one."

He looked at her, as though he expected her to go on—to say something about the man of this kind, or men, who'd found her, perhaps.

"You couldn't have prevented it, Sean," she said. "Not at fifteen. Not at any age. I hope you know that by now."

"I know it," he said. "It doesn't mean I wouldn't go back and kill him if I could."

"I know you would."

They fell silent again. She looked at her watch—she should be on her way, let him go on his.

"Did you tell her about it?" she said.

"Who?"

"Denise Givens."

He shook his head.

She watched him. Then she stood and smoothed out the back side of her coat.

"I wish you luck, Sean Courtland," she said, and began to walk away.

"There's one more thing, Detective."

She turned back.

"I never told Dan about the three little boys. Those rumors about Devereaux."

She stood looking at him. "You never told him?"

He shook his head again. He lit his cigarette and held the smoke, let it go in a long blow. As if he'd unburdened himself somehow. And maybe he had.

"Why didn't you tell him?" she said.

"Because I didn't want him to get spooky."

She watched him. "Because you needed him to help you finish that job and get out of there."

"Yes ma'am. I needed him so I could get out of there."

He sat in stillness, studying the ember of his cigarette, and she remembered then that Dan Young was still on her phone—his picture. As was Holly Burke. Two people she'd never seen when they were alive.

She shook her head—both to dispel a shiver and in refusal of it.

"But Dan was spooked," she said.

"He was spooked."

She watched him.

"Not you, though," she said, and Courtland looked up. He met her gaze briefly and looked down again. The smoke unspooling from his ash and twisting on the wind.

"I never said that," he said.

When she left him he was still sitting there, and as she drove away she saw the floating Christ move from behind his left shoulder to his right, then withdraw with distance, leaving him alone and precarious somehow on the stone wall, and that image—the stained-glass icon, the sitting solitary man—remained with her.

Two days later she drove up to the Coulee animal shelter north of town, and there a tiny bright woman began flipping through the sheets of a three-ring binder, softly whistling some made-up tune. Soon enough she stopped whistling, smoothed her hand over the sheet and turned the binder on the counter for Viegas to see. It was a form with many lines of handwritten data and a printed color image stapled to it and the image was of a brown-and-black German shepherd sitting alertly, uneasily, with large erect ears, and eyes that had gone white as snow in the camera flash. The dog's name was written down as Bonnie and the form was stamped, in red: ADOPTED!

"She was that dog they found out at the old Devereaux place," the bright little woman said. "Just the saddest old thing you ever saw. Couldn't see the food in front of her. Wouldn't touch it anyway, put it right under her nose. So sad.

You wonder about the things she must've seen out there at that house—when she could see. The things she might tell you."

"Yes," said Viegas, declining to point out that the *things* the woman was alluding to had happened—to the extent they'd happened at all—four decades ago. Instead she kept looking at the form, as if she'd not already read it from top to bottom. "And the man who adopted her?" she said without looking up.

"Yes, ma'am. I wasn't here, but Rhondelle says he took one look at her back there in the kennels and said he'd take her. Said he knew her, and she sure seemed to know him, Rhondelle says, so that was a no-brainer. She just kinda skipped over the whole application process. I mean, who else was going to take her—sad old thing like that? If it were me I wouldn't have even taken his money, but he paid the hundred dollars and signed his name and she walked on out with him to his truck, Rhondelle says."

Viegas closed the binder and pushed it back toward the woman.

"Sad old thing," said the woman. "Gosh, I hope he's good to her."

PART IV

42.

April 2018

"MR. DEVEREAUX," SAID the young woman, stepping with purpose into the old man's room.

"Mr. Devereaux," she said at his bedside, "it is time for you to eat a little something."

She placed the tray on the overbed table and stood watching the old man's gaunt and sallow face. After a moment his eyelids parted, slow as an old lizard's; the yellow sclera rolled and two watery blue discs descended and brought the young woman slowly into focus. Her name was Natukunda Jones, and she wore the blue scrubs top and black scrubs bottoms that identified her in that hospital as a nurse's aide. Although one day she, Natukunda, would be the doctor in her own white coat. *Dr. Jones.* Striding from room to room, examining, comforting, healing.

The old man's lids closed again and his face lapsed back into its habitual look of unconscious, languishing defeat, though his vitals were stable.

"You are fooling no one, Mr. Devereaux," said Natukunda. "You are hardly getting any pain meds at all, and I hear your stomach growl like a tiger."

Nothing.

"Do you know what today is, Mr. Devereaux? Today is chocolate pudding day. No regular dinner, only chocolate pudding. Here, I will help you." She peeled back the foil lid and stirred the pudding with a spoon and reached a glistening dollop toward his face. She waved it under his nose.

"You smell that? Doesn't that smell good?" She bumped the pale and cracked lower lip with the spoon. "Go on, now. You know you want to." Daubed a bit of the pudding on his upper lip.

"No? Nothing? Oh, you are a stubborn man, Mr. Devereaux." She set the spoon in the pudding and returned the cup to the tray and plucked a tissue from the box and wiped the pudding from his lip and stood staring at his face. He'd been brought in by the police after a body was found in his basement, it was said. It was said he had killed his uncle and put him behind a wall in the basement and there the uncle had stayed for forty years.

It was said he had killed three little boys who had gone missing, also forty years ago.

All right, people could say anything they wanted. That was not her business. He was a patient in her hospital, on her shift, and the only thing that mattered to her was that he open his mouth for the pudding.

She took a deep breath and let it out again for him to hear. "What if I told you I would stand here and talk to you until you took one spoon of the pudding? Hmm? Do you want to hear my story—my life story, Mr. Devereaux?"

Devereaux went on breathing, raggedly, wheezingly, despite the nasal cannula.

Natukunda checked the oxygen level. She checked the two IV bags and flicked the drip chambers with the nail of her middle finger, two flicks each.

"Too bad," she said. "I do not have time today to stand here and tell you my life story, much as you would like to hear it. I have other patients." She fussed with his bedding. She rested the back of her hand on his spotted forehead. "But I will come back later, Mr. Devereaux, and if this pudding has not been touched I will tell you everything you want to know. All right? Beginning with the very earliest days of my girlhood in Uganda. How does that sound?"

Devereaux lay wheezing, the balls of his eyes unmoving under their veiny skins.

"Think it over, Mr. Devereaux." She patted the bone of his forearm, then turned and left the room as she had entered it, with purpose.

DEVEREAUX HEARD NONE of it. His mind had become detached from his body's present and confining circumstances and gone journeying freely and widely. Not unconscious and dreaming of long-ago times, not consciously cycling through memories, but floating in some third and more vivid realm where a man of no determinate age who was indisputably himself—the age-less essential being that was Marion Devereaux—beheld himself at various ages, various times and places, with the weird duality of experiencing, or re-experiencing, the moments as he had lived them, and also of witnessing them as this floating, timeless Devereaux.

At the moment the young nurse's aide touched his arm, the unrespon-sive old man was observing himself standing on the back stoop of a house at night while piano music played through the grid of the screen door. A younger Devereaux standing transfixed, his nose pressed to the screen as though he would pass through it like the notes themselves and thereby enter the music, live in that sound, and pulling back from the screen only when a pretty young woman came to the door and smiled at him, and though he knew it was she who had been playing the piano, still the piano played as she stood before him—the pretty young woman standing before him and playing the piano both—and Devereaux the man and Devereaux the witness can smell her perfume through the screen.

On a bridge of smell the old man's brain crosses from the porch to a gym-nasium where Devereaux the janitor pilots the great mop dampened with Zep's solution, and while he pushes the mop from one end of the floor to the other, kids dash about to either side of him, yelling, screaming, their sneakers screech-ing on the bright wet floor, and a volley of red rubber balls sail by his head and he can smell these too as they pass, he is in the middle of a game of dodgeball and he understands that the children are not throwing at each other but at him, and he looks to one team of kids and he looks to the other and they are all rushing to the line to throw—all but one boy, a thin and copper-headed boy who leans against the back wall with his hands behind him and simply watches Devereaux's progress amidst the rubber balls as they go flying and humming past his head.

A small basement window shatters and a length of two-by-four punches out the remaining glass and a boy contorts himself into the frame and swims through it and tumbles out onto the frosted grass in his jeans and nothing else, gets to his feet and walks away from the house with a strange, uneven gait. He stops and turns around and stands picking glass from his skin, bleeding in the cold and dark while a darker smoke disgorges from the basement and the bright glow of fire moves from window to window on the ground floor. This boy, young Marion, age eleven, looks up and down the street, where no other houses, no other lights, can be seen, and finally he goes up the porchsteps and takes hold of the knob—and draws his hand back with a cry and shakes it in the air. He steps down off the porch and backs away from the house for a better view of the second-story windows. He looks at the ground and turns a circle and stops, and pulls like a tooth from its socket one of the small decorative stones that line his mother's flowerbed and, taking aim, pitches the stone into his parents' bedroom window. The stone passes cleanly through the glass and in the next instant, as if by the sudden change in pressure, a window on the ground floor explodes, spewing glass and flames out into the night. Upstairs, no one comes to the window. Fire hisses and roars and moans. The boy steps back from the heat. Steps back some more. Black smoke boiling from the windows. Flames climbing the exterior of the house like monkeys on fire. Furniture and everything else bursting. Fire screaming in the seams of the house—

Momma!

—the smell, the terrible greasy black chemical stink of a burning house.

Don't you just sit there and stare at that hamburger, boy, that cost me two dollars at the butcher, highway robbery if you ask me but who asked me? Who ever asks me?

The old woman watching him, then turning away still talking, busying herself at the stove while the boy sits at the table staring at the hamburger in its bun.

I don't think he's hungry, Ma. I don't believe he's got his appetite back yet.

He'll get it back or he'll starve. You mind your own business.

The older boy, his uncle, Frankie, sitting there chewing, watching him. Thin makings of a mustache above his lip. The calculating meanness of a sixteen-year-old in his blue eyes. Then, leaning close and taking a sniff of his nephew, another sniff, he says low with hamburger breath, *I can smell the smoke on you, Marion. You reek of it. Did you know that? I know she washed those clothes and I know you've taken about a hundred baths since you been here but—phew. You got the stink of fire and death on you.* Uncle Frankie shakes his head slowly. *He's a talky one, Ma. A real chatterbox. How long's he gonna be staying here?*

You know how long. Don't be so smart. He's family. He lives here now.

Lives here? Here?

Of course here.

Couldn't he stay out in the garage?

The old woman turning with a two-prong fork in her grip. *Frankie, you are trying me. Why are you trying me?*

I'm just asking questions here, Ma.

She sighs and turns back to the stove. Frankie reaches forward and picks up Devereaux's hamburger and takes a great bite and sets the burger down again and sits chewing open-mouthed.

Hey, Ma.

Don't you hey me.

Ma.

What.

He ate a bite. Flexing his eyebrows at Marion.

Told you. Eat or starve.

Uncle Frankie leans in close again. *Hey, Marion. Anybody gives you shit at school or anywheres else, calls you firebug, calls you gimpy—you let your Uncle Frankie know, all right? I won't have anybody talking shit about any nephew of mine. All right?*

Marion sits there. Then he nods, and Uncle Frankie leans back again.

Hey, Ma.

The old woman at the stove says nothing.

Ma, says Uncle Frankie.

What, Frankie.

Ma. Just curious. We got fire insurance?

The sound of the bat, the fat smack of wood on the ball, the cries of the boys when you come out at the end of the day and the sun is still up in the west and they are out in the cool, mud-smelling dusk—seven, eight, ten of them out on the diamond. Forget about the mud of the infield, forget about the soggy outfield, the boy on the mound winds up, hurls, the boy at the plate swings, and the crack of the bat on the ball is the same, no matter the mud, no matter the time of year, no matter the age of the boys . . . Athletic boys, tough boys, no girls in this game, *Why not? Um, cuz yer a GIRL? And no little brothers, yer too little, and no redheaded fruity-tooties either, you can all just stand back and watch . . .* Watch us with our leather mitts, our jaws chewing our wads of Topps bubble gum, the sugary pink bubbles we blow awaiting the grounder up the middle, awaiting the sweet double play we can see so clearly in our minds it's as if we make it happen . . . Something going on now out toward left field, everybody looking—*Shit, it's the Creep. Don't look at him too long, he might smile at you, might follow you home like a dog!*

Devereaux passing well beyond the boys in the outfield and the boys all pausing to watch him make his way and then turning from him with smirks, pounding their mitts harder, yelling louder, spitting, wagging the bat slugger-style and—*Throw me one down the middle, goddammit, betcha anything I can hit him, just throw it already*—the crack of the bat and the ball sailing, rising, but falling far short of Devereaux, far short of any boy's wildest dinger dreams, and from way out there you can see that kid standing at the edge of the woods watching, his hair in the setting sun like a wig of copper wiring, same kid he tried to help one day and what did he get for it but an earful of nastiness?

Same kid toting that barn post into the yard, letting it drop. *Come back when you can and we'll finish the job,* says Uncle Frankie but the kid never comes back, not that Devereaux ever saw.

That boy ever come back around here?

What boy? Uncle Frankie not looking up from his magazine.

That redheaded boy was helping you with the barn post.

Uncle Frankie sitting there. Turning the magazine page. Looking up finally at Devereaux. *You best stay away from them boys, Marion, redheaded or otherwise. You know what people say about you as it is.*

They don't say anything about me.

Uncle Frankie taking a puff and blowing the smoke. *Right. And you quit that job at the junior high.*

Devereaux shaking his head, turning, walking away.

Don't get mad at me, Marion—I ain't the one talking. And you can just unball those fists of yours while you're at it, buckeroo, you know you ain't gonna use 'em. Jesus Christ, Marion, don't be so goddam sensitive.

In the late sunlight and cold grass of spring, first afternoon of spring, his mother chases down the ball laughing, turning in her skirt, laughing and throwing the ball back to him, girl-like and pretty, bright fin of water spinning from the ball in the sun before it punches so deep and solid in the mitt—the new leather smell of the mitt he loves already, covering his face with it when the ball is not in it, breathing it in as she scrambles again for the wet ball, popping up from the grass and setting herself once again for her throw and laughing, and both of them waving at the car, the old blue Ford, as it turns into the drive—he is home. Dirty from the factory, smelling of engines, bent with the long day, slamming the car door and standing with the black lunch pail in his grip, *Come play with us,* she calls, but not in her voice of just seconds ago, not with that laugh, and he stands looking at them, saying nothing, and goes on into the house.

Later it's just their voices, rising like heat through the bare floor, up through mattress and pillow, *What were you thinking, buying him a mitt?*

What a question! He's a boy. He wants to play. He loves that mitt!

You know goddam well he can't play baseball.

Why can't he?

You know goddam well—do you know what those boys will do to him the second they see him run on that leg?

The doctor said he can play sports. He can have shoes for that too.

I've seen those shoes. Don't you think he's had enough humiliation? Why are you setting him up for more?

A long silence then. Long. Silence. Then: *Whose humiliation are we talking about here?*

Fire screaming in the seams of the house—

Momma!

And then he is standing on the cellar steps watching the old woman at the sink as she wrings the neck on a dingy pink T-shirt and the pink dripping on the white porcelain and circling with the suds and burbling down the drain.

She straightens, and without looking up says, *What you want, sneaking up on me like that?*

Just bringing down these clothes, Gramma.

Well, bring 'em down then, don't just stand there like a ghost, like to give me the heebie-jeebies.

The boy comes down and stands beside her. Fifteen, sixteen years old. Tall as her now, but she is not tall. He stands watching her. The wet, powerful hands.

What? she says. Turning to look at him.

Nothin.

Nothin is right. Your Uncle Frankie had an accident, got blood on himself.

Marion looks over at the canvas army cot near the old cellar steps. As if Uncle Frankie might be lying there, bandaged and watching. A rusty iron standing lamp with no shade leans over the empty cot. Old magazines on the concrete floor. *Guns & Ammo. Field & Stream.* An opened can of Hamm's beer.

Is he OK?

He's fine. But the blood . . . , she says, and turns the T-shirt under the faucet. *Working on that old tractor, God knows why. Says he sliced himself somehow under there. Says he thought it was oil dripping on him. When he walked in I thought . . .* Shaking her head. *I don't know what I thought.*

Abruptly she turns and looks at the boy, as if she'd forgotten him.

Marion, ain't you got something to do with yourself other'n standing there watching me wash clothes?

No, ma'am.

Well—find something. Standing there like a ghost, she says. *Giving me the heebie-jeebies . . .*

The night a hoot owl got him out of bed—years later now, the old woman dead. The owl hooting and hooting and just would not quit and finally he had to get up and go down and see if he could see him in the moonlight. Hot July night anyway and at least he might cool off out there, get cool and tired enough to sleep when he got back to bed. They had buried the old woman, and Uncle Frankie was sleeping in the cellar and Devereaux went through the house in bare feet and didn't turn on any lights. Crossed through the kitchen in the moonlight and opened the screen door just as quiet as was possible and likewise shut it again behind him. The hoot owl was out there in the trees by the garage—he could just about see him by the sound—but the second Devereaux's foot hit the grass the owl stopped.

Dead quiet. The moon bright and lopsided in the southern sky so must've been two, three in the morning, and something, some sound that wasn't the owl made him look away from the moon and he saw them: two boys, stepping from the woods like deer. The bigger boy holding the smaller one's hand. Brothers, perhaps.

The bigger boy leading the smaller one along, encouraging him because the smaller one was holding back, scared . . . And as the boys came along, Devereaux moved closer to the house to get out of the moonlight and when the boys passed out of sight behind the house he crept alongside the wall in his bare feet, past the back door until he got to the other corner. Standing still and quiet as the moon itself, he could hear them moving again, their sneakers in the dewy grass, their whispers, and the little one's whimpering. They were struggling somehow, and Devereaux eased his face around the edge of the house, saw nothing, eased farther . . . a little farther . . . and there they stood, just beyond a dim yellow light spilling upward from the open bulkhead.

The bigger boy had a grip on the smaller one's hand and the smaller one was leaning back with all his little weight and shaking his head and crying, and the older one whispered at him fiercely but lightly, playfully, *Come on, don't be a baby, you said you wanted to see it and here we are, we made it, it's right in here, Harlan . . . Come on, just a few steps more, you won't even believe it there's so much of it. Snickers, Reese's . . . You like Reese's, don't you . . . ?* The little one shaking his head and tugging his arm and the older one finally giving him such a yank the little one cried out, and without knowing he would do it Devereaux moved. He stepped out from his hiding, and the bigger one saw him. Looked right at him and Devereaux looked right at the bigger one and it was then the kid's hair turned red, or seemed to turn red: the moment he saw Devereaux.

And Devereaux would know that kid, that hair, anywhere, in any kind of light, and he stepped toward them. But just then the light from the cellar changed—darkening with the shape of a figure moving into the source of the light, a looming man-shape rising up out of the earth step by step as if out of some crypt. The smaller boy screamed and jerked his arm and the older boy, the Parnell boy, in his own fright, perhaps, let go. The little boy fell and bounced back onto his feet and was gone like a jackrabbit dropped from the claws of a bird, the great night owl itself, and nothing but the whites of his sneakers as he dashed away into the trees.

Devereaux standing there, his chest pounding. The Parnell boy staring at him. Not at the rising figure—at him. The boy white-faced, his legs rooted in the turf where he stood, and first came the voice: *Davy—what in the hell is going on out here?* Then the man himself, *Ah, shit, kid, what did you—*And that face, the shadowed eyes, following the frozen boy's stare and the man stopping, not taking the next step, halfway risen from the bulkhead and turning to Devereaux.

Marion—? Uncle Frankie looking at Devereaux, then at the boy again. A long while. The boy looking from man to man. Devereaux paying no attention to the boy anymore. His eyes on Uncle Frankie. The three of them in their quiet triangle and their brains racing from point to point until at last Uncle Frankie turned away from the boy, slowly, and put his gaze once again on Devereaux.

Marion—what in the hell have you done?

Devereaux, watching his uncle—watching him—shook his head. *It wasn't me.*

Uncle Frankie did not take his eyes from Devereaux. *Davy, what's he gotten you into here, boy? Huh?* Then, turning suddenly on the boy: *Speak up, it's all right. He can't hurt you now.* The boy shaking his head, that red hair, the tears shining on his face in the light from the cellar. *Davy, listen to me. Listen. You need to go catch that kid and make sure he gets home, you hear? You need to catch him and make sure he don't say a word about you—you understand? He talks and you are in big, big trouble, boy. Hear me?* The Parnell boy standing there shaking.

Go! says Uncle Frankie and the boy jumps, the boy turns and runs—careening, stumbling back the way he came, vanishing into the woods until there's no sound of him anymore. No sound at all but Devereaux's own breathing. Uncle Frankie standing in the bulkhead, absolutely still—then taking the last steps up to stand at his full height on the grass, half-lit in the yellow light. Jeans and boots and no shirt. Pale ribs and chest. The stark shapes of scars. He is turned toward Devereaux and somehow, from out of nowhere, there is the flash of the knife. The great blade moving side to side in the light, slow and dreamy as a snake.

You've really done it now, Marion. You've really screwed the whole mission. We are just sitting ducks out here—do you realize that?

He steps toward Devereaux, the blade passing through the light as though to slice it into thinnest ribbons, and Devereaux, hardly understanding his own intentions, moves to his left, toward the side of the house, where something lies in the weeds that climb the foundation, a thing seen so many times it has ceased to register on the mind and has all but vanished anyway in the untended growth—is it even still there?

It must be. Why would it move? Where would it go?

They are going to talk about this night, Marion. Man, are they gonna talk. Ol' Marion Devereaux, they'll say, that boy never was right in the head . . . A very strange boy—the blade weaving in the moonlight, winking at Devereaux like the eye of a salacious dragon—*burnt up his own folks in their beds while they slept, so no wonder. But don't you worry, little nephew, I won't pour gas on that fire. I won't have people—where you headed now? What're you looking for? Ah, lookee there, I wondered where that old thing went off to. Hell of a strange time to dig a hole, Marion . . . But I won't put you in the ground, I'll leave everything just like it is so the sheriff and his little deputy can see what happened, how I caught you out here creeping around. I won't even mention 'ol Red there, only how you went berserk and came after me with a goddam POSTHOLE—hey, there you go! Good swing, Marion, good effort!*

The length and weight of the tool, the effort to swing it, spins Devereaux nearly around before he catches himself and turns back, the digger held athwart his body. He takes one step back in his bare feet for each step Uncle Frankie takes forward.

You know what, Marion? That's a good idea. I'ma let you clock me one with that thing, that'll look better.

Where are the other ones?

What—? What did you say?

The other boys. Where'd you put 'em.

Uncle Frankie staring at him, incredulous in the moonlight. *See, Marion, it's shit like that. It's shit like that that got us here. Your twisted mind, your twisted little creep mind. I shoulda slit your throat in your bed a long time ago, in memory of my dear dead sister, and we wouldn't be in this mess. OK, here, take your shot—right now. Come on, slugger . . .* turning his back but not his eyes, the welts of long-ago wounds like puckered code on the pale flesh, wormish runes in the moonlight. And Devereaux draws back the blades of the digger, drops his right hand to join his left and steps into his swing, but the ball he swings for is low, not high, and Uncle Frankie cannot react in time. The longwise edges of the curved blades land crackingly on the outside of the right knee and he crumples instantly, dropping to that knee with a howl and nearly pitching to the ground before stopping himself with one arm—his right arm. His knife hand. *Holy Christ! Yow. Jesus . . . just—back off a second there, slugger. That really hurt . . . I think you broke her.*

Devereaux holds his batter's stance, the digger half-cocked for the next pitch, and his uncle cranes to look back at him. All the hardness and evil gone from his face, he looks like nothing but a pitiful man in pain, in dismay at that pain, how it has befallen him, at whose hands. *Jesus Christ, Marion—what'd you go and do that for? Did you think I was gonna cut you? I was just messing with you, son. Come on, now—stop fuckin around and help me up, shit, I may have to go to the hospital . . . Here now, give a man a hand, goddammit . . .* reaching out toward Devereaux with his free, his left hand.

Devereaux stands uncertainly, the digger still half-cocked but already a little lower, perhaps an inch or two. As if it were growing too heavy for him to hold in that position. It drops again, and when the blades are at the level of his own knees he lets go with his right hand and reaches out and Uncle Frankie snatches at his hand and seizes it as the king snake seizes the mouse. In that same instant his other hand whips around like a second, quicker snake to slash at Devereaux's bare forearm. The movement is so quick and smooth it seems he's missed altogether, but then a dark smile spreads across the meat of Devereaux's forearm and blood begins to run from the opened skin.

Uncle Frankie draws back the knife and jerks at Devereaux's arm and Devereaux is nearly thrown off-balance, but he gets one foot forward, planted in the wet grass, and jerks back. His uncle's grip is a bear trap. An alligator. There's nothing to do but swing the digger one-handed, left-handed, in an upward arc, and if there's no great power behind the swing there's accuracy—the edges of the blades catch his uncle on the chin and the blood flows from the gash and Uncle Frankie lets go Devereaux's hand and topples backwards into a sitting position in the grass.

He cups his chin in his free hand and looks at the blood and looks at Devereaux, then holds his hand under his chin to catch the dark string of blood, the blood pooling black and thick in the palm. The blood overspilling the Vs of his fingers and drizzling like paint from his knuckles to spatter the cloth of his jeans.

O'right, says Uncle Frankie. *O'right now'm mad.* Something in his mouth has been knocked loose—teeth, tongue, jaw. *Now you really piss me off, fucker. Just gimme goddam second get my feet, tough guy.* And Devereaux does. He takes his batter's stance once more as his uncle groans about on the ground. As he pushes himself up slowly and stands hunched over his bent legs, buttressing his upper body with hands on thighs, elbows locked. The knife still in his hand.

At last, holding this position, he lifts his head—lifts it, then cocks it far back on his neck, as if to give Devereaux the best possible view of the blood that has striped his underjaw, his throat and upper chest, like the tattoo scrollwork of an island warrior, or high priest—a fierceness at odds with the slackened face, the dulled and torpid gaze. He grins, baring his teeth to Devereaux, and stands erect again. And raises the knife once more.

OK, Marion, he says—and that is all. For Devereaux has swung the posthole digger round and crashed it squarely into the side of his uncle's skull, just above and behind the left ear. The head keels to one side, the body staggers. Blood jets from the skull in a thin dark spray. The head rights itself but one eye is out of true, staring off into the woods, while from the other eye someone, something no longer Uncle Frankie, stares at Devereaux. The body staggers again, it back-steps, it instinctively tries to stop itself but with the next backstep it encounters the bulkhead door thrown open on its hinges and the body trips—arms windmill in the air and the knife blade goes flashing away into darkness and the body slams down dumbly onto the door. The upper body sloughs into the opening and thuds upon wooden steps and goes no farther. The legs remain above, bent at the knees, the boots at rest on the bulkhead door, the worn and dirty soles splayed to either direction. It is all very clownish and final.

Or not quite final. When Devereaux steps up to the bulkhead and looks down, his uncle, or what had been his uncle, is looking up—directly up, with his one good eye. And smiling. Not some terrible grin of pain and death, but the smile of a man pleased with what he sees, and Devereaux looks up at the night sky, the starry heavens. He looks at the stars, then down into the bulkhead again. His uncle's good eye roves as if the stars were in motion. Blood pumps in small gouts from the side of his head, darkening one wooden step, dripping down to darken the next, a slow, dark waterfall.

Devereaux raises the blades of the digger to the cellar light and studies them closely, turning them this way and that, and finally he stands the tool against the side of the house. He inspects his wound: deep, but not so much blood now. There is gauze and tape and peroxide in the upstairs bathroom.

Marion . . .

The call is so faint he thinks he's imagined it. He steps once more to the bulkhead and looks down.

Uncle Frankie is staring up at him. He speaks but Devereaux can't understand. Devereaux gets down on his haunches with his elbows on his knees, hands hanging loose.

What did you say? he says.

Leave'm be, Marion.

Leave who be?

Daby, says his uncle.

Davy?

Din't do nothin.

Did he bring that other boy here? Billy Ross?

Uncle Frankie rolls his head slightly on the step. *Just . . . the one,* he says.

Where are the others?

Din't know, says his uncle. *Din't know nothin. Just a dumb . . .*

And that's all. Devereaux on his haunches watches the last of the light dim from his uncle's eyes. The blood ceasing to pump.

The deputy when he comes in the morning will not even mention this other boy, only the redheaded boy who hangs himself in the tree.

And why'd he go and do that? Devereaux will wonder.

Because, he'll reason, he thought the other boy—Harlan—would tell on him.

But Harlan says nothing, ever. Too small, too scared to know where he was. Or else Davy caught him and scared him even more.

Or did Davy think Devereaux would tell?

And if Devereaux had never heard that hoot owl and come downstairs, would Davy still be alive?

Would Harlan be dead?

Again he hears his uncle's words:

Din't know nothin.

Was that true? When had the redheaded boy first started hanging around with Uncle Frankie? It wasn't long after that day on the school playground, when the bigger boys were picking on him, that he'd come to help Uncle Frankie sink a barn post for a basketball goal. Same day the deputy first came out looking for Billy Ross, the third boy. Missing for two days.

No, thinks Devereaux, the redheaded boy didn't help with Billy Ross. Or Teddy Felt or Duane Milner either. Harlan was the first, and Davy didn't even know what he was doing—not really, until he saw Uncle Frankie come out of the cellar bulkhead. Until he saw Devereaux. Then he understood. The fear that came into his eyes. The panic.

Got him a rope and it was all over before he could get a grip on himself, before he could calm down and figure some other way out.

His parents having no idea, all these years.

And that was better. Better than knowing what their boy had been mixed up in.

Better than the whole world knowing.

In the morning the deputy will show Devereaux the Zippo lighter, that's all, Uncle Frankie dead in the cellar the whole time, then walk away and never come back.

But that is hours away. Hours. And here is Uncle Frankie, lying just so under the stars.

Devereaux in his squat sits a long while looking at the body on the steps. The dark blood on the steps. All the mopping in the world will never get it out. A long, long while he sits—Devereaux then and the Devereaux who is Devereaux always, looking on.

The hoot owl begins hooting again in its tree.

Dirt. Dirt will cover—

"Mr. Devereaux..."

The hoot owl speaks.

"Mr. Devereaux."

In the late sunlight and cold grass of spring, first afternoon of spring, she chases down the ball laughing

A third time: "Mr. Devereaux, come on now!"

In late sunlight she chases the ball laughing, turning in her skirt, throwing the ball back to him, bright fin of water spinning from the ball

The monitor is sending out its alarm. A nurse rushes in and takes over, all but pushing the young nurse's aide aside. The nurse begins compressing the bony chest. Breaths huff from the open mouth.

Both of them waving at the car, the old blue Ford—he's home

The monitor is in distress. The doctor strides in in her white coat. She commands the nurse. She looks at Natukunda and commands her too. The doctor opens the old man's gown and takes the paddles in her hands.

You know goddam well he can't play

"Clear," says the doctor, and the old ribcage jumps to the charge and drops again.

Why can't he play

You know goddam well—do you know what those boys will do to him the second they see

"Clear," she says, and the ribcage jumps. A full two minutes this goes on, but without great urgency, and less hope. He is an old, busted-up old man.

And a murderer.

"Clear."

No one comes to the window. Fire hisses and roars. Boy steps back from the heat. Black smoke boiling, flames climbing

Momma!

Turns and runs down the sidewalk, bare feet slapping unevenly on cold concrete, he can think of nowhere closer than the Grindell house, though the boy there hates him, teases him at school, calls him The Gimp

Two full minutes and now—the doctor calls it—he is gone. All he is, all he ever was, all he ever thought or remembered or dreamed.

Bare feet slapping cold concrete, slap slap slap

Devereaux the living, conscious being in this world ceases and there is nothing left but the dead tissue and bone. Nothing but the old Devereaux house out in the bluffs and the difficult, violent Devereaux history, the entire truth of which was known to none but Marion Devereaux himself, now deceased.

43.

ANDANTE, LENTO . . .

Viegas read the sheet and played the notes but it was all mechanical—her fingers could not make the music she heard in her head.

She looked at the keyboard and tried it from memory. Muscle memory. Better, but she could only go so far before her fingers stopped and had no idea where to go next.

"Ugh," she said into the deadened silence. The practice rooms were sound-proofed, and yet she could hear someone playing, a beautiful and fluid melody she'd never heard before. An original composition, probably. Some twenty-year-old college kid. A prodigy.

She sat listening, and her thoughts progressed from notes and chords to Sean Courtland and Dan Young. To Blaine Mattis and Henry Givens. Denise Givens.

Unthinkingly she began to play *Moonlight Sonata*, her father's favorite.

Devereaux in his hospital bed. William Ross—one old man trying to get another to tell him where his son was.

And now Devereaux was dead and would never tell anyone anything.

She banged out two bars of "Chopsticks" and held the last notes until all sound, the least vibration, had died away.

She looked at her watch. 6:35. She had the room for another twenty-five minutes but what was the point? Her mind wasn't in the right place.

Truer to say her mind was someplace else altogether.

6:35. Forty-five minutes, maybe an hour of daylight.

But by the time she got out to the bluffs, dusk was already in the trees.

She parked on the shoulder and ducked under the yellow tape and walked the gravel drive, her boots loud in the silence, and stepped into the clearing. The old gray house in the gloom of sundown was as bleak and forsaken as any she'd ever seen. The ground-floor and basement windows had been boarded up, the doors fitted with hasp latches and padlocks. Nothing but darkness in the upper windows.

The makeshift tomb where Devereaux's uncle had been found was now enclosed by sections of barricade fencing lashed together at the corners with white zip cuffs, more police tape woven through the links. She got out her Mini Maglite and walked its beam down the steps where the corpse had lain all those years—those decades—and on into the basement. No green tubs from that vantage nor any vantage; they lived in the evidence room now.

Something moved in an upstairs window and she looked in time to see a bat fly mutely from the second story. Another. The glass had been pierced by a stone. More than once. All the windows had. Kids, come to prove their arms and their nerve to each other, to speak the haunted names out loud:

I see Teddy Felt.

Crash.

I see Duane Milner.

Crash.

I see Billy Ross.

Believing they indeed saw the boys' faces in the panes of glass they broke.

The tractor sat where Dusty and his guys had dragged it, aimed back toward the garage with the look of some forlorn creature, waiting only for the sections of fencing to be removed before it returned to its rightful place under the sagging joists.

Viegas stood at the fencing, looking into the garage. Poking her beam around. The ages of old junk. The packed dirt floor and the pit where the dog, or coyote, had been buried.

She fingered the zip cuffs tying the two sections of fencing together and knew they were the same as those in her coat pocket, with the box cutter.

She put her beam on the pit again.

Why would you bury a dog or coyote in a garage? Under a tractor.

She didn't need to cut the zip cuffs: the outer posts of the sections were not fastened to the garage in any way but stood freestanding on square metal bases. Genius. She dragged one post away from the garage and stepped through the gap into the darkness.

She swept her light from one piece of junk to another. Old wheelbarrow. Old basketball backboard. Agrarian tools from another era leaning together in a kind of stall: shovels, rakes, a posthole digger. A pickaxe such as she hadn't seen since her days running barefoot on her grandfather's farm.

She stood at the edge of the pit, thinking the darkness and the bright, narrow beam might pick up something that could not otherwise be seen, but she saw only dirt, rocks, some idiot's tinfoil gum wrapper.

Then she looked up. Played her beam over the darkened and mottled undersides of large sheets of plywood where they lay on the great bowed ribcage of the ceiling joists.

Sean Courtland had said something about the ceiling joists in the basement—something Dan Young had noticed. Something off. She stood looking at these awhile.

The extension ladder was gone but her light found a series of wooden dowel rungs behind more junk, and after a minute's dirty labor she had raised the old ladder from the floor and stood it upright between the joists. Just the right height.

She put her weight on the lowest rung, bounced on it, and climbed.

At the top she skimmed her light over the three planes that formed the triangular space, the two pitched walls of the roof and the sheets of plywood. The big four-by-eight sheets might once have been stacked but had long ago fanned out over the joists in a filthy and warped kind of floor on which other lesser pieces had been tossed—or else had fallen from the rafters above, for the rusted nails stood up sharp and bristling in her light, and of length enough to pierce the human foot clean through. Good-size bootprints in the dust marked where a cop or deputy had taken two steps onto the ply and two steps back.

Viegas stepped onto the ply and stood hunched under the rafters. Where the plywood did not cover the joists she could see through the open spaces to the dirt floor below. She made a small juking motion in place and set the burdened joists to swaying. If the fall didn't kill you, the roof crashing down would finish the job. Her poor father's face when they told him she'd been found in a pile of wood out at the old Devereaux place: disbelief and grief and embarrassment all at once.

She moved on, choosing her steps with care, until she reached the center of the attic where the headroom was greatest and she could stand at her full height, barely—her scalp so close to the peak she could feel the day's heat radiating from the roof. A hot pungency of dust and wood.

The thick old rafters sloping away from either side of the ridge beam were spaced perhaps two feet apart, the bays they created some six or eight inches deep, and here and there they'd been sheathed over with those lesser pieces of ply that lay on the floor nails-up. Some erratic approach to mending, or cryptic scheme for sheathing the whole that had gone only so far before being abandoned.

Her light paused at the edge of one piece of sheathing and her heart kicked. An animal lay asleep in the warmth of the bay, its furry backside protruding.

She moved closer. Not an animal. She poked it with her finger and a thin talus of grit and mouse droppings rained to the floor. It was fiberglass insulation, and it appeared to fill the box of the space—and the others—for some reason she couldn't imagine, since so much of the roof remained unsheathed and uninsulated.

She thought she was looking at some form of madness. A handyman who'd lost his mind. The same one who'd built a false wall in his basement as a tomb for his uncle.

But that had been a different kind of work—mad, yes, but far from mindless. That wall had been built with care. With skill. The work of a pro.

She stood following the spot of her light where it roved. The strange sheathings. The open bays. The dark corners where the pitched roof met the joists on which she stood. Her light passed over a large section of sheathing and then came back—two full sheets of plywood, in fact, fastened longwise across the rafters, one at floor level and the other above it, offset by one rafter. Insulation bulging from the bays.

She toured the light around to be sure: no other full sheets anywhere on the rafters. And looking again at these, her gut dropped through space. The hair on the back of her neck stood.

"No way," she said. "No fucking way."

Had the two sheets been attached to a vertical wall and not the slant of the roof, she could not have reached the top edge of the top sheet without a stepladder. As it was she needed only to step forward, hunching again, to touch the insulation, and this she did—working her fingers into it as if it were some filthy head of hair, and with a soft ripping sound yanked up a good chunk of it from one of the bays. Debris and droppings rattling at her feet. A glistening cloud of fiberglass dust.

She put her light on the chunk: where it had ripped it was still pink at its center. She dropped it and reached deeper into that darkness thinking mice, thinking rats, and with greater care worked free another piece, this one a good two feet in length, and squared at the far end. Either a new piece began below it, or there was no more below it. No more insulation.

Her heart was thudding.

She stuck her head up into the bay, pressing her skull to the roof decking, into the points of roofing nails, and tipped the Maglite over the lip of the ply and lit the boxy space—but could see nothing for the cloud of glittering dust. A shape down there, maybe. Something. Not insulation. So much fiberglass in the air she began to cough and could not stop. She moved to improve her view and doing so drove a roofing nail into her head and cried out and dropped the Mag. The light went tumbling down the bay, knocking and slashing in the bright dust and stopped, not at the bottom but at some midway point—four, five feet from the floor—and aimed up at her now so there was no chance of seeing what had stopped it. She tried to get her arm down there, waiting for something to sink its teeth into her fingers, but felt only empty space, wood, the points of the roofing nails.

She stood staring at the box of light in the rafter bay. Coughing. Rubbing her head.

She gripped the edge of the sheet of ply with both hands and jerked at it. Nothing.

She hung all her weight on it and did not think what would happen if it came suddenly free, the entire sheet swinging down, herself thrown backwards onto some ungodly bed of nails. But it did not come suddenly free. Did not even budge.

For a moment she didn't cough and there was dead silence. Then she coughed again.

She went down the ladder, and some minute or two later she came back up with no coat, no jacket, and the pickaxe in her hands.

The old iron head was long and curved with a flat kind of chopping blade on one end, a skinny point on the other. She put the flat end into the bay, seating it on the ply, centered the pointed end on the edge of the rafter, and pulled back on the handle. The ply creaked, it bowed, but then the pointed end skated off and she took a hop to keep from falling over. Stood still, holding her breath while the restless joists settled.

She studied the problem.

She changed her grip on the handle and placed the flat blade where she wished it to land, drew back the axe-head and swung it forward—and the blade buried itself between the ply and the edge of the rafter, a good inch before it struck a nail. She levered the handle to widen the seam, the nail groaning—*Yes*—but then something cracked and the blade swung down and chopped the ply so near to her left boot she watched for the blood, waited for the pain, her stomach turning.

When she stood again a piece of the ply in the rough shape of the blade was missing, had gone flying off somewhere. Dust wheeling in the box of light.

"God damn you," she said. She had sweated through her blouse. Her mouth was coated in rancid dust, insulation fibers.

Why didn't you think to bring water?

Maybe because you didn't know you'd be swinging a pickaxe in a garage attic.

She stood there. Then in frustration she raised the tool alongside the bay's other rafter and jerked down and closed her eyes against the burst of debris and when she looked again the ply had come away from the rafter.

"Holy shit."

She raised the axe and brought it down. More space.

She hauled insulation from the bays to either side and raised the axe-head and brought it down. The ply had been nailed every two feet or so along the rafters and with each set of nails the sheet dropped, the mouth opened. Her light down in the middle bay shifted but there was nothing to see but the empty spaces, the insulation, the spinning, bright dust. When the sheet was halfway pried from the rafters she set down the axe and took hold of the ply and purposed her weight against it. The sheet yawned with a cry of nails, and with her next effort it dropped suddenly away from her like a drawbridge and her light rolled down the ramp of it and the bay went dark, but she had already seen—or thought she'd seen. Her heart pounding, pounding, as she scrabbled for the Mag and trained it on the middle bay. On the bays to either side.

Three of them. Held in place by the remaining sheet of ply, the dusty heads fallen slightly forward. As if eager after all this time to have a look around.

The dimensions of the plywood and the bays already suggested children, each of whom had once stood a little over four feet; the skulls left no doubt: the big front teeth and the gaps where the smaller incisors and canines had not come in. Smiles of nine-, ten-year-olds. Shocks of hair that, dusty though they were, any mother would know by sight. By touch.

Three boys like brothers put to a single bed, tucked in by the sheet of ply, all roused by a sound, or voice.

Teddy Felt.

Duane Milner.

Billy Ross.

Viegas reached as if she would touch the wasted, leathered faces. "Little boy," she said quietly, not touching. "Which one are you?"

Forty-one years. Before she was even born.

She took up the pickaxe—then set it down again. If she brought down the next sheet they would tumble out facedown on the floor, the nails.

She stood there, trying to make sense of it. Not buried, not sunk in the river with stones, not burned, not bricked in behind a wall. *This.* Who would think of such a thing?

The same person who'd bury a dog or coyote under a tractor: Let the dogs sniff there, let the men dig there. Keep the attention down, not up.

Devereaux.

She'd looked into the old man's eyes and she'd seen the cinderblock wall, the murdered uncle—but this? This was a level of calculated crazy she'd not seen.

The lonesome faces gazed down at her. She hated to leave them, but her phone was in her jacket and her jacket was down below.

She descended the ladder and crossed the dirt floor on legs that felt as if they'd not been on solid ground in a long time. Legs of a sailor just back from her yearslong voyage.

Water, she was thinking—cold, gushing water. The spigot at the house. They wouldn't turn it off until the bill was past due, and the old man had not been gone long enough for that.

Out in the clearing it was night. The air incredibly clean and cool. A nearly full moon balanced on the tips of the evergreens. 8:14, her phone said. Past dinnertime but before bedtime.

Oh God, she thought. *William Ross. The other parents. The mothers.*

She put the phone to her ear and felt it move as if with heartbeat—it was her own thudding neck.

He answered on the second ring. "Detective," he said.

"Where are you?" said Viegas.

"One guess."

"Good. I need you to do something for me, Victor."

Samuels heard it in her voice; she heard that in his silence.

"OK," he said. "What have you got?"

It didn't take long, and would not take long for Samuels to mobilize the city's forces and agencies, the entire crime-scene apparatus. She had ten, maybe fifteen minutes before the site was no longer hers.

The boys no longer hers.

She drew the air into her lungs and lifted her face to the light of the moon, as if there might be some warmth or nourishment in it she'd not found before. Then she crossed to the house, the water spigot—*Jesus, let it work*—thumbing her phone as she went.

"Detective," she heard for the second time, and this one flooding her chest. *Counselor,* she was supposed to say. But she couldn't.

"Corrie—?" her father said. "Are you all right?

"Yes, I'm fine."

"You don't sound fine. Where are you?"

"I'm out at the Devereaux place."

"The Devereaux place—?"

"Is she all right?" That was Martin, standing close. These good men.

"Sweetheart, what on earth are you doing—"

"Dad—" she said.

"Yes?"

She waited. She wanted her voice to be steady. "Dad," she said. "I think you need to come out here."

44.

IT HAD RAINED in the night and the lawn shone greenly in the morning sun. Robins with their breasts aflame stood head-cocked in the wet grass, listening. Stepping. Listening, then stabbing with their beaks and shaking free the worm, jerking it quickly down their throats. Clouds of blackbirds dropped like leaves into the silver maple and rose again as suddenly, leaving the branches bare as winter.

The second Friday of April this was—one month to the day since he'd been shot on that porch by a former student, and although Givens could now hold a cigarette in the fingers of his right hand, he could not lift the cigarette to his mouth without a ripping pain in his shoulder. He must do so anyway, said the therapist—he must lift through the pain. She'd not been speaking of cigarettes, per se, but lifting was lifting. And the smoking made the lifting worth it.

He lifted, grimacing, and held the smoke. Let it go. Rested.

He watched the robins—watched them startle and fly off, and he turned to the sound of an engine, an old green truck slowing in front of his house, pulling into his drive and not backing out again.

He knew the truck, with the rusting Knaack box in the bed. Knew the driver. Had thought he'd never see either one of them again.

He was watching the truck, watching Sean Courtland behind the wheel, when someone rose up in the passenger seat and looked out the window.

Not someone. A dog. The long nose and erect ears of a German shepherd.

Courtland spoke to the dog, then got out and shut his door in some particular way and it was then Givens saw, and understood, the damage to that side of the truck.

The carpenter took the brick path to the foot of the steps and stopped there.

"Mr. Givens."

"Mr. Courtland."

"How are you doing, sir?"

"I'm still here." He watched the younger man, then looked at the Chevy. "Is that a dog I see in your truck?"

Courtland glanced back. "Yes sir. That's Bonnie. She used to be Mr. Devereaux's dog. I got her from the shelter."

Givens studied him. "I assume you know the old man died."

"Yes sir, I heard that."

"And the rest?"

"And the rest. Yes sir."

Givens nodded. Courtland stood looking at the ground.

"So what brings you out here today?" Givens said, and the younger man looked up.

"I was over in Madison," he said, "at my dad's, and I remembered there was something I forgot to do back here."

"And what was that?"

Courtland stood with his left arm bent slightly at the elbow, in something of the attitude of a gunslinger.

"I forgot I needed to help a man with a project," he said.

"And what was the project?"

The carpenter gestured toward the ramp. "I noticed you've got some treads need replacing."

"Yes," said Givens. "Pretty much all of them. It's on my small-but-nonzero-chance list."

Courtland looked at him.

"That's my list of things that have roughly the same odds of getting done as I have of getting hit by an asteroid today. And that was before this." He lifted the cigarette.

"Yes sir. Well, I've got some decking in the back of the truck and a box of decking screws."

"Do you."

"Yes sir."

"Pressure-treated?"

"Yes sir."

"I see. Buy the materials and show up at a man's house. Is that how you find jobs these days?"

"No sir. This isn't a paying job."

"Pro bono."

"It's just something I wanted to do."

Givens sat thinking.

"How about time and materials," he said. "Whatever your going hourly is."

The carpenter hesitated, but agreed.

"When can you start?" said Givens.

"Start right now, if that works for you. If not I can come back."

"You wanna get started, get started."

"OK," said Courtland. "There's just one thing."

"What's that?"

"I could use a hand."

Givens laughed. "I hope you don't mean me. I've only got the one, and it's not even my good one."

"I could use it." Courtland lifted his own bent elbow.

"Yeah," said Givens, "I heard about that too."

"I figure between the two of us we've got two good hands."

"And four wheels. Hell, son. I'd just get in your way."

Sean stood there. Then he said, "Mr. Givens, there's something I've realized about myself since I left here."

"You're a dog person?"

Sean smiled. "I realized I don't like working alone."

"I never did either."

"You think you can reach these old screws with the cordless?"

Givens leaned to look over the side of the chair. He reached toward the floorboards with his left hand, as he might for a glass of wine, a bottle of beer. "Yes, I believe I can."

"Is the truck all right there in the drive?"

"It is."

"OK, I'll grab some tools."

"I'll wait here," said Givens. Then, calling to Courtland: "Let that dog out, if you think she won't run off."

"She won't run off."

It was slow going. Givens was out of practice, not left-handed, and in a wheelchair. The old Phillips drive screws were rusted and he stripped them, or the heads snapped, and Courtland would have to Sawzall them from below. But as he progressed from tread to tread Givens found the best way to position himself on the ramp, the best leverage with the cordless, and the screws began to come up, squealing and entire from the old decking.

Sean, working from the tailgate of his truck, paid no mind to the terrible sound of stripping screwheads, and neither did the shepherd other than to prick her great ears. She sat in her sphinx pose on the lawn and watched Sean with her foggy eyes as he cut the new treads with his father's old worm-drive Skilsaw, as he predrilled the wood against splitting the end grains and got the new star-drive deck screws started.

Around noon they went into the house, the three of them, and Sean pulled cold cuts, pulled lettuce and cheese from the fridge with his heart going, expecting Denise to walk in the door any minute. He'd not mentioned her and neither had Givens and he thought about the various reasons why the older man hadn't, and among them was the idea that Givens wanted him to do exactly that: think about it.

Givens filled a bowl with tapwater and they returned to the porch and Sean sat on the bench swing with his plate and his beer and they watched the dog lapping up the water.

"Should've thought of that sooner," said Givens, and Sean said, "She's all right."

When the dog was done drinking she began snuffling at the floorboards, where Sean could see that the painted boards had been scrubbed. Scrubbed almost to the raw wood. Blood. Givens was sitting now as he must've been sitting that night, while his daughter was out with him—Sean—eating and laughing. While she washed his hands at the old sink with her own smaller, finer hands. And with those same hands she'd washed these boards—who else?—down on her knees with some industrial cleanser from the tavern. And still the dog snuffled at that place, and finally he called to her and it was Givens who said, "She's all right."

Sean held a bit of turkey out and she came to take it from his fingertips. "Lie down now," he said, and she did. She licked her chops and watched him.

As did Givens. "Forty-one years," he said.

"Yes," said Sean.

"I try to imagine what it must be like for those parents—all those years of not knowing, and to suddenly know. To have their boys home. But I can't. I can't imagine it."

"I can't either," said Sean.

Givens was silent. Then: "I'm sure it's occurred to you that those boys might still be out there, up in those rafters, if you'd never done what you did."

"Yes sir, it's occurred to me."

"Wills and fates," said Givens.

"Sir?"

"'Our wills and fates do so contrary run, that our devices still are overthrown. Our thoughts are ours, their ends none of our own.'"

Sean sat there. "Shakespeare?"

Givens's face lit up. "Yes."

Sean looked at the sky, or what he could see of it from where he sat.

He said, "Did you know we only have starlings in this country because of Shakespeare?"

Givens, raising his beer, paused. Then took a swig. "Go on," he said.

IT WAS THREE in the afternoon before they made the turn and began working their way down the ramp's lower run, and it was getting on to five, the day growing chill, when she pulled up in the red Honda.

The shepherd lifted her head from her paws and growled.

"Quiet," said Sean. "I'll move that truck," he said to Givens, and Givens said, "Don't worry about it. She can park there for now."

The two men gave her a wave each in his own manner, and as they were in the middle of setting a tread they went on working. She sat in the car. At last she got out and opened the rear door and began lifting plastic bags from the seat.

The shepherd sniffed at the air.

Sean stood from his work. "Can I help you with those?"

"No, thank you." She got the bags in her hands and shut the door with her hip and came up the brick path to the foot of the steps and there she halted. The shepherd had gotten to its feet.

"Who's this?" she said.

"That's Bonnie. Sorry. Come here, girl."

The shepherd stayed, her tail sweeping, and Denise came up the steps and set down half her bags and let the dog sniff her knuckles, and while it put its nose in the bags she ran her hand over its head and ears.

"Yours?" she said. Watching the dog.

"Yep," he said.

"Used to be Marion Devereaux's," said Givens.

She stroked the dog's head, then stood and looked at Sean. "Strange turn of events."

"Yeah." He stood looking at her.

Givens, still leaning over the arm of his wheelchair, looked at her too. Then he looked at the next tread in Sean's hand and revved the cordless and Sean turned to the sound. "Sorry," he said, and got down in his crouch and fitted the tread in place. He held it while Givens mated the star bit to the screwhead, bore down on the cordless and sank the screw down tight.

When Sean looked at her again she was watching him. Her eyes so green in the late afternoon light.

"Are you and Miss Bonnie staying for dinner?" she said.

"I hadn't planned on it. I wasn't—"

"Are you staying for dinner?"

"Sure. That sounds great."

"Good. It's possum night."

"Dibs on the tail," said Givens, and sank another screw. He set the cordless in his lap and moved the wheelchair and picked up the cordless again.

"Dad?"

"What?" He was leaning over the arm of the chair. Finally he looked up.

"Don't overdo it," she said.

"Overdo it," said Givens. He sank the next screw. "This is child's play."

She stood watching them, each man focused on his task, both silent. Then she picked up the bags and crossed the porch and hauled open the stormdoor and stepped into the house, and for the time it took the door to close there was no sound other than the long slow wheeze of the pneumatic closer, and when the door clicked home there was no sound at all, and no Bonnie either, for the dog had followed her into the house.

Sean looked at Givens. Givens at Sean. Then Givens, leaning again, drove the screw into the wood, and Sean fit the next tread into place.

ACKNOWLEDGMENTS

Along the way I felt the constant company of doubt:
my lack of talent, my impostor's syndrome, my fear of boring others.

THE SUPERB WRITER Teju Cole is talking about his photographic project in Switzerland ("Far Away from Here," *Known and Strange Things*), but since I happened to read this sentence while I was thinking about what I wanted to say here, I've copped it—not just as affirmation that such doubts are, if not always then at least pretty often, part of the creative act; but more by way of remembering, *acknowledging*, the distance that this particular act, *Distant Sons*, has travelled from its long-secret drafting in the company of doubt (its *long* incubation in a laptop folder called salvos), to the most surprising of outcomes, which is the book in your hands. That journey is the story of the simple and beautiful alchemy of *other people*—from first brave reader to agent, to editor, to so many other good people along the way that the word *acknowledgment* just doesn't cut it. More like *Astonishment. Wonder.*

In that spirit I wish to thank especially:

Chris Kelley, fellow writer and carpenter, whose importance as first responder and friend cannot be overstated. **Amy Berkower**, guardian agent for over ten years now and who, along with **Genevieve Gagnes-Hawes**, composes a reading and editing supertandem that has helped me transform three novels before the manuscripts even left the premises. Plus all the other dedicated and talented people at **Writers House** who do more than I even know. **Betsy Gleick**, who took over as my new editor at Algonquin at a time of seismic changes in the Algonquin/Workman world and yet demonstrated nothing but total devotion to this book, bringing her keen sensibilities as a booklover and a human being to bear on every aspect of the story. Plus everyone up and down the publishing staircase of **Algonquin**: managing editors and designers and publicists, marketers, and everyone else working so hard to bring good books to readers. **Elizabeth Johnson**, returning copy editor, whose intensity of attention has spared the reader countless grammatical and stylistic departures (and for any that remain, I alone am to blame). **Chuck Adams**, legendary editor who so gracefully shepherded my previous two novels through the mountains and across the rivers, and from whom I have learned so much. **Joe Veltre** and (again) **Amy Berkower**, steadfastly and deftly managing the film side of things.

In the camp of other writer/reader friends and family who read drafts or otherwise lent aid and comfort: **Michael Koryta, PD Mallamo, Tyler Johnston, Tricia Johnston, Randy Larson**, and **Ian Marron**.

I wish to heap special gratitude on **America's independent booksellers** and its **librarians**, who are the keepers of the light.

And lastly and again: **You**—the reader, in whom this story finds its last and most true life.